Trial of a Warrior

by

Mary Morgan

Legends of the Fenian Warriors
Book 3

This is a work of fiction. Names, characters, places, and incidents are either the product of the author's imagination or are used fictitiously, and any resemblance to actual persons living or dead, business establishments, events, or locales, is entirely coincidental.

Trial of a Warrior

Cover Art by *Debbie Taylor*

The Wild Rose Press, Inc.
PO Box 708
Adams Basin, NY 14410-0708
Visit us at www.thewildrosepress.com

Publishing History
First Fantasy Rose Edition 2018
Print ISBN 978-1-5092-2358-9
Digital ISBN 978-1-5092-2359-6

Legends of the Fenian Warriors, Book 3
Published in the United States of America

The smile in his eyes contained a sensuous flame, and she was drawn to him. A soft breeze billowed around them. She ached to press her mouth against his. Just one kiss.

As if reading her thoughts, Liam cupped her chin and stroked his thumb over her bottom lip. "Your mouth begs to be kissed, princess."

She swallowed and did the unthinkable. "Then kiss me, Liam MacGregor."

His groan echoed around them as he took possession of her mouth. The kiss sent the pit of her stomach into a wild swirl of delicious sensations. Abela's body yearned to touch him, so she wrapped her arms around his neck. The contact of his skin against her chest ignited a burning desire for more.

Liam grasped her firmly around the waist with one arm and deepened the kiss. When his silken tongue sought entry, she opened fully to the seduction, tasting wine, apples, and his own scent. His moan resonated deep within her, and she found her body responding to a rhythm as old as the land they lived upon.

Never did Abela imagine the power behind a kiss—seductive, enchanting, shattering, and she craved more.

Liam demanded and Abela surrendered.

When he finally broke free, Liam's breathing was labored.

"Do not stop," she pleaded.

His eyes glittered with the light of the stars. "If I continue, I will claim you here upon the ground. I shall take your body and all you have to offer. Are you ready for the claiming?"

Praise for Mary Morgan

"The author pulls you in, and you can feel the world evolving around you, and see it in your mind as you read along. A new-to-me author and it feels like I found a new favorite".

Cyrene for Uncaged Book Reviews

~*~

"I love Mary Morgan's Dragon Knight series, but I believe this is the best she's ever written. Weaving mythical lore within a historical romance, blending both Irish and Scottish storylines, I was swept away."

~N.N. Light Book Heaven

~*~

"Well crafted with great world building. The storyline is unpredictable, intriguing and captivating."

~April

~*~

"Mary Morgan is fast becoming my new favourite romance author. *DRAGON KNIGHT'S SWORD* is an evocative tale that combines historical with fantasy, modern day with old, and it will keep you turning those pages right until the end."

~Mary Yarde

Dedication

To Celtic musicians
who have inspired and fueled my imagination.
My stories reflect the melody of your ancient tunes.
You are my muse.

Glossary of the Fae Realm

Dear Readers,

For those so inclined to learn more about my fantasy Fae Realm and the Fenian Warriors, please refer to the glossary below.

CATHEDRAL OF TREES: A place of worship and where royal ceremonies are held.

COURTS OF THE FAE: Special chambers where the Fae Order discuss and advise on the laws of the land.

FAE APOTHECARY: A special healer and a place where one can purchase or create medicinal herbal remedies.

FAE COUNCIL: A group of nine Fae members who proceed and advise over the laws, especially those governed by the Fenian Warriors.

FENIAN WARRIORS' POWERS: The powers granted to the Fenian Warriors upon their initiation into the Brotherhood mainly consisted of the ability to travel between Earth's centuries and to live among the humans without ill effects from the human world. Along with their Fae elemental powers connected to the land and other magical abilities, these warriors were also far stronger than their counterparts in the Fae realm.

HALL OF REMEMBRANCE: A place where the Fae can visit to reflect on their life's journey through mirrored images.

KEEPER OF KNOWLEDGE: Archibald McKibben, Bard of the Fae. He is responsible for keeping a historical record of all events pertaining to the Fae within both worlds—human and Fae.

LIBRARY OF THE ANCIENTS: All the knowledge the Fae brought with them to Ireland.

PLEASURE GARDENS: A vast, luscious, sensual garden where the Fae may find others for sexual pleasures.

REALM OF SORROWS: When a Fae becomes trapped in his own misery and sorrow. Ultimately, they become a shadow of their former self and go mad.

ROOM OF REFLECTION: The Fae prison.

ROYAL HOUSES: On the planet of Taralyn—the Fae homeland—each of the nine continents maintained a royal house and family. These houses governed their own continents, but all were ruled by the King and Queen of the Fae.

STONE OF AGES: The magical capabilities of the stone could transport members of the Fae royalty to any time-period within the human world. It remained in possession of the Fae King Ansgar until his son Conn's five hundredth year and then was presented to him.

Prologue

In the beginning…when the world was new, Fae and humans lived peacefully together, but as the centuries passed, fear and distrust evolved. The Fae continued to love the humans, but they believed it was time to safeguard the realms. Therefore, they appointed the Fenian Warriors to protect the domain between human and faery. But most importantly, these warriors were only to assist the humans and steer a new course in the mortal world.

When evil threatened to destroy a clan, country, or civilization, the Fae council called upon these warriors. This group of elite Fae had the power to travel through the Veil of Ages, supporting those in need. They were not to alter the timeline or what the Fae believed to be the life strings of a human. To do so, would be catastrophic.

Ancient and powerful, the Brotherhood of the Fenian Warriors was second only to the Fae King and Queen's powers. They have lived amongst mortals for thousands of years—watching, aiding, guiding. They could live in the guise of a professor, lawyer, knight, tavern owner, or a simple farmer.

Whatever was required, the warriors did so without complaint.

Yet, even these great warriors had their weaknesses as with any race. Though they used their powers for good, there have been times when a select few deemed it wiser to interfere *without* the knowledge of the Fae council. They twisted the laws to suit their own purpose and changed the course of time.

When three Fenian warriors left the Brotherhood to aid a clan—the Dragon Knights of Urquhart, they brought the fury of the Fae down upon their heads. Their punishment should have been swift, but the Fae always believed in redemption—even for one of their own.

A trial was ordered for all three Fae. Conn MacRoich and Rory MacGregor have given their accounts. Their judgments have been pronounced. Now the third Fenian Warrior, Liam MacGregor, must face the Fae council and give his report. However, the council is concerned with only one action this Fenian Warrior dared to defy.

When Liam took Fae Warrior, Aidan Kerrigan—an outcast among his own people—through the Veil of Ages, he broke a sacred law. The council gave no care that Aidan was once their most elite Fenian Warrior. Nor did they concern themselves with Aidan's plea to rescue his daughter trapped in medieval Scotland. Therefore, Liam deemed his loyalty was greater to his mentor and granted Aidan's request.

He evaded his trial for several years, until he was captured by the Fae guards after the great battle against the evil druid, Lachlan. Though Liam's punishment would surely be death, the council must still hear his account before he is sentenced.

However, deep within the realm, another Fae can no longer watch from the shadows. She is one who will not let Liam suffer death's blow by her own people. No matter the severity of his crimes, she cannot allow him to die. Her mind and heart can find no other solution. She will risk her own life and her freedom to release him from his chains.

Time is fleeting. She must act swiftly. If she succeeds, she may well bring about the destruction of both worlds—Fae *and* human.

All for him. All for love.

Chapter One

Beneath the Hill of Tara, Ireland—Winter, the season of contemplation and meditation in the Fae Realm.

Snowflakes danced in a prism of muted colors over the top of the glass dome. They glittered from the weak sunlight, casting an eerie glow inside his prison. Each snowflake in the Fae realm was unique, existing for a solitary moment in time until they became one with the others. Their beauty was a constant he had always taken for granted and *disregarded.*

Now they mocked him with their freedom, melting in a puddle of water and rolling down the sides of the walls.

As Liam stood rooted to the ground, he continued to become fixated with the swirling mass above him. Envy and bitterness dug their claws into his soul, and his gut soured.

How many seasons had he witnessed? Was it a full four? Time no longer concerned him. He understood his fate. Yet, he could not fathom why the Fae council made him endure an isolated existence in the Room of Reflection. Death should have come swiftly upon his return.

When he first arrived, Liam had prepared himself for the welcome of death's embrace and fought with his guards when he was placed inside his prison. No news was given to him. Only food, drink, books, and writing materials were provided. Even his attempt to reason with his captors only brought silence from his guards.

Days, weeks, and months bled into the next, and he cursed them all for abandoning him here.

With each new season, the tide of melancholy wove its way into his soul—splintering more of the Fae warrior. However, he refused to give into despair and shadows. His anger became a fortitude of strength. His control became his shield. He harnessed and fought back the anguish within his soul. Often times he lashed out at Mother Danu, begging for advice. And she responded in riddles, confusing him further.

"Stone me, flog and strip the skin from my bones, but do not leave me in this pit of despair and silence. I am ready for my death. Let it be done!"

Letting out a frustrated sigh, Liam lifted his hand upward and stretched his fingers as far as he could extend. "I may not feel the icy sting of your touch, but I remember."

He balled his hand into a fist and lowered his arm. The elements tormented him within his soul, and he shook with rage. Anger at those who continued to ignore him. Anger at the injustice of laws he sought to change during his lifetime.

His own people kept him a prisoner in a cell, tormenting Liam with what he could not control. The ability to manipulate his own fate and to touch the passing seasons. His prison was a mockery.

Nonetheless, each day he honored the passing of the light and dark. He remained steadfast in his training, and refused to succumb to the darkness—tempting his soul to lash out at any who came near him.

Defeat was not an option. It had been drilled into him since his induction into the Brotherhood. Though the great warrior was dead, Liam heard the words repeatedly in his mind by their leader and mentor, Aidan Kerrigan.

"I will not fail you, Aidan. *Ever.*"

Turning away from the glass dome, Liam walked to his desk. As he braced his hands on the smooth wood, he tried to center his soul for the day. If he could control his mind, his heart and soul would follow. He stilled the thoughts of fury and anguish, attempting to calm his breathing and prepare for another day.

During the daylight Liam wrote in the journals, recalling everything Aidan had taught him. From ancient lore, research, archaeology, and the history of the human world. Hours passed in study, and when the sunlight slipped into darkness, Liam trained his body as that of a warrior. Because he required little sleep, his mind and body were kept sharpened in this fashion of exercise.

When the council saw fit to retrieve him, Liam would walk to his death as a strong warrior. There would be no softness or despair to show them.

Although in retrospect, there was one sliver of regret that haunted him. He had made his peace, but often times, he questioned his decision in agreeing to take Aidan back in time to rescue his daughter. Liam never considered the action would result in his friend's death. They both had understood the risks, but never fathomed death would be the outcome.

"Would I do it again?" he muttered into the silence of his chamber and shook his head. "By the Gods,

Aidan. What were you thinking?" He chuckled with a dry and cynical sound. "Yes, I know. You would have done anything for your daughter, Aileen."

Liam sat down slowly. His fingers brushed over the quills and parchments. Images from another time seeped into his thoughts, reminding him that his friend sought to travel the Veil of Ages by any means. Though he had been stripped of his powers and immortality, Aidan still possessed his Fae blood—his heritage. Liam often mused if the great warrior would have requested assistance from the elders, or even Mother Danu herself if he had refused to do as Aidan asked.

"By the hounds, you must, Liam!" Aidan paced the grounds of Arbroath Abbey, intent on getting his demand granted.

Liam raked a hand through his hair. "You dare to ask me to tamper with the Veil of Ages? You who were—are my mentor."

Aidan's steps stilled. He pierced him with a look of savage fire. "Did I ask you to alter a timeline? No! Only to take me to my daughter." He pointed at the ruins. "She has vanished to an unknown time! One where danger lurks everywhere. How can she survive?"

"Did you not consider that this is her destiny?" Liam snapped and confronted his friend. "She has already made a connection to the Dragon Knight when she saw him on the tapestry in the Great Hall."

"I'll kill him, if he touches one finger on my daughter."

"Listen to yourself. You're not speaking as a Fenian Warrior!"

"Because I'm no longer one, or did you forget?"

Liam clenched his hands. "How many times have

you spouted that even though the Fae stripped you of your powers and markings, your blood and oath as a warrior will never falter? Now, because you don't like certain events, you will disavow all your oaths?" He stepped nearer. "You are not a human, Aidan."

"No. I am a father! Duty bound to shield and protect my child." Aidan glanced over his shoulder at the ruins. "She is all I have left of her mother. I can't lose her like I did Rose."

Unable to fathom his friend's feelings, Liam remained silent. Even after the passing of years, he still found it difficult to understand why Aidan defied an entire kingdom to marry a human. He had no words for his friend when he was banished long ago, and now he fought the growing fury at Aidan's request to break more Fae laws.

Aidan returned his attention to him. "If I gain permission, will you take me through the Veil of Ages?"

Liam snorted in disgust. "How can you seek authorization when you have been barred from the realm?"

There was a faint glint of humor in Aidan's eyes. "Aye, I am unable to enter my former world, but that doesn't mean I can't communicate with my family. Are we in agreement?"

Folding his arms over his chest, Liam replied, "If the request is granted by another Fae, I will escort you through the Veil. But be warned, in doing so—"

Aidan clamped a hand on his shoulder. "Could bring about both our deaths? Yes, I understand the consequences, but I intend to return and clear your name. I shall not allow any harm to come to you. This is my decision."

Liam rubbed a hand across his forehead. "You did return, old friend, and I watched you die in your daughter's arms."

Reaching for one of the rolls of parchment, he unfurled it slowly and placed two crystals at the top corners. Retrieving a quill, he dipped the end in green ink and sought to banish the past with a legend of the mighty first king of Scotland—Kenneth MacAlpin, King of Dalriada. A strong, fierce, and loyal leader, the Fae judged the man perfect as an alliance between their realm and the human world. Since he was already descended from a Dragon Knight, they sought to have him on the elite board to oversee rules to keep both worlds safe.

A council was convened in the human year of 844 Anno Domini. Those present were four Fenian Warriors, four Dragon Knights, four high chieftains from Ireland, King MacAlpin, and one elder from the Fae council. Laws were suggested, argued over, and then finally written down in the annals of Fae and human laws called the Feahan Treaty.

Liam was one of the Fenian Warriors present, along with Aidan. It was an honor to witness the signing of new laws. Afterward, a great feast was held in honor of the historic event. The king summoned other Dragon Knights from across the seas, and the kingdom rejoiced in an alliance that would forge a stronger world for both peoples. Celebrations continued for a full year.

Yet, the tide of the new religion was sweeping across the land. Wars broke out in the smaller villages against the Fae and their dragons. They sought to rid their land of the demons who were in league with what some called the devil. Words and lies became a plague that journeyed across the sea to Eire.

There were those among the Fae who sought to alter timelines and wipe away memories of their existence with the humans. But the laws were precise, and the Fae King refused to go against what was agreed upon at the council.

Liam's hand hovered above the parchment. "And I was the first to break one of those laws. I took another through the Veil for his own gainful purpose." Frustration seethed within him, and he snapped the quill in half.

Rubbing a hand vigorously over his face, Liam tried to squelch the fury at a man long gone. The past was vanished—elusive. There would be no future for him. Today was all he had.

And his impatience grew.

As Liam reached for another quill, he considered it wiser to focus on another year of events. In particular, the great battle with the evil druid, Lachlan. He was one of three who witnessed and participated in wiping the world of a gruesome monster, and Liam was determined to give his account. The council might not want to bother with his knowledge, but someday another Fae warrior would need the record of what transpired.

"Evil always slithers back from the cosmos," he uttered with disdain.

With slow and meticulous detail, Liam gave a full account of the battle with his fellow Fenian brothers and Dragon Knights—beginning with his time at Aidan's castle and meeting his daughter, Aileen.

Hours slipped by, and he gave no notice to the food

and drink that magically appeared on a nearby smaller table. His duty to preserve a written document consumed him. He wished for no interruptions—save one—his trial.

The last ray of sunlight shimmered off the glass dome and onto his desk. He blinked and raised his head from his work. *Another day has ended.* After placing the quill back in its holder, he gathered the reams of parchment and neatly rolled them together, securing them with twine.

Standing, he stretched out the muscles in his shoulders and back. He removed his tunic and draped it over his chair. Making his way to the center of room, he then knelt on one knee and waited for the last sliver of light to leave his prison.

When the first shaft of darkness settled around Liam, he stood and prepared for his evening ritual of exercise. The training was an attempt to keep him centered, focused, and to rid the growing anger. When he had used all his strength, he would partake of food and drink.

It did not matter that he had been stripped of his Fenian markings or powers. Even when death claimed Liam MacGregor, he would take his last breath as a warrior.

****

Staring at the eerie night shadows slithering across his room, Liam tried to find some rest. Sleep was not a welcome companion, but a required one. He closed his eyes, longing for a brief respite. As his mind drifted, he sensed the faintest whisper of power within his chamber. The Fae guards would never enter without announcing themselves first, so Liam's curiosity grew

11

as the power increased.

As he slowly opened his eyes, he cast his gaze outward. He almost chuckled at the absurdity of the situation. Whoever had dared to enter his prison hovered in the far corner, and he waited for them to approach. After several moments, he grew frustrated at the intrusion and shifted his body to a sitting position.

"Is there a reason why you cower in the darkness inside *my* prison?"

Liam tried to suppress his growing anxiety. Was this to be his executioner? No trial? Only a swift end to his life? Where was the honor?

He stood and flexed his hands. "If you have come to pronounce my judgment, do me the honor of stepping forth from the shadows and allowing me to see your face. It is my right."

The figure complied and stepped forth. The person was cloaked from head to toe in a hooded garment, concealing almost everything. The only spark of light came from eyes that pierced straight into his soul. A flicker of familiarity wove through him.

"Who are you?" he demanded.

When the person gave no response, he took a hesitant step toward them.

Instantly, a blast of power sent him stumbling backward. Uncertainty filled him as Liam righted himself. He clenched one hand, prepared for whatever was next. "I will not go without a fight. If you are here for justice, then I have the right to face the council and give my account. Either you explain this intrusion, take me to the council, or battle me in combat."

"I am here to set you free," replied a soft feminine voice.

Liam's mouth dropped open in shock. Snapping it close, he folded his arms over his chest. The voice was one he tried to recall, yet, she cloaked the sound. "Why?"

"Must you seek a reason for a gift? Your freedom is not enough?"

He snorted in disgust. "Surely you are aware of my crimes. Death awaits me outside my prison."

Her eyes grew wide. "Do you long for death's embrace, Fenian Warrior?"

"No!" he conceded and shifted his stance. "But why are *you* doing this?"

Silence stretched between them.

"Because I have no wish to see you die," she whispered.

Liam narrowed his eyes. He tried to recall the voice but failed. "Who are you?"

She angled her head as if listening for something. Tossing a cloak to him, she added, "Time is fleeting. We must go now." The woman surprised him further by sliding his sword across the floor.

"Not until you tell me your name."

After giving him a passing glance, she withdrew a slim crystal dagger from her cloak. Waving her hand in an arc, the room shimmered to reveal another realm. Ancient words poured forth from her as the realm continued to expand. She held out a gloved hand to him. "Freedom or death? Which do you seek?"

The temptation to flee was great, but Liam was honor-bound by an oath as a Fenian Warrior. He picked up his sword. "To run is cowardly. I am a warrior, trained by ancient laws and edicts."

"Do you honestly believe the council will listen to

your account?" Her gaze bore into his. "They are determined to keep you inside this prison until they can consider how to terminate your life. You are a fool if you deem otherwise."

Liam glanced over at his scrolls. All that occurred was written down, yet, he believed he would have been given the right to confront the Fae council. Indecision plagued him. "What about my brother, Rory? I cannot leave him."

"He is no longer in his Room of Reflection and yes, he lives. Now, may we go?"

"And Conn?"

She laughed nervously, and again Liam tried to recall where he had heard the voice. "He has been freed."

"Interesting," he replied dryly.

"We must hurry, before others sense the shift of power inside your prison."

He moved slowly toward her. The lure of freedom was a heady one. "You do realize the situation will be dire once we leave the Fae realm. Any possibility of telling me where we are going? I cannot go willingly, if I don't know the destination."

She grasped his hand. "Of course. To the year 844, prior to the signing of the Feahan Treaty. We need to rewrite a certain law."

Before Liam could utter a complaint, a brilliant flash of light blinded him and sent him spiraling through a dark abyss.

Chapter Two

"All good intentions are often times fraught with bad decisions."

~*Chronicles of Liam MacGregor*

Shards of pain continued to torment Liam as he leaned against a tree for support. The moment he could see, he was going to throttle the impudent Fae. Whatever power she used to transport them had horrific side effects. She was unskilled when it came to moving through time and distance. He could hear her pacing several feet away, tossing out a litany of curses.

He massaged his temples in an attempt to soothe the throbbing ache and calmed his breathing. When he opened his eyes, he cast his sight around them. Frost hovered on each breath he took, and fog shrouded the treetops. A crust of hard ice covered the area as far as he could see. Weakened from his time in the Room of Reflection, Liam blew into his hands and rubbed them together to ward off the chill. It would take time for him to regulate his body temperature to the elements. And even then, they could ill afford to stay out in the harsh weather. "Are we in the Kingdom of Fortriu?" Liam asked as he moved away from the tree.

She shook her head and dropped to the ground. Removing one of her gloves, she placed her palm onto the ice.

Liam fisted his hands on his hips. "Moot Hill at Scone?"

"Silence," she hissed out.

He ignored her order and crouched down in front of her. By the hounds, he wanted to rip the hood off her face. "You don't have a clue where we have landed, do you?"

She met his hard stare. "The land will reveal its origins."

Not only are you untrained, but foolish. "Sorry, but that's not how it works." Liam stood and surveyed their surroundings. Yes, they were indeed in Scotland, but he could not determine the year. The land spoke to him, but obviously, this Fae was unable to make a correct calculation. Without his Fenian powers, he was useless to assist. If he were in control of those powers, he would be able to transport to any time and any country with a single thought or wave of his hand to open the portal.

He closed his eyes and lifted his hands upward in search of any possible signs of human life. After several moments, he lowered his arms and let out a curse. They were in a desolate part of the country.

"Take my hand," she demanded.

Liam glanced over his shoulder and arched a brow. "I'm not going anywhere with you. Your directional compass is skewed."

"How dare you? In case you have not noticed, we are no longer inside your prison. I would have thought any place you were free would be desirable."

He gestured outward. "And this is better? Can you at least tell me the year?"

"I cannot gather the knowledge from the land." She

moved past him and placed her palm upon a pine tree.

Rolling his eyes, Liam tried to control the bite of anger in his voice. "The trees will not give you their wisdom."

"They will to me," she answered while keeping her back to him.

His curiosity now stoked, Liam stepped near the tree. "Do tell."

"Thurso? Sweet Goddess, no!"

"Viking territory?" Liam's hand automatically went to his sword. "And the year?"

After uttering a prayer of thanks, she walked away and lifted her head to the sky. "Unsure. The tree is young."

"Sweet Mother Danu! You do realize how much the Vikings despised the Gods and Goddesses of the Celts."

She waved a hand dismissively at him. "They would never dare to strike a Fae. I do not fear them."

He stood in gaping silence. Was she demented?

"I shall attempt to move us nearer to Castle Dunkelp. Is it not located by Moot Hill near Scone?"

Liam folded his arms across his chest. "No."

Her eyes narrowed. "But I understood it to be—"

"*No*. I am not going anywhere with you. It is obvious to me that you don't have the skills to properly transport us within the human realm."

"Might I remind you that without your Fenian powers you are helpless among these people?"

"At least I am fully aware of what I can and cannot do, unlike someone who has never ventured outside her own homeland. I still have control of the elements and other magic."

"That's not true," she argued, and turned her back on him.

Liam moved closer. "When? Where? The last time you ventured outside the realm?"

"I have nothing further to say to you...you *stubborn* man! After all I've risked, this is my thanks?"

Dark fury burst inside Liam. He yanked her by the arm to face him. "I never asked to be rescued! My fate was sealed the moment I took Aidan Kerrigan back through the Veil of Ages. Since that day, I have prepared myself for the inevitable." He shook her. "But you're the one who stole into my prison and took my fate from me. Thanks? Not likely. And while we're having this fascinating debate, I'd like to know the face behind the hood. Only cowards hide while spouting their tirades."

"You bastard," she snapped, and Liam could see the indecision within the depths of her lavender eyes.

"I shall save my remarks until after you have removed your hood." His grip tightened as he prepared for her to fight him.

"Release me," she demanded.

"Shall I do the honors?" he asked and lifted his other hand.

"Absolutely not!"

Liam released his hold but refused to back away.

Her eyes glittered like shards of steel as she reached up and pulled her hood free. After tossing it to Liam, she tilted her head to the side. "Happy now?"

He was too stunned to move or speak. Never in his existence had he thought to see *her* again. They moved in different circles within the Fae realm. He was a Fenian Warrior. And *she* was not supposed to be his savior.

"What? No words of a joyous reunion?"

Liam fought the wave of emotions coursing through his mind and body. She was too near. Her scent of honeysuckle invaded his pores, reminding him of a memory long ago. Quickly slamming the door on the vision, he took a step back.

He dipped his head out of respect. "*Princess* Abela."

She tapped her foot in irritation. "Do not address me thusly. I gave up my right to the kingdom when I entered the Temple of Mother Danu as a priestess."

"*What?*" his question came out as a garbled word. "Preposterous! Insanity on all levels! What in the Gods' names are you doing outside the sacred temple?"

Abela glared at him. "Saving your life!"

"Why? It is forbidden to leave the sanctuary. And *why* would you ever think to enter the temple?"

"Either your memory is failing due to your age, or you did not believe what I told you back inside your prison." Abela directed her gaze to a lone deer ambling within the thick pines. "I had no wish to see you die. Furthermore, it is an honor to become a priestess of the temple. You had your path and I had mine."

Liam blew out a frustrated breath. "Regardless, you still are a princess of the Fae realm, priestess to Mother Danu, daughter to King Ansgar and Queen Nuala, as well as *sister* to Conn. You should not have interfered. Eventually, we all must die."

A frown marred her features as she returned her attention to him. "You should die with honor after many lifetimes. The Fae council meddles where they should not."

"Yes. It is a complaint we have discussed among the Brotherhood, but how does this concern you?"

She flipped her long ebony braids over her shoulder. "There is much you do not comprehend. The Fae realm is changing—expanding. New laws have been initiated into the Fae annals."

"Change has always been good for the kingdom," argued Liam.

Her mouth twitched in humor. "I am in agreement with you. Although, there are some who see this shift as a division and fight against the tide of change."

"What exactly are you *not* saying?"

"It does not pertain to you, so for now, let us close the door on this conversation."

Liam pinched the bridge of his nose to temper his anger. He would have thought a hundred years apart would have softened her tongue, but no, she still managed to twist words and take control of every situation. How he'd forgotten the battle to remain civil in front of her.

He lifted his head at the sound of her soft laughter. "Would you care to share your amusement?"

"I can see nothing has changed between us. Whenever you grew weary of our discussions, you would forestall your rage by pinching the bridge of your nose."

Liam hated that she knew him so well. "Return me to my prison and go home, Abela."

All traces of humor vanished from her features, and she walked away from him. "Not possible. The abyss that opened for me has now been sealed. I had no wish for anyone to sense the direction we were traveling. Even if I wanted to return, I cannot."

"Transport us to the Hill of Tara in Ireland. We can seek entrance through the ancient oak," Liam suggested.

She snickered. "That portal is permanently sealed. There was an...*altercation* many moons ago."

"Sweet Brigid! What happened to the kingdom in my absence?"

"A lot."

Regardless of what happened during his time in seclusion, Liam realized they needed to journey away from the northern end of Scotland. Uncertainty filled his next decision. He held out his hand. "Concentrate on moving toward a fixed location."

Abela's eyes widened in excitement. "You will assist me?"

"Us," he corrected.

After taking his hand, Abela took a deep breath in and released it slowly. The air warmed, and they vanished in a blur of light—arriving near the edge of a forest.

Abela dashed ahead, scanning the area. "Are we near Moot Hill?"

"Nowhere near," he replied in the frosty air.

When the first snowflake landed on his cheek, Liam judged it wise to take control of their current predicament. If snow was falling, they required shelter. Even a Fae could suffer from the elements. Since he was unable to transport them through the Veil of Ages, he needed to seek out other traveling arrangements.

He knelt on one knee. Placing his fist upon the ground, he called out to the animal kingdom. Rabbits skittered into their burrows as an eagle cried overhead. Liam sent out the message for any horses in the surrounding area and prayed at least one would respond.

"What are you doing?" asked Abela coming alongside him.

"Snowfall is here. We need to remove ourselves from the harsh elements. I'm seeking traveling companions." Liam stood and scanned the area. "We shall keep to the trees for protection until aid arrives."

"No. I shall attempt to take us to Castle Dunkelp."

"Absolutely not! You have proven to be unskilled when moving through the Veil," he challenged.

She darted him a look that would have frozen any hardened warrior. "Can you blame me? It was my first attempt."

"Nevertheless, I deem it unwise to move forward until we can judge the year." He gestured her onward into the forest.

Abela hesitated and then nodded.

He kept stride with her steps, listening to any news from the animal kingdom. Without a sense of place, year, or his Fenian powers, Liam had to squash the growing fear that he alone was now responsible for the princess of the Fae realm. One who was headstrong, obstinate, *and* stubborn. He could handle those irritating qualities about Abela. Yet, there was another concern that plagued him. She tempted him beyond reason. When Liam entered the Brotherhood, he assumed his feelings were only those of a young man.

However, the instant she removed her hood, those lustful emotions slammed back into Liam. The woman who walked beside him was one who had grown into a vision of beauty. Why had she entered the Temple of Mother Danu? Did she not want to marry? Her brother

Conn had relinquished his right as prince when he entered the Brotherhood. So what would make Abela renounce the throne?

Enough! To open the door on their past lives would only encourage an attraction. And Liam wanted nothing to do with her. Onward they traveled, and his mind continued to plague him with the past.

"You're thinking too much," she scoffed, stepping over a fallen log.

"I'm sorting out our situation," he lied.

She cast him a skeptical glance. "Remember, I can always tell when you're lying."

Liam ducked under a branch, refusing to offer any more comments. The woman was infuriating. "Do share."

"Why? Then you'd try and correct the problem."

"If you cannot divulge your observations, then I must presume you're the one lying."

Abela halted and pushed against his chest. "You know me better than that."

Liam fisted his hands. "And you presume too much. We are no longer in our youthful years. The decades have changed us both." He noted the hurt reflected in her eyes, but refused to soften his tone or approach. "I could say the same about you. Always making *false* assumptions."

"You, *you* ba—"

"You've already stated I was a bastard. And for the record I did have two, loving parents. Though I'm curious why you are using a *human* curse word."

Abela drew the hood of her cloak over her head and turned away from him.

Stepping back, Liam scanned the sky. Smoke

billowed in the frosty air high above the treetops. As he closed his eyes, he searched outward with his Fae senses. After several minutes, he detected one human life within a stone structure.

He opened his eyes and glanced over his shoulder. "We shall proceed north. There is human life."

She kept her back to him. "How far?"

"Ten kilometers."

Turning around Abela held out her gloved hand. "I can take us there. Permit me to try again."

For a moment, he considered traveling on foot. The exercise in the frigid air might help deplete both of their tempers.

"*Trust* me," she pleaded.

Letting out a groan, he complied and grasped her hand.

The scenery blurred in muted colors, and they arrived tucked behind a grove of oaks.

"Nicely done," he acknowledged, and leaned against one of the trees. Noticing the Ogham markings, Liam traced his finger over the grooves in the bark.

"Druid," she pronounced and moved away from the protection of the trees.

"Agreed." He strode forth and stood alongside her in front of the stone cottage.

"What now?" Abela asked.

"We wait for him to acknowledge us. He already senses us."

"Powerful?"

"One of the most commanding druids you shall ever meet in the human world."

"You know him?" Her question was one of surprise.

"Yes."

The door opened to reveal a tall, elderly man. His gray beard was neatly trimmed, but his eyes were as bright as the day Liam first met the druid. In addition, he gathered the time was nowhere near the ninth century, confirming his suspicion and cementing his reasons why Abela was an untrained traveler. She should have never tampered with going through the Veil of Ages. They were most likely in the thirteenth century and years after the great battle had been fought.

The druid inclined his head. "Greetings. What brings ye to my door, Fenian Warrior?"

"We seek a favor. Do you have any horses we can borrow?"

The man slowly turned his attention to Abela. "Great Goddess! Why do ye travel with royalty?"

Abela gasped. She quickly composed herself and stepped near the druid. "How do you know?"

He chuckled softly. "Ye have the look of another. Your brother, Prince Conn."

"Prince?" echoed Liam. "What is the year?"

The druid frowned in concentration. "I will only answer your one question, Liam MacGregor. 'Tis obvious ye are without your powers. Aye, I have a horse to lend to ye"

"You dare to defy me?"

Abela held up her hand to halt Liam's words. "I deem you are correct, druid. Do not answer the Fenian Warrior. We are traveling together to undo an unjust judgment." She dipped her head in courtesy. "You were correct. I am royalty. My name is Princess Abela. And you are?"

Liam gestured toward the druid. "Let me introduce

you to Cathal, druid to the Dragon Knights and brother to the once evil druid, Lachlan."

Chapter Three

"The first kiss broke the innocence."
                    ~Diary of Princess Abela

The cry of a black falcon heralded the arrival of a lone horse, and Abela smiled. *Praise Mother Danu. All we require is another. We shall not depart with one horse. Never will I put my arms around Liam MacGregor again.* "Can we trouble you for some water and food, Cathal?"

"I would be honored to have ye join me." The druid extended his arm to her, and Abela accepted it with a smile.

"I suggest we continue on our journey. The land will sustain us," argued Liam.

She gave him a skeptical look and proceeded to enter the druid's cottage.

"Grant an old man an hour of your time," Cathal spoke over his shoulder.

Liam grunted a curse, but complied.

Abela removed her cloak and went to the hearth. She wished to know more about this human who was revered in the realm. Many of the Fae bards spoke eloquently of his mighty deeds in assisting the Dragon Knights and offering his wisdom to the Fenian Warriors.

Whatever was cooking in the pot over the flames

caused her stomach to rumble, and she inhaled deeply. "Smells divine, Cathal. What tempting fare have you prepared?"

The druid ambled about, collecting plates and cups from a shelf. After setting everything down, he went to a cupboard and brought forth an earthenware bottle. "A mixture of kale, onions, and wild mushrooms. Though I fear 'tis a meager fare for ye, Princess. The winter can be harsh here in the glen."

"I favor the hearty meal," she replied. Smiling inwardly, she waved a hand over the pot, increasing its contents.

"Wine?" asked Cathal.

"Most definitely." She beamed and made her way to sit at the small table.

Cathal poured some into their cups. "Let me also bring ye some bread. 'Tis wondrous that I made several loaves yesterday."

"Thank you."

Liam stood by the entrance, rigid as a stone pillar. How she longed to bring a smile to his features. What had happened to him? Had she expected gratitude for helping him escape his doom? Yes. But that wasn't what bothered her. When she removed her hood, he appeared horrified to see her. Furthermore, his verbal assaults were the worst. Gone was the Fae of laughter, poetry, and song. In his place stood a hardened warrior. And then Abela recalled seeing her brother Conn for the first time in many years. He appeared to possess the same demeanor. What did these warriors witness for them to lead such cynical lives? Abela could not fathom and her heart wept at the thought.

There had to be a way to crack the exterior of this

warrior. Abela smiled and patted the chair next to her. "Please come sit, Liam. We shall not tarry long." She swallowed, hating the lie she was about to tell. "I have not eaten in over a day, and I find my strength ebbing."

His features softened, and he nodded. As he took a seat beside her, he stole a quick glance at her.

Abela frowned. "Is something amiss?"

"You should not be wearing trews," he whispered, taking a sip of his wine.

She bit the inside of her mouth to keep from laughing. So he did notice her female form. Interesting. She waited to respond until after Cathal placed the bread on the table and departed to the hearth. "It would not have been proper dashing about in gauzy gowns." Abela lifted her cup and added, "I would have been forced to rip the material to my thighs."

Liam choked on his wine, and she turned her head away to shutter her features.

Cathal returned with bowls of soup for each and took a seat across from them. Bowing his head, he offered a prayer of thanks.

"Yes, all praise to Mother Danu for providing food and shelter," echoed Abela. She tore a piece of bread from the loaf and dipped it into her soup. Closing her eyes, she savored the flavors.

"Ye favor the broth?" asked Cathal.

Abela opened her eyes and smiled at the man. "I must commend your use of thyme with the other ingredients."

"You flatter me, princess."

"And you honor us by sharing. Where is this place?" asked Abela, reaching for her cup of wine.

Cathal settled his gaze on Liam, but continued to

eat his soup.

"The Great Glen. Specifically Urquhart land and the home of the Dragon Knights," replied Liam.

Abela sipped her wine, letting the warmth spread throughout her limbs. The stories of the Dragon Knights were legendary as well. Then she recalled all the stories, especially those of Cathal and deduced they were not in the ninth century. She would not misjudge the next time they went through the Veil.

Cathal settled back in his chair. "Is this your first time in the world of humans, Princess?"

"Yes." She swirled the wine in the cup, praying the druid would ask no more questions. Let him keep his interest on Liam.

"And ye journey with a Fenian Warrior without a chaperon?"

Smiling sweetly, Abela finished her wine and placed the cup down. "There are different rules within our realm. Women are treated as equals and do not need to have supervision."

"Truly?"

Liam grumbled a protest. "The Princess was in error not to bring along her attendants."

Her hands twisted within her lap, longing to rip out his tongue. "And as a princess, I have the right to travel with only *one* guard."

"Is this a new rule in the kingdom?" Liam challenged as he reached for the jug of wine and filled his cup to the brim.

She fidgeted within her chair. "You forget your absence has been lengthy. Or has the time of solitude addled your brain?"

Cathal leaned forward and placed his hands on the

table. "If I may ask Liam, what happened at your trial? When we last went our separate ways several years ago, ye were in shackles."

Abela noted the dark fury rising in Liam's features and body. She never knew the precise time he entered his confinement within the Room of Reflection. The whispers had reached her deep within the temple many moons after she had met with her brother. She had shared too much and now had no wish to bring shame to him in front of the druid.

"Liam has chosen to escort me on a journey of knowledge. It is part of his time spent in serving the royal household. The trial has been delayed."

Cathal rubbed a hand through his beard. "Interesting."

"How are the Dragon Knights?" Liam asked, before drinking deeply from his cup.

The druid eyed them both with curiosity. "They are almost done with the building of Aonach Castle and will make the move from Urquhart to their new home come late summer."

"Perchance one day—"

"No!" Liam cut her off with a wave of his hand.

Why must he continue to spare words with me? She directed her attention to Cathal. "As I was saying, I pray one day the Dragon Knights all find peace in their new home."

"There shall always be conflict, Princess. But ye are kind to offer your prayers. Surely, Mother Danu listens to ye more than the others."

Surprised by his last declaration, Abela said, "The Great Mother listens to all equally."

"Agreed," he acknowledged.

Liam stood. "Thank you for your hospitality, Cathal."

"Ye may find my horse in a shelter behind the cottage. Her name is Epona."

"A Roman name? I am surprised you named her thus," replied Abela, standing.

Cathal chuckled softly. "She was a gift from another druid and it suits her."

Liam inclined his head. "We shall return her after our travels here in this time." He grabbed his cloak and handed Abela her own.

Abela watched as Liam strode quickly out of the cottage.

"'Tis a dangerous path ye are on, Princess."

She met their host's searching gaze, but refused to divulge their true purpose for being here. The druid was inquisitive. "All journeys are fraught with danger, Cathal."

"This one can lead to both your deaths."

A tremor of unease skirted across her skin. His scrutiny was unnerving. "I can assure you no one shall die."

"A *priestess* outside the temple—unheard of. What would ye call this path you are on? A pleasant journey in the human world?"

The food in her stomach soured. "I appreciate your concern, but it is not warranted. It is obvious the years have passed here in your world, and you have come upon this knowledge of me as a priestess in the temple from my brother. I have recently left the order and now seek to obtain information."

He dipped a slight bow. "My apologies. When ye return, give my regards to Prince Conn."

If he ever speaks to me again. "Of course. It was an honor to meet you. The stories told in my kingdom speak highly of you."

Cathal gestured her forward. "Ye flatter me once again."

As they stepped outside the warmth of the cottage, Abela smiled. Not only would they have the use of Epona, but also the stray horse that stood munching on some tuffs of grass between the frozen parts of the ground.

"'Tis good ye have called another animal. And one in fine form," remarked Cathal.

She lifted her hand in front of the horse. "We shall return him to his master once we are done."

"Safe journey, Princess, and heed my words."

"You are very kind, Cathal." Clicking her fingers, the horse followed her down the path.

****

The bitter cold wind slashed across Abela's face. How she yearned to return to the cottage. What possessed her to think she could travel with the same endurance as a warrior during the harshness of the human's wintertime? Yes, she was trained in the art of blades and arrows, but she had not the stamina needed for now or in battle. In addition, what made all her sensibilities flee whenever she was around Liam? Had not her time serving Mother Danu help to temper her tongue and quiet her mind?

All her training, wisdom, and purpose were tossed aside when she drew near him. Never in her life did anyone rile her good judgment like this man. She spouted human curses, stomped her foot in agitation, and dared to push or poke him in the chest.

I am a princess—a priestess! Quiet the mind, still the beating heart, listen to the words of truth.

Abela straightened her back, inhaled the frigid air, and sought to bring warmth into her body and soul. She settled her gaze on Liam's back. He kept a steady pace as they galloped across the land. Did he not understand why she risked everything for him? "Foolish thought," she murmured. How could he empathize?

Liam was correct. The years had changed them both. Nevertheless, her heart had maintained a vigil all those moons. What had occurred over a century ago meant nothing to him, but she was unable to banish her feelings. Only when she entered the temple of Mother Danu was she able to seal the chains of emotions she felt for the Fae warrior. At least she believed it to be so. When the whispers of his predicament brushed against her cheeks one autumn day, the force of the words knocked her to the ground. She never knew who sent her the message, but death was not an option for the man who dared to give her a first kiss.

Abela lifted her gown and dipped her toes into the sparkling stream. She let out a sigh. The water was warm, soothing, and eased the strain from her limbs. The exercise with her tutor this morning was rigorous. She insisted on training Abela in her gown. When she tripped for the umpteenth time on the material, her tutor suggested the healing waters of the stream.

"Why not remove your gown and go for a swim?" Liam suggested, leaning against a rowan tree.

She gasped, unaware anyone was in this particular area of the glen. Of all the Fae, Abela was not prepared to be alone with Liam MacGregor. He stirred things within her—made her heart beat wildly, and her skin prickle with heat. His silver blue eyes roamed over her, and she fought the temptation to do what he'd suggested. Liam MacGregor was sinfully seductive, but forbidden to her. She'd heard the rumors he was destined to enter the Brotherhood of the Fenian Warriors, and she refused to enter into a dalliance. Her parents—no her brother would kill him and seek answers later.

Turning her back on the intruder, Abela stepped into the stream. She kept her focus outward and enjoyed the water lapping against her legs.

His footsteps retreated and for a moment, Abela regretted his departure. She stole a glance over her shoulder and gasped for the second time. He'd removed his tunic and rolled up his pants. He strode with intent and entered the stream, halting beside her.

Abela lifted her chin. "What are you doing?"

"Testing the water."

"Are you jesting with me?"

"Never, princess."

She studied his profile—one of power and ageless strength. The sun danced off his dark auburn hair, and Abela ached to brush away a lock that was forever falling across his eye and cheek. And his lips, oh my. No man should ever possess such full lips. Abela often fantasized on tasting them. Would they be soft? Or firm?

Liam kept his attention riveted on the stream. "The water is soothing."

"Agreed." Her gaze traveled the length of him.

He turned toward her. "Is there something wrong with my body?"

Abela felt the heat rise from her neck to her entire

face. "No," she whispered, unable to turn away.

His hand brushed against hers. "Do you find it...pleasing?"

A tremor of longing to be kissed filled Abela. She should flee this instant, but her feet refused to listen to her mind.

Liam reached out and tucked a stray curl behind her ear. His finger trailed down the side of her neck, and she shuddered. "You have not answered me."

"Yes," she replied rapidly.

The smile in his eyes contained a sensuous flame, and she was drawn to him. A soft breeze billowed around them. She ached to press her mouth against his. Just one kiss.

As if reading her thoughts, Liam cupped her chin and stroked his thumb over her bottom lip. "Your mouth begs to be kissed, princess."

She swallowed and did the unthinkable. "Then kiss me, Liam MacGregor."

His groan echoed around them as he took possession of her mouth. The kiss sent the pit of her stomach into a wild swirl of delicious sensations. Abela's body yearned to touch him, so she wrapped her arms around his neck. The contact of his skin against her chest ignited a burning desire for more.

Liam grasped her firmly around the waist with one arm and deepened the kiss. When his silken tongue sought entry, she opened fully to the seduction, tasting wine, apples, and his own scent. His moan resonated deep within her, and she found her body responding to a rhythm as old as the land they lived upon.

Never did Abela imagine the power behind a kiss—seductive, enchanting, shattering, and she craved more.

Liam demanded and Abela surrendered.

When he finally broke free, Liam's breathing was labored.

"Do not stop," she pleaded.

His eyes glittered with the light of the stars. "If I continue, I will claim you here upon the ground. I shall take your body and all you have to offer. Are you ready for the claiming?"

The rational side of Abela awoke, and she took a trembling step back. She had no words to give the man. Their destiny was on two separate roads—warrior and princess. He was not hers to claim, and Abela would not surrender her virginity so easily. By the Goddess, how she yearned to be someone else and not royalty.

He placed a chaste kiss on her forehead and turned away, retreating into the trees.

The air cooled considerably, but she refused to leave the water. Her body and mind ached with the loss.

Abela's mind relived the velvet warmth of his mouth, and she raised a trembling hand to her lips. "Never again, Liam MacGregor."

Chapter Four

"Rules are a foundation for life. If you believe yourself to be above them, you must be able to fly. Otherwise, the ground beneath you will be hard when you fall."

~Chronicles of Liam MacGregor

Liam brought his horse to the crest of the hill and scanned the valley below. Snow continued to fall, and the landscape was blanketed. He shifted to get a better view of their surroundings.

"Where are we going?" asked Abela, giving a firm pat to her horse.

He pointed in the distance. "Beyond those trees are the ancient Pictish standing stones. We can utilize them to travel back to the Fae realm."

Shock registered across her features. "No."

He almost laughed at the absurdity. This was his life, not hers. "I will not continue on this path, Abela."

She twisted the reins of her horse. "Why are you so eager to die?"

"My life was doomed the moment I took Aidan Kerrigan back in time to rescue his daughter." His tone remained resigned, and he looked away from her.

"Are you so sure?"

Liam snapped his attention back to her. "It is the law! No Fenian Warrior can alter the timeline to suit their own needs."

Her mouth thinned in disapproval. "Those *needs* were Aidan's—not yours."

"You're twisting the meaning of the words. You seek to bend the laws for your own understanding."

"Then let us return to when the Treaty of Feahan was written and change the one law," she encouraged, leaning across and touching his arm.

He shook his head solemnly. "Again, we are attempting to alter something which occurred on a timeline. Furthermore, even if I wanted to do so, I cannot."

Abela straightened. "Explain."

"You forget I was present at the signing of the treaty. One must never return to the exact moment in time they once occupied. You would split the very fabric of the universe, bringing about death to everyone and skewing the timeline irrevocably. In addition, there are many variables to attempting to go near the time-period. We must procure the document after it was signed."

She wiped a hand over her brow. "I...I had no idea."

"You are not at fault. This knowledge is only contained within the Brotherhood. You are not a Fenian Warrior." Liam noted the blue tinge to her lips. They had spent too long out in the frigid weather. His last remaining duty was to see her to safety. "Abela?"

She lifted her gaze to meet his. "Yes."

"Thank you for your efforts, but I deem it is wise to return home. The Fae guards will soon find me missing. I have no wish to do battle in the human world if they come charging at us."

Her eyes gleamed with a far-off look—one Liam understood well.

"I have another plan," she announced.

"Abela," he warned, raking a hand through his hair. "I do not want to come upon guards with you by my side."

She dismissively waved away his concerns. "We are both in trouble with our kingdom. First, I left the temple without permission. I violated a sacred trust. Do you know the judgment, if I should return?"

"Do tell."

"Banishment. My eye color has already receded to lavender and no longer contains the vibrant hues of all the gems of our world. Second, I broke the law by using the temple's magic to set you free. Do you want to know the punishment?"

"I am afraid to ask."

"Stripped of all my powers. Forever. And then I would be sent to a remote part of the realm. *Forever.* Third, I dared to defy my own people by breaking into a prison and releasing the notorious Fenian Warrior, Liam MacGregor on trial for death." She narrowed her eyes. "I don't believe anything like that has ever been attempted in our kingdom. Do you?"

"No," he replied dryly.

"Now do you see my predicament? We cannot return."

"Great Goddess! Then please state what we *can* do!" He pointed a finger in warning at her. "And do not tell me we are traveling back in time to rewrite the treaty."

Her eyes held mirth as she tapped a finger to her luscious mouth. "No, but why not include a provision to the treaty? Did not others do so down through the centuries?"

Liam wanted to throttle her. Apparently, she knew enough about the lore and facts of the treaty already. "Your knowledge is correct, but again, we cannot venture back to the time—"

"As you have professed many times," she interrupted, and quickly added, "but we can journey forward a few years of the signing, correct?"

Intrigued, he asked, "Exactly what law are you seeking to rewrite?"

Abela tapped a finger to her chin in thought. "Did you volunteer to take Aidan back in time?"

"No."

"He sought you out and asked your permission?"

"Not exactly. More a demand."

She pursed her lips. "He forced you?"

"Must I remind you, Aidan no longer possessed his powers? All he had was brute strength, and the blood of the Fae lineage."

"He exercised his right as a leader, correct?"

Liam blew out a frustrated sigh. "He presented me with a condition. If he could get permission from one Fae, I would grant his request and take him through the Veil of Ages."

Her brow furrowed. "Who granted him permission?"

"I am unable to divulge the name of the Fae. I took a vow of silence—one which will die with me."

Abela shifted on her horse, excitement flaring within her eyes. "But don't you understand? We don't need to add an amendment to the treaty. Why not ask this person to step forward and be a witness at your trial?"

"Did you not hear my words? A vow of silence. To my death!"

She gaped at him in horror. "Well, I would like to say a few words to this Fae for putting you in this predicament. Shameful."

Liam settled his gaze beyond the trees. Her idea of adding an amendment to the treaty was appealing. He'd known of several during the past few centuries. Furthermore, they were amended by the royal houses of the Fae, not by a Fenian Warrior. He brushed a hand over his chin. In truth, it was senseless to continue on this journey. Both were now doomed. Abela for leaving the temple and breaking him free. For himself, agreeing to leave with her and considering an alternate possibility to his current situation. If he hadn't, then perhaps she would have abandoned her irrational plan. Did he long for death? No. Yet, there truly was no other alternative.

He returned his attention to Abela. Even in the harsh weather, her profile was regal. Out of all the Fae in the kingdom, she was the only female to twist his guts and make his blood burn. This journey was fraught with uncertainty, but having her by his side might prove to be his greatest challenge as a warrior. She had stirred the ashes of feelings he had buried when he recited his vows and received his markings as a Fenian Warrior.

I will not succumb to the lure of your beauty, princess. You are not mine to possess.

Slowly, Abela angled her head to meet his intense stare. "I have no wish to return. We have come this far, so will you dare to see how much we can tempt fate?"

Her words ignited something Liam had not felt in

many moons. *Hope.* "They will track us. They will not stop until we are captured."

"They can try," she challenged.

His decision made, he said, "You must learn quickly, Abela. With your powers and my guidance, we can travel through the Veil. Heed my words and do not deviate. If there is any error, we could travel from one century to the next without achieving our destination. Or worse, we could become separated." He refused to scare her further with the possibility of entering into another dimension—lost within the fabric of the universe.

Her mouth twitched in humor. "You will find me a quick learner, Fenian Warrior." She pulled forth a pendant from around her neck. The red oval stone glimmered in their stark surroundings.

Liam tried to contain his shock. "You have the Stone of Ages from our homeland?"

"I am the keeper, yes. This will make it easier to travel within the Veil. But I require your aid."

"Why is it not with your brother, Conn?"

"As I have stated, much has occurred in your absence. The relic has been entrusted into my care. This is all the knowledge I shall share with you."

What happened to Conn? When Cathal had referred to his friend as the prince, Liam had to control the questions spilling forth from his mind. What terms did they give Conn at his trial? The Fae Warrior had always been adamant about not seeking his heritage and claiming the throne. Yet somehow, Conn became the Prince of the Fae and would eventually be their king. *His king.*

"Answer me this, Abela. How did Conn step back

into the role of being the prince?"

She pulled the hood more firmly around her head. "It is not my place to discuss his journey."

"Can you share anything?"

"No."

Snow fell more heavily, and Liam slammed the door on his questions. "We must retreat from the bitter elements."

"Agreed," she muttered.

"Then let us proceed to the standing stones." Liam gave a nudge to his horse and off they rode.

By the time they reached the ancient giants, the snow had turned into a fierce blizzard. Abela slid off her horse, eliciting words of comfort to the animal and led him near the tallest stone pillar.

Liam withdrew his sword. "Hold out your palm. Since you are royalty, your blood with help transport us through the Veil of Ages."

She removed her glove and held her hand out in front of him. Her gaze never wavered from his, and Liam noted the trust within those beautiful depths.

He made a small incision in the middle of her palm and smeared a portion of the blood on the stone. "Keep your focus on me. Do not falter for a second. The lights will tempt you."

"I understand, Liam. The realms in between are a delight to behold, but the most dangerous and deadly."

He sheathed his sword and wrapped an arm around her waist.

"And the horses?" she shouted.

The wind howled around them, and Liam raised his voice. "You will send them back the moment we leave this century."

There was no room for doubt. Liam required utter concentration. To transport them both through the Veil was a risk he dared to take. His fate was already decreed, so another law broken wouldn't matter. If only he had his Fenian powers, they could have been there in a whisper of seconds. Now he needed to create an opening.

He drew in a deep breath and released all his anxiety on the exhale.

When he uttered the first words in their ancient language, the ground rumbled beneath them. Mother Danu was not pleased. Abela leaned her head against his chest and fisted her hands in his cloak. Liam continued to chant the words as lightning splintered the sky and slashed over their heads. He refused to retreat and raised his voice over the clamor of thunder.

The vortex opened to reveal a swirling mass of fog. "Send the animals back!" he shouted.

He heard Abela snap her fingers and then grasped her hand. He kept his attention riveted on their destination as he pulled them along. One year. One place. One king. And this all depended on Abela's focus to get them there. Lights danced all around him. Echoes of other timelines. The air grew heavy, slowing their progress, until Abela stepped in front of him and lifted the Stone of the Ages.

The mists retreated, and they were swept off their feet in a giant swoosh of air. The magic catapulted them through the void, and Liam grunted a curse as his back hit solid ground with Abela landing on top of him. A resounding clang echoed around them as the vortex slammed shut.

"Ears...hurt," gasped Abela, trying to draw in a

breath.

Liam cradled her head against his chest. "It will soon pass."

"Is it normal?"

"Yes, when traveling unconventionally." In truth, Liam considered them fortunate to have survived the journey. Never had he attempted this method of traveling the Veil.

She lifted her head. "And we have to do this again? Through the stones?"

He strangled on a burst of laughter. "Unfortunately, yes. It is the only way. To venture through the land might prove far more dangerous."

"Sweet Goddess, that was deafening," she complained.

Liam reached up and pushed the hood of her cloak back from her head. Color had returned to her features. He was unable to turn away from staring at her lips. They were full and as red as the berries he had eaten many moons ago during a Midsummer feast. Her body was soft, warm, inviting, and desire shot through his veins.

Abela's eyes widened, and she quickly scrambled off of him. After rolling in the opposite direction, Liam sat up and surveyed their surroundings. He clasped his hands over his bent knees and tried to calm his swollen erection. Lush grass and wildflowers as far as he could see wrapped around them. He deemed it might be late spring or early summer. Shielding his eyes from the sunlight, he smiled. Castle Dunkelp glimmered in the far west. Though it only contained one large keep surrounded by other round houses, it was a splendor to behold from a distance.

"We have arrived near Moot Hill at Scone," he announced and stood slowly. When Liam got no response from Abela, he peered over his shoulder. She stood several feet away. Uncertainty clouded her features, and he regretted his earlier lustful attentions.

"Abela..." he started forward, trying to form words of an apology.

She quickly masked her emotions and held out her hand. "I am ready to take us near the castle."

He clenched his jaw so tight he feared it would snap. Taking her hand, he gave her a curt nod of approval.

She whisked them away in a sliver of light, and they emerged within a cluster of pine trees. Abela instantly dropped his hand and waved her fingers over her body. Gone were the trews and tunic. She was covered in a gown of ivory edged with silver trimmings. With a snap of her fingers, a cloak materialized in her arms. She slipped the garment over her figure. Liam watched in awe as the princess tapped a finger to her head, and her ebony tresses cascaded in soft waves down her back. Elegant, refined, and noble. All for the King of the Scotland, he mused.

Abela gave him a sideways glance. "Can you prepare yourself, or would you like me to do the honors?"

Liam took in his appearance and with a wave of his hand transformed his ragged clothing into those of his homeland.

"Are you ready?" she asked, holding out her hand once again.

Liam stepped in front of her. "One rule to commit to memory is a Fae never appears by magic in any king or chieftain's castle."

"Duly noted. Have you considered the speech you will present to the king?" she asked, moving to his side.

He had little time to ponder what he would say to King MacAlpin. Yet, one thought came thundering through his mind. It was a preposterous idea, but would provide the necessary argument. The only problem he foresaw was Abela might contest the plan.

"Yes. Before we enter through the gates, I require your acceptance in this scheme."

She let out a groan. "Pray continue and don't keep me in anticipation."

Liam squared his shoulders as if preparing for a speech. "My reasons are simple. We have come to amend a law and require the original treaty."

"That's your explanation?"

He kept his attention on the keep. "In order to amend the treaty, not only do I require the original, but the other three copies. This is only the first step. If I speak the true reason, the king will not part with the treaty. I must pledge a vow to return it to him."

"So what untruth are you going to spout?"

Liam turned his gaze to Abela. "I am requesting a marriage contract with the Princess of the Fae and have been given a quest from our council." She gasped, and he continued, "I seek to rewrite the laws of the Fenian Warriors, specifically the one about traveling through the Veil of Ages for certain gains. I wish to make an amendment in the case of an extreme emergency, so other Fae or humans can travel the Veil with the assistance of the Fenian Warriors. Of course, I would present this in a language the king would comprehend."

"Surely, you have gone mad." Her tone was one of

astonishment. "Why would the king consider your reasoning?" Abela rubbed at her temples. "I am not prepared to accept this falsehood about a…*marriage contract.*"

Liam waved a hand outward. "Think, Abela. Never before has a Fae female entered the mortal realm of men. King MacAlpin is shrewd and calculating. He will want to know why you are at my side. In addition, he might favor your pleasing company and grant my request." He folded his arms across his chest. "*Or* you can stay behind in the trees while I visit with each human who holds the treaty."

"Absolutely not!"

"Good, since I judge it wise to not separate. If you sense the smallest vibration of another Fae, we must flee immediately."

This time Liam held out his hand to Abela. She hesitated briefly and then grasped his fingers. Her touch was warm, soft, and he fought a wave of emotions. This was all an act. *A lie.* Never would the Princess of the Fae realm belong to a renegade Fenian Warrior.

Slamming the door on his heart, Liam escorted them toward the gates.

Chapter Five

"My entire life was based on truths and beauty. But I would spout any lie for the Fae who ignited a firestorm with one kiss."

~ *Diary of Princess Abela*

Fae Realm ~ Gardens of Prince Conn, leader of the Fenian Warriors

Conn lifted his daughter into his arms, smiling as her laughter brought forth all the hummingbirds to swirl in a colorful parade around them. "Do they sing a song of praise, lovely Sorcha?"

She babbled in her own language and held out a tiny plump finger. One of the smaller hummingbirds landed serenely, and she bent to blow a kiss over the delicate bird. He watched in fascination, until they all circled in a crown over her head and then spirited off to the flowers.

"You are their queen," he uttered softly, and placed a kiss on her forehead.

Slowly, Conn made his way through the peaceful garden, heading toward the balcony and his wife, Ivy. An open book lay in her lap as she slept. The sun shimmered off her features, and his breath caught. He never tired of seeing the lovely vision of his beloved.

He gently placed Sorcha in her carriage. Turning

toward his wife, he knelt beside her. Her eyes fluttered open, and she smiled.

Yawning, she whispered, "It was difficult to keep my eyes open."

Conn stroked a finger across her cheek. "The sun beckons one to rest. You are still recovering from your birthing."

Ivy closed the book on her lap and attempted to sit. "Humph! Might I remind you, I healed in no time many months ago. You are pampering me far too much, my Celt."

"I call it *loving* my wife," he argued and kissed her soundly.

She moaned as he slipped his tongue inside the warmth of her mouth. When he broke free, her eyes darkened with desire. "You can pamper me with kisses anytime."

His hand skimmed down her arm. "Would you care for—" He paused and stood abruptly.

"What's wrong?"

He hissed out a curse and closed his eyes.

Ivy grasped his hand. "You're scaring me, Conn. Talk to me."

His anger barely contained, he shook free from her embrace. "Liam has escaped from his prison. I am to appear before the Fae council immediately."

Standing, Ivy muttered, "Oh, my stars. How?"

"Unknown, but he had to have assistance."

They both turned at the pounding on their chamber doors. As Conn quickly made his way to the entrance, the sky darkened, and thunder rolled in the distance.

"I've never witnessed that color in the sky before," observed Ivy.

He glanced over his shoulder. "Nor I."

She bundled Sorcha into her arms and entered the chambers with Conn. When he opened the door, Ronan and Taran stood there with grim looks and dressed in battle clothing.

"May we come inside?" asked Ronan.

Conn stepped aside and gestured for them to enter. "What—"

Taran shook his head and placed a finger against his mouth as he passed by Conn.

As soon as Conn closed the door, he turned abruptly toward the two Fenian Warriors. "Explain."

"The news is spreading throughout the kingdom," replied Taran. "We had no desire to speak in the hall."

"Yes, I've received the message that Liam has escaped. I am ordered to appear before the Fae council immediately."

Thunder crashed all around them, and Ivy stumbled. Conn grasped her firmly to his side.

"There's more," stated Ronan in a hushed voice.

"More?" Conn snapped and settled Ivy and Sorcha in a nearby chair.

Fisting his hands, he glared at the warriors. They both looked at one another before turning their attention back to him. Conn noted the hesitation and feared his next question. "You know the name of Liam's accomplice?"

Ronan shifted his stance. "Before we divulge the name, ye must swear an oath ye will not kill Liam."

Uneasiness settled within Conn. Had he not worked tirelessly to find a solution for Liam? "Your request makes no sense. I would never bring harm to Liam. He's escaped, not committed a crime against me."

"Then I shall take that as an oath of confirmation."

Once again, thunder roared above them, and this time Sorcha screamed. Conn swiftly glanced at his wife. Ivy's sight had shifted to one of a seer—pale and unfocused, and he went to her side. Kneeling down, he placed a soothing hand on his daughter's back. Her cries soon turned to soft whimpers.

"Can you share your vision, *mo ghrá*?"

"You must not interfere with the destiny. A new beginning has been forged across the realms. You may long for his death, but it is not yours to take. War has begun. Battles will be fought. What you deem in the name of justice will only incite both realms, human and Fae. You, Conn MacRoich, Fenian Warrior, Leader of the Brotherhood, *future* King of the Fae, must do battle with both. Protect the innocent."

Ivy blinked and wiped a hand over her brow. "Mother Danu has spoken."

Confused by her words, he grasped her hand. "Why does she not speak to me? To the Brotherhood?"

Tears misted her eyes when she lifted her gaze to Conn. "Her heart is broken."

"Is this the reason for the darkness and thunder?"

She nodded and clutched Sorcha more firmly against her chest.

Conn kissed her lips and stood. Anxiety clawed inside him. "Is she angry with Liam? Us?"

Ivy's lips trembled, and she looked away.

He began to pace the room, trying to understand his wife's words, Liam's escape, and the disturbance with Mother Danu. Conn halted and lifted a single thought outward to another for answers. He waited, attempting to curb his growing rage when his sister did not respond. When silence greeted him, he turned toward the warriors.

"Who assisted in Liam's escape?" His question came out in a growl.

"Remember your vow," warned Taran.

Conn pointed a finger at him. "Name!"

"Abela," offered Ivy softly.

An anguished cry ripped forth from Conn, and he staggered from the blow of his sister's name. The pain of betrayal sliced deep into his heart. His friend had allowed his sister to help him escape. Allowed a priestess of the temple to do the unimaginable. Allowed this transgression, knowing the pain it would cause within the kingdom. Liam should have halted this horrific plan. He was no longer a brother. No longer a friend.

Ronan moved toward him, and Conn's eyes blazed with ferocity. "Do not take another step."

The warrior clasped his hands behind his back and halted his progress.

Conn turned from them and braced his hands on the stone mantel. His body shook with fury and it took all of his control not to unleash it outward. He burned to cleave out the heart of the Fae he once considered his brother. "How did you come upon this knowledge?"

"The king sent for us," Ronan responded. "They— the king and queen—were notified immediately when Abela's presence was no longer felt within the temple."

"Does the Fae council know?"

"No. And the king has requested the information to be kept in silence."

"Good," he gritted out, turning to face everyone.

"The king has asked for you to join him in his inner chamber."

"No. The Fae council awaits, and I judge it wise to squash their effort to form an army to pursue Liam."

Taran stepped forward. "What do you recommend?"

Conn tried to temper his sizzling anger. "*We* will go after him. Order Rory to return. He's currently at Aonach Castle with Adam and Meggie MacFhearguis."

"A grand idea," Ronan proclaimed. "His blood brother can track him."

Conn started for the door. "Agreed. Since he will be the only person who can keep me from taking Liam's life."

Ivy's gasp lingered within his mind long after he left their chambers.

****

As Conn stood before the nine Fae council members, he tried to calm his breathing. Presently, three things disturbed him—having his wife witness his fury, Liam escaping with his sister, and returning to a room that made him nauseated. Yet this time he was not the one on trial, though, he sensed they would argue otherwise.

Per Conn's earlier request, he had asked the council to give an alternate form of punishment for Liam, instead of the death sentence. He petitioned and reminded them of the request to spare the lives of himself, Rory, and Liam made by Meggie MacKay MacFhearguis after the final battle with the evil druid, Lachlan. They argued for days, concluding they required more time to offer an alternative punishment for Liam.

He laughed inwardly at the irony. If they had acted swiftly with another sentence, he would not be standing here before the members.

Conn glared at them as they continued to whisper in hushed tones, ignoring him. His patience was lacking and their behavior unjust. He judged it prudent to take control. "As we are all aware, Liam MacGregor has escaped his prison in the Room of Reflection. I have assembled a group of Fenian Warriors to go after him."

The leader of the Fae council, Seneca, eyed him skeptically. "We are not ready to hear your account."

Conn dared to take a step forward. "Regardless, I am done with standing here while you proceed to talk in muted voices. I am *not* on trial here. I came at your request, so either you speak now, or I shall take my leave. The king has requested an audience with me."

"How dare you—" objected one of the council members.

Seneca silenced the Fae with her hand. "Enough."

The Fae slammed his hand onto the marble table. "Must we be subjected to this intolerable lack of respect?"

Conn despised the council member known as Tulare. He slowly turned his attention to the Fae. "And why must the members continue to show their *lack* of respect for the Prince of the Realm? You kept me waiting for an hour outside this chamber. Furthermore, once summoned inside, you refused to acknowledge my presence."

Seneca stood. "Clarify. Are you here as our prince or the leader of the Fenian Warriors?"

He arched a brow in mock severity. "Both."

Several of the members gasped but remained quiet.

She tapped her finger on a golden leaflet. "We are at an impasse on what to do. We must work together for the good of both worlds."

"I concur. If there is nothing else—"

"You will take five of the council guards with you," interjected Seneca.

"We are not searching within the realm," he countered. "You can have the guards sent to the royal household. They can assist them."

She narrowed her eyes. "And where are you going?"

"To the human world. Unless something has changed, I believe only the Fenian Warriors can travel through the Veil of Ages."

"Are all your warriors accounted for?" Tulare demanded.

Conn gave the man a heated glance. "Yes. None from the Brotherhood freed Liam MacGregor."

"Any thoughts on the accomplice?" asked Seneca.

"None," he lied.

As Conn turned to leave, Seneca's voice sent a chill down his spine. "It is the determination of the council members that when the warrior is found, his trial will be swift and death the punishment. I realize there might have been an argument to spare his life and issue him another punishment, but now that will not happen. There will be no argument, Prince Conn. Do you understand my words?"

He refused to comment and did the unthinkable in front of the members. With a wave of his hand, Conn vanished.

Appearing in front of his father's royal chambers, Conn proceeded along the corridor to the right. He tried to calm his breathing. Being among the council members had only increased his agitation. Since he was unable to fathom his father's reaction, he deemed it best to temper the beast within his own soul. As he took the crystal steps leading downward, he pushed aside his emotions.

Coming to a halt before the massive door, Conn lifted his hand and pressed his fingers over the smooth wood.

"You may enter." King Ansgar announced within Conn's mind.

The door opened, and golden light spilled out. Conn stepped inside and closed the door with a single thought. Warm mists surrounded him as he followed the path to the inner chamber. He ducked through the hollow of an ancient oak tree and emerged inside. His father stood leaning against his desk, staring at the giant map on the wall of the Fae realm.

Conn's heart clenched. It looked as if his father had aged overnight. The gray at his temples was more pronounced, and lines he'd never witnessed before now creased his brow. He paused before the desk and waited patiently for his father to acknowledge him.

"Once long ago, the prophecy spoke of a time when the Fae would welcome the arrival of twins to the kingdom. They heralded this as a sign from the Gods and Goddesses. Light and dark—a balance for both worlds. It would bring about a change of enlightenment. Never did I consider they were foretelling our destiny." His father's laugh was bitter. "I'd love to hear what the Fates have decreed with this new path, especially the one for your sister."

"We will find Abela," reassured Conn.

King Ansgar slammed the wall with his fist. "Not in this world!" He turned away from the map and leaned his hands on the desk. "Has she gone mad? She left the temple of Mother Danu without consent. And what possessed her to free the warrior and enter the human world?"

"What are mother's thoughts?"

He raked a hand through his hair—something Conn had never witnessed from the great Fae. "When word reached us about Abela's absence from the temple, your mother left immediately. She has yet to return. And before you ask, I do not know where she went." Letting out a heavy sigh, he approached Conn. "I can only surmise she went to visit the Seer."

"Then perhaps she can give us insight as to where Abela has fled."

"And the warrior," snapped his father. "I believed him to be honorable! Why would he risk escaping with Abela? Does he not understand her predicament?"

Conn shifted his stance. "Sadly, since Abela is royalty, he might reason she is able to dwell in the mortal world. He is unaware the Brotherhood and the Master Apothecary are the only Fae able to live among the humans and travel the Veil of Ages. Even for a time, I thought all Fae could travel to the human world."

"A poor assumption on any warrior's part," the king protested. "This is why I entrusted the Fenian Warriors with the ability to travel through the Veil. I considered it wise to have only one group of trusted warriors with this power. I removed the ability from the Master Apothecary centuries ago, yet, they are permitted to live above in order to obtain herbal knowledge and pass on their lore to humans who are gifted."

Conn nodded. "I must make ready. How much time does Abela have in the human world?"

"Time moves differently in the other world. And since it has never been tested, my daughter will be the first to tamper with *her* strings of life. With each shift through the Veil, her essence will begin to fade." He waved his hand in the air. "Can you find a reason for this insanity?"

"None. My concern is to find Abela and bring her back to the realm. I have entrusted Liam into the care of the other Fenian Warriors. I fear it will take many to hold me back from doing bodily harm to him."

His father's features hardened. "His sentence has been ordered. There is nothing I can do, Conn. I might have reasoned with the council before for his freedom, but no longer. I cannot forgive this reckless and dishonorable action." He placed a hand on Conn's shoulder. "Have you tried to contact your sister?"

He stiffened, fearing his father would ask the question. "She has severed our link—our bond as twins."

Dropping his hand, his father went back to his desk. "Do whatever it takes to find her and the warrior. You have my permission, my power in the human world to seek them out. You are her only hope, my son."

"You do realize she has the Stone of Ages in her possession, and it will be difficult to track her. Although, I don't believe she has the knowledge to use the stone properly and would never dare to remove it from our kingdom."

The king opened a small marble box on his desk. He drew forth an obsidian pendant and handed it to Conn. "I've infused the stone with some of my powers. You will be able to track her more efficiently. Be warned, though. Your sister will know when any Fae are near. You will have to have sharper wits."

"I am a trained warrior—"

"Do not underestimate the strength of your twin, Conn. She did not have the training of the Brotherhood, but her power is cunning, and she can command the land more than you. She has been among the priestesses for a long time. Her knowledge of the abyss between both realms is vast. If you recall, she brought you and Ivy back through one of them, so you could save her life in our world. In addition, if she freed a warrior from his prison, what will prevent her from using the Stone of Ages?"

Conn clutched the pendant to his chest. How little he knew of his sister. Warrior, priestess, princess, and female. Deadly combinations and he had no desire to do battle against his twin. If only he could find a reasoning to her madness.

He inclined his head to his father. "I shall not fail you."

King Ansgar smiled sadly. "You never have, my son."

Chapter Six

"I allowed my twin brother to be birthed first into the realm, so he could prepare my entrance into our world."

~*Diary of Princess Abela*

The torches flickered and snapped as Abela and Liam made their way along the narrow corridor to the main living area of King MacAlpin. She had never experienced the human world and so far, this experience lacked in design and hospitality. Yet, their visit with the Druid was cordial. The guards had left them outside the gates far too long before allowing them to enter. Abela had read the tales of the great king and the humans in the Library of the Ancients. Excitement had flared inside her at meeting this honored man. However, her spirits sagged when he chose not to present himself at the gates. Perhaps she expected more from this human male. She thought it best to reserve any further judgments until they had spoken in person.

Nevertheless, it did not prepare her for the reality.

As they entered the long narrow passageway, the area opened to reveal a blazing fire centered in the middle of the room. Abela lifted her gaze and watched as smoke trailed out of a small hole in the roof. Benches and tables flanked either side of the fire pit and several dogs slept on the ground. She scanned the rest of the area, searching for the king. Shields adorned the walls around them, and Abela was intrigued. Some held carvings of deer, horses, and Celtic symbols.

When she tripped over some carcass on the floor, one of the animals let out a low growl and raised itself. Horrified, she lifted her hand and sought to bring reassurance to the dog. She was not here for his meal and made it known within his mind. The beast let out a sigh and slumped back onto the ground.

Abela twisted her hands in front of her. After the guards departed, she turned her displeasure toward Liam. "Is this how the great king lives? Along with the animals? Where is his grand castle? Why is he not present to greet his guests?"

"Either he is returning from a hunt or bedding his current mistress. This is his meeting room." There was a trace of laughter in his voice

Abela's stomach lurched. "Hunting…as in *animals*?"

Liam leaned near her. "Humans like to eat meat."

She swallowed and put a hand over her stomach. "Barbaric."

He shrugged and bent to ruffle the fur of one of the dogs. "It is their custom. There are a few humans who I have encountered who only eat what the land provides—fruits, grains, and vegetables."

"Then I can assume those individuals have evolved into higher beings. All animals are sacred to the Mother."

Liam coughed into his hand and turned from her.

Abela wandered near a giant chair at the back of the chamber. Its regal position spoke volumes within the space. Large armrests depicted two dragons and she smiled. She traced a finger over the Celtic spirals that were carved into their backs, marveling at the craftsmanship.

"Do ye favor the beasties?"

Startled, Abela turned abruptly. The man's commanding presence surrounded her. His dark eyes bore into hers as they twinkled with mischief.

She inclined her head in respect. "You have done justice to our dragons, King MacAlpin."

He took a hold of her hand, and Abela fought the urge to pull away. "Ye grace us with your beauty."

Liam emerged and placed a comforting hand on her elbow. "May I present Princess Abela."

The king's eyes widened. "Truth?"

"Yes," Abela confirmed.

His thumb brushed over her knuckles. "Why would a *princess* dare to leave their world?" He settled his gaze on Liam, refusing to release her hand.

"She desired to make the journey with me, before the princess becomes my *wife*."

Abela quickly took the lead. "I yearned to learn more about the world my future husband has spoken so highly of." She pulled away from Liam and smiled demurely. "It has always been a wish of mine to meet the honored king and Dragon Knight."

"Only half," corrected King MacAlpin. "My mother's kin were related to the knights." He steered her away from Liam. "Surely you would not be traveling without guards, Liam. Not with such a precious cargo as the princess."

She tapped him on the arm. "They are by the entrance to the giant rowan tree bordering your lands."

"Do all the Fae females speak for their men?" He asked tersely.

"Only this one," Liam replied in a dry tone.

King MacAlpin roared with laughter.

Abela grimaced. "Forgive me. I am not schooled in the laws of…human males."

"I have overlooked the manners. Your striking beauty allows for the misgivings."

By the Goddess, she fought the barb settling on her tongue. The man thought himself a charmer, but in reality, he was a brute. With a single thought, she could reduce his size to one of his dogs. "Where are we going?"

King MacAlpin paused by the entrance and released her. "Nowhere." He closed the massive door to the room and folded his arms over his chest. "Why are ye here, Fenian Warrior?"

"I have come for the treaty. I am proposing an amendment to one of the laws. As you are aware, I cannot present my case to the King of Fae without your copy and those of the others."

"Aye. But which law?"

Liam clasped his hands behind his back. "That in a harsh time to both worlds, a Fenian Warrior may escort another Fae *or* human through the Veil. There will be no profit, merely to protect."

The king blew out a curse. "Did we not argue over this many moons ago? Why would I agree to this *change*?"

Abela held her breath. Human males were as stubborn as their Fae counterparts. She stole a glance at Liam.

"It shall only be used during troubled times and

would apply to both worlds."

"The same law, only different words."

"But one that is important. Think of those in the future." Liam's expression was tight with strain.

Abela noted the censure in the king's eyes. He was indeed shrewd. Liam had not presented his case. It was weak. Liam required something more to stir this man.

"Nae. I cannae agree and hold firm as I did at the signing."

Liam's eyes blazed, and he shook his fist at the king. "I fought the battle with the Dark One, along with some of my other brothers. Good men on both sides of the worlds—Fae and human died. And it wasn't only the one battle. There were several over a period of many moons."

The king straightened from the door. "The outcome?"

"The Dark One and his companions have been vanquished. The evil that plagued the worlds has been destroyed for another thousand years. I cannot share anymore. Nevertheless, I thought you would value the account."

King MacAlpin scratched his beard, moving away from the door. He traveled along the length of the room staring at the fire. "I have heard the bards weave the tale of the last battle with the Dark One. Even some of my hardened warriors grew pale listening to the account. If I give ye my treaty, ye ken I must sign it last, after the others have added their mark."

Abela let out a sigh of relief. Her Fae warrior had done well.

"I give you my word I will return the treaty with the others' marks. I understand the formality."

King MacAlpin retrieved a jug off the table by his chair. He returned with two cups. After filling them, he presented one to Liam. "Your pledge as a Fenian Warrior."

Liam took the cup. "My vow to you."

The king took a sip. "Ye ken the battle ye might have with the others?"

Great Goddess, she was merely an ornament here. The man ignored her completely. *Your manners are horrid.* "Who are they?" she asked.

The king's expression was one of pained tolerance. "The MacAoidh in the Great Glen, Niall across the sea, and your own people."

Liam regarded her over the rim of his cup. "The Niall is part of the great O'Neill clan."

Abela nodded in understanding.

King MacAlpin placed a foot on the stone near the fire. "Ye may find getting Niall's mark challenging. He has changed."

"Are you at war with him again?" Liam drained the contents of his cup and placed it on a nearby table.

"Nae. He has welcomed a traveling monk and is learning the new religion. We are now thought of as heathens."

Liam scowled. "Then gaining entrance might prove thorny."

The king took a fist to his chest and let out a belch. "Aye."

"Nevertheless, the journey must be made."

King MacAlpin settled his gaze on Abela. "Traveling is dangerous."

She lifted her chin in defiance. "We have the protection of the Goddess, Mother Danu."

His eyes roamed down her body and then returned to her face. "'Tis a pity ye cannae prolong your stay."

Liam drew her to his side. "Our time is short, since the princess must return soon to prepare for the wedding."

"Ahh…the work of a woman. Allow me to go fetch the treaty."

Abela gritted her teeth as she watched the king leave the room. The fire snapped, the blistering sound mirroring her mood. "Rude man."

Liam placed a finger over her lips and leaned near her ear. "The man has spies everywhere. Wait to speak until we are free from this place."

The breath of his words warmed her face, and she glanced into the fire, praying he did not notice her reaction. Quickly composing herself, she made ready to depart. "A pity we cannot snap our fingers and vanish." She turned toward him. "Any objections?"

"Sadly, it is not to be done."

She clucked her tongue in disapproval.

Fortunately, they did not have to wait long. King MacAlpin returned and handed Liam the rolled parchment. "Remember your vow, Fenian Warrior."

Liam tucked the treaty inside his cloak. "Thank you."

Abela gave the man her most charming smile, though she doubted it reached her eyes. "Long life and good fortune, King MacAlpin."

The man dipped his head. "And a good marriage bed to ye."

"I can hardly wait," she responded, happy to see his smile replaced by one of astonishment.

Liam gripped her arm and escorted her from the

castle. As soon as they cleared the gates and entered the woods, Abela yanked herself free from his grasp.

She hurried down through a narrow path. "Infuriating man! He did nothing but leer at me the entire time. Not once did he ask us to sit *or* offer us food." She halted and held up a finger. "Banish the thought of food. I've witnessed the floor. Yet, I would have enjoyed some wine. At least *you* were offered a cup."

Fisting her hands on her hips, Abela tried to bring her breathing to normal. After several moments, she glanced over her shoulder. Liam was leaning against a tree, trying to contain his fits of laughter. "Men," she muttered, fighting the smile forming on her lips.

With a wave of her hand, she magically replaced her gown with trews, tunic, and a cloak. Snapping her fingers, her unbound hair became two braids once again. Folding her arms over her chest, she waited for Liam to compose himself.

As he pushed away from the tree, he raked a hand through his hair. "Oh, princess, you are in the world of humans. Contrary to how we treat our women, the men here view their females as those to be bedded and provide heirs—especially in this century. And your quick words about longing for the marriage bed only whetted his appetite for *you*."

Her face heated as Liam moved closer. "I was not about to be the one shocked. In addition, I thought I did well in controlling my tongue. The comment was merely a parting barb."

He stroked a finger over her cheek. "Are you truly longing for the claiming? The marriage bed?"

Shocked by his words, Abela smacked his hand

away and turned from his smoldering look. *You will never know how I yearn for you, Liam.* "Once, but no longer. Furthermore, you know what I meant when I spoke those words. I had no wish for him to shame me."

"Then you will never marry?"

She swallowed and twisted her fingers around one of her braids. "What is the point? When I return, banishment will be my future. I have brought dishonor to my family, the temple, and Mother Danu." Walking over to a pine tree, she placed her hand on the rough bark. "Even now, she refuses to acknowledge me. In time I pray she will forgive me, along with everyone else I may have wronged."

"We both walk the path of unknown futures, Abela," Liam added, and placed a gentle hand on her shoulder. "Even in the darkest moments of my life as a warrior, Mother Danu was always there. Out of all our people in the kingdom, you should understand this wisdom."

Tears misted Abela's eyes. "This is why my grief is so great."

Liam wiped away a tear that spilled down her cheek. "You should not have freed me."

"If given another chance, I still wouldn't have deviated from my original plan. Death was not an option for you," she protested softly.

He took a step back. "It was not your decision to make. Eventually, we all end up on death's path."

"But not today."

His smile was as intimate as a kiss. "For now we live and continue *together* on our quest."

She pushed away from the tree. "Where to now?

The MacAoidh?"

Liam chuckled. "Yes. Let us travel to the home of the Dragon Knights. You will find their manners more hospitable. Alexander is the current leader."

"I favor meeting them. I've heard so many good tales about these men." She lifted her head as they emerged forth from the trees. The sky was blue, and a warm breeze brushed over her face. She glanced at Liam. "Would you rather walk back to the standing stones?"

"Are you sure, *princess*?"

Abela rolled her eyes. "I am fully prepared to make the trek back. If you recall, Aidan Kerrigan trained me. His grueling hikes through the rugged hills of Locheesh were ones I mastered."

"Did you know Aidan was forbidden to train you?"

Abela kept a steady pace with Liam. "Yes. One of several heated arguments with my father alerted me to that fact. He considered it unwise for a princess of the realm to be training with a Fenian Warrior. Although, I did argue that Aidan was their leader. The battle of words with my father lasted for several days."

"Why did you wish to endure harsh training? For what purpose? Insight into the warriors?"

Snorting in disgust, she responded, "I sought to learn why the Brotherhood held interest for Conn. I never dreamed he would enter the prestigious group. He was the prince—our next king. Another item you forget, Liam, I am Conn's twin. In many ways, we are a reflection of the other. I might be female, but my power, strength, *and* stubbornness can rival his on any day." Abela slowed her steps. "I am in error. His brute strength is vastly superior to mine. Yet, magically…"

She shrugged and picked up her pace.

"Aidan was one of our greatest warriors," he uttered softly.

"The entire kingdom felt his loss keenly. I still find it difficult to reason he is no longer with us. We—my parents and I, never met his wife. I have heard his daughter, Aileen, is a beautiful and kind human. This knowledge came from Conn."

"Yes, she is. I was honored to be her guardian. How long did you train with Aidan?"

"Not long. After Conn entered the Brotherhood, I went through a phase of mourning. I then sought out a female to spar and train with during those dark days."

Liam sighed. "I never knew."

Abela darted a glance at him. "You and I discussed other items of interest. Conn was not on the agenda."

He halted in front of her, causing her to stumble and slam into his chest. "What exactly was on your *agenda*, Abela?"

"You didn't have to step in front of me," she protested, embarrassed by his question. Not sure how to answer him, she stepped around him and proceeded toward the stones.

However, the man was swifter and reached for her hand. "Was it a game for you in the beginning? Was that *your* agenda? If you couldn't train with a warrior, why not toy with one?"

Abela tried to pull free. "Game? I don't know what you're referring to. We teased, flirted, and enjoyed each other's company, then simply moved on."

Liam's expression stilled and grew serious. "So I meant nothing to you?"

She squirmed under his gaze. The man asked too

many questions she was unprepared to answer. "I'd like to reach the stones before nightfall."

He dropped her hand as if he had been burned. "By your refusal to answer my question, I can assume I speak the truth."

"Can we not discuss our past, please? It was so long ago. You left for the Brotherhood and I...well, I became a priestess." She tried to soften her reasoning and reached for his hand. "Let us not quarrel, Liam. Not only is time fleeting, but precious. The past is gone—"

"For us," he interjected sternly. "And we had no chance to write a future. Let me be clear, Abela. I teased, flirted, and enjoyed only the sexual contentment of other Fae in the Pleasure Gardens. That is where I played *my* games. It meant nothing more. As for you, let me say that we shall never find where the road might have led."

Abela released his hand, the pain of his words opening a wound she thought scarred over and healed. She knew about his time in the Pleasure Gardens. She knew about his sexual tastes and prowess.

And she knew Liam MacGregor was the only one who could fulfill her every fantasy. Had she meant more to him than she perceived?

A pity their relationship had ended too soon.

Chapter Seven

"Training can harness and improve the body and mind, but the heart cannot be shielded or protected from the onslaught of love."
~Chronicles of Liam MacGregor

Why did he find Abela's words disturbing? *Because you believed there was more at the time and you were the fool.* Liam bristled at his own thoughts. No matter how much he remained focused, she wove herself under his skin. He required absolute concentration. Their mission was risky and filled with danger. There was no time for lustful thoughts or conversations regarding their past. It was over. Dead.

Though he did ponder why she risked everything to break him out of his prison. Abela had a talent for avoiding pertinent questions or situations she was unable to dictate. It was an irritating side to her character. Regardless, they had a mission to fulfill. There was no point in dredging up ancient memories. It only complicated their circumstances.

As they approached the stones, Liam withdrew his blade. This time Abela understood and held out her hand for him to make the incision.

Afterward, she let a few droplets of blood grace the bottom of the largest stone.

Liam sheathed his sword. "Keep your focus on the

Dragon Knights of Urquhart. Again, do not deviate from our path in the abyss."

"I am ready." Abela blew across her palm, sealing the wound. Withdrawing her pendant, she nodded to him.

He tensed in preparation. As he spoke the ancient words, the air stilled, and the ground remained silent. His voice grew louder with each chant, letting the power build. When the swirling vortex opened, Liam grasped her hand and moved forward.

The mists shimmered before them. "Push the thought of the Dragon Knights forward beyond the haze.

Abela stumbled. "Pain."

"Ignore and concentrate," he ordered.

The Stone of Ages glowed as she held it outward. Again, her steps faltered. Liam wrapped an arm around her waist as he fought the whispered sounds of the other realms around them. A tendril of song flitted nearby, and he ignored its luring melody. "We're almost there," he encouraged, dragging her forward.

She let out a strangled cry as the mists parted and an internal blast of energy propelled them through the abyss. Liam tried to hold on to her, but the force separated them. He tumbled past the stones, smacking into a pine tree. He quickly brought himself to standing and scanned the area. Abela was on her knees, emptying what little she had in her stomach onto the muddy ground.

He rushed to her side and collapsed next to her. Placing a soothing hand on the back of her neck, Liam spoke healing words.

She wiped her mouth with the back of her hand.

"I'm so weak."

Liam rolled her onto his lap. Worry infused him. Her features were pale and drawn. "Was the pain worse this time?"

"Yes." She coughed and attempted to scoot away from him.

"No. Stay and rest until you have gathered your strength."

She gave him a skeptical look. "Why are you not feeling the same?"

He gave her a wink. "Fenian Warrior, remember?"

"But you are without your powers," she argued, rubbing the heel of her palms against her eyes.

Liam continued to massage her neck. "I had training. I am able to block out the pain and harness the energy to stay strong."

Abela frowned. "It was worse this time. I thought my heart was going to stop beating. The air in my lungs pressed like a vise against my chest."

Guilt plagued Liam. What if traveling through the Veil brought harm to her. "Perhaps we should wait twenty-four hours before we journey to the next time-period."

"Absolutely not," she protested and pushed away from him.

Liam stood, bringing her with him. "I deem it a wise decision. A few days here or there will not hamper our plans."

"Regardless, was it not you that had no desire to be caught with me? I can only shield us for so long." She brushed the dirt and leaves from her cloak.

Stunned, he turned her around to face him. "You are shielding us? By the Gods, no wonder you are weak!"

She shrugged. "I am feeling better, so we can continue."

"Is there anything else I need to know, Abela?"

"I have now told you everything, so wipe that scowl off your face." She glanced around the area. "Where is Urquhart?"

Liam pointed in the direction over her shoulder. "North, by the loch."

"Perfect." She reached for his hand. "Are you ready?"

"Maybe we should walk part of the way," Liam suggested, moving away from her.

She looked affronted. "I am much better."

You're as stubborn as your brother. Liam stepped over a fallen log and surveyed the area. The trees were different. He knew this land well. Abela continued to march down the hill. His mouth clenched as he digested the news of their surroundings. "Stop!"

She shot him a haughty glare. "What now?"

Liam made quick strides to her. "We are in the wrong century."

"Sweet Mother Danu," she whispered. "Are you certain?"

"Absolutely. And it's spring, *not* winter."

Abela grimaced as she retraced her steps back to the stones.

"Where are you going?"

"To take us back," she responded tersely.

"No."

She halted, and her stance became rigid. Liam sensed the wave of anger from where he stood. "I am strong enough."

Liam seriously doubted she was powerful enough to make another journey so soon, but he was not about to argue. The constant sparring of words left him frustrated and wanting to do certain pleasurable things to her body. An idea blossomed, and he smiled. "Would you care to visit Aidan's daughter, Aileen?"

When she turned around, Abela fought to contain her surprise. "Is this her time in which we have landed?"

Liam nodded. "Your thoughts must have been on our earlier conversation, and this is where your power directed us."

Abela dashed down the hill. "How fortuitous," she blurted out, passing by him.

Her enthusiasm was barely contained, and it wove a thread through Liam. Perchance this was a more suitable destination. They were traveling between centuries, thwarting any attempts of the Fae to find them. He made rapid strides toward her. "Let us walk part of the way and then I will have you take us to the entrance magically."

"Perfect." She brushed her hand over a group of tall wildflowers. "Ahh…beauty and rebirth in spring. The air smells divine." She cast him a sideways glance. "Isn't this better than the harshness of winter?"

Liam noted the rosy glow to her cheeks, relieved all traces of her earlier condition were now gone. "If I recall, spring is your favorite season."

Her mouth slacked open in awe. "You remember?"

"Did I not just say so?" he countered and sprinted ahead. Coming to a cluster of violets, Liam bent and plucked one. As she drew near, he held the flower out to her. "And I believe these are your favorite, though their color is far more opulent in our realm."

Abela's hand brushed against his as she took the violet. "Yes…*yes* they are."

He watched as she twirled the tiny flower between her fingers. "Their hue is no match for the color of your own eyes."

She squirmed under his gaze. "As you once stated," she whispered.

The air grew warm around Liam. *Claim one kiss.* He took a step forward. "My favorite season is summer, especially Midsummer. When the fields are ripe with flora and the air is heady with their scent."

"A time of planting more seeds and joining with the land," Abela added.

Liam walked in a circle around her, a dance of seduction as old as time. "It is one that calls out to us." He tugged gently on her braid. "The seeds of life are planted within the womb."

She followed him with her eyes as he came to stand mere inches in front of her. Placing a hand on his chest, she said, "Spring and summer's luring song is one that is hard to ignore." Her tongue darted out, tempting him beyond reason.

Desire shot through Liam's veins. As he dipped his head to feast on what he dared not take, the screeching of a bird startled them both.

Abela was the first to withdraw and shielded her eyes to gaze upward. "Angry bird."

Liam surveyed the hawk, trying to control his lustful inner beast. He was beginning to hate all the seasons. "Shall we proceed?"

Did he detect hurt within her eyes when she glanced his way? Regardless, Liam had to regain his control. His behavior was one of a callow youth and not a hardened warrior. He gestured her forward. "When we get to the water, you can transport us the rest of the way."

Without a word, Abela stepped past him.

Several hours later, they approached the loch. Sunlight glistened like gems over the water. The energy of the Great Dragon brushed over him. She grew curious, not angry, and Liam walked to the edge of the water.

"Great Goddess," Abela whispered. "This is where she dwells?"

Liam knelt on one knee. "Yes." He fisted his hand over his heart. "Greetings, Great One. I cannot pass by without paying my respects, for I do not know when I shall again."

The Great Dragon rose in an arc of glittering jeweled colors. "Welcome, Fenian Warrior."

Abela removed her cloak and pulled her boots off. Stepping inside the loch to her ankles, she opened her arms wide. "Greetings, Great Dragon—*Finola Fyean mo ghrá*. Do you remember me?"

The Great Dragon bobbed gently with the rhythm of the water. *"Yes, Priestess Abela. Welcome, daughter of King Ansgar and Queen Nuala."*

Shaking her head, Abela whispered, "I am no longer called by that name."

"Until Mother Danu releases you, this is your name. Why do you journey with the Fenian Warrior?"

"To resolve an issue with The Treaty of Feahan," Liam interjected and stood.

"A dangerous path you have chosen, Fenian Warrior. Nevertheless, the question has yet to be

answered fully by the princess."

If he revealed more of their situation, whispers of their conversation might travel to those in the kingdom. Even though the dragon spoke within his mind, he did not want to tempt fate. Liam walked a path of indecision—one he did not understand himself.

"I deemed it my duty, Great One," Abela blurted out. "My destiny was shown to me in a vision. I beg you to keep this wisdom within your own heart. As I'm sure you have seen within mine and know the truth." Abela dipped her fingers into the water. "Tell Mother Danu I have not forgotten."

Silence greeted them both as they waited patiently for her to speak.

"You run in the shadows without permission. You dare to walk in the light, refusing to grasp the emotion. Sorrow reigns and only the truth shall set you both free. Your mind clouds the decisions of your heart and you refuse to accept the inevitable. The timekeepers have recorded the journey. Others shall follow."

Heavy mists gathered around the dragon as she descended back within the water.

Her parting words sent a stinging arrow to Liam's heart, and the air cooled considerably. He had no time to contemplate her wisdom.

Lowering her head, Abela let out a choked sob. "I have failed her."

"Then let us right the wrong," Liam offered, and reached for her hand.

She lifted her head. "Even you railed against my idea in the beginning. Why are you fighting to resolve this?"

"Fenian lesson number one. When you make a

choice, follow through to completion. Do not waver. Do not question your reasoning. If you continue to plague yourself with doubts, the mission will fail."

Her luminous eyes widened in astonishment. "There shall be no more talk of failing," she stated with conviction and retrieved her cloak and boots.

Returning to his side, she grasped his hand and they vanished within the mists.

When they emerged by the ancient oak outside the gates of Urquhart, Abela hastily changed into presentable clothing and fashioned her hair. Liam tried to hide the mirth from his features. He found this quality endearing as she was now fashioned in a pale green gown, trimmed in silver knotwork along all the edges of the material. Her hair cascaded in soft waves down her back to her bottom, and Liam had to settle his sight elsewhere.

"Do you not wish to present yourself as a Fenian Warrior to the Dragon Knights?" she asked, her tone commanding.

Liam searched for a plausible explanation. Rubbing a hand over his chin, he sighed. "These knights are my friends. The last time I came unannounced, it was to ask for their help in the last battle against the evil druid, Lachlan. Conn, Rory, and I stood here in our royal garments. I have no desire to do so again." He turned toward her. "Do not worry, Abela. I do not intend to ask questions concerning my brother or yours. We tread on dangerous ground within the timelines."

Her face clouded with uneasiness. "Are you fearful of the year? Should I not enter first?"

"No. I have searched the castle. The children are older, and a couple of the wives are heavy with bairns.

We are safe, though I will introduce you as Abela and not as the princess. These Dragon Knights were never made aware of your brother's heritage."

Abela surprised him by tucking her hand in the crook of his arm. "Then let us go greet these good people."

As they approached the gates, one of the guards stepped forth. "Do my eyes deceive me, Liam MacGregor? Are ye truly here?"

"Your sight is correct, Matthew. It is good to see you are still here with the Dragon Knights."

Matthew swept his gaze toward Abela. His mouth gaped open, and then he snapped it shut. "Have ye married?"

Abela's body shook as she attempted to contain her laughter. "The warrior has agreed to a marriage pact."

Liam inwardly groaned. "We seek entry into Urquhart, so if you would be so kind as to alert Angus."

The guard rubbed a hand over his nose. "Ye need no permission. After the last battle, all Fenian Warriors were granted access. Ye will find the laird in the Great Hall or his solar."

"Thank you." Liam escorted Abela through the main gate and into the bailey.

A heated debate greeted them, and they both halted at the commotion that ensued near several horses. Liam nudged Abela and placed a finger over his mouth for her to remain silent.

"I cannot believe you're keeping me from riding out along the loch. I can still manage to mount my horse, so quit acting medieval," protested Aileen, before poking her husband, Stephan, in the arm.

"Ye keep spouting the word *medieval*, which ye

have explained its meaning, but I refuse to have ye bring harm to ye or our bairn—"

"By riding a horse?" She tapped her foot in obvious irritation.

He crossed his arms over his chest. "Might I remind ye that ye fell from said animal several months ago."

She gave an impatient shrug. "I had not broken my fast. I got dizzy."

Stephen reached for her, and she stiffened. "Can ye not take an easy walk?" His voice softened, and he trailed a finger over her cheek. "It would soothe my fears."

Aileen's features softened. "Why must you worry? I am strong and if you recall, I carried two at once the last time I was with child."

Grasping her around the waist, he nuzzled her neck. "Husbands always fear for their wives. I have another suggestion."

"I can only guess." Aileen chuckled low and wrapped her arms around his neck.

Liam determined it was time to announce their presence. Coughing into his fist, he waited for the couple to turn toward them.

Shock registered on both their faces. Aileen was the first to withdraw from her husband's embrace. With her arms outstretched, she ran to him. "By the Goddess! Liam MacGregor!"

He captured the woman, embracing her in hug. "Happy to see you, too, Lady Aileen. Might I add my congratulations on the impending birth?"

She drew back and studied him. Her eyes misted with unshed tears. "The trial? It's over?"

"We are working to resolve the issue," Abela responded.

Aileen quickly composed herself and took a step back. "You have the look of another." She gasped as if coming to the conclusion on her own. "Conn MacRoich."

"Should we expect him to follow as well?" Stephen asked, sweeping his gaze around the bailey.

"No," replied Liam. "May I present Conn's sister, Abela." He turned toward her and added, "And this is Aileen and Stephen MacKay."

Abela dipped a curtsy. "I am honored."

Reaching for Abela's hand, the woman said, "Please do not bow before me."

"The tales of you are written in verse and song. You are heroes among our people." Abela squeezed her hand in return.

Stephen gave a puzzled expression. "Why would the sister of Conn MacRoich be traveling with another warrior?"

The Dragon Knight was observant. Liam shifted his stance. "We are—"

"Betrothed," answered Abela, taking Liam's arm and darting him a reassuring smile.

"Praise the Goddess," Aileen uttered in a shocked tone. "You must confess everything, especially Conn's reaction. Please come into the Great Hall."

Stephen took his wife's hand. "Aye, agreed." However, his tone sounded skeptical.

They risked staying long at Urquhart, and Liam sought to soften the blow of their visit. "Sadly, our time is short. I must speak with Angus."

"He is in his solar going over a message from

Alastair," Stephen replied as he gestured him forward. "He seeks to alter plans on the building of Aonach Castle in the north. Both Alastair and Duncan are in agreement, but I fear Angus disagrees."

As they made their way into the castle, Abela's steps slowed. "Aonach? Why would they flee their home?"

Liam pulled her aside. "A request from a family member in the future when they were there helping to rid the world of the vile monster."

She shuddered visibly. "When we return, I intend on reading the scrolls of the last battle. There is much I would like to learn."

"It was horrific. Nothing can be gleaned from reading about a battle that saw many lose their lives," snapped Liam.

"Forgive me. I forgot you were also a witness at the battle."

His jaw clenched. "No, Abela. I *battled* alongside the knights. I fought the demon threatening to invade both realms. The stench of the conflict will always remain with me."

A frown marred her features. "You are more of this world than of our kingdom. I apologize for my ignorance." Releasing her hold on his arm, Abela followed Stephen and Aileen.

"How wrong you are, princess," muttered Liam as he continued to stand in the cold entryway.

Chapter Eight

"A journey can be one of truths, revelations, and wisdom. My path with the Fenian Warrior is none of these, merely strained."

~*Diary of Princess Abela*

When Abela entered the Great Hall, she marveled at all the colorful tapestries that adorned the walls on either side of the room. These were the proud Dragon Knights. Powerful and descended from her own people. Her recollection of meeting the first clan heralded in a new beginning between the Fae and humans. Joyous celebrations marked the occasion for many months.

She strolled along the side, touching each one in reverence. Four brothers and one sister. As she approached the last tapestry, she narrowed her eyes in confusion at the sixth tapestry.

A woman and man stood together with hands joined. Behind them, a boy stood on a hill with a sword raised and the Fire Dragon hovering above him. His eyes blazed with the inner power of the beast. Abela lifted her hand, but drew it back at the last moment. "Your destiny is filled with shadows and darkness. Beware the power you possess," she uttered softly.

"They are the new bloodline of Dragon Knights," stated Aileen, coming to stand next to her. "Some of the women at Urquhart and Brigid, Duncan's wife, created this new tapestry."

"I recognized the woman from the younger version of her in the other tapestry. She is the sister of the Dragon Knights." Abela studied the threaded image, trying to sense more.

"The man is Margaret's husband, Adam, and that is their son, James. He will become the leader of the Dragon Knights in the future," offered Aileen. "We wanted to honor them. It is our only link to them."

"I can empathize. My brother and I were apart for many years." Abela gave her a wistful smile.

Aileen massaged her swollen abdomen. "Is Conn your only brother?"

"Yes. He is my twin. There are no more in our family." Abela studied the beautiful woman. "Does the babe bother you?"

Aileen chuckled and shifted her stance. "Often, but not as much as when I carried my twins."

"I can't even comprehend. Should you not be lying in bed?"

"Absolutely not. Do the Fae women keep to their chambers?"

Abela burst out laughing. "No. It is a time of celebration and honoring the women who carry the babe."

"I know you were privy to our earlier conversation in the bailey. All I wanted was to ride out to where the other women and children were having a picnic. I was late joining them this morning." Aileen pointed to her husband's tapestry. "I tried to sneak out and someone saw me leading my horse out of the stables. They dashed off to inform Stephen."

"Overprotective," Abela mentioned.

"Positively."

"Yet, he loves you, but I sense your inner strength and wisdom. The women here have traveled a great journey to be with the men they were destined for."

Aileen closed her eyes. "A path I have never regretted."

Reaching outward, Abela brushed her fingers over the woman's cheek. "I believe your father approved as well."

When Aileen opened her eyes, they shimmered. "You knew him?"

Abela linked her arm through her hostess and traveled along the hall to a nearby table. She motioned for Aileen to take a seat. Settling herself next to her, Abela straightened the folds in her gown. "I had the privilege of training with him for a year."

"You did? Why? Is this the custom in the Fae world?"

"In truth, yes *and* no," she responded dryly. "When my brother considered entering the Brotherhood, I sought to find a reason why the place held such a fascination. Of course, no females are permitted inside the inner chambers, but training with a Fenian Warrior is possible. We have other elite programs for the women in the kingdom." Abela folded her hands in her lap. "Aidan Kerrigan was the elite—the best of all the warriors. At the time, he was also their leader."

Aileen sighed. "There are times when I wished my father would have shared his lineage earlier in my life. I only learned of his Fae blood months before he died." She glanced away, placing a hand against her heart.

"If he shared the knowledge with you from the beginning, would it have altered how you feel for him?"

"No. I was privileged to know a fraction of his life, but nothing about my own past and where I came from," she answered with staid calmness and turned toward Abela. "Even though the Fae banished him from his home, I know absolutely nothing about his world *or* family."

Abela smiled, reflecting on the knowledge she held and was about to impart to this woman. It was odd no one had told her before. "His family was vast, Aileen. He was one of the rare Fae not born here, but instead, on our home world of Taralyn. The royal bloodline flowed heavily within him. He was the firstborn. Two other siblings followed many years later—a brother and sister. Both his parents have passed over into the land of eternal youth." She paused, letting this small fragment of information process within the woman.

"Royalty," she whispered. "He never mentioned anything."

"There is more, Aileen."

She blinked. "Don't hold back now."

Abela's mouth twitched in humor. "Aidan was my mother's brother, and my uncle."

Aileen stared at her in shocked silence. Abruptly standing, she paced in front of the giant fireplace. "All this time...Conn never said one word." She smacked her fist into her palm. "Not...one...bloody...word!"

Standing slowly, Abela clasped her hands together. "Conn swore an oath to never reveal the information to you. A request from the king and queen. They understood he traveled the Veil of Ages, but I don't fully understand why they made this demand. In truth, Conn revered Aidan as his leader and mentor. His admiration was vast, and not once did he call him an uncle. Conn saw our uncle as a great Fenian Warrior."

Aileen glanced up. "And you?"

She approached the woman. Taking her hands, Abela tried to ease the tension. "I made no such vow, *cousin*. I judged it wise to share the knowledge. You should not be cloaked in the darkness without knowing the truth."

Letting out a choked sob, Aileen asked, "Are there any more secrets you need to reveal? I don't think I can handle anymore."

Abela shook her head and released her hands. "Only stories to be shared about your father. Sadly, there isn't much time."

"Wait until I tell Stephen." The woman clamped a hand over her mouth to stifle the laughter.

"Does this mean he'll permit you to ride a horse in your present condition?" Abela arched a brow.

Aileen rolled her eyes. "No. He believes the bloodline of the Dragon Knights is superior, as do his brothers."

"Truly? Now I am the one shocked."

Both women burst out in laughter. After composing herself, Aileen moved to another table. "I've completely forgotten my manners. Would you care for some wine? Food?"

"Only if I may assist you in the preparations." Abela held her hand up in warning when the woman narrowed her eyes. "I make this offer as a sign of respect and wanting to spend as much time with you before we have to leave. Not because you are heavy with child."

"Then I welcome your help."

As they made their way out of the hall, Aileen

turned toward Abela. "Thank you for sharing this knowledge. Of course, if I ever see Conn again, I'll have a few choice words to impart on my dear *cousin*."

Abela embraced the woman. "I fear you may never see him again. His duties require him to maintain his position within the kingdom."

Taking a step back, Aileen slowly moved along the corridor. "What exactly are his duties? I'm presuming his trial is over, correct?"

Abela had shared so much, but there were certain facts best left unsaid. Liam was still on his journey. "I am not able to discuss his present circumstances. However, I can share that my brother is well and happy."

"And Rory?"

The aroma of freshly baked bread greeted Abela as they entered the kitchens. "His journey has led him to happiness, as well."

"And now you're here with Liam." The woman smiled at a passing servant and pulled down two large trenchers from a shelf.

"Correct."

Aileen pointed to a pitcher and cups. "If you could gather and place them on one of these, I'll prepare the food items."

Abela busied herself with the task, praying Aileen would not pry with more questions.

"What do your parents think of this engagement between you and Liam? Surely Conn is overjoyed since Liam is a close friend, right?"

Abela shuddered. *Conn might take a blade to his heart.* She had never fully realized the extent of her decision. What her actions would do to her family. She sought to save only one person. It blinded her reasoning. "Yes, they're jubilant," she lied.

"Are you all right?" Aileen stared so intently that she feared the woman's vision found the lie.

"Of course. I must return soon to make our plans for the ceremony." She moved the cups to the side and set two pitchers on the trencher.

"Weddings are always exciting, but nerve-wracking." Popping a berry into her mouth, Aileen asked, "Can you share why you are here?"

Abela shrugged and continued moving the items about. "It is a matter dealing with a treaty between all the realms. Liam is seeking to alter one of the laws. It cannot be done, unless the original documents are presented to the King of the Fae."

"Did you want to make this journey with him? I am stunned you're traveling without guards or Conn. I'm sure he's a very overprotective brother."

She could feel the scrutinizing gaze of the woman. *You are intuitive, my cousin.* Abela straightened. "This was my decision. I yearned to visit the human world before Liam and I are settled. Originally, our plans were to travel to another century, but I am happy our path led us to you. Never did I imagine meeting my human cousin."

"And never did I dream on being related to Fae royalty," added Aileen.

Sorrow reflected in her eyes, and Abela walked to her side. "I make no promises, Aileen, but I shall try to return and tell you more stories of your father."

Aileen hugged her arms around herself. "Part of me is angry—upset with the Fae for forcing him to make a decision. Of course, he chose my mother and love in the end. I can't imagine never seeing my husband and children again, so I don't know how he battled the emotions. My mother and father are dead, and the knowledge buried with them."

"My heart ached after Aidan left the realm."

Letting out a sigh, Aileen placed the bowl of berries on the trencher. "Did you know Liam worked with him in Scotland on archaeological digs? I'm sure there were other Fenian Warriors who visited him on occasion, too."

Abela shook her head. Her time had been spent deep within the Fae realm serving Mother Danu. She was unable to fathom Liam's reasons for working with him. "I was not privy to any news pertaining to the warriors or your world."

Placing a hand against her side, Aileen slumped into a nearby chair and let out a groan. "Enough of the past. We only have this brief time, so share how you and Liam first met. Was it love at first sight? What will the ceremony be like? What will you do after you're married? Will he still be part of the Brotherhood? And you must tell me more about my father."

Abela grew dizzy from the onslaught of the woman's questions. Taking a seat beside her, she deemed it best to give her a skewed, but partial truth.

****

The leader of the Dragon Knights leaned against the arched window, surveying him. Liam couldn't detect if it was Angus searching for the truth in his words after requesting the Treaty of Feahan, or the Fire Dragon that dwelled within the man. Out of all the knights, Angus MacKay had mastered complete control of his beast.

Did he know Liam was without his powers? Could the man sense his weakness?

I walk a dangerous path with this one.

Liam folded his arms across his chest. "By your extended silence, am I to assume you are calculating the risks? Or preparing an argument?"

Stephen drummed his fingers on the desk. "Ye have yet to share what happened at your trial."

Why did this particular branch of the Dragon Knights believe they held the upper hand? Did they not understand the strength of a Fae warrior? Thank the Gods Duncan and Alastair MacKay were absent. He had no wish to battle words with all four Dragon Knights.

Angus pushed away from the wall. He reminded Liam of a lion. "Because the trial is ongoing, correct?"

Liam stiffened, but remained composed. "I can offer no information."

Smacking his palm on the oak desk, Angus blurted out, "Yet, ye arrive asking for our Treaty of Feahan based on your account? We ken the laws set down by our ancestors. Our father counseled us wisely. Is this to save yourself? Or another?"

This time Liam narrowed his gaze in warning. "You are aware—"

"We ken why," Stephen interjected. "If ye recall, I was there. Ye took Aidan Kerrigan back through the Veil of Ages. Aileen has shared the knowledge that ye broke a Fae law in escorting her father back in time."

"It is no secret," Liam protested. "I require the treaty to argue for an amendment. If you deem it unreasonable, you can voice your grievances, and I will forward them to the Fae King."

Angus snarled. "Ye ken we are not the original signers. Why not journey back and have Alexander give ye the treaty?"

"Does it matter?" argued Liam, unfolding his arms. "We are here, and you have in your possession the parchment. Nowhere in the bylaws does it state that in order to amend a law the original signers must be notified."

"Horse dung," muttered Stephen.

Growing weary of the discussion, Liam moved to a chair. Resting his hands on his thighs, he glanced at both men. Did not they battle for the same cause? How could he reason with them? "I have spoken the truth with you. Yes, I am doing this to save myself. Aidan Kerrigan was one of my closet friends and mentor. Did he see his death? No. He fully intended to return and give his account on why he required traveling through the Veil of Ages." He blew out a frustrated breath and leaned back. "Perchance at the end of the battle we fought, he foresaw his own death."

"Dinnae forget your oath to me, too," reminded Stephen. "I made ye swear a vow that if the fight were to turn brutal and not in our favor, ye were to return Aileen to the future."

Liam nodded slowly. "Let me be clear. I have no regrets. In addition, the politics of the Fae kingdom are complex—*thorny*. There is no assurance I will succeed in my world with my request."

Angus rubbed a hand through his beard in thought and walked back to the window. "Ye were outnumbered during the battle, especially with only Duncan and Stephen to help ye fight Lachlan."

"You and Alastair were still on your own quests for

redemption," noted Liam.

Angus's expression was of pained tolerance. "A dark time indeed."

"Aye," agreed Stephen quietly.

Liam had stated his plea more fully than he intended. He understood the risk if Angus decided against giving him the treaty. His and Abela's journey would end at Urquhart. His hope was she would accept the decision and return back home with him.

Silence permeated the small chamber as the earlier sunlight turned to gray skies, putting a damper on his already sour disposition.

"I will give ye the Treaty of Feahan," Angus announced.

Liam tried to mask his surprise. "Thank you."

"On one condition." Angus smiled slowly.

Letting out a curse, Liam nodded though feared the request.

"The *truth* as to why Conn's sister is with ye."

Why did Liam keep finding himself backed against a wall? First with Abela and now with these knights. Regardless, these men were his friends, and he found it taxing to continue with the injustice to Abela. Liam had no time to ponder their reaction to what he was going to reveal. His patience was limited.

Standing, he went to the mantel and viewed the shield mounted above. "Strange, but I never fathomed on being set free from my prison by a woman, much less, the daughter of the king and queen. You were never privy to the information regarding her brother Conn. He renounced his right as the next king when he entered the Brotherhood. And for reasons I'm unable to fathom, Conn has now claimed his *right* to the Fae kingdom. I do not know his purpose, but I am sure it has something to do with his own trial *or* quest. Princess Abela can be as stubborn as her brother, and refused to listen to my protests against leaving the prison. She can be quite convincing. I should know since we had a history. Thankfully, one that I've buried. I have no wish to hinder our journey with the past."

Liam glanced over his shoulder to face the stunned looks he knew were on their faces. Yet, he was unprepared for the strained expression and hurt reflected in Abela's gaze as she stood in the doorway.

"I agree," she stated brusquely, removing herself from the room.

Chapter Nine

"Her radiance is one of sunlight and moonlight, and I am no longer the hardened warrior in her presence."

~Chronicles of Liam MacGregor

Liam started forward and then paused. What good would it do to go after Abela? She'd lash out at him with biting words, and he did not have the stomach for an argument with her. He was unable to fathom why her emotions countered the words she spouted at him. Their tryst consisted of several kisses, games along the river, and a picnic that ended in terse words. There was a time he ached for more from her, but she denied him the opportunity on their last day together.

He was the fool. But no longer. His heart had hardened during his many years as a Fenian Warrior. The past was gone. There was no hope of a future for them.

"Aye, we can see how ye both have *buried* the past," Stephen scoffed and stood. "Ye look like ye could use a drink."

He stared into the empty corridor. "It would be welcomed. Damn. She must have heard everything."

Angus stepped past him. "I shall retrieve the treaty and meet ye in the hall." Pausing at the door, he half-turned around. "A word of warning, Liam. Dinnae share any more information with us. My gut tells me we shall receive a visit from Conn, and I for one, will not lie to the warrior."

"Will you tell him about the treaty?"

"Aye. I have nae desire to do battle with a warrior *and* prince. Does he ken about his sister?"

"A muscle flicked angrily at his jaw, and Liam fought the urge to wipe his hand across his face. "Most certainly."

Angus arched a brow. "'Tis good ye are carrying a sword."

Liam watched the man depart from the chamber. "Do you wish to add to your brother's advice?"

Stephen chuckled as he approached him. "Nae. I can see ye have endured enough torment."

As they made their way to the hall, Angus' words about Conn gnawed at him. He had to speak to Abela about her ability of cloaking. How much longer would they be able to avoid the Fae? What were the risks?

Entering the Great Hall, Liam spied Abela laughing with Aileen. They appeared to have bonded, chiding one another and speaking as if they had known each other for years. The revelation as to why slammed into his thoughts when he heard the word cousin mentioned. His steps faltered as he neared the table.

"By the hounds," he spat out. "You shared Aileen's lineage?"

Abela shot daggers at him. "Yes. She has a right to the knowledge. Aidan is no longer with us, so it is within my right as her cousin. Regardless, you told these men we are *not* engaged, and I had to offer my apologies to Aileen for telling her a lie!"

"*Cousin*," echoed Angus and Stephen.

Liam fisted his hands on his hips. "It was proclaimed throughout the kingdom that no Fae would share the knowledge. All made a pledge to the king and queen."

Standing abruptly, Abela pointed a finger at him. "Then I must not have been present when the order was given, for I made no such oath. I was only privy to the one Conn made to our parents. I had no knowledge of this proclamation."

Stephen went to his wife's side. "You...*you* are related to Conn?"

Smiling, Aileen took his hand. "Apparently so."

"Do ye have a title?"

"No," interjected Abela, and added, "since she is half-fae there is no title granted. Is it not enough for her to know her heritage?"

"I have no words," muttered Stephen, taking a seat beside his wife.

"Nor I," replied Angus, rubbing his hand down the back of his neck.

Liam wanted to throttle the woman. "We can add another item to the list of broken laws." He turned to Angus. "If you don't mind, I'll take that drink now."

"Agreed," mumbled Angus, retrieving a pitcher. After pouring a hefty amount into the cups, he then handed one to Liam. "To *your* health, my friend."

Liam wasted no time in tossing back the drink. Wiping his mouth with the back of his hand, he went to the farthest chair from Abela. He barely registered her question to Aileen regarding the children at Urquhart. His mind reeled with this latest disaster. Yet, it was not his fault the princess opened her mouth and deemed it necessary to spill the information. At least Aidan

101

Kerrigan had kept his mouth shut.

He brushed a hand over his brow and slid the cup toward Angus. "If you would be so kind."

"Have something to eat, Liam," encouraged Aileen.

Giving her a feeble smile, he reached for some bread and cheese. Even the aroma of the vegetable stew did not entice his appetite. Eating his meal in silence, he half-listened to the conversation. Reaching out with his inner Fae senses, he searched for any others beyond Urquhart. By the time he had finished, his head pounded.

"I will stall Conn as long as I can," Angus offered as he refilled his cup.

Liam straightened. "Thank you. Our journey might come to a halt soon."

"Then ye best leave after the meal." He shoved the rolled parchment across the table. "If ye succeed, I would be honored if ye were the one to return the document."

"I fear our rate of victory dwindles with each passing hour." Liam retrieved the parchment and tucked it inside his belt.

Angus' expression stilled and grew serious. "And if ye recall, *our* path to redemption was a grueling one."

"Yet, victorious."

"Aye." His somber tone was now replaced with one of mirth. "Stephen, I am going to go fetch my wife down by the loch. Ye are in charge."

"Wait," Aileen protested. "I wanted to go, too."

Placing an arm around her shoulders, Stephen whispered into her ear. Aileen's complexion turned to a rosy glow, and she giggled. She waved dismissively to

Angus. "Tell everyone I've decided to remain here. I'm positive the children are having a wonderful time without us."

Peace and prosperity had reigned at the home of the Dragon Knights, and Liam uttered a silent prayer it would continue until their dying breaths.

****

Saying farewells to new friends and family was difficult for Abela. There were no promises stated for return visits. In their brief time together, she had done her best to fill Aileen with good stories and memories of her father to be passed down to the children. Her heart ached at not being able to meet them, but for as long as she lived, Abela would treasure this time spent with her cousin and two of the Dragon Knights.

She stole one glance over her shoulder as she crossed through the gates of Urquhart. Blowing Aileen a kiss, she imparted a prayer on the breeze. *Long life, happiness, and may you always walk with the Fae. I shall remember you always, sweet cousin.*

Returning her attention to the downward path in front of her, Abela blinked to avoid the tears from spilling down her cheeks. *No regrets. Remember your pledge, no matter the cost.*

Liam kept a steady pace ahead of her, and she judged it best if she walked behind him. His rigid stance told her everything. Nevertheless, his words earlier in Angus' solar still ripped through her heart, and she pondered why it bothered her. It was the truth she had known for many years. She was only a passing fancy to fill the time before Liam entered the Brotherhood. Yet, the sharp pain of betrayal and emotions she once harbored continued to linger in the deepest part of her heart. Why did her heart refuse to listen to her mind?

Onward they traveled. Liam avoided going near the water and kept them traveling along a path within the trees. A rabbit skittered past her and birds chirped in song within the branches. Golden sunbeams streamed down through the thick canopy of leaves. The late afternoon air was warm on her back. She inhaled deeply, trying to absorb the serenity of the place.

When Abela's gown snagged on a tree limb, she laughed at the absurdity. She had not changed into appropriate clothing for traveling. "Liam, wait," she called out to him.

As she waved her hand over her body, her gown was transformed into trews, tunic, and boots. Snapping her fingers, a belt was secured at her waist and a cloak was draped across her arm. She took her hand to her hair and magically transformed her heavy locks into braids.

Abela surveyed the area and frowned. "Did the man not hear my words? Or did he choose to ignore me?"

"Yes and no," replied his low voice behind her.

She twirled around so fast, her steps faltered. Liam was at her side in two strides, catching her before she could tumble down the hill.

Placing her hands on his chest, she lifted her gaze. Worry reflected back from his silver blue depths. "How did you get behind me?"

"I didn't. I heard you calling my name and retreated to you. As you were magically changing, your body shimmered and shifted." He brushed a strand of hair from her cheek. "Are you in control of your magic?"

"Other than being slightly dizzy, yes," she answered calmly.

Liam eased back from her. "Perchance we ought to return to Urquhart and spend the night."

"I am all right," she reassured, giving him a smile.

He regarded her for several moments and then swept his gaze to the water. "The path by the loch will lead us to the stones in less time. I sought the trees for cover, and I had no wish to encounter the Great Dragon and banter words again."

Having no desire to spar words with him, Abela replied, "I think that is a clever plan, but I sense she is not in this part of the land."

Darting her a surprised look, he nodded. "I'll lead and you follow in my steps."

"Perfect. If I take a tumble, you can soften my blow when I land on you."

Liam coughed into his hand to suppress the outburst of laughter. "My pleasure, princess."

With skillful ease, he maneuvered down the incline. Abela followed, grasping tree limbs for support along the way. As she neared the water, she slipped on a mixture of mud and leaves, but managed to quickly right herself. Stepping over a boulder, she kept stride with Liam as they made their way along the water's edge.

Silence became the companion between them, and Abela found it disturbing. Yes, the years had changed them both, but she recalled the ease of those earlier conversations.

She tugged at the collar of her cloak. "Is the air always so warm here in the Great Glen at this time of year?"

"Per Angus, they are having an unusual spring," he answered with a chuckle.

"What's so funny?" She was happy to hear a thawing in his voice. Her stomach clenched when he spoke harshly.

"Angus almost ordered Duncan to produce another storm to temper the heat before he left for Aonach."

Her eyes grew wide. "He's the one with the power over the skies."

"Correct."

"Why didn't he?"

Liam waved his hand upward. "Angus determined it was a sign from the Goddess, and he deemed it wiser to keep to her plans, instead of interfering."

Abela smiled knowingly. "He is a great leader and sensible man."

"I can think of no one greater since the inception of the Dragon Knights."

"Truly?"

Liam sighed, and his steps slowed. "Yes. He has mastered his beast, even in the darkest moments of his life. His own failing was his guilt at not steering a clearer and firmer course for his brothers after the death of their father."

"Hmm…It's a shame we could not have prolonged our stay. I would have enjoyed visiting with the rest of the family. I do believe Aileen has chosen wisely with Stephen. She did share with me that he has the power of water." She darted a glance at Liam. "Can you share something with me?"

"Do I have a choice?" he asked, his tone resigned.

She smacked at him playfully. "Yes. You may

agree or not."

"What do you wish to know?"

"Why did my parents forbid anyone speaking to Aileen about her heritage? Even her father remained silent."

His brow furrowed in concentration. "One does not question the commands of the king and queen. It was a joint decision on their part to issue the demand. Therefore, I'm sorry to state I don't know the answer. How did you come upon the knowledge?"

Abela hesitated, unsure how to answer the man without revealing too much. "When last I spoke with Conn, he shared the proclamation." She held up her hand in warning. "Do not ask me anything further."

"As you have previously stated," he responded dryly.

She settled her gaze on the path ahead. What a pity to deny a beautiful person their right to a certain lineage of information. But this was a half-human. She knew little of the reasoning behind her parents' decision. *One day, I shall present the issue to you. If you'll ever speak to me again.*

"May I ask you a question?"

Startled out of her thoughts, she turned to Liam. "Of course." Her heart pounded waiting for him to proceed.

"Why did you not hear the decree?"

Abela blew out an exasperated breath. She was hoping for something else. "Since I was a priestess in the temple, we were not allowed any news from the kingdom. As you are aware, the priestesses do not venture outside the temple unless there is a wedding or important ceremony to preside over." Walking over to a

107

boulder, she sat down. "However, there were times when the breeze carried the whispered conversations of others to me deep within the temple. They were fleeting, and often times I was able to grasp their meaning."

He approached and stood before her. "I apologize for my earlier behavior. I truly did not understand. You and the priestesses were surely the only Fae not to have received a summons to listen to the proclamation. The king and queen were adamant in their declaration."

"Nevertheless, you would have thought it important for all to hear." Standing, Abela removed her cloak. She held out her hand. "Ready for me to transport us to the stones?"

He shrugged. "If you are not too tired, I would welcome the journey back on foot."

"I am refreshed from my time at Urquhart." She tossed the cloak outward, watching as the material vanished before their eyes.

They remained quiet on their journey to the stones, and Abela took this time to settle her thoughts. Nature bloomed all around her. She drew forth from her training by noting every new leaf, flower, bumblebee, butterfly, and animal that darted or flew out in greeting. The effect was intoxicating, and by the time the stones came into view she felt one with the land.

"Why the broad smile?" asked Liam.

Abela stretched out her arms. "Quieting the mind with the beauty that surrounds us."

When he smiled fully, her pulse raced. His entire demeanor transformed into the Fae she knew from long ago. Playful, talkative, and giving her those smoldering looks. Being a warrior changed Liam, and her heart ached. Why must everything alter? Yet, Abela already knew the answer deep within her soul. In order to grow, one must accept each new transformation. The land had taught her this, as did her training with the other priestesses.

"How did you hear about me?" he asked softly.

She strolled over to a blackberry bush ripe with fruit. Plucking one from the vine, she held it out to Liam. His fingers brushed hers as he accepted the fruit. Abela tried to ignore the tingling sensations and glanced away. What harm would it be to tell him?

"I first felt the brush of Conn's energy when he entered the kingdom. As a twin, we have always had this bond."

Liam popped the berry into his mouth. "Yes, I do recall you mentioning the connection."

Nodding, she moved along the bush removing more of the berries. "He refused to acknowledge me and instantly sealed the door on our connection. Obviously, I was crushed. I had not seen my brother in over a hundred years." She glanced at him sideways. "I bided my time with him. Nevertheless, messages from the kingdom of three Fenian Warriors doing battle with the Dark One reached us in the temple. Confusion filtered within the communications—ones of anger, rogue warriors, defiant Fae who had abused their powers. It tore the realm into a divided kingdom." Abela turned to face him. "I knew if Conn had faced dire circumstances, you and Rory would be there to protect him. He might not have been the prince then, but you both swore an oath at your initiation into the Brotherhood to always protect him. Your pledge betrayed you with words of protection not only for the warrior, but for your *prince*. A part of you would always see him as the heir to the Fae kingdom."

Liam fisted his hands on his hips. "How do you know what pledge we made? You were not present."

She regarded him with sadness. "I was there, hidden in the back."

He took a step near her. "Just to be clear, Rory and I asked Conn to help us thwart the evil monster and the druid, Lachlan. We concluded he would eventually try to fight the battle on his own, so we presented him with a solution. Nevertheless, you have not said how you knew I was in prison. Did Conn tell you?"

Her hands clenched together, crushing the berries. "No. On my first transgression, I used my own magic and those of the temple to search for you within the realm. It took many days of solitude and concentration to find you." *I did not eat, drink, or sleep during that time, but you shall never know. And then I heard the whispered words of your transgression and death penalty.*

He cupped her chin. "Why?"

The juice of the berries dripped from her hands. "I already told you. I had no wish to see you die."

Gently, he stroked her bottom lip with his thumb. "One day you will tell me the true reason, *Abela*."

Liam withdrew his hand and strode toward the standing stones.

Her body trembled not from his touch, but from his words. Why did her resolve always weaken around the man? "You would flee the moment you heard the truth, Liam MacGregor, just like you did so many years ago."

With a flick of her wrists, the stains from the fruit vanished from her hands and this time, Abela slammed the door on her emotions.

Chapter Ten

"The second kiss awoke a passion that had been dormant, and I could no longer contain the emotional bleeding."

~Diary of Princess Abela

Lifting her hand, Abela waited for Liam to make the incision. She winced slightly at the pain. "The year 844 in Ireland and to the great Niall, correct?"

"Yes, though I fear what we might expect from the man. I do not want to do battle with a man on the path of his new-found religion."

She smeared her blood on the base of the tallest standing stone. "Do not all beliefs guide one to love? And to the great spirit?"

"It is what the druids state."

As she straightened, Abela sealed the wound. "Let us remain positive." Removing her pendant, she nodded to Liam.

The first brush of power caused her to stagger when he began to chant the words. She tried to keep her focus centered, but her thoughts drifted. The wind bellowed like a banshee, and she became giddy, embracing the magic. *Take me home, Ireland.*

"Concentrate," ordered Liam, placing a protective arm around her waist.

She blinked, trying to see the landscape as he

pulled her through the vortex. Lights mirroring the hues of rainbows encircled them. Whispers of other realms tickled her skin, and she giggled.

"Control your emotions," demanded Liam, his breath hot against her cheek. "If you continue to waver, we will fall into the abyss."

"I cannot…"

"Bring forth your training!"

Abela shook her head to get rid of the luring images, and she drew her gaze toward the stone. It glowed with the power of the ancients. Onward they traveled along a path she could no longer see. "You must be my eyes," she shouted. Her legs began to tremble as the land beneath them sprouted vines to snatch at them from below.

His protest echoed all around them, and Liam lifted her into his arms. "Keep holding the pendant in front of us!"

She raised her head. *Help us, Mother Danu. Do not let us fail.*

A sudden burst of power propelled them through the vortex, and they landed in a meadow of wildflowers. The heady floral scent engulfed Abela, and she stretched her arms outward, caressing the petals. She remained flat on the ground, unable to speak or open her eyes. Bees hummed around her, and she smiled.

"Liam," she uttered in a hoarse voice.

"Here," he announced, tucking her against his body. "Pain?"

"I am floating."

"Center yourself, feel the land, breathe the air."

She giggled again.

"Now, release the energy back into the ground." He stroked a finger across her cheek.

"What if I don't want to?"

"Abela, I will only ask once." His tone even more severe this time.

"You're no fun," she huffed out, but complied. Keeping her palms on the soft grass and flowers, she eased the residual power from the pendant into the ground. A chill came over her, and she shivered. Opening her eyes, she smiled at him. "That was lovely."

"No it was not," argued Liam, and took her hand into his. His look was one of concern.

"What happened?" she whispered.

He laced his fingers with hers. "You were beginning to fade."

She let out a choked sob. "I could have led us into—"

"A place of no return," he interrupted and quickly added, "but you did not. You held us firm until the last few seconds."

She struggled to sit up, and Liam placed a firm arm around her shoulders. "Yet, I experienced no pain."

"Because we are in Ireland," he stated. "A part of our home dwells beneath. It is always easier to travel between time and space on this land."

A soft whinny alerted them they were not alone. Abela twisted to view the intruder. The horse grazed several feet away, paying no heed to them.

"How fortuitous. Don't you agree, Liam?"

Standing, he held out his hand to her. "It depends on if he has an owner."

She accepted his assistance and stood. "Regardless,

he is here, and we require transportation." She waved her hand outward, and her cloak appeared. Placing the garment around her shoulders, she peered at Liam. "Can you tell the year?"

"Not exactly and I'm unsure of our location."

One of these times, I'm going to lead us precisely to our destination. She strode past Liam and approached the horse. She dipped her head and raised her hand. "Greetings, my friend."

The horse shook his head and moved forward for her touch.

"Ahh...so you were abandoned? A fine animal to be left on your own. I see plenty of food, fresh air, and the land to roam."

"Do share why we require a horse to transport us?" asked Liam, approaching from the side.

"I hate to divulge this, but I am too weak to magically escort us to the Niall."

Worry creased his brow. "You need rest. Since our journey began there has been none."

"Yes, if only for one night." She continued to soothe the horse with her touch, ignoring Liam's penetrating gaze. "And yes, I am able to maintain the shield around us."

"We should have remained at Urquhart," he protested, moving away.

Anxiety clawed at her. Abela did not know how much longer she would be able to control the shield. She prayed it would hold until they completed their last quest, and then she could return them both to the Fae realm.

"Should we ride for a while to determine our location?"

Liam glanced in all directions. "The Niall's home was north, so that's where we will journey."

Abela turned to the west and sniffed the air. "I sense the sea is near."

Letting out a groan, Liam retraced his steps. "Follow me."

"Why do I think we are nowhere near the Niall," she muttered to the horse.

They traveled for several miles finally reaching a dirt path, and she dismounted. The salty tang of the ocean teased her senses as they made their way into a wooded area of thick pines and a narrow path. Liam kept silent during their journey, glancing back at her every so often. After giving him a reassuring smile she was well, he would venture onward.

Brushing away pine branches, she made sure her new friend was not lingering on the path and paused long enough for the horse to nudge her gently on the back. Soon, Liam's curses removed the smile from her face.

Abela made quick strides, jumping over a fallen log, and emerging forth from the trees. What greeted her was not to be expected. Yet, she was neither surprised. She lifted her face to the soft sea breeze and warmth of the sunlight. "We're on the west coast of Ireland."

"Correct," confirmed Liam.

"Instead of the east coast, the home of the Niall."

"Bravo, *princess*."

By the hounds, how she hated when he referred to her in that sarcastic tone. *So far, you have struck out on all your destinations. I wonder how long it took any Fenian Warrior to manage traveling through the Veil.*

The horse snorted behind her in obvious amusement to their situation. She pointed a warning finger at the animal. "It shall be a long arduous journey to make our true destination, so do not speak to me in that manner."

Liam stormed past her and retreated into the woods. "Are you coming?"

She nodded reluctantly and followed him.

As the late afternoon sun settled behind them, Liam came to an abrupt halt. Several cottages stood out in stark contrast to the rolling hills of lush grasses and flowers. Sheep grazed in a large pen nearby. Wood smoke drifted by them, and he lowered his head on a sigh.

Regret filled her when she realized they were most likely in the wrong century. Stepping near him, she shielded her eyes to inspect the view. "Sorry." It was the first time she'd uttered an apology in decades.

"Not your fault." He glanced sideways at her. "Remember, unskilled." And his gaze danced with mirth and not with a scolding.

"What now?"

He pointed to the south. "See the structure beyond the cottages?"

"Yes. The one without a roof?"

"This is where we shall spend the night."

"But...*but* should we not attempt to go back to the stones?" Abela blurted out. The idea of spending an entire night in Liam's company made her cheeks burn.

Without warning, Liam lifted her into his arms and placed her on the horse. "I will not risk going through the Veil so soon. As I've stated before, you—"

She raised a brow in argument.

"Let me clarify. *We* require rest and food, if only for part of the evening."

Satisfied with his correction, Abela smiled. "It would be lovely to sit for a while and gain strength from the land."

"Good. Then we are in agreement."

Abela waved him forward. "Lead on, my warrior."

He inclined his head. "By your command."

She chuckled softly as they followed Liam away from the cottages and dirt path. Her horse gave no objection when the warrior led them across a small stream, steadily making their way to the ruins of a cottage. By the time they approached the place, the last ray of light danced off the white and gray stones.

Liam eased her gently from the animal. "I am going for food and water. Make yourself comfortable inside."

Startled he was leaving her, she grabbed his tunic. "What if there are humans living inside?"

He placed a comforting hand over hers, warm and strong. "I magically inspected the cottage before I mentioned it earlier."

"Oh." She bit her lower lip, feeling foolish.

After releasing his hold, he gave the horse a pat. "Guard the princess in my absence. For your services, I shall return with food for you."

The horse stomped the ground and ambled toward the side of the cottage.

Abela pulled her cloak more firmly around her body as she watched Liam dart away. "Do not tarry."

She turned and surveyed the cottage. Ivy and moss trailed a path within the crevices of the stones. There were no shutters in the window and the door was broken, hanging to the side.

Entering the small structure, she lifted her palm. "*Illuminate*." Light shimmered inside, banishing the shadows. Rats scurried from their protective places, angry at her intrusion. With a wave of her hand, she removed the cobwebs and dust inside the interior. Broken pottery littered the place, and the room was void of any furniture, so they would have to be content with sitting against the wall.

She tapped a finger in thought. A fire would bring warmth and cast out the dreariness. Walking to the hearth, she held her hands outward. "Fire and flame, spark the light, let no others witness the bright."

Flames burst forth from the charred wooden remains. Placing her hands outward, Abela allowed the warmth to seep into her. Liam was correct. Her body was weary from all their travels. All she longed for was a few hours of sleep, and they could be on their way.

Settling down near the blazing fire, Abela stretched out her legs. She watched the flames spark up through the aged chimney. A year ago, she was in the peaceful, bucolic womb of the Fae realm. Never had she imagine this incredible journey. The human world was indeed a strange and complex land. Yes, there was beauty, but it was raw and untamed. In truth, she prayed they would not have to travel to anymore human realms. A prickle of unease developed within her. Her shield of protection was fading over them.

"Oh, please let this be our final destination."

Liam startled her when he stepped inside the cottage, and she drew forth her dirk.

He eyed her skeptically. "Are you preparing for a battle?"

She quickly sheathed her blade at her side. "It's always best to be on guard in strange surroundings."

Dumping a satchel on the ground, he removed his sword and sat down next to her. He proceeded to pull out bread, apples, cheese, and a flask. "We have landed in the late 17th century. I procured our fare from a nearby farm, along with another stray horse."

Reaching for an apple, she drew forth a *sgian dubh* from her boot and sliced off a piece. *Praise the Goddess for another animal.* "Do you know who has the treaty in this century?"

His expression was a mask of stone as he tore into the bread. "Yes."

Abela waited for him to finish and tell her who this person was, but he continued to eat in silence. The bit of apple lodged in her throat, and she reached for the flask. Taking a sip, she sputtered in disgust. "Sweet Mother Goddess. What foul liquid did you bring back?"

Liam took the flask from her hand and sniffed the contents. "The mortal's version of ale."

"I suggest we dump the remaining contents and fill it with water from the nearby stream. This is horrid."

Liam stood abruptly and made for the door.

"At least wait until after you have eaten. I did not intend for you to rush off and do my bidding," she pleaded.

"No worries," he replied, leaving her once again.

Reaching for the loaf of bread, she tore off a piece and slumped back against the wall. A wolf howled in the distance. *Be gone from this place.* She waited for a few minutes, sensing the animal's indecision to venture near them, and then he turned in the opposite direction from the cottage.

"Wise choice," she mumbled.

Liam soon returned with fresh water. Maintaining his vigil of silence, her nerves twisted like vines within her stomach. Tossing her apple core into the fire, she turned toward him. "Who has the treaty in this century?"

"Tinkers. Specifically, the O'Malley of the Irish Travelers. He is their leader and descended from the Niall."

Abela shuddered visibly. "Say no more. I've heard the accounts of how certain travelers have attempted to steal the powers from the Fae during the centuries, especially those of Fenian Warriors."

He regarded her with intensity. "So if you have heard the tales, imagine when they realize you are *royalty*. This particular leader was known for his cruelty toward anyone who could see or speak to the Fae. The holy wells precious to the Fae were guarded by his own people. They spied on any who they thought could communicate with us."

Swallowing the lump in her throat, Abela glanced into the firelight. "What do you suggest?"

Liam rubbed a hand vigorously over his face. "A couple ideas. We could stay for a few days until you regain your strength and then return through the stones."

She did not like the first option and feared what she had to tell Liam. "Tell me the other one."

"We attempt a meeting with the O'Malley. I deem it unwise, though."

"Let's take our chances with him," she suggested, placing her blade back within her boot. "As soon as possible. My protection over us is fading. To attempt another passage through the stones in my weakened condition will most likely shatter my shields and alert everyone to our presence."

"All right. Furthermore, if we are to meet the O'Malley, I want you fully rested. Not only is he shrewd and calculating, but extremely observant."

Abela could only nod. The strain of the past few days had now reached its zenith. In truth, it began when she made the decision to defy everything and everyone to rescue Liam. Weeks of preparation, fraught with meticulous details had gone into her planning. Leaving little time for sleep or food.

"Lean your head against my shoulder," Liam encouraged, his breath a warm caress across her cheek.

Mumbling a word of thanks, Abela complied and drifted off to sleep.

Chapter Eleven

"Upon entering the Brotherhood, I silenced the luring seduction of her lips. If I required pleasure, I sought my release in the Pleasure Gardens."

~Chronicles of Liam MacGregor

As he stared into the flames, Liam contemplated their plan with the O'Malley. Never would he have imagined ever having to bargain with the leader of the travelers. He was a ruthless man and would do anything to achieve power. The man would require something of value from him in return for the treaty. Had he not made a vow with the man that he would seek nothing from him? He gritted his teeth at the long-forgotten memory.

Liam dusted his hands off and surveyed the edge of the hill. His captors were sent scurrying in various directions. "You may think you've saved my life, but you are in error."

O'Malley scraped the dirt from his fingernails with his dirk. "Ye are wrong, my Fae friend. I could have sat back and let those men rip the limbs from your body."

"Seriously?" He folded his arms over his chest. "With a single thought, I could have banished them from this place."

The man gave him a passing glance and shoved his dirk into his belt. "And show your powers? I think not."

"Do not underestimate your foe, O'Malley," warned Liam.

O'Malley's gaze sharpened. "When did ye become my enemy?"

Taking a step near the man, Liam replied, "The day you attempted to steal a jeweled dagger from my brother, Rory."

The man shrugged and held his arms outward. "Thieving is not an act of war."

"You're wrong. It is if the one you're stealing from is a Fae. We—Rory and I—came at your request. The summons was one of dire importance. However, I sensed the real reason was one of deception." Liam's words were as cool and clear as ice water.

A muscle flicked angrily in the man's jaw. "Are ye calling me a liar?"

"Never," responded Liam flatly.

O'Malley's smile never reached his eyes. "Then let us not quarrel further."

"Nevertheless, I would not think this act of saving me is one that needs to count as a debt of payment to you."

He regarded him for several moments. After spitting into his hand, he held it outward. "Deal."

Liam narrowed his eyes. "No, only in agreement. A Fae makes no deals with the leader of the travelers. I seek nothing from you that requires an exchange."

A flash of anger showed briefly over the man's features and then vanished. Wiping his hand on his shirt, O'Malley turned to leave and then stayed his steps. He glanced over his shoulder. "All men have need of something, even you, MacGregor. Beware the words you have spoken here today."

Liam watched the man descend the hill in steady strides.

Bringing his attention to the present, Liam understood the predicament he faced with the O'Malley. He had one item of value on him. As he absently brushed his hand over the hilt of his sword, he thought of other ways to appease the man. Abela had two blades, so maybe she would be willing to part with one. In his recollections, the O'Malley did favor any weapon from the Fae realm.

She slept soundly next to him, soft snores escaping every so often. His minx was exhausted from traveling through time. Yes, her landings were unskilled, but she did manage to see them through. He worried more about her strength and ability when they met with the travelers. They were known to weave their own charm over the Fae, and he did not intend to let Abela fall prey to this group of humans.

Liam rested his head back on the stone and closed his eyes. *One more treaty and we can return home.*

For the next several hours, he kept his Fae senses alert, but allowed his body to get the required rest. An owl hooted nearby, so he sent out a message to the bird to alert him of any intruders. When the flames dwindled, Liam blew across his palm and ignited the dying embers. Heat and light flooded their small enclosure.

Abela snuggled more against him, wrapping an arm around his waist. Gently, he brought his arm out and placed it around her shoulders. Her honeysuckle scent filled him. Even after all these decades, he yearned for her. Time, battles, and other liaisons had not diminished his emotions. He deemed he sought out the Pleasure Gardens in the Fae realm to rid her essence from him. Yet, he left feeling empty, and one night he vowed to never return.

Taking the end of her braid, Liam wove the soft hair around his finger. Black as ebony, the lock glistened in the soft glow of the fire. She'd tempted him beyond reason. Once, he thought there might have been a destiny for them, but her words of rejection slammed the door on any possibility. If she had no desire to claim him, why did Abela come to his initiation?

"Why witness my ceremony?" He let out a frustrated breath and brought the braid to his lips.

"Because I never said goodbye," she uttered softly. Lifting her head, her eyes sought his and her cheeks colored from the heat of his gaze.

Liam was unable to look away from her beauty. "No. I recall harsh words and tears."

"We were young—*naïve*."

"Stubborn and set on a path of adventure," he added.

"But our roads have led us to this fork, so to speak."

He cupped her chin. "Was it destined?" He felt her tremble from his touch.

"I am not a seer," she replied, darting her tongue out along her bottom lip.

His mind screamed at him to move away. She was a princess—a *priestess*. But the temptation to taste her lips once more seeped into his being. Liam bent his head and placed a feather-like kiss on the corner of her mouth.

A small breathless whisper escaped her lips, "More."

Her invitation sparked a desire that had remained sealed. Cupping the back of her head, he continued to kiss her tenderly on the eyes, nose, and forehead. As he shifted his position, Liam brought his arms around her and dared to feast on something that was forbidden. If death was his future, he wanted one more kiss to take with him.

He moved his mouth over hers, devouring its softness. He reveled in the heady sensations as his tongue sought entry into her velvety warmth. Her moan entered his body, and Liam crushed her against his chest. His kiss became more urgent—demanding, and she met his fierce possession with her own. He craved Abela like no other, and the passion of claiming her consumed his thoughts.

When he brushed a hand beneath the folds of her cloak, he cupped her breast. She drew her head back and arched into him. Her heat surrounded him, and he longed to strip the clothes from their bodies. "Take it off," he demanded in a hoarse voice.

She tugged at her cloak, pushing the garment free from her shoulders. Her eyes blazed with passion. He gasped when she quickly straddled him and tugged at the lacings on his tunic. "I have longed to touch your skin," she teased, stroking a finger across his collarbone.

"You're playing with fire, Abela."

Aware of his growing desire, she moved against him. "We have been playing this game for some time, I believe."

He let out a groan and recaptured her lips. This time he let his hand slip under her tunic. His fingers grazed over the taut nipple as he explored the softness of her breast. Liam ached to bury himself deep within his minx. Possess her body and soul. Take her to the stars and beyond. Fill her with pleasures she never knew existed.

Breaking free of the kiss, he grasped her bottom and nudged it over his swollen cock. "Is this what you crave?"

Her breathing was labored, and she rocked in a rhythm as old as time.

"Answer me," he ordered.

"I have *always* desired you," she confessed. "Is that what you want to hear?" She lifted her hand. "With one word, I can remove our clothing."

Liam's heart pounded, the words slamming into his mind and heart. His eyes clouded with images of the past. "Then why did you send me away when I came to your chambers that summer evening?"

Abela blinked in confusion. "You were leaving."

His hands shook as he shifted her off his body. Standing, Liam raked a hand through his hair. Placing his fists on the stone mantel, he glanced over his shoulder. "One word, Abela. *One* word from you and I would have stayed."

She stood slowly, and he watched the play of emotions on her face.

"You can't even answer me," he stated in disgust and moved away from the hearth. Grabbing her cloak, he tossed the garment at her.

As he made his way out of the cottage, her words caused him to pause.

"I wanted you for more than one night, Liam."

He stormed back to her and grabbed her by the shoulders. "Did it not occur to you I desired the same?

You never gave me the chance to say what was in my heart."

Abela shirked out of his embrace. "I'm supposed to believe the words from a Fae who frequently visited the Pleasure Gardens?" Fury sparked within the depths of her lavender eyes.

He raked his gaze over her. "I guess we shall never find out, Abela. And let me make this clear. I did not *once* visit the Gardens while we were together. I sought only to spend time with you. I don't know where you came upon your information, but that particular one is false."

"My brother would never lie to me," she claimed.

Liam took a step back. "You are a fool, Abela. Conn would have done *anything* to make sure you were protected and see me enter the Brotherhood."

Her chest heaved with anger. "I don't believe you!"

"Sadly, that has always been your problem." Liam blew out a sigh of frustration and walked out of the cottage.

Storming away from the place, he wanted to distance himself from Abela. The cold stream beckoned him to cool the burning rage he had for Conn. He no longer cared if the entire Fae realm descended upon them. Actually, he wished the Fenian Warrior would present himself right now. He'd have a few colorful words for the bastard, along with a fist to his face. All these centuries and not once did Conn mention knowing about his relationship with Abela. Or did he fill her mind with foul lies, so she would spurn him? Regardless, the deed had been done.

As he approached the stream, he stripped completely. When the first icy sting of water touched his skin, he bit back a curse. Submerging his body, he released the tide of ferocity into the stream. He swam swiftly with the current.

By the time he returned to the land, not only had he closed the door on his anger, but also on his lustful feelings for Abela. Once, they might have had a future. She had chosen her path, and he walked another. Even now, their futures were strained, undetermined. The focus had to be in obtaining the last treaty and returning to the kingdom. Emotions and lust only clouded their mission.

Nevertheless, the day of reckoning with Conn MacRoich was an absolute certainty.

****

Conn tried to temper his impatience. Never could he have imagined the difficulty of finding two Fae. From the moment they entered the human world, all traces of his sister and Liam were non-existent. Each Fae carried an elemental signature, but for some unfathomable reason, they were unable to find any. He had no knowledge of where they would flee, and this made it difficult.

Pacing the outer edges of the forest, he tried to recall fragments of past conversations with Abela. Even his recent discussions had been fleeting. He'd thought of her as one with Mother Danu, safe and off limits within the temple. Was it all a ruse to remain hidden? When he sought entrance at the temple doors to speak with the elder priestess about his sister's disappearance, she refused to offer him an audience.

Even Rory could offer no viable explanation for Liam's behavior. His brother had never spoken about Abela. The two shared their conquests in The Pleasure

Gardens, but nothing else.

Conn knelt on one knee. Placing his palm upon the ground, he searched the land, stretching his magic in a wide arc. He swept along the veins deep within the earth, probing for the smallest speck of essence from her. Silence greeted him, and he smacked the hard dirt. Standing, he fisted his hands on his hips. This was going to be a tedious journey.

He studied the landscape. Memories of being in this exact spot over a year ago consumed him. His journey began in Ireland on an uncertain future. Now he found himself contemplating his own sister's future. She'd actually assisted him through one of the darkest moments in his life with Ivy.

"Why Liam?"

Ronan approached quietly by his side. "Nothing from the animal kingdom."

He kept his sight on a lone hawk hovering in the distance. The bird had sought out its prey as the rabbit skittered out from within a bush. If it had remained hidden, the hawk would have flown to another part of the land.

Conn narrowed his eyes in thought. "Camouflage."

"Explain."

"Abela is shielding herself and Liam. It's a form of magical camouflage—one she is extremely good at performing."

Ronan brushed a hand across his brow. "The king and queen possess this power—"

Conn placed a hand on his friend's shoulder. "So does my sister. It's one of her varied gifts. I had forgotten this peculiar power."

"Then we are at an impasse," stated Ronan.

Releasing his hold, Conn clasped his hands behind his back. "She cannot maintain the shield much longer, given she is in the human world. Time moves more swiftly here. Soon, it will collapse, and we will be able to find them both."

"Where do you think they went? If they are on foot, they are not far. Let us each take a direction and search," Ronan suggested.

Conn shrugged as he continued to view the lazy circles of the hawk. "When I returned last year, I found a horse to take me near Dublin. Abela or Liam could have done the same."

"There were none," countered Ronan and stepped away.

His anger grew as he turned toward the warrior. "No! I will not accept the alternative."

Ronan's eyes widened as if he came to the same conclusion as Conn. "Did they travel the Veil of Ages?"

"By the hounds!" snapped Conn, recalling the earlier words of warning from his father within his mind. "My sister is proving to be one step ahead of us. If she has the Stone of Ages, she *might* be able to travel through the vortex."

"Especially if Liam speaks the ancient words. A strong possibility," added Rory, appearing magically through colored mists with Taran following closely behind him.

"Anything?" demanded Conn, trying to temper his fury.

"No. Yet, I'm beginning to agree with your theory," replied Rory. "They must have known how foolish it would be to remain in the present here in Ireland."

Conn threw up his hands in aggravation. "What is their purpose? To avoid death? Why didn't Liam thwart this plan? Was he not the honorable warrior we all believed him to be?" He glanced at the warriors gathered, each remaining silent. They held no answers. There were only two Fae who could give an accurate account to this sheer madness, and he was determined to search to the stars for them.

Rory shifted his stance. "My brother has always been one to maintain control in any situation, regardless of his emotions. One of his greatest battle qualities, but this is beyond my comprehension."

Conn drew in a breath and released it slowly. "Time is fleeting. I now share this knowledge with you. It is unknown how long Abela can survive in the human world. As you have recently learned, we—the Fenian Warriors—are the only Fae who are allowed to travel away from the kingdom and through the Veil of Ages. Apparently, the king sought fit to inform me of this new revelation."

Rory started to protest, and he held his hand up to still his words.

"It is an ancient law and one that is written down in the annals of some tome. I have ordered it to be joined with the other volumes of knowledge within the Brotherhood."

"It is an important piece of Fae information we should have known," complained Rory.

"Agreed," echoed the other warriors.

"Regardless, we must proceed quickly," commanded Conn. "I suggest we travel to the nearest standing stones. There will be residual energy, something Abela did not factor in when she concocted her scheme."

"But where did they go?" asked Taran. "The humans have a saying—it's like searching for a needle in a haystack."

"I believe this one is worse," argued Conn, turning toward Rory. "Any time period your brother favored?"

Rory tapped a finger to his mouth in concentration. "Hmm...Liam is more scholar than warrior, so toss out anything relating to battle times. He enjoyed visiting and working with Prince Albert on designs for locomotives in Victorian England. Then there was the time he talked for hours about his time with Leonardo DaVinci—from paintings to inventions." He chuckled softly. "Yet, he favored most the time spent with Aidan Kerrigan on the archaeological digs. Remember, he was Aileen's guardian."

"*Still*," corrected Conn. "He has maintained a vigil over her and Stephen, especially after the death of Aidan. He thought it was his duty to the warrior."

Rory nodded. "Then I deem we have our first point of origin to search for them. Yet, what year do we venture to?"

"We follow their trail through the stones," responded Conn tersely.

Chapter Twelve

"I dared not risk my heart being shredded like the petals of a flower during a thunderstorm."
~Diary of Princess Abela

The air hummed with energy as they galloped closer to the Irish Traveler's camp. Abela had heard all the tales, some even spoken in whispers among her people about these Irish folk. Long ago, when the Fae dwelled with the humans, the travelers lured many with song, food, and drink. Although there were some who were good decent men and women, others schemed to procure the powers of the Fae. They used dark and twisted methods to coerce many. Some succeeded with their drug induced potions and spells, leaving those Fae immobile, or worse dead.

A sense of unease washed over her as she darted a glance at Liam. He had warned her of the danger, so she made a vow to keep her tongue silent and permit him to do all the talking. If any questions were directed toward her, Abela would give curt and concise answers.

The O'Malley had a keen inner sixth sense.

As they crossed the stream, Liam directed them southward. The area opened up to reveal a sprawling landscape dotted with cottages here and there. Farmers milled about their chores and some gave a passing wave. Abela forced a smile, and she gripped the reins of her mount more fully as a man tipped his cap to her.

Her heart remained bruised from Liam's slashing remarks last evening. How could they have gone from passionate kisses to biting words in a matter of moments? Liam had given her no promises. He only spoke of desires, wants, and needs. She was confused, wary. When she sought out Conn for advice about his friend, he warned her to stay away. He professed the man liked to dabble in sexual favors within the Pleasure Gardens. Additionally, he shared that Liam's brother, Rory, was a frequent member of the Gardens as well. Trusting Conn, she went back to her chambers and refused to see Liam anymore and sent him curt messages. She'd chastised herself for many days, until she heard about his initiation into the Brotherhood. Her heart broke fully on that day.

"Was it all a lie?" she asked, lifting her head to the sky. She returned her sight to the man riding ahead of her. "Was there more? If so, I am the fool."

Regardless of her past emotions, Abela had to close the door forever. Bitterness had replaced joy. Now that Liam knew what happened, there was no point in going forward. She only prayed this course of direction they were taking would set him free.

For the next several hours, the scenery blurred past them. Abela kept a slight distance behind Liam, ignoring the dwindling magic she used to keep the protective shield around them. As the land dipped below them, she noted the forest in the distance.

Liam brought his horse to a light canter. Coming alongside him, she shielded her eyes from the mid-afternoon sun.

"The O'Malley keeps to the trees, specifically the

area known as Drewbrae. He considers this his land and retreats here until early summer."

Dropping her hand, Abela asked, "You seem to know a great deal about this man. Have you had many dealings with him?"

Liam eyed her warily. "Many, and our last conversation did not end well."

"Goodness." Abela shifted uneasily on her horse. "What do you require from me? Are you presenting me as your betrothed?"

"Most definitely. Act submissively around me."

She snorted. *That will be a challenge.*

"Again, this is a mission, and I'm presenting my case for the treaty. It will be fraught with difficulties, since I stated once I would require nothing from the man. You are merely on this journey to tour Ireland. To see the landscape of your ancestors."

She nodded slowly. They were so close to obtaining the last treaty. "What clothing is appropriate?"

He looked at her for the first time since they left the cottage. "Dress as one of the lower houses of the Fae realm." Leaning forward, he tapped the stone that was hidden beneath her cloak. "Embed the relic inside your gown. If they even suspect you're garbed in finery or gems, they will snatch them from you. When offered drink or food, partake of small quantities only. Let the drink touch your lips and nibble on the food."

Abela laughed nervously. "I do realize these people are cunning, but you're acting as if they have more powers than we do."

"Therein lies your mistake. I've witnessed the power in a curse and fought off the tempting lure of a melody at a campfire."

A soft gasp escaped her. "Do they have magical capabilities? Where did they harness this power?"

He stiffened at the question. "We are in Ireland. There were some Fae who did mingle with the people before we descended underground. The elders are in agreement that the bloodline of the travelers is mixed with ours. Even a drop will produce a lasting effect in a human's genealogy. However, I do trust the O'Malley and some of his people more than other clans."

"Interesting," she mused, sweeping her gaze to the trees. "I shall be on guard and weave a stronger thread of protection around us."

"Only if you are strong enough. Do not tax yourself." He reached out and grasped her hand.

Startled by the warmth of his touch, Abela darted a glance at where his fingers rested. "Have no fear, I have no desire to fall prey to their alluring charms."

"Good. I believe it's a few years in the future since I last visited with this clan. Let us move out of range, so you can change without prying eyes."

Turning to leave, she asked, "Do you fear them, Liam?"

"I have learned on my many travels in this world to always be on guard around *all* humans. Yes, we are powerful, but not once have I underestimated these people. So heed my words, Abela."

"I understand."

After they found a place for her to transform into presentable clothing, Liam escorted her into the forest of Drewbrae. The energy she experienced earlier now cloaked her. Instantly, she whispered a stronger shield over them. A raven swept down from a branch, cawing as it flew over them.

"Eyes of the people," Liam explained quietly.

She looked affronted. "It did not impart greetings like the others in the animal kingdom."

Liam chuckled. "Because it has no need. It belongs to them."

"I find this disturbing."

"Curb the feelings and assumptions," he warned and slowed his pace.

Light filtered through the canopy of trees, illuminating the path in front of them. The forest was devoid of birdsong, and a trickle of unease slid down her spine. She felt the sharp gaze of eyes from the humans within the trees.

After bringing his horse to a halt, Liam lifted his hand for her to move beside him. She complied, and they waited in silence. Were they waiting for him to speak? She knew they were observing them, so why the subterfuge?

Minutes ticked by, along with her impatience. She stole a glance at Liam, noting the rigid posture and tick in his lower jaw. This was almost as bad as waiting outside the gates for permission from King MacAlpin. Yet, she attributed that time to one of rudeness and the particular century.

Abela fought the smile when a whisper of greeting floated by her on a breeze. It came from a small child. Inwardly, she smiled. She could ill afford to acknowledge the wee human, yet. They had not been acknowledged by anyone, including the elusive O'Malley.

A swoosh of wings alerted her to the presence of the raven. The bird had returned, perching itself on a nearby branch. Its beady eyes surveyed her oddly. Tilting its head to the side, its gaze never wavered. Since the bird had not imparted a greeting, Abela returned her attention to the path in front of them.

The crunch of leaves signaled someone was coming. *Finally.* She was tempted to steal another look at Liam, but refrained.

Four men appeared, and two others stepped out from the trees on either side of them. Was this their welcoming committee or guards? She found their clothing vibrant among the greenery.

One of the men stepped forward. "State your business."

"I request a meeting with the O'Malley," replied Liam.

"Name?"

"Do not insult me in front of your men, Colm," warned Liam, glaring at the man.

A sudden icy contempt flashed in the man's eyes. "They are not familiar with ye, *or* your kind."

Abela tore her gaze from the man called Colm to rest on Liam. His insult reflected in his tone, and she fought to hold her tongue. Were the Fae considered specimens among the travelers? To the others Liam appeared calm and composed, but she'd gamble all she owned that his mind was shouting vile obscenities at the man.

"Then introduce us." Liam's tone cut sharp as the steel he carried by his side.

Colm spit onto the ground. "Ranald, go tell O'Malley that *Liam* MacGregor requests an audience."

As the man complied, he sent a leering look at Abela in passing. The other men nodded and made crude comments toward her as well. Some even went so far as to emulate vulgar gestures with their bodies. She fought the ire growing within her. Never in all her existence had she faced this type of barbaric behavior. *Wrong, there was King MacAlpin*, she chastised herself. *But at least his manners were a wee bit more civil.*

Liam steadied his hand on his blade as he swept his sight outward. "Do I misspeak when I say I thought the manners of the O'Malley clan were better than I have witnessed? To utter lewd comments and barbs to my betrothed brings dishonor to your people *and* leader."

"No harm was done," Colm argued, patting the man who instigated the remarks on the back.

"Ye are correct in your observation, MacGregor," admitted a tall, muscular man striding forth.

His long, red hair was tied back, and Abela noted the deep crescent-shaped scar starting above his left brow and ending at his mouth. He strode with intent toward Colm and without warning, slammed a fist to the man's jaw.

Abela gasped, unprepared for the assault on the man.

Colm staggered but remained standing. He rubbed a hand over his chin and lowered his head. "Forgive me, O'Malley."

"If ye cannot control your men while on patrol, ye are of no use to me. Return to the camp."

Colm gave O'Malley a curt nod, though he managed to glare daggers at Liam before he stormed through the trees.

"O'Malley turned toward Liam and folded his arms over his chest. "I am surprised to see ye on my lands *and* with your woman. I believe our last conversation was a terse one."

"Did you hear everything in the shadows of the trees? Are we welcome?" asked Liam, his face a mask of stone.

"Ye have never been banished, but since these are your rules—" He extended his arms, adding, "I bid ye welcome." He took a step forward. "And the *shadows* have always provided excellent protection."

Swiftly dismounting, Liam came to Abela's side. He gave her a wink. Grabbing her around the waist, she let him help her dismount. He lifted her hand to O'Malley. "Before I discuss my reason for being here, may I present my betrothed, Abela. She has agreed to make this journey with me."

O'Malley's smile was disarming, and she found herself unable to resist by giving him one of her own. Allowing her hand to slip free from Liam's hold, she allowed the man to take it in his grasp. O'Malley placed a kiss along her knuckles, though his eyes never left hers. "*Abela.*" He rolled her name off his tongue in a leisurely manner.

She dipped her head. "I am honored."

He lifted a brow in challenge. "I cannot fathom why, since I believe the Fae consider they are far more superior." Leaning near, he uttered softly, "Mayhap, 'tis only the men in your world?"

"I would not be privy, since this is my first time in your realm." Abela struggled to contain her words. How she longed to speak more with this man, but Liam was correct. In just a few short minutes, she'd deduced his cunning character. Had he truly been watching them the entire time from the trees?

O'Malley took a step back and roared with

laughter. Recovering his wits, he pointed a finger at Liam. "A wise *and* beautiful woman ye are marrying."

"Thank you," remarked Liam and placed a protective arm around her waist. His grip was firm and warm.

Abela stiffened, but managed to smile at O'Malley. "You are kind, sir."

"Ahh…flattery is rewarded, Abela. Let us retreat to my camp. Surely ye can join us for a meal and drink. My men will fetch your horses." The man continued to ramble on as he stooped beneath a cluster of pine branches and disappeared through the forest.

She stole a glance at Liam and he nodded. "Trust me. This will give us extended time to rest," he whispered against her ear.

Abela pulled him aside. "Will I be there when you speak to him about the treaty?"

He shrugged. "It depends. Most of my conversations with O'Malley have been short, fueled by drink—limited on my part—questions about the world, and what he required by the way of assistance in handling a situation. Nevertheless, you have made an impression on him."

"And this is good, right?" She frowned, pursing her lips.

"Yes, it is, but what troubles you?"

"Are ye coming?" O'Malley bellowed.

"Let us not tempt fate," suggested Liam and started forward.

"Wait. I have one more question."

"Which is?"

She darted a glance behind him to make sure O'Malley did not reappear. "Are all the human males crude when it comes to women? Their gazes wander to parts of our anatomy, instead of keeping their focus on our eyes. Why must they speak in vulgar languages? The animals who roam the land have more manners. It's indecent and disrespectful, and I'm repulsed by human males." Drawing in a shaky breath, she released it slowly. "At times I'd like to smack them, and you know I'm not prone to violence."

Liam drew near. His eyes skimmed over her features. "No. It depends on the man, century, and what he has been taught. Here you will find the men love their women beneath them—for pleasure, along with other domestic duties." He lifted a stray lock from her cheek, trailing a finger to her jawline. "You are beautiful, Abela, and it will take all my strength to keep from taking my blade to anyone leering at you during our time here." Stepping back, he added, "Does this answer your question?"

Her face heated, unable to recall anything she'd said to him. He had a way of melting her to a puddle of honeyed ambrosia with his words and touch, and all she could do was agree. "Ye...*yes*."

Smiling broadly, Liam turned and parted the branches for her. "After you, *my love*."

For a moment, Abela could do nothing but gape at the man. Finally recovering her senses, she moved through the trees, realizing he was only playing the part of her beloved.

Once again, she told herself it was only a pretense.

Soon this madness will be over, and the vow I made to save you will end my duty to you.

Chapter Thirteen

"My word given in loyalty shall always remain. If I break the promise, it's because you have leveled the blade against my heart."

~Chronicles of Liam MacGregor

The crowd parted in hushed tones as Liam and Abela entered the clearing keeping a close pace behind O'Malley. Caravans and tents were sprawled out in a circular fashion with their leader's wagon tucked under a huge pine tree.

Their reaction to Abela was disturbing. Some actually dipped a curtsy, especially the young children. Had they sensed her true identity? Or were they enchanted by her beauty? What was he thinking bringing a Fae female amongst these people? Abela was stunning, even in her simple garments. Even though Liam towered over these people, he realized many had never seen a woman of her height.

But he could not have left her wandering the countryside by herself. Nor would she allow Liam to be separated from her. *I should have waited until you had rested and attempted to travel through the Veil of Ages. This is madness being here.*

Stealing a glance at her, he saw she was smiling. One of the wee girls had dashed out to present Abela with a bunch of foxgloves. The princess gracefully bent down and accepted the gift. Murmuring soft words of appreciation, she stood and continued walking alongside him.

He reached out and touched one of the flowers. "They mirror the lovely shade of your eyes."

Abela looked stunned at his comment. "Thank you."

Did she not understand he spoke the truth? He gently moved her away from the crowd and to the wagon belonging to O'Malley.

As they entered the wagon, another woman approached and gestured for Abela to take a place on a bench away from the men. O'Malley was speaking quietly to two other men—one his brother, Malcolm, and the other his strongest guard, Adam MacDonald.

"It is their custom that the women are not involved with the politics of the men," Liam uttered softly.

"Of course. I shall observe from a distance," she reassured him.

He brushed a kiss along her cheek and drew back. Her lips parted in invitation, and Liam quickly averted his gaze. *This is only a ruse, Abela.* Yet, he deemed the statement was more for his well-being and not hers.

"I have been working on a batch of wine for the Midsummer. Would ye care to sample a cup?" asked O'Malley as he settled himself along the cushioned bench.

"Definitely," Liam acknowledged, taking a seat across from the man.

"Midsummer?" Abela blurted out, clutching a hand to her chest.

Her outburst brought the light conversation to a halt.

"Surely ye were aware of the season," declared O'Malley, handing Liam a cup of wine, though his gaze was leveled on Abela.

"Our travels have been many, and my beloved lost track of the seasons," stated Liam, giving her a reassuring grin. *By the hounds! How could he have misplaced the season? It was one of the primary ones for the Fae and the priestesses.*

Abela placed her hands in her lap. "You are correct, Liam. When you are done, I shall require time alone."

Giving her a curt nod, he reined in the questions he longed to toss out at her. Returning his attention to O'Malley, he asked, "How soon to Midsummer?"

The man's mouth twitched in humor. "Three days. I assume ye will want to take your leave before then to return for your own celebrations."

"Indeed."

O'Malley took a sip from his cup. "What do ye seek, MacGregor?"

Good. I have no time for small talk. "I require your Treaty of Feahan. I am preparing an amendment in regards to traveling through the Veil of Ages."

The man drained his cup and placed it on the table. His gaze was sharp and assessing. Folding his arms over his chest, he leaned back. "Am I the first ye have visited?"

"No." Liam surveyed him over the rim of his cup.

"Second?"

"Last."

He dismissed him with a wave of his hand. "This conversation is for my ancestor, Niall."

Liam brought the cup to his mouth, letting the wine

147

brush against his lips. The tart fruit teased him to take more, but he set the cup on the table. "I am unable to talk with him at this time. Niall is on another path in regard to religion. I have no wish to descend at a time when he might consider us heathen individuals."

O'Malley shrugged. "Then find the right year. Ye should not be asking this request from me."

Liam placed his hands on the wooden table. "Time is critical. I seek to bring justice for another—"

"Fae?" interrupted O'Malley. "I am not interested in your affairs."

Technically, Aidan Kerrigan was mortal. "It is for both human and Fae," he countered.

"I find this amusing." Refilling his cup, O'Malley swirled the contents. "Ye and your brother were so arrogant. Now ye come here making demands."

"No. A simple request. Ye can either help us or not. This is your choice."

O'Malley pounded his fist onto the table. "Nothing is *simple* with the Fae."

"Might I remind you of the times we have assisted you and your people?"

His eyes narrowed to slits. "Have ye come for payment of your deeds?"

Liam pushed the cup away. "On the contrary, I am asking for aid in this matter."

Adam leaned near the man and whispered into O'Malley's ear. Though the man showed no signs of relenting, a smile curved his features. He gave Adam a curt nod. "These are difficult times for my people. Are ye willing to barter for the treaty?"

Liam glanced around, noting the lush interior and heartiness of the people he had witnessed. The man was one of the richest travelers in this part of the country, and he found their host's statement contrary to what he witnessed. "I have nothing of value on me."

O'Malley pointed to his sword. "I will accept the blade at your waist in exchange for the treaty."

Abela stood abruptly. "Will you consider my dirk?"

"I admire a woman who can wield a blade," remarked O'Malley. He lifted his hand. "May I?"

She stepped forward and handed him the weapon. Liam clenched his fists at his side, trying to retain his composure. Did she not comprehend his instructions to remain silent?

The blade was stunning in its craftsmanship. Silver and etched with Celtic knots and symbols. Liam would have preferred handing the man her smaller *sgian dubh* blade.

O'Malley gestured for her to sit, and Abela took a seat next to Liam. "Is there magic forged within the metal."

She smiled charmingly. "Magic can only be found in the land, air, sea, and fire."

He brushed his fingers over the engravings. "However, it was made in your realm, correct?"

"Yes."

Liam gritted his teeth and snatched the dirk from the man's hands. "I will bring you another when I return with the treaty."

"But I have not granted ye the treaty, yet."

"Those are my terms. A gift from my home in exchange for the document." Liam glared at the man, daring him to challenge his offer.

O'Malley shook his head. "No. I want the blade

belonging to your woman."

Abela touched Liam's arm. "It is of no personal value to me. I would be honored to let him have the dirk."

Her grip told him otherwise. *You lie, Abela, and we are in a dilemma.* "If my beloved has consented, then I have no objections."

"Excellent." Retrieving the dirk, he tucked the blade within his belt at his side. "You will have the treaty in a couple days."

"Unacceptable," Liam protested. "If you are not willing to hand over the document now, we shall leave." He held out his hand. "The dirk, please."

Chuckling softly, O'Malley withdrew the blade and handed it back to Liam. "The document is not here. My younger brother, Peter, has it in his possession. If ye recall, he is the scholar within our clan. He arrives the day after next, Midsummer's Eve. Business in the south prevented him from joining us."

The man's iron will held firmly around Liam. All he required was the bloody document. *Two days...two more days.* He stood slowly. "Then we shall spend the night. Would you have an empty caravan for Abela?"

She clasped her hands together. "I have no objection to sleeping—"

Liam glanced sharply at her. "Preferably a wagon away from the others." He had no intention of having her sleep under the trees.

"I will have one of my women make the arrangements." O'Malley stood and motioned to the woman sitting on the far bench. "I believe the birthing wagon will not be needed for some time, correct?"

"Aye," conceded the woman.

O'Malley pointed to Malcolm. "Take two men and move the wagon away from the others."

His brother grunted his acknowledgment and left the wagon.

Liam rose from his place. "Thank you for your hospitality."

The man broke into a leisurely smile. "Ye have honored my clan by accepting an invitation to stay with us. I am quite certain the bard will tell the tale of how two Fae dined with us." He wandered over to Abela and took her hand. Placing a kiss along her knuckles, he stated, "Please join us later at the campfires."

Liam noted the hesitancy on her features and wrapped a reassuring arm around her shoulders. "It will be our pleasure," he affirmed.

O'Malley released her hand and gestured for them to step outside. "The wagon is being placed south, near the river. I give ye my word, no one will bother ye."

"Thank you," stated Abela and quickly added, "You have been generous."

He winked. "Always to the Fae."

Liam watched him cross to a group of men gathered around one of the fires. He tugged on Abela's hand. "Let us move away from the camp."

She made no sound as he ducked under some branches. Liam continued to move them along a narrow path toward the river. Not once did he release his hold on her. The area curved, and they descended through the trees, revealing the river below. He wasted no time in moving her toward a smooth boulder.

Letting out a sigh, he raked a hand through his hair. He had no concept how the priestesses prepared for the feast day. "What do you require for Midsummer? Can I take you somewhere?"

She sat, mesmerized by the water below them. Her silence bothered him, and he knelt in front of her. "Speak to me."

Her eyes were filled with sadness when she looked at him. "I should have prepared a week ago." Abela wiped a hand across her brow.

Confused by her demeanor, he grasped her hand. "But we were enjoying spring, not summer. Jumping through the Veil multiple times is difficult for Fenian Warriors, so I can't imagine what it would be like for someone who has not had the proper training."

She withdrew her hand from his. "You cannot fathom why I'm upset. I have trained for decades to sense even the tiniest whisper of the feast day."

"Your focus has been on other things," he countered.

"Again, you did not hear me. We trained and honed our keen insights against distractions. The exercises were intense, often without rest for weeks. We had to always be one with the land, regardless of what was happening around us." Her voice rose. "This was a test, and I have failed. You cannot begin to understand, just as I am unable to comprehend your own training."

Liam was plagued with guilt. He should have never agreed to venture out of his prison. His life was ruined, but now hers was as well. "I should have banished you the moment you stepped forth from the shadows inside my cell." He shook his head in remorse and turned away.

Abela gently touched his face. "No regrets, Liam MacGregor. This path has already been woven."

Slowly, he returned his gaze to hers. "Was my life

so important to you?"

"It has always been thus," she whispered. "I am truly sorry I sent you away so many moons ago."

Lifting her hand, Liam placed a kiss on her palm. "I am, too. Yet, it is done. Over." He stood, bringing her to her feet. "What can I do for *you*?"

She leaned against him and looked outward. "With Midsummer approaching, I will be weaker. The veils between the realms will be thin, so I have no wish to draw attention by moving through the land. We celebrated by feasting, dancing, and planting more seeds for rebirth in the land."

"Understood." Wrapping an arm around her waist, he added, "The traveler's camp is the perfect spot to remain hidden. I pray O'Malley's brother arrives before dusk on Midsummer's Eve. If you'd like, we can venture farther away from the camp near the river. It will provide you with more tranquility for meditation."

Abela chuckled softly. Placing a kiss on his cheek, she moved out of his embrace. "I think it best if we are separated and wise to return on Midsummer's Eve."

He arched a brow in challenge. "Do you not trust me?"

She gaped at him. "At this time of the season? No. The song of the land is powerful and difficult to resist."

"You forget. I am a trained Fenian Warrior, skilled in fighting the alluring temptation of sexual pleasures during this time."

"So the Gardens were used upon your return for your...release?" Her tone implied teasing.

Liam placed a fist over his heart. "I am here to protect and guard you."

"Yet, can I trust myself around you? I am new to

being outside of the realm of security."

Her question startled him. Desire bolted through him, and he turned away from the intensity of her stare. With one look, she had stripped away the warrior, and now the man ached to possess the woman. Liam glanced over his shoulder. "If I must, I'll chain you to the wagon."

"Sounds enticing," she purred, and strolled down to the river.

He gaped at her in utter dismay. One moment, she was sorrowful and in agony. The next, a tempting vixen, inciting a riot between his body and mind. "I must be the stronger one," he muttered.

Shaking his head to rid his lustful thoughts of the woman, he followed her down to the water. By the time he approached the bank of the river, O'Malley's men had maneuvered the wagon to a cluster of trees not far from the bank. Their horses had been tethered to a nearby tree and Abela went to free them, leading them toward refreshment.

She lifted her arms and stretched. "I have no problem sleeping under the stars."

Settling his body against a tree, Liam studied her. "You and I both know the wagon is better suited for your needs, especially so close to other humans."

Shrugging, Abela glanced up at the first star of the evening. "Do you believe the ancients are angry with us?"

"The dragon guardians are wary. I sense their watchful presence. If we had disrupted anything, I am certain a blow would have been delivered."

"Disrupted, as in the timeline?"

"No. What you did in freeing me."

She nodded in understanding and pointed upward. "A crime within the realm, but maybe they comprehend."

Liam fingered Abela's dirk at his waist. Retrieving the blade, he examined the etchings in the fading light. "Who gave you the dirk?"

Her faint smile held a touch of sadness as she walked toward him. She held out her hand. "May I?"

Handing the blade to her, he waited.

Abela traced a finger over the symbols. "Aidan gave it to me on our last day of training together. It was a parting gift for being a worthy student. He forged the steel from the waters by his home."

He patted the ground next to him. "Tell me more."

She hesitated, uncertainty shown within her gaze.

"I promise not to touch you," he affirmed.

"I envy your training," she uttered softly, taking a seat next to him.

"Don't, Abela. You were destined to become one with the land. I pray you will be able to continue once we return. Whereas, I am hardened by decades of training and can silence the call within me." He pointed to the dirk. "Continue."

"Ever since he presented me with the dirk, I have carried it with me. The priestesses saw no objection when I entered the temple, carrying the blade at my side. It was the sole item I possessed and regarded it more deeply after he left our world. Not only was Aidan a great warrior and leader, but he was *my* uncle. When the news of his death reached the kingdom, I wept for days near the waterfall that leads to *Tir na Og*."

An ache of remembrance stabbed at his heart. "We

all did on that day. Conn refused to acknowledge him as an uncle, preferring to see him as the great Fenian Warrior."

"So sad," she whispered.

"No, Abela. It was out of a high regard for Aidan. In truth, Conn had no desire to seek favors due to his blood lineage. I witnessed many conversations between the two."

"My brother is always in control."

For a moment, Liam longed to ask more about Conn, but recalled his vow. In due time, he would come upon the knowledge. "Did you know I was there when Aileen scattered his ashes in the waters of Loch Ness in Scotland?"

Her eyes were misted with unshed tears. "No."

"All the Fenian Warriors arrived to pay tribute to him. I will never forget the scene." He placed a hand over hers. "We are not going to turn over this dirk to O'Malley."

She scowled and removed her hand. "A bargain was struck."

"I will offer another gift. Give me your *sgian dubh*."

"Like this is going to pacify the man," she scoffed, removing the smaller blade.

"Ahh...but look how it glows." He tapped a finger against the hilt, turning the wood to silver.

"Impressive, but not as big. In my short time among the males, I'm guessing they like their blades huge and decorative."

Liam stared at her. Even in the faint light, her cheeks started to turn a rosy glow as she caressed the length of the blade. Images of her hands on his body ripped through him. Stirrings of lust shot through his blood, and the land urged him to take her upon the ground, swift and claiming.

Standing abruptly, he shook while trying to bring his emotions under control. He had to move away from her and clear his mind. "Try and get some rest."

He had only taken two steps when her voice drifted by him. "Rest comes to those who don't understand what we feel."

Liam kept walking and the more his steps carried him away from Abela, the more he ached to possess her.

Body and soul.

Chapter Fourteen

"Even in the remote parts of the temple, I understood that the ripple from tossing a stone into the water can mirror the first taste of a kiss."
                              ~Diary of Princess Abela

Sleep was elusive within the confines of the wagon. From the parted curtains, Abela counted the stars in this strange world and attempted to trace outlines with her outstretched hand of all the various constellations. When she argued with Aidan one day that he should teach her about the human world and its stars, his denial was swift. It was often a topic of heated conversations.

"Why this interest in the humans?" he argued, piercing her with a stern look.

"Did we not once live among them? You did. Certainly, you can share your knowledge. I don't know why it's forbidden," countered Abela. *"If I must, I'll seek out the Library of the Ancients."*

Aidan halted in front of her. *"There are no records of the constellations of the human world in any tome. It is merely the sacred texts of our people."*

"I have heard otherwise."

"By whom?" he demanded.

"I do not divulge my sources."

"Name the Fenian Warrior." His order came out

as a growl.

Never would she speak his name. He was gone. Dismissed from her life. But he had manage to share fragments of the human world he had heard from his brother during training.

Abela dared to defy her uncle. "Why is it so wrong?"

His chest heaved in frustration. "So you present me with a question and refuse to answer my own?"

She waited, praying his temper would cool, refusing to show no fear in front of him.

Minutes ticked by in agonizing torture. She would not relent and considered this information a part of her training.

Aidan snapped his fingers beside her. A parchment appeared in his hand. "This is a map of the constellations in the northern European hemisphere during the summer months. If you are intent on learning the stars' alignment, you'd better study."

Her fingers trembled as she took the map. "Thank you."

Turning away from her, he started for the garden outside the chamber and paused. "Abela?"

"Yes, Aidan."

"If you ever disobey an order again, I will end your training." He glanced over his shoulder, glaring at her. His eyes had shifted to pure shards of crystals.

All she could do was nod.

"One more lesson for you to learn, Abela. You may not have answered my question, but all the Fenian Warriors are under my command. I shall find the man. It would have served you better to disclose his name."

Never before had she witnessed the intensity of his

anger. Abela vowed on that day to never incur the wrath of her uncle ever again.

When he left the chamber, Abela trembled. All she had wanted was to witness the stars in the world Liam would eventually travel to, along with her brother. Was it too much to ask?

Swallowing the lump in her throat, she deftly opened the map upon the table and spent the entire day committing to memory every detail of the constellations.

Sighing, she shook her head at the long-forgotten memory. "Did you ever find out it was Liam, uncle?"

Abela brought her knees to her chest and inhaled deeply. A cool breeze kissed her cheeks as she watched the last star wink from sight. The new day rose with a pink hue across the treetops. "It's almost Midsummer's Eve," she murmured. "How am I going to move through these days?"

Tossing aside the coverings, Abela stepped forth from the wagon. As she turned toward the east, she lifted her arms in welcome to the new day. "At the stone we sing and gather. Brush a hand over the first breath of dew's kiss." She bent and touched the ground in reverence. "We awaken this day."

Rising slowly, she waited for any message from Mother Danu. Abela sensed it was a futile effort, but attempted the contact. Hugging her arms around her body, she tried to banish the ache of loss. Would the great Goddess ever reach out to her again?

Birdsong was her only greeting. The tiny sparrow flitted about in welcome. After giving her feathered friend a small smile, Abela made her way toward the river. Removing her shoes, she bunched up her gown and stepped into the water. Its icy sting vanquished the weariness from her body and cleansed her mind. A powerful urge to strip her clothes and submerge her body deep within the waters was immediately squashed. Too many prying eyes, she suspected. She quickly splashed her face with one hand and then retreated to the wagon.

"Good morning." The timbre of Liam's voice was low and sent her nerves skittering.

He stood leaning against the entrance of the wagon. She brushed past him to grab her cloak and weapons. "Yes, it is."

"Plans for the day?" he inquired and pulled the cloak from her arms. After draping the garment over her shoulders, he tilted her chin up with his finger. "You did not rest."

"I counted the stars and the constellations," she confessed.

"You do realize they are different in the human world." His eyes brimmed with amusement.

Abela stared at him. Why did the man look positively gorgeous, especially in the early morning hours? "It was part of my training."

A flicker of surprise flashed briefly on his features. "Only the Fenian Warriors are privy to the knowledge."

She adjusted her cloak and tucked her blades in their respective places on her body. "Aidan gave me the parchments to study." Stepping around him, Abela moved down along the river.

"You seem to have been Aidan's favorite," he proposed, coming alongside her. "Or did you blackmail him? Do tell."

She was furious he would think she'd do anything so appalling. Ignoring him completely, Abela went in search of fresh berries.

He darted in front of her, halting her progress. His eyes danced with mischief. "Is it your secret? Did Aidan share other information about the humans?"

She gave him an exasperated snort. "Who are you? And where is the stern Fenian Warrior from yesterday?"

"In front of you," he responded dryly.

"Humph! You're behaving strangely this morning." Pushing him aside, Abela continued on her path.

Again he fell into pace alongside her. "I decided to embrace these next few days. It might be the last we have of our freedom."

Abela stole a glance at him. "Either your brain is addled from too much sleep or you have been drinking the O'Malley's wine." Halting abruptly, she grasped his tunic and searched his face. "That's it. You're drunk on the wine. I must find protection for you from the travelers."

He tugged on her hands. "No. Not one drop this morning. In truth, I did not get any sleep. My thoughts were of my life. Journeys I should not have traveled, and ones filled with contentment."

"Oh." Slowly, she released her hold on him. "Did you draw any conclusions?"

Liam bent and picked up a stone. He tossed it casually into the air. "That I have no regrets."

"Why?" she asked, surprised by his declaration. She thought he might have one or two.

As he tossed the stone across the river, they watched it skip over the water. Ripples fanned out in a wide arc. "Each decision I made led to the next and had an impact on another life—be it human or Fae. I cannot undo the past. My destiny is linked to the destinies of others in this universe."

"But what about Aidan?" Her question barely a whisper.

Frowning slightly, he answered, "I deem he understood the risks. Besides, I was his daughter's guardian. He would have trusted no one else to assist him through the Veil. I had to put myself in his respective position. *If* I had a daughter, I would have moved the stars to protect her."

"How can you be so sure?"

Liam sighed heavily. "There are times when I think the man foresaw his own death. In addition, he had aged tremendously after the death of his wife, Rose. The moment Aileen came to Scotland he demanded I take extra care in watching over her."

She studied his features. "You came to this revelation all within a night?"

"I made my peace long ago with what I did for Aidan. His death was an honorable one, though heartbreaking for his daughter."

Looking away, Abela watched several geese make their way across the river. *Your death would have cleaved my soul in half.* Closing the door on her emotions, she resumed her trek in search of food.

Once again, Liam took his place by her side, and she fought the temptation to utter a groan. The sun had now risen and warmth flooded the area. A doe ambled through the trees foraging for its early morning meal. Inhaling deeply, she tried to detect any scent of fruit.

"Why don't you ask?" His tone was one of teasing.

His joyfulness was irritating and amusing at the

same time. "I can assure you I can find what I'm searching for."

"You're wandering in the wrong direction."

Determined to ignore him, Abela kept on ambling along the side of the hill. Perhaps if she reached the top, the area would open to reveal fields of fruit. One could only hope. However, this was the human world and not her home.

"I spotted a huge blackberry bush earlier this the morning," announced Liam, strolling casually away from her.

Blast him! "Are you certain that's what I'm after?" She paused and sniffed the air again.

Liam plucked a wildflower and held it out to her. "They are your favorites in the morning."

Startled he had recalled the memory, Abela tried to compose herself. "Your recollection is correct." She walked slowly toward him and accepted the dainty flower. "Thank you."

He grasped her hand and tucked it in the crook of his arm. "Let me show you."

Instead of fighting the offer, she let him lead her to the area. Heat radiated off him. Abela found this side to the warrior fascinating. It reminded her of the man before he'd entered the Brotherhood. She tried to bring down the barriers of protection surrounding her heart and enjoy the moment. Nevertheless, Abela feared what would happen when they returned. It haunted her now.

"You're thinking too much," observed Liam, pushing aside pine limbs for them to pass under.

"What do you suggest I do?" she blurted out, furious he kept reading her thoughts.

"You're a priestess—"

"Was," she corrected.

He shook his head. "Have you forgotten the teachings from the temple?"

"No!" she affirmed, spotting the blackberry bush sprawled out beyond the cluster of pines. Quickly removing her hand from the warmth of his arm, Abela made her way up the hill.

Smiling, she held her hands over the lush fruit and uttered a prayer of thanks for the bounty. After gathering as many as she could, Abela darted back down toward the water, passing Liam along the way.

She settled herself on the ground, gazing outward while she ate the juicy blackberries.

Liam returned with more in his hands and sat down next to her. "In case you're hungry for more," he explained.

Chuckling softly, she fixed her attention on the water and scenery beyond. "Ireland is a beautiful land," she admitted between bites of the fruit. Holding up one of the berries, she added, "Even the fruit is tasty."

Dumping the contents from his hands onto her lap, Liam leaned back on his elbows. "Much of Ireland is mirrored in our own world."

"I wish I could remember the time I spent here," she mused.

"You were an infant when we descended underground after the great battle."

Abela glanced at him, enjoying his leisurely posture. Again, he surprised her with how much he retained of their previous conversations. "Didn't you mention they had to drag you away, since you fought leaving your home here?"

"Ahh...yes. Not a fond memory. I screamed and

kicked the ground, refusing to leave. A glorious temper-tantrum for all to witness. Rory was furious at my childish behavior and refused to speak to me for weeks."

"You were only two and Rory was how old?"

"Four. Nonetheless, we were men of the world then."

She laughed. "Indeed."

Contentment filled her as they sat in silence. If only the peacefulness could last. For now, she would take Liam's cavalier attitude and enjoy their brief time here.

"Abela?"

"Yes," she muttered, keeping her gaze on the ripples of the river.

"Thank you."

Casually brushing her hands on the soft grass, she asked, "For what?"

"As much as I do regret allowing you to rescue me, I will be eternally grateful."

"Yo...*you* are?" she sputtered, turning to face him.

He sat and brushed the back of his hand across her cheek. "Yes. Always. If anything, this has given us time for closure."

The word smacked of finality, and she placed her palm over his lips. "Stop. Use another word for closure." Touching him sparked a wild frenzy in the pit of her stomach, but she was unable to resist. He smiled against her skin and prickling sensations broke out along her arm.

When his tongue darted out and licked her fingers, Abela gasped. She was powerless to resist the temptation. Cupping his face, she pressed her lips against his and then gently covered his mouth. He tasted of the land, and she couldn't get enough.

It was meant to be a simple kiss, but the heady rush of passion burst inside her. Liam swiftly turned her onto her back and thrust his tongue inside her mouth. She wrapped her arms around his neck, bringing the kiss deeper into her. His hand skimmed along the side of her waist and then up to fondle her breast. She arched against the possession, aching for more.

Loud coughing brought them both out of their lustful trance. Liam broke free, but remained positioned over her. His eyes glittered like crystals.

He lifted his head. "Is there something you seek, *Adam*?"

"O'Malley wishes to inquire if ye would care to break your fast with him."

"Tell the man I'm occupied, but will join him later."

"Will do."

The man's laughter could be heard as he left through the trees.

Abela uttered a groan. "How embarrassing."

"Why?" asked Liam, placing a tender kiss on her forehead. "We are betrothed, remember?"

She stewed on his words and looked away. "Right, only a ruse."

His grip was firm on her chin, forcing her to meet his eyes. "Truth?"

Abela's chest heaved. "Always."

"I have constantly desired you—wanted you. This is no pretense."

"I know," she admitted. " Nevertheless, you and I long for more, and sadly, we cannot go any further."

Liam leaned his forehead against hers. "Then I will take your sweet kisses with me, even when I draw my last breath."

Chapter Fifteen

"I can only serve one master, and I chose the path of a warrior over love."
~Chronicles of Liam MacGregor

What a foolish notion Liam pondered as he kept his sight on Abela who moved from one wagon to the next. He desired more than her kisses and believed he would never be happy until he possessed her completely. A part of him had always remained fractured. Once she had spurned him, Liam was never fully the same. He sought release with those who never warmed his heart or burned a fire in his soul.

Happiness? A whisper on the breeze—fleeting and inaccessible.

Her laughter filled the camp, and he found himself grinning. The children clustered around her like honeybees, and they were spellbound. She radiated a beauty that could not be contained, filling the area with enchantment.

He expressed his opinion to keep her hidden from these people, but it was not in her nature. She required the freedom to explore, and he doubted any would consider her to be of royalty. Liam had spent part of the evening surveying all the men and women within the camp—from old acquaintances to the new faces in the clan. And he sensed no threat here.

In the twisted adventure they were on, he tried to grasp a sliver of peace. Liam deemed it was only a matter of time before they were captured, but last night came a revelation. A vow to treasure these last remaining days with Abela.

"I have a riddle for you dear children," her voice rang out through the camp.

The children clapped their hands in glee, giggling with delight.

Abela tapped her finger to her mouth. "This is one that was told to me long ago, so listen carefully. I was meant for the air, but love the ocean. I am from the land, but belong to the stars. Who am I?"

Each of the children gazed at her with the light of youth, trying to determine an answer. Abela blew a kiss across her palm over them. "Ponder the puzzle and let me know if any can solve the riddle." She moved along the path as the children trailed after her.

"Ye are a blessed man to find a treasure in the woman," noted O'Malley, nudging him on the arm. "She has honored us to walk among the children and women. The storytellers will spread the tales for years to come."

If only she was mine forever. "A gem among our realm," he acknowledged.

"A messenger arrived early this morning with news Peter is unable to get here until Midsummer or the next day."

The news squashed his contentment, and Liam glanced at the man. "Do you know where he travels? Perchance we can meet him part of the way."

"Ye forget. I am required to *sign* the parchment."

Liam wiped a hand across his brow. How could he

have forgotten? His thoughts were on a certain Fae minx. "Of course."

"Ye can withdraw to your realm for your own feasting and return the next day," suggested O'Malley.

"Unfortunately, I cannot return until it is in my possession."

The man surveyed him skeptically. "Is there more ye want to share regarding your journey?"

That my life is at stake, and we're fleeing from the entire Fae kingdom? "No."

"Ye are most welcome to join in our celebrations."

"Thank you for the offer, but I judge it wiser to stay away from the merriment."

O'Malley inclined his head and started forward.

Liam returned his attention to the princess wandering the area with her wee attendants following closely. Every now and then, one of the small girls would touch her dress in laughter, and their whispered words reached his hearing.

Instantly his features hardened, and he strode across the camp. So focused on her bewitching Fae aura, he had never considered the small children. Reaching for her hand, he pulled her away from her admirers. Words and sighs of complaints were issued from the children, but he ignored their minor protests.

"What is wrong?" demanded Abela, tugging to free her hand from his grip.

He refused to answer her until they were away from prying eyes and ears. Rabbits skittered out of their path as he steadily kept on moving through the trees.

"Liam, stop!"

No! Now be quiet!

Abela yanked hard, finally freeing herself. "How

dare you speak to me within my mind. Did I ever give you permission? You're behaving like a human."

Liam fisted his hands on his hips. "Humans cannot project their thoughts into each other's minds."

"Obnoxious man," she hissed out.

"Forgive me. I judged it wise at the time."

Her eyes blazed with fury. "It was not appropriate."

"Then you will not accept my apology?" he challenged.

"No, because you don't mean it. Your actions are beneath you and your training."

Turning from her anger, Liam cast his sight to the valley below and the river. *You're losing control and she's correct. Quit thinking of possessing her.* He let out a frustrated breath and went to a nearby tree for support. He darted a quick glance at her. "The children know you are royalty."

Abela looked appalled. "You're wrong."

"Trust me, they do know, and I'm in error for not realizing it sooner. I watched as some dipped a curtsy and whispered princess to each other. The human children tend to have the gift of sight until they reach a certain age. Then they choose to ignore the images, discounting them as childish faery tales when they are older."

She maintained her rigid stance. "Regardless, you had no right invading my mind."

"You are correct. I misplaced my control."

A smile tugged at the corners of her mouth. "Do you require aid in maintaining your direction of what a proper Fenian Warrior should do?"

He snorted. "I am positive you will be there to alert

me of my misgivings."

She eyed him suspiciously. "It depends on if you'll listen to me."

Pushing away from the tree, Liam shook his head. "I have never stopped."

She drew near him. "What do you propose we do now that the children suspect?"

"Nothing." He waved a hand outward. "I'm confident we are safe here with these people."

"The children are harmless, Liam."

He pointed a warning finger at her. "They are the young bards here. All listen to them."

Abela linked her arm through his. "We will have the treaty tomorrow. By evening, back in our kingdom."

"There's a snag in the plan."

Her shoulders slumped. "Do tell."

"O'Malley informed me earlier Peter will not be here until Midsummer *day*. Or maybe the next."

A horrified expression passed briefly over her features. "Then we must spend the evening before here?" Releasing her hold on him, she crossed to the edge of the clearing.

"Would you be more comfortable with the women?"

She shook her head adamantly. "Absolutely not. The heady mix of emotions will be too much for me."

"Tomorrow is Midsummer's Eve. If you'd like, I can request that the wagon be taken across the river. It will provide more seclusion away from the festivities. In addition, I will ask for some bread and cheese. We can gather fruit from the land."

"Yes...*yes*, that would be more agreeable," she

responded quietly.

He started for the camp. "Good. I'll go inform O'Malley."

"There's one more problem."

Liam halted his stride and glanced over his shoulder. "I believe we can manage anything, as long as it's not the appearance of your brother and his guards."

Her features were strained. "I am unable to magically change my attire."

He was at her side in two strides. "When did you notice?"

She wrapped her arms around her body as if she was cold. "Several hours ago."

"And the shields?" Liam held his breath, fearing the answer.

"Holding. Do you think it has anything to do with traveling through the Veil?"

"The magic we possess has no limits." Liam rubbed a hand down the back of his neck, trying to sort out this latest crisis.

"Apparently mine does here in the human world." She touched his arm. "Have you ever experienced this *weakness*?"

"Never. I have all my powers, except for the ones from the Brotherhood. And I cannot fathom why this is happening to you. I can draw no conclusions. Why didn't you mention this at the time it occurred?"

Abela looked away. "Actually I was stunned, confused, and frightened, Liam. When I was pacing back and forth within the trees after I ate a light meal, some of the smaller children came scampering toward me." She laughed nervously. "They are so like our Fae children. Carefree, smiling, and full of light."

"You were carried away by the wee sprites," he chided, aching to reach out and take her in his arms.

"Yes. They helped soothe the worries, though only temporarily."

"Would you like me to request a garment from one of the women?"

Abela turned back around and brushed her hands down the front of her gown. "No. I favor this green gown, and it will be easy to blend in with the trees. I don't want to draw attention with some of their more colorful clothing."

Liam reached out and traced a finger over the neckline of her gown. "Yet, you have managed to add the ancient pattern of our people in the silver trim."

She visibly trembled from his touch and took a step back. "It was one of the oldest gowns I could think of wearing."

"Are any of your other powers dwindling?" he asked.

Shaking her head, she replied, "No."

Clasping his hands behind him, Liam smiled. "A few more days, Abela, and then we can go home. However, if you sense any other changes or shifts in your magic, do not hesitate to come to me."

Her mood suddenly appeared buoyant. "*Yes*, you are correct. I will take this time to honor the land."

"Excellent."

Taking a hold of his arm, Abela steered him toward the trees and the camp. "I will accompany you while you make the request for the wagon to be moved. Do you think they can give me some food as well? Come the morning, I deem it wise if I stay away."

"Midsummer's Eve," he acknowledged, lifting a

pine branch out of their way. "Yes, I can fetch us some food."

"Will you be staying within the camp?"

"Absolutely not."

Abela halted their progress. "Then what are your plans?"

Liam had no intention of falling under the spell of Midsummer or the bewitching minx studying him with her glittering lavender eyes. His gaze lowered, and he yearned to taste those pouting lips. His iron control was beginning to falter. "I will sleep under the stars far away from everything *and* everyone."

She arched a brow skeptically. "Where?"

Tapping a finger against his head, he responded, "It's a secret."

Her eyes narrowed. "Do you not trust me?"

"I hear a challenge in your question. If I divulge I am nearby, will the knowledge scare you?"

She looked affronted and pushed away from him. "Of course not. I don't know why you're being secretive."

He watched her progress through the trees until she had entered the camp. It was going to be a long two days. As he slowly made his way to the O'Malley's wagon, Adam emerged from the side, blocking his path.

Liam shifted his stance. "Is there something you require?"

"If ye are seeking an audience with O'Malley, ye must wait."

"Then I'll direct my request with you. I require the wagon for Abela to be moved across the river. In addition, if we could partake of some food it would be appreciated."

The man frowned and scratched the side of his face. "Again ye wish to move the wagon?"

"Yes."

Uncertainty flickered within his eyes. "I will ask O'Malley."

"If there is a problem, I will do the chore myself. No need to bother O'Malley with this undertaking. I will let him know I handled it on my own." Liam didn't want to debate a simple task with the man and started for the main part of the camp.

"Nae!" shouted Adam, barking out orders for several of the other men to follow him.

His annoyance now tempered, Liam nodded. "Thank you."

The air was heavy with wood smoke and meat, making Liam queasy. Steadily moving away from the main part of the camp, he came upon young lads playing a game of knucklebones. Their enthusiasm was contagious, and Liam marveled at the competition between two of the boys.

"I dare ye to pick up all five and flip them from the back of your hand to your palm," challenged a lad with a mop of red hair.

"Can ye do the same?" asked the boy who was challenged.

"Aye," he boasted.

Watching in fascination, Liam settled himself against the bark of a pine tree. One of the other boys caught his gaze and nudged another sitting next to him. All conversation and playing ceased.

"Do continue," encouraged Liam with a wave of his hand.

The lad with the red hair shook his head. "Are

there any here ye favor?"

Stunned by the lad's question, he replied, "Why would that matter? This is a game of skill."

"Ye…ye might use *magic* on one of us." The boy peered around the clearing, fearing someone would hear him use the word.

"Aye, he might," echoed the others in the circle.

Liam shrugged dismissively. "In any competition, the rules of the game are set. I merely wanted to observe. If I favor one lad over the other, it is simply because of their skill. I have no desire to use magic, but to find out who is the champion."

"Should we bind his hands?" asked another boy.

Narrowing his eyes, Liam shook his head. "Not a wise choice. Would you feel more comfortable if I was not present?"

The lad with the red hair smiled. "If my father doesn't fear ye, then we will not."

Liam had already surmised O'Malley was his kin by the eyes, jut of the chin, and mannerisms. "Are you sure?"

His smile faded, and he swallowed. "He says ye should never show fear to your foe."

"Am I your enemy?"

"No! But…ye are different."

Folding his arms across his chest, Liam countered, "We are all unique, and I am not your father's enemy."

The lad appeared confused. "Then what are ye?"

Liam chuckled. "We have a mutual partnership. Do you understand the word? And I am positive your father has explained who I am."

"I do," blurted out another boy. "I ken the meaning."

"Good," acknowledged Liam and pointed to all of the boys. "When you are older, remember this conversation. You might have need of my services or another warrior from my realm. You will age and fade from this world, but I and my people are forever beneath the land." He leveled his gaze on the red-headed lad. "And when you become leader, be very careful who you call an enemy—regardless how *different* they appear."

All the boys nodded in unison.

Relaxing against the tree, Liam gestured outward. "If you don't mind, I'd like to observe this game of knucklebones. It's been many years since I've played."

The red-headed boy exchanged looks with the other lads and then stood. Approaching Liam, he held out his hands with the knucklebones and ball. "My name is Dylan. Would ye like to play?"

"I thought you'd never ask," responded Liam in a casual, jesting way.

Chapter Sixteen

"Once upon a Midsummer, I ran barefoot through the soft meadow carpeted with fragrant wildflowers and swam with the dolphins in the waterfalls near the creation of life."

~Diary of Princess Abela

Departing the wagon before the first rays of sunlight kissed the land, Abela ran barefoot through the trees. When she reached the clearing, she opened her arms in greeting. The chill of the morning seeped through the soles of her feet, but her heart basked in the warmth of the approaching dawn.

"Midsummer's Eve," she uttered softly. "Your daughter welcomes the turning of the season."

Regardless of where she stood, Abela could still feel the pulse of the land. The human world wasn't as opulent as the Fae realm, but it had an exquisite beauty of its own. Trees swayed in the breeze around her, moving in a peaceful rhythm. She hugged her arms around her body and watched the new day beginning.

A stag emerged from the trees, majestic and proud. She bowed her head in welcome. The noble animal wandered to her side.

"Greetings, my friend. Will you stay and hail the new day with me?" Abela gently touched his forehead with her fingers.

His whisper of acknowledgement brushed across her mind. Letting out a sigh, Abela turned from the animal and waited in silence as the sky turned a rosy hue. A few clouds gathered in the distance, but it did not distract from the shimmering beams of light. She closed her eyes and reached out with her Fae senses, drawing the energy into her body, and then released it back into the land.

Abela remained rooted to the ground for some time. When she opened her eyes, her new-found friend had silently slipped back into the trees.

This was what she had missed. Her daily ritual of welcoming the new dawn. She'd forgotten how centering the action was on her mind and body. Quickly checking her shields, Abela knelt on one knee. Placing her palm on the ground, she murmured a silent prayer of thanks and protection over the land.

A four-leaf clover caught her attention, and she passed her hand over the delicate leaf. "For luck and long life," she uttered softly. "It is enough that you have presented yourself, and I will leave you for another to snatch into their care."

She stood and continued to enjoy the quiet solitude. Once again, sleep had been elusive. She yearned to rest under the stars and not be confined to a wagon. However, when she suggested the idea to Liam, he quickly cut her off and demanded she return to the wagon's safety. Abela fought the harsh words she threatened to spew at him. Yet, she never closed the covering and enjoyed a partial view from her shelter.

Glancing at her gown, she drew in a long breath and released it slowly. Passing a hand over the front of her, Abela concentrated. The energy shifted, but she was unable to magically transform the garment into another gown.

"Nothing?" asked the low voice behind her.

"Only a slight tremor of power." She kept her gaze on the glowing ball of light ascending into the morning sky.

"Would you like me to fashion one for you?" The timber of his voice sent a delicious thrill down her back.

What was wrong with her? Her nerves skittered with him being so close. "I thought you liked this gown?"

Liam stepped to her side. Though the morning was brisk, the heat of his body surrounded her. Abela wanted to lean against the man.

His hand skimmed across her arm. "What would you like to wear on Midsummer's Eve?"

Abela visibly shuddered. "Pale yellow and silver for the coming light," she replied softly.

He kissed her cheek. "Done."

She gasped and fingered the material. Glancing at Liam, his smile was as intimate as their kisses. "Thank you."

"All my pleasure." He swept his gaze outward. "It never changes, does it?"

"What do you mean?"

"The beauty of a new day. As a Fenian Warrior, we began each morning and evening, honoring the light and dark. The ancient words flowed within me, no matter where or what I was doing."

Abela studied his features—from the chiseled jaw to his eyes, which mirrored the shimmering stars and oceans of their home. His dark auburn hair glinted in the early morning light. Her hand twitched, aching to touch the strands.

He returned his attention to her. "Your emotions are showing, Abela. You might want to seal them."

She blinked in confusion and took a step back. Did he invade her thoughts again?

"Midsummer's Eve is a potent time. A time of feasting, sowing seeds, *and* making love," declared Liam.

Her face heated. "I was *not* thinking of lovemaking," she argued, though she was sure her thoughts would have eventually led her to desiring his lips. "Merely observing your features. A strong chin, mesmerizing eyes, and dark auburn hair that captures the radiance of sunlight."

He broke into a leisurely smile. "But nothing about my mouth?"

"Egotistical Fae," she teased and started forward.

Liam reached for her hand, pulling her against his chest. He lifted her chin with his finger. "The lure of the land is potent this day and the next."

Abela was conflicted, but his earlier statement entered her mind. "Seal the emotions, Liam."

Slowly, he released his hold. "Touché."

"Have you been to the camp?" she inquired, grateful he had moved away. His nearness brought out desires Abela was finding hard to control.

"Yes. I have deposited a basket of food in your wagon. The travelers have already started their feast. It's one I deem will last for days."

"As it should," she acknowledged. Noticing a patch of wildflowers, Abela crossed the open area toward them.

"What are your plans for today?"

Sweet Goddess. One moment he looks like he wants to devour me, and the next, he's telling me to seal my emotions. Can the man not make up his mind? "Midsummer magic has muddled your thoughts, Liam MacGregor," she muttered.

"I heard that!" he shouted.

She shrugged dismissively and decided to head back toward the river. The water lapped at the stones and boulders near the bank, its soothing sound calmed the burning desire to fling off her clothing and dance playfully on the lush grass.

A splash brought her attention to the center of the river. She gawked at Liam making long strokes in the water. Was he insane? He had stripped to his trews, and Abela could see every muscle in his torso ripple with each movement.

"Not fair," she protested.

He halted his progress and glided across the water toward her. "Then join me."

"I can't."

"Why not?" He splashed playfully at her.

"Are you addled?" she asked, avoiding his intense stare. "Go away, Liam." *I can't be near you now.*

Abela continued along the bank, sealing off her thoughts about the enticing man.

"I dare you to step into the water," he challenged.

She froze. Never one to back away from a dare, Abela bit her lower lip. She couldn't look at him. "What do you want?"

Silence was her answer. Darting a glance over her shoulder, she saw the answer reflected in the depths of his eyes.

"To spend the day with you. Talking, swimming, learning about your life in the temple," he responded. "If you'd rather be alone, I will understand."

Uncertainty filled her, and she bunched her hands at her sides. Droplets of water trailed down his chest as he stood in the water, and she became mesmerized by the sight. She should run away and hide herself in the wagon. Gathering her thoughts, she replied, "I will spend part of this day with you, but I am not swimming in the river."

His eyes danced with mischief. "Why not?"

"Nothing to wear."

"I can always fashion something for you." His hands glided back and forth in the water.

"I will be content with dipping my feet in the river, but no more. When the first star blinks in the evening sky, I shall leave you." Abela climbed onto a nearby boulder and dangled her feet into the water.

Liam dove back under and then emerged floating on his back. He made lazy strokes in the water. The sun rose higher in the sky, warming her skin. She could spend the remainder of the day in this blissful silence. Yet, she had questions, too.

"Were you happy, Liam?"

"What do you mean?"

"Being a Fenian Warrior? With your life? Did you find contentment working for the Brotherhood?"

He remained quiet as he steadily made his way toward her. When he neared the riverbank, he stood and raked a hand through his wet hair. He took a seat next to her on a fallen log and kept his gaze outward. "I enjoyed working with the Brotherhood. It was challenging, interesting, and I made a few human friends along the centuries. Was I content?" He shrugged. "Part of me."

Abela frowned. "What was missing?"

Liam leaned forward, bracing his hands on his thighs. "*You.*"

Abela's lungs constricted, and her heart ached. Their time had slipped away, all because she refused to see him that night so long ago. She yearned to reach out and touch him. "Why are you sharing this now?"

He swept his gaze toward her. "Because I owe you honesty. Once we return, our paths will separate. You and I need closure, Abela."

Again she hated that word. There would never be a happy ending for them, but she would always be in love with Liam MacGregor. She had spent decades in isolation, trying to seal the wound left open by his departure. Yet the moment she had known of his return and imprisonment, her heart beat wildly. "Thank you for sharing," she whispered.

"And you? Was the temple a rewarding place of knowledge and admiration?"

Smiling fully, she nodded. "Indeed. The beauty is exquisite. Beyond what you can imagine. It took many years to adjust to the opulent foliage, dazzling lights, and the air. It's intoxicating."

"I pray they will allow you to return."

She shook her head slowly. "No. Even if it is possible, I do not want to go back."

He looked stunned and straightened. "Why ever not?"

Abela sighed, clasping her hands in her lap. "Like you, I was never fully happy. In truth, I deemed I sought out the temple more as a haven. I required a time of peace and reflection. Away from the burdens inside my heart."

Liam stood and came to her side. "Did I cause this pain?"

"It was my fault. Not yours," she reassured.

Turning his back on her, he fisted his hands on his hips. "Because of Conn's words," he uttered tersely. "Damn him."

Standing, Abela touched his arm. "Don't blame him. I could have asked you. More to the point, he has suffered from a few poor decisions."

He looked at her incredulously. "The great Conn MacRoich? I doubt we're talking about the same Fae *prince*."

She pinched him and began walking along the path away from the river and toward the wildflowers. Her emotions were wound so tight around Liam. "Again, you don't know everything."

He caught up with her in two strides. Taking her hand, Liam tucked it in the crook of his warm arm. "You are correct. But without the current knowledge of the man, I can only deduce my own conclusions. Trust me, when I do see him there will be words."

She tried to pull her hand free. "So stubborn."

"One of the many qualities you admire."

Abela fought the smile forming on her mouth. "Egotistical."

"Yes, as you've stated many times."

"Your assumptions will get you into trouble, Liam MacGregor."

He halted their progress. "Tell me, Abela, was I wrong about us? Could you have seen a future? If you can't answer, then I have made a grave error in assuming we might have found happiness together."

Shielding her eyes from the sunlight, she watched as a pair of geese flew overhead. How could she answer him? So much time had passed, yet, she knew in her heart how she still felt for him. "Someone once told me that to look back on past deeds in hopes of seeing another future can result in a skewed present." She dropped her hand. "Can we not move forward?"

"A wise person, indeed, but not the answer I was seeking." Liam strolled along in front of her.

Following slowly behind him, she was determined to enjoy every second they had together. "Can you guess who told me those words?"

He darted a glance at her over his shoulder. "Aidan?"

"No. My mother." She ran up alongside him. "She had come upon me weeping by the fountain in front of the chambers of the Brotherhood."

"Why were you there? Conn?"

"My mother assumed my tears were over the loss of my brother, since we never spoke before he departed." Abela sighed and knelt on the patch of flowers. "I could not speak *your* name. Only within my heart. I was too late in reaching you."

Liam halted. When he bent down beside her, his smile was one of sadness. "What am I to do with you, Abela?"

Her heart already knew the answer, but she had allowed fear to guide her the moment she set eyes on him again. Their past was already written. There were no promises of tomorrow. This moment in time was all they had left—a tiny thread here in the human world. There would be no others to dissuade her on paths of the heart and life decisions.

Abela grew weary of fighting her own battle of restraint. For the first time in her life, she would take what she wanted, craved, and desired.

She closed the door on her rambling thoughts that forbade her to do the unimaginable.

Liam MacGregor was the only Fae she had ever loved. There would be no other.

Abela took his warm, strong hand into hers and smiled. "Spend the day with me and..." She paused, fearing he would flee once she spoke the words out loud.

"*And*?" he echoed.

"The night, as well."

Chapter Seventeen

"I heard the call of love, but cast it aside as foolishness. It was an emotion foreign to other warriors, but I was one of the few to capture its alluring first spark."

~Chronicles of Liam MacGregor

Liam pressed his palm on the ground between them. Violets in a variety of shades of lavender spread out in a carpet around them. He banished the thoughts of a warrior, screaming at him to leave her presence. They had become annoying, cluttering his heart and soul with the same rigorous training he had honed his body and mind for centuries.

There had been a void in his life and only one could fill the emptiness. *Abela.*

He brought their joined hands to his chest. "I noted your statement is a declaration and *not* a question. Therefore, I will be with you until the sunlight dances within the sky on Midsummer morning. There will be no regrets, Abela, come the morn. Can you live with only one night with me?" She had to know for certain he would claim all of her.

Her eyes glittered like lavender crystals, and she gently lowered herself to the ground. Her hair fanning out against the flowers was a feast for his eyes. His hand shook, aching to strip off her gown.

"But will you have regrets, Liam?" she asked softly. "I will not. However, you are honor-bound by laws and edicts within the Brotherhood and as a Fae."

"No." The answer came swift and sure, and he lowered himself beside her. "Yet this will be no simple lovemaking, Abela. I will take you here upon the land, binding you with the ancient words of our people. If you expected a casual dalliance of sexual pleasure, then you need to seek out the Pleasure Gardens."

A secretive smile softened her lips. "If I had wanted sexual release with another Fae, I would have done so many decades ago."

"You have waited for me?" Liam's groin tightened. "Always."

Liam wasn't ready to utter the words in his heart. Not yet. The realization that she was presenting him with the gift of her virginity made him love her all the more. His love for her had been hidden, kept locked away in his heart. He'd denied it over the centuries. But no longer.

Keeping his focus on her face, Liam trailed his fingers down the side of her neck and to the valley between her breasts. Her heart beat rapidly against the material touching his skin. "Your heart shall be joined with mine."

"From the first heart-beat to the last," she added. "Forever yours."

"Abela…" His mouth sought her lips in a fiery possession, demanding entry into the velvet warmth of her mouth. The kiss sang through his veins, opening all the emotions he had kept locked away. She filled a void he was unable to fill for centuries.

He cupped her breast, massaging the pert nipple

between his fingers. Her moan filled his body when he deepened the kiss. She tasted of the land, urging him onward as she wrapped her arms around his neck and stroked her tongue against his.

Liam broke free and nipped her gently on the side of her neck with his teeth. Glancing around, he swiftly took in their surroundings.

"Don't stop," she pleaded and rubbed against his swollen erection.

Her eyes glittered with passion. "I'm looking for a more intimate location."

"I like it out here in the sun," she argued, and stretched her arms overhead. Her lips pouted in invitation.

Drawn to her once again, he clasped her wrists together with one hand. Slowly, he teased his tongue over her bottom lip. "We shall, but not here."

"Then decide quickly," she demanded, squirming beneath him.

Liam chuckled softly. "You love to give orders."

She paused. "A flaw?"

He kissed the dimple on her right cheek. "No. One of many enduring qualities I've admired about you."

Her eyes twinkled with mischief. "Then what are you waiting for?"

Liam stood. Upon extending his hand out to Abela, she grasped it firmly, and he brought her to standing. "The river is soothing, but I know of a better area."

"Do you want me to move us there?"

Scanning the area, he replied, "Keep your magic for the shields." He pointed north. "If we take the path along the river toward the hills, there is a stunning waterfall that spills into a small lake."

Abela leaned against him. "I'm intrigued."

He glanced at her. "You should be. The humans have named it the Fae Pools of Glynn."

"Truly? Have you seen them?"

"Once. When I required solitude after a battle and was unable to return home. I heard an elderly woman speak of the enchantment of the land." He brought her hand to his lips and placed a kiss along the vein in her wrist. "Whenever a human mentions a particular place that is named after the Fae, it brings out the historian in me. I had to see it for myself."

She trembled from his touch. "Show me."

Smiling he complied, and led her toward the hills. An hour later they reached the secluded lake. Liam lifted pine limbs for Abela to enter. Upon stepping into the clearing, Liam watched her entire face light up with pleasure. The waterfall cascaded down a steep cliff face into a foamy pool. Their haven was bordered by trees, ferns, wildflowers, and rocks carpeted with emerald green moss.

"It truly has earned its name," she declared, moving into the sunlight. "I believe one of the Fae has graced this place with magic."

"Beauty in all directions," he remarked. However, the treasured gem was the one standing barefoot in front of him.

She gasped in delight. "Look at how the water gracefully flows down into the lake. It is so peaceful and serene. The sunlight dances off the rocks like shimmering crystals in a rainbow of mosaic colors. And look at all the foliage. I never knew the human world had these hidden gems of landscapes."

Liam stepped forward and wrapped his arms

around her waist. She leaned her head against his shoulder and sighed. "Make love to me."

Her words undid him, and he turned her around to face him. Brushing back her ebony locks, he sought out her sensual lips, devouring their softness. His hands skimmed down the side of her body, and he cupped her bottom, bringing it against his hardened cock. Desire hummed in every pore within his body. He tasted, teased, and took his time with the kiss until the tide of passion exploded, and their kisses became a wild torrent. He ached to touch her skin and explore all her hidden treasures.

As if reading his thoughts, Abela drew back. Her eyes mirrored the lust he knew shown in his own. She gave him a bewitching smile and took a step back.

Liam started to reach for her, but she held up her hand. Slowly she turned her back on him. He froze, and his chest constricted as she gradually slid the straps over her shoulders. When her hands paused at her breasts, he let out a growl. "Remove the garment, or I'll be forced to rip it from your body."

She glanced back at him seductively, letting the material slip all the way to the ground. After stepping free from the gown, she ran her fingers through her locks. Her hair cascaded down her backside, caressing the top of her lush bottom, and Liam became mesmerized. When she turned fully toward him, her rosy nipples teased him.

"You are an enchantress—a vixen who steals the breath from my lungs." He stripped free from his tunic and removed his boots with a wave of his hand.

Her gaze traveled over his body and then back to his eyes. Stepping toward him, she trailed a hand over his chest. He trembled from her touch. "And you are perfection. All that I have ever wanted, Liam."

He allowed her to continue her exploration as she marveled at the markings on his body. When she kissed the Celtic knots near his heart with his name emblazed in the center, he let out a groan. "I have never been with a man, but when I've touched myself, your name has been on my lips."

His cock swelled more at her confession. "Not only a vixen, but a brazen one."

She moved nearer, her nipples brushing against his skin. "Do I shock you?"

In all his lifetime, no one had made his blood boil like the woman standing before him. "*Never.*"

With a snap of his fingers, he magically removed his trews. Her eyes widened as he brushed his cock against her skin. Waves of tingling sensations traveled through his body, and he clenched his jaw, trying to maintain control and not spill his seed.

Lowering her gaze, her hand lifted. "Impressive," she whispered.

"Do not touch me there." His demand sounded hoarse even to his own ears.

Without giving her time to react, Liam grasped her firmly around the waist and covered her mouth hungrily. He sought to teach her the ways of lovemaking, but he believed he would be the one learning. She was a tempting feast, ripe for the plundering, and he would take all she had to offer.

He broke their kiss to feast on her ivory breasts. She dug her fingers into his scalp as he teased one nipple with his tongue and then the next. Her skin tasted of honey and all the flowers from their realm.

The heady floral scent drove him to madness. He couldn't get enough and desired more.

Dropping to his knees, he grasped her thighs. "You are intoxicating, *mo ghrá*."

"Wh…what are you doing?"

Nudging her legs further apart, he responded, "Bringing you pleasure."

Her chest rose and fell with each breath. "Oh…"

She squirmed, but he held her firmly. "Are you not curious?" He placed a feather-like kiss on the inside of her thigh, her scent filling him. When she refused to answer, Liam continued to kiss her all around her nest of curls. He slid one hand slowly down the back of her leg and then up to her bottom.

"You're tormenting me," she blurted out, her legs trembling.

He needed no further invitation and slipped his tongue between her delicate folds until he found her center. Liam teased and nipped, feasting on her forbidden nectar. She uttered a guttural moan and placed her hands on his shoulders, moving in a rhythm that drove him mad.

Liam's body roared for release, but he refused to do so until Abela sought hers. His entry into her body would be a harsh one. When he dipped a finger inside her, Abela moaned.

"Too much," she whimpered. "I can't grasp…"

"Let go, *mo ghrá*. Allow me to taste your pleasure," he murmured against her thighs and went back to her intimate center, making lazy circles with his tongue.

"Liam!" A scream of pleasure ripped free from her as she dug her nails into his skin.

After collapsing into his arms, Liam brought her gently down upon the ground. He continued to lavish her body with kisses and brushed his hand over the curves of her body. When she wrapped one of her legs around his waist, he needed no further invitation, and nudged his swollen cock between her thighs. Her heat invaded him as he tried to move slowly into her.

Abela cupped his face, her eyes the most beautiful he had ever witnessed. "Don't prolong the agony. I know there will be pain, but I have dreamt of this moment for a long time. Permit me to guide you."

He groaned as her delicate hand stroked and guided him into her. With a powerful thrust, Liam entered fully into Abela. She let out a hiss and closed her eyes. Slowly, he withdrew and entered her again.

"More," she pleaded.

"Open your eyes," Liam demanded.

When she did, Liam moved in a primal dance as old as time. With each kiss, brush of his hand over her breasts, and words of endearment, he watched her embrace the sensual passion. As her desire built, his expanded. The blood pounded in every fiber of his body, and his cock throbbed to release all he had into the woman he loved.

She was beauty beneath him.

His thrusts became urgent and beads of sweat broke out along his brow. His control failing as the tide of passion began to sweep him away. Unable to hold back, Liam shook as the pleasure exploded and vibrated all around them. His roar of release echoed throughout the land, along with her own. Iridescent lights shimmered around them in a rainbow when he took her mouth with savage intensity capturing her own

pleasurable sighs.

Liam couldn't move. His body heavy and spent. The residual fervor rippled over his skin.

He could feel her heart beating against his skin, and the air cooled around them. Sunlight faded, and he slowly lifted his head. Unable to focus on their surroundings, he rolled over and brought her still quaking body against his chest. He tried to calm his own rapidly beating heart and closed his eyes. When he finally did open them, he glanced upward.

"Where is our sunshine?" asked Abela, her question muffled against his chest.

He stroked a hand down her back. "The sun and moon are as one."

Abela visibly shuddered, her eyes growing wide. "No," she whispered.

Liam wiped a finger across her worried brow. "What troubles you? It is only a solar eclipse."

"Have you not heard the legends about a Fae witnessing the appearance of both—sun and moon—at the same time?"

"I believe it is only a tale told of—"

"Two Fae who defied the kingdom and married," she interrupted.

"And they were banished," he concluded, kissing her lips. "It is a story about a couple on *our* homeland, Taralyn. I do recall it was when the moons crossed with the sun. We are in the mortal world."

She pursed her lips in concentration. "Yes, you are correct." Glancing over her shoulder, she added, "Yet, can this similar occurrence be an omen?"

Liam cupped her cheek, forcing her to meet his stare. "Again, we are in the human world and not our own. This does not apply to us." Tucking a strand of hair behind her ear, he asked, "Are you truly worried? Have I brought you shame?" He held his breath, fearing her reply.

"No, *no*," she whispered against his lips. "I have waited a lifetime to be with you, Liam. My heart is yours. It has always been yours. Why do you think I freed you?" She swallowed. "I love you."

He swept his gaze over her lovely features. "I have never known love...until *you*, Abela. From the first moment I saw you walking with Conn, I watched, waited, and yearned to claim you for my own. Though I understood your parents had most likely chosen another for you to spend your life with, I was unfazed. However, time and circumstances prevented us from being together. And as all young Fae do, we sought out other pleasures." He blew out a frustrated breath. "It wasn't until our paths crossed again a few years later near the time I was thinking of joining the Brotherhood that I had hoped you might consider choosing me for a life partner. If you had, I would never have enlisted."

She laughed softly. "You did seem boastful and arrogant at the time. However, I was intrigued. My parents did choose someone for me, but I was adamant in my protests that I find my own love. They finally relented. When I saw you leaning against the pillar by The Library of Ancients, my breath caught."

Taking her hand, Liam placed it in the center of his chest. He banished all negative thoughts. He would not believe in ill omens or legends of forbidden lovers. And in their own ancient language, he uttered the sacred words to bind his soul to hers. "From the stars we came, to the stars we shall remain. Heart to heart, I am yours.

Blood to blood, we are one. I weave my soul into your soul with the thread of our lovemaking. When I take my last breath, your name shall be on my lips. Until we gather at the Tree of Life in *Tir na Og*."

Abela's eyes misted with unshed tears as she took Liam's hand and placed it in the center of her chest. "From the stars I call home, to the stars I shall be with you for eternity. Heart to heart, I am yours. Blood to blood, we are one. I weave my soul with yours with the thread of our lovemaking. I will claim you once more at the Tree of Life in *Tir na Og*."

After placing a kiss over his heart, Abela added, "I love you, my warrior."

Liam wrapped his arms around her, cherishing the overwhelming sensations inside of him. The sun parted from the moon and glorious sunlight filled the area around them. "I love you, too, my princess," he uttered softly against her ear.

In those quiet moments, Liam realized he would move the sun, moon, and stars to have Abela by his side.

Not only for today, but also for all eternity.

Chapter Eighteen

"When I watched the last of the sun's legs dance gracefully out of the land on Midsummer's Eve, I looked for the first star of the evening, and made a wish."

~Diary of Princess Abela

Floating high on euphoria, Abela basked in the land beneath her body and the warmth of the sun on her skin. Birdsong, bees, and the waterfall near them filled her with a joy she had never known. As she lay on her stomach with her head resting on her arms, she drifted. Right before she succumbed to a peaceful slumber, she twitched as she felt something brush over her bottom. Her limbs were too weak to swat at whatever was tickling her.

"Go away," she mumbled.

"Never," responded the low male voice.

She cracked open her eyes, and her breath hitched. Sunlight illuminated the man beside her. "You remind me of the God, *Angus Og*. Virile, sexy, and wickedly handsome."

He arched a brow seductively. "Be careful. He may consider me competition. I have no wish to become a target of his jealousy."

"My lips are sealed." Letting out a sigh, she closed her eyes.

Liam chuckled softly.

Once again, a feather-like touch brushed against her bottom. She squirmed. "What are you doing?"

"Brushing a flower over your skin."

Abela started to laugh. "It tickles."

"But does it make you feel good?" Liam bent and placed a soft kiss on her shoulder.

"Hmm...now that does." She yawned and rolled onto her back, stretching her arms outward. "Are you not sleepy?"

He brushed the delicate flower between her breasts. "With you around, never. Especially when you are now presenting me with a glorious view."

Abela smiled seductively and rolled back onto her stomach. "Then I won't bother you with any more viewings."

Liam brushed his fingers down the middle of her back until they rested on her bottom, and then swept them up to her shoulder. He pulled her hair back from face and teased the soft spot below her ear with his tongue. "You are just as seductive in this position."

She quivered under his touch. "Truly?"

He remained silent and traced patterns over her skin with his tongue. His burning touch sparked the passion within her. When his lips touched her lower back, she moaned. "Liam."

Gently he rolled her onto her back. "Yes, *mo ghrá*?"

Noticing his desire for her, Abela parted her legs and opened her arms in invitation. Liam bent and suckled on first one breast and then the other. Her hands dug into the soft grass, enjoying the pleasurable sensations coursing through her body. His hand caressed the curves of her hip until they rested between her sensitive core and she sighed. Abela yearned to have him in her, but he kept on with his ministrations.

Tossing her head back and forth, she pleaded, "Inside me."

He grazed his teeth along her rib cage, and she arched against him. "I can't get enough of tasting your skin."

"You're torturing me."

"I believe I am giving you pleasure." He laughed—his breath hot against her skin.

The blood in her veins burned as he continued to tease and torment her. Without giving him any warning, Abela pushed him away from her. When he landed on his back, he gave her a look of surprise. She swiftly took advantage of his prone position and straddled him.

Placing her hands firmly on his chest, she winked. "Two can play this game."

Reaching out, Liam squeezed one of her pert nipples. "Did I tell you that I love games?"

She hissed at the heady sensation—an equal mix of pain and pleasure. "I do recall you mentioning your fascination with foreplay many years ago."

Liam grinned mischievously. "You are a minx, princess. I never once mentioned *seductive* foreplay."

Abela moved against his rock-hard erection, marveling at the pleasure. Though he wasn't inside her, she enjoyed the pleasure of rubbing against him. So soft and yet, hard as steel. "Oh, I guess I misunderstood."

He grasped her hips and began to rock in a rhythm with her. "Does this bring you desire?"

She nodded, unable to speak as she delved deeper trying to catch the elusive spark within her. Her breathing became labored as she focused her gaze on the man beneath her. Shifting her position, she slid down his cock in an unhurried fashion, and marveled as his eyes turned to shards of silver. His guttural groan echoed around her.

Abela became fixated on the slow movements, relishing the feel of the man. Powerful and in control, she continued to move in a leisurely rhythm.

"Now you're the one torturing me," he growled out.

Abela bent and teased her tongue across his nipple. "You taste of the wildness of the land."

He thrust upward. "And you are driving me to insanity." Taking his fingers, he brushed them over her intimate area.

Trembling from the slightest touch, she whispered, "More."

As Liam continued to touch her down below, she moved in a more powerful pace. With each thrust, moan, and touch, he brought her closer to the flame. "Feels so...good."

"You are my Goddess," he admitted in a gruff voice. "I am losing control."

When his body began to quake inside her, Abela exploded in a thousand tingling sensations. The release so powerful, her heart stopped beating, and the day became night. Stars filled her sight until Liam's cry filled her being, and she floated back into his arms.

He immediately rolled her onto her back and took swift possession of her mouth. His thrusts became more urgent, and then he shuddered violently—calling out her name. Desire rolled in another wave inside her, and she went crashing along into its abyss.

Cradling his head against her breasts, Abela stroked the corded tendons in the back of his neck. Strong, ancient, and all hers. She didn't know what their future held, but she did understand one fact. Liam was hers forever. She had claimed him. Took him into her body, heart, and soul.

Even when they returned, she would fight any who attempted to take his life. Tears smarted her eyes, and she was helpless to stop the flow down her cheeks. By the Goddess how she loved this warrior.

Liam lifted his head, a frown marring his features. "Do not cry, *mo ghrá*."

Abela cupped his cheeks. "I will fight the entire kingdom to keep you safe."

"Ahh…not only a Fae minx, but a warrior as well."

She hiccupped and looked away. "Peace, knowledge of the land, and understanding the elements was my path. I am not one to condone violence, but I will oppose any who step in my way."

Liam rolled off her body, and she shivered. "It is not your fight."

Turning on her side, she placed her hand against his chest. "Do not tell me what I can do, Liam MacGregor. I took you into my body and soul, and I will not let anyone utter the words of death over you."

"Sadly, it is not your choice—*nor* is it mine."

A chill of foreboding swept through her. What if he was correct? Yet, her mind screamed at the situations already resolved with Conn and Rory. Each was able to make their own choices—from their destiny and life mates. If only she could share what happened with them with Liam. Would he understand the hope she had allowed to blossom in her heart? She drew her hand back and stood.

Liam joined her and placed his arms around her waist. He nuzzled her neck, and she leaned against him. "Let us not speak of the future or what the council will pronounce. Remember, we are attempting to alter the treaty. Fortunately, we can do so soon and resolve the issue of my trial."

"I would like to be present at your trial."

When he remained silent, Abela glanced up at him. Love shone in the depths of his eyes. "Thank you," he uttered softly.

Smiling, she turned in his arms and kissed his lips. "Did you not mention swimming as part of our plans for the day?"

"Yes, I did." He bent and kissed her earlobe.

"Hmm...I wonder what it will feel like to play in the water with you." She pushed out of his arms and gave him a wink.

Liam fisted his hands on his hips. "Have you not had your fill of me?"

Abela watched in a lust-filled haze his growing erection as she walked slowly back. "I have only begun, my warrior." She bent and picked a wildflower. "Or maybe you're tired and require more rest?"

He grabbed his cock, and Abela let out a gasp. "Contrary to what you might believe, I am aching to enter your honeyed sweetness again."

She brushed the flower over her breasts. "Then you'll have to catch me."

Chuckling low, he shook his head. "I can run faster."

"But I can use magic," she countered, dropping the flower and snapping her fingers.

In a flash of colors, she transported herself near the edge of the lake. Shielding her eyes, she could detect Liam's garbled curses as he ran across the open meadow of flowers. Dipping her toe into the cold water, she was tempted to forgo the swim. Yet, with any problem, there was always a solution. She bent and brushed her fingers over the water. "With the beat of my fingers, so I shall bring forth the heat." The magic came gradually and she realized the risk, but threw caution to the winds.

Standing, she smiled, just as Liam smacked her on the bottom and lifted her into his arms. He strode with intent into the now heated lake. "You must learn that magic is not the remedy for everything and any attempt to use your power might weaken you further. Besides, you cheated."

Wrapping her arms around him, she placed slow, lingering kisses on the vein alongside his neck. "I *never* cheat, only manipulate."

"And for that, you will be punished."

"Should I be scared, worried, or aroused?" she teased, nipping on his chin.

Liam crossed along the edge of the lake to a boulder and placed her down. The water lapped at her calves as she leaned against the warm stone. "Turn around," he ordered.

Clucking her tongue, she complied. "What now?"

"Spread your arms over the boulder."

After doing as he demanded, Abela glanced over her shoulder. "Are you going to spank me?"

Without giving her time to react, Liam grabbed her hips and entered her in one thrust. The pleasure so exquisite, she closed her eyes on a moan. He withdrew slowly and then pounded deeply back into her. His movements were driving her mad with desire as she longed to reach the peak of pleasure. She yearned for him to move faster, but he kept torturing her with his slow process.

Gripping the side of the stone, her body tingled from her head to her toes. "Faster," she growled.

"No."

"Liam, you…you're killing me." She was helpless under his possession.

He slapped her bottom. "Never cheat."

She moaned as the first wave of ecstasy lifted her, and she let out a cry when the second slammed into her body. Abela barely registered Liam's groan of release as the pleasure continued to vibrate throughout her.

Swiftly turning her over, Liam captured her mouth with savage intensity, stealing the breath from her lungs and giving it back to her mixed with his own. She clung to him, giving him all she had and more. He was her lover. Her warrior. *Her husband.*

Their kisses continued for some time, before Liam broke free and lifted her into his arms. Striding back toward the edge of the lake, he waved his hand outward and lush grass filled the area by an old oak tree.

"I thought we were going swimming," she muttered against his chest.

Kissing her forehead tenderly, he responded, "After you rest."

Lifting her head, she placed her hand against his rapidly beating heart. "Are you saying I'm exhausted?"

"Can you dress magically?"

Her smile faded. "No."

"Until you can, I shall make sure you do rest."

"With plenty of lovemaking thrown in, too?"

He arched a brow seductively. "How could I say no?"

Beaming, she replied, "I love you."

Liam brought her gently down to the soft, dewy grass. He sat against the bark of the tree and cradled her onto his lap. "And I love you. Regardless, I will not risk weakening you any further, so don't attempt anymore magic."

She pouted. "I will do my best."

"No. You *must* follow my orders."

His stern tone and look brought their dire situation into focus. He was correct. Her magic was fading. Even heating the water made her weak. She didn't dare tell Liam, deciding to wait until later. This was a time of celebrating the land and each other. Tomorrow she would tell him.

Cupping his face, Abela brushed her lips over his mouth. "I will follow your orders."

"Good. You have just declared a vow."

"Truly?" Abela blinked trying to mask her amusement. "Did I mention a promise?"

Liam looked affronted. "Most assuredly. Especially when you sealed it with a kiss."

"Then I shall be true in my convictions to you."

He nuzzled her neck, speaking words of endearment. Abela reveled in his warmth and touch, tossing out all negative thoughts and enjoying the pleasure of being with the man who had stolen her heart forever.

They spent the next several hours talking about their lives. There was no mention of the future. It was unwritten. Yet within her heart, she held on to a sliver of hope. And when the first star winked in the twilight, Liam made love to her tenderly all over again.

Chapter Nineteen

"As part of the final preparation into the Brotherhood, a warrior is required to spend one year among the humans without the use of magic. I chose my time assisting Aidan Kerrigan."

~Chronicles of Liam MacGregor

Urquhart Castle, Scotland ~ Early spring 1209

Conn surveyed the entrance to the home of the Dragon Knights, trying to do his best at containing his fury. His hand clenched the sword by his side, longing to pull it forth and tear out Liam MacGregor's heart. What possessed the warrior to take Abela? Why would he think to bring shame to her? Had he missed something when it came to the Fae during all their years together?

"Loosen your grip," muttered Rory beside him.

Conn kept his focus on the portcullis. "Why? Do you fear I'll harm your brother?"

"Worse. The fire in your eyes tells me you seek to end his life."

Tightening his hold, Conn smirked. "Do you think to order me?"

Rory stepped into his view. "Yes. You're letting your feelings for your sister cloud your judgment on dealing with the situation. If you storm into the castle and react on your current emotions, I will be forced to fight you. In addition, our wives will be sorely pissed if one—or both of us are slain. I for one, have no wish to return to Ivy with your dead body over my shoulder."

Conn arched a brow in amusement. "So, you have already declared yourself the winner of our battle?"

"Of course. I believe my constant training has me at an advantage."

"Now you insult me further by insinuating my *lack* of training?"

Rory rubbed a hand over his chin. "When was the last time you were in the Fae lists?"

Conn snorted. "Three days ago."

"And when Ronan came to fetch me from Aonach Castle, I was sparring with Adam MacFhearguis."

"A human."

"A Dragon Knight."

"Oh for the love of the Goddess, will you both stop this bantering of words," demanded Taran, pushing away from an oak tree. "I believe the question is, how much longer are we going to stand here gaping at the entrance?"

"I concur," stated Ronan. "Can ye sense your brother, Rory?"

Taking a step back from Conn, he answered, "No."

Conn inhaled and exhaled slowly. "Time to pay a visit to the Dragon Knights."

"Finally," mumbled Taran.

As he started forward, Conn glanced at Rory. "I give you my word, not only as your prince and leader, but as your friend I will not put my blade into your brother. Yet, do not attempt to thwart me when I take a fist to his jaw."

Rory's mouth twitched in humor. "Deal."

Approaching the entrance, they waited for the Dragon Knights to appear, so they could ask permission to enter. However, the massive iron gate lifted on a groan and one of the guards motioned them forward.

"Strange, we always had to wait for permission to enter from at least one of the Dragon Knights," declared Ronan.

Conn narrowed his eyes as he spotted Angus MacKay near the entrance of the castle. "Why do I sense they were waiting for us?"

"Liam *was* here," uttered Rory quietly. "I can detect a faint trace of his blood."

"Past tense? Then they are no longer here."

Conn made quick strides toward the leader of the Dragon Knights. As he approached, Stephen stepped into view, his hand on the hilt of his sword. A glimmer of contempt shown in the man's eyes. Conn halted in front of Angus and gave a curt nod. "You honor us by opening your gates."

Folding his arms across his chest, Angus responded, "I would never bar my gates to the *Prince* of the Fae realm."

Conn clenched his jaw. "You have seen Liam and my sister."

"Aye," replied Stephen and added, "She was forthcoming about her knowledge in regard to Aileen. Mind ye, the shock was great to my wife."

"That information was forbidden!" snapped Conn, leveling an ominous look at the Dragon Knight.

"Why? Her own father withheld so much, but ye…" Stephen pointed a finger at him. "Ye should have spoken to Aileen."

"I was not permitted," Conn argued.

"She is your kin! Did ye not consider it wise in all your discussions to share this knowledge with us? Or with Aileen?" shouted Stephen.

"I could not go against the orders of my king and queen."

Stephen bit out a curse and stormed off into the castle.

Conn coolly surveyed Angus. "Nothing to add?"

"Ye have not offended me."

"Good to hear. Now, may we enter and discuss why Liam and Abela sought the home of Dragon Knights?"

Angus shifted his stance. "On one condition."

Conn tempered his anger. "Which is?"

Starting for the massive oak doors, Angus answered, "Before I give ye an account, ye must make amends to Aileen. I dinnae care what oath ye swore to your king and queen. This is our home—our world, and ye will make this right with her." Angus glanced over his shoulder. "Ye are fortunate it wasn't my wife, Deirdre. If it were, I would have taken a blade to your throat."

"What a warm welcome from the Dragon Knights," professed Taran. "At least their leader portrays a sense of calm."

Conn tilted his head toward the Fae. "Let me give you a slight warning. Never underestimate Angus. Regardless of his control over his beast, his elemental power is fire and you were a fool not to notice his eyes were blazing the color of amber."

A shocked looked registered briefly over Taran's features. "Duly noted."

As Conn stepped inside the castle, old memories surfaced of their time here before the great battle with the Dark One and Lachlan. All appeared the same, though he sensed a calm, peacefulness within their home. Approaching the Great Hall, they proceeded toward the long table near the hearth. Aileen stood by her husband's side, her hands clasped together. Her silver blonde hair and lavender eyes denoted her Fae lineage.

For the moment, he had no words of comfort to offer her. All his life he had known about the human link to royalty in the Fae realm. When the whispers reached the kingdom that Aidan had sired a daughter, his parents ordered a declaration that no one would ever divulge her true heritage to her. And Conn never questioned their decision. Even refusing to be her guardian. He willingly handed over the duty to Liam. He had no desire to forge a bond with her.

Another dilemma to add to the growing lists of concerns.

Aileen broke the tension in the room by stepping away from her husband. Smiling, she walked past Conn and opened her arms to Rory. "I'm so happy to see you. Abela also shared you were happy."

Rory embraced the woman. "I truly have found happiness, and I'm married."

She withdrew from his arms. "Praise the Goddess. You must tell me all about her later." After greeting Ronan, she stood in front of Taran.

The Fae took her hand and placed a kiss along her knuckles. "I am called, Taran MacLean, and I'm honored to meet you. Your father was my mentor as well."

"So many friends," she whispered.

Taran nodded and dropped her hand.

As Aileen turned toward Conn, her smile faded. She placed her hands protectively over the babe she was carrying. Conn waited patiently for her to speak. Minutes ticked by in agonizing silence, and the air grew heated with everyone watching them.

Letting out a sigh, Conn held out his arm to her. "Show me your garden?"

After she reluctantly took his arm, he led her out of the hall. Recalling the garden was near the kitchens, he walked along the corridor to the left. Silence continued to linger like an unwanted companion between them. When he pushed open the door leading outside, the cool air and her simple touch helped to ease the tension inside him.

Scents of rosemary, sage, and dill filled his being as they wandered among the kitchen garden herbs. "You have expanded," he confessed, scanning the rest of the garden.

"Yes, but sadly we have had to halt any further planting," she affirmed, slipping her hand from his arm. She strolled toward a cluster of chamomile, heady with bees. Plucking a dainty flower, she twirled it between her fingers.

"When will the building of Aonach be completed?"

Arching a brow, she responded, "This year, hopefully late summer."

"It is quiet," observed Conn. "Where are the others?"

Grinning, she replied, "Brigid went to assist Nell with a birthing of one of the villager's horses. Of course, Duncan is there to oversee everything. Alastair and Fiona took all the children for a picnic in the hills." She paused and narrowed her eyes in thought. "And I believe Deirdre is waiting for Angus to join her along the loch to teach her how to fish. In case you didn't notice, Angus is upset at having to be detained."

Tired of discussing the state of the garden and whereabouts of the other Dragon Knights and their families, he approached her. "I was forbidden to speak of our lineage. An order from the king and queen."

Tossing the flower onto the ground, she faced him. "Did they think I would make some demand to the throne? I find this horribly distasteful. It's like I was considered a bastard, and the birth brushed under a mat. Did my mother know?"

Conn shrugged. "I cannot answer your questions. Considering how much your father loved your mother, I can only surmise that he did indeed share his connection to the Fae royalty with her."

She shook her head and crossed the garden to a bench. Taking a seat, she eased back against the bark of an elm tree. "Too many secrets. First my parents and now you. I am finding I don't like the Fae people. From my impression, they consider themselves above humans. It's a form of discrimination." Pausing, she took in a breath and released it slowly. "Let me rephrase, I do adore your sister, my cousin."

Conn winced at her words. Again, he found himself unable to offer any words of comfort. How could she possibly understand the rules and edicts of their kingdom? An earlier conversation with his beloved Ivy entered his thoughts, and he chuckled softly.

Aileen glared at him. "So now you insult me

217

further with laughter? Honestly, Conn—"

"I was recalling a similar conversation with my wife, Princess Ivy. She would be in agreement with you," interrupted Conn, strolling near her side. Taking a seat beside her, he leaned his forearms onto his thighs.

"Seriously? Then I've added another Fae to my list of those I like."

"Ivy is only part Fae."

Her eyebrows shot up in surprise. "Like me?"

Rubbing a hand down the back of his neck, he responded, "Not exactly. When I first met Ivy, she was human. After an incident where she was near death, I gave her my blood to aid in her healing. As a result, she carries the traits of both—human and Fae."

"Do you love her?" she asked in a hushed tone.

Smiling fully, he nodded. "With all my heart. Her soul called out to mine, and I accepted."

Aileen looked at him in amused wonder. "A mere mortal took down the mighty Conn MacRoich."

"She has been the only one," acknowledged Conn.

"A pity I can't meet this woman who has captured your heart. Although, I am curious. Why didn't you mention you were heir to the Fae kingdom? I can try and process why you kept my lineage from me, but I don't understand why you wouldn't say anything about you being royalty."

Shrugging, he explained, "At the time, I wasn't the prince. I had given up all rights when I became a Fenian Warrior. In order to save Ivy's life, I made a bargain with my father, the king. I would take my rightful place by his side and leave the Brotherhood, *if* he allowed the blood transfer to save her life."

Aileen gestured outward. "Yet, here you are

leading the other warriors."

His mouth twitched in humor. "Agreements were discussed and renegotiated *after*."

She smiled knowingly. "You are ever the diplomat."

This time Conn barked out in laughter and leaned back.

Aileen stared at him in stunned fascination. "Sweet Goddess…"

"What?" he asked, wiping a hand across his brow.

"I have never heard you laugh."

He winked at her. "Don't tell anyone. It will tarnish my image of a hardened warrior."

Narrowing her eyes at him, she poked him in the arm. "I happen to like this side of you. Goodness, between you and Angus, I don't know who is worse."

"It must be the leader qualities in us," teased Conn.

"At least I know where I stand with Angus. But with you…" pausing, Aileen glanced at a squirrel darting between some of the bushes beyond the garden.

"I shall always be your loyal friend," stated Conn.

She turned slowly toward him. Wariness reflected within her eyes. "But no more?"

Conn blew out a frustrated breath and stood. He directed his gaze on the shimmering loch below. What he had felt eons ago, no longer applied to the man he was. Love had entered his life, making him see things in a different perspective. "As a Fae, I am honor-bound to uphold the laws of my king and queen." Turning his attention back to her, he added, "However, as your *cousin*, I shall love and treasure our bond forever."

Returning to her side, he knelt in front of Aileen. He placed his fist over his heart. "I pledge an oath to always honor and protect you, Lady Aileen, and your descendants. Not only am I honor-bound by your marriage to a Dragon Knight, but by my right as your cousin. Your blood flows with that of the Fae, especially my own." Reaching outward, he took a hold of her hand. "Forgive me?"

Tears misted her eyes. "There is no need. I only wanted to hear your explanation. I realize this might be hard to fathom, but I do love you, Conn. You, Liam, and Rory stood by our side during one of the darkest times on Earth. You risked so much. Actually, I was angry, but I am not one to hold grudges."

Conn stood bringing Aileen with him. Embracing her in a hug, he whispered, "Thank you."

As they strolled back toward the castle, Aileen remarked, "Your sister is fascinating as well as beautiful. I so enjoyed our brief time together."

His peaceful demeanor now dampened with the reality of their situation. "Why did they seek out this place?"

Halting their stride, Aileen studied him. "You truly don't know."

Conn fought the urge to clench his fists. "Not one bloody clue."

Aileen placed a hand on her chest. "Oh, my, I thought you did. Though they did express worry if you arrived here. At the time, Abela was not concerned. They had been moving from place to place."

"For what purpose?" demanded Conn.

"To acquire the Treaty of Feahan, so they could offer an amendment," she stated softly. "I'd advise holding any further questions for Stephen and Angus."

His mind reeled. "Shit!"

Aileen rolled her eyes and proceeded him into the castle.

Doing his best to hold his tongue, he followed along in silence. When they entered the hall, Conn stormed to the table by the hearth. Angus sat back in his chair, drumming his fingers over the top of the table. "Have ye made your amends?" the man asked him.

"Yes. He has graciously made an apology," answered Aileen, taking a seat beside Stephen.

Conn pointed a finger at Angus. "Did you turn over the Treaty of Feahan to Liam?"

"By the hounds," hissed out Rory.

Taran grumbled a curse, and Ronan stood slowly.

"Aye," acknowledged Angus.

"Why?" demanded Conn and took a step toward the Dragon Knight.

"He wishes to make an amendment."

Conn braced his hands on the table. "In order to do so, he should have sought out the first Dragon Knight present at the signing, which is not you."

Angus arched a dark brow and stood. "They missed the correct year when traveling the Veil of Ages. Furthermore, he did obtain the original from King MacAlpin."

"Sweet Mother Danu," expressed a shocked Ronan.

Pushing away from the table, Conn went to the blazing hearth. "What changes is he wishing to make?"

"To alter the one about taking another Fae through the Veil, one not connected to the Brotherhood."

Conn pounded his fist onto the stone. "He seeks to make right his reasoning for taking Aidan Kerrigan back in time to aid Aileen."

"Aye," responded Angus.

"If I recall, humans made a point to put this strict rule within the bylaws of the Treaty, so why would you and King MacAlpin turn over the parchment?"

"Because he has conditions to present to the king and believes they are just. Furthermore, ye ken it was *your* king that suggested this to be a wise law and was totally in agreement. I don't believe Liam has a chance with your king, but I would grant him anything after his aid in obtaining victory over the evil druid. As I would with ye, Ronan, and Rory."

Conn pushed away from the stone and clasped his hands behind his back. "Regardless, he has broken out of prison and as the leader of the Fenian Warriors, I must retrieve him." He pursed his lips. "But what I cannot fathom is my sister's involvement."

"She's in love with him," announced Aileen, chuckling softly. "In addition, I believe Liam is in love with her, also."

"I'll kill him!" roared Conn.

Chapter Twenty

"I have walked along the abyss of death and left fear behind. Yet, I dread what love can do to my heart."
~Chronicles of Liam MacGregor

"Wake, *mo ghrá* and welcome the new dawn of Midsummer," murmured Liam against Abela's cheek.

The stirring of summer entered his veins as he stood. He witnessed the sky transforming from night into day, the rose-colored tone luminous against an azure background.

Abela yawned as she linked her arm with his. Leaning her head on his shoulder, she whispered the words of greeting, "All sweetness of summer we herald your new song. Rise forth and anoint us with your gift of warmth, light, and new beginnings. As the cycle weaves onward, so we honor this day. You are the crowning point at this time of year. Good morrow to thee."

Liam squeezed her hand. "Let the song of Midsummer fill us today. Open our souls to the bliss of Midsummer's kiss."

"What a stunning dawn," observed Abela, removing her hand from Liam's arm. She moved away from the protection of their tryst and opened her arms. "Beauty everywhere."

Liam watched in fascination as she moved in a

spiral dance. With each step, wildflowers sprouted more in abundance. She was one with the land—a beauty in her own right. Contentment filled him. However, a nagging thread of regret kept entering his mind. What would happen when they returned? Would the council even consider listening to his argument? He tried to banish the thought, but it had returned with a vengeance when the first stirrings of dawn awoke him.

I will fight for our convictions. We shall not be parted.

As if sensing his thoughts, Abela turned, a frown marring her stunning features. "Do not tempt the Fates."

Crossing to her side, Liam wrapped his arms around her waist. "Did I leave my mind open to you?"

She twisted her fingers in his hair. "Now that we have uttered our binding vows to each other, it comes naturally listening to each other's thoughts." Abela tapped a finger against his temple. "We must learn to close the link between us."

He kissed her nose. "And only use the connection in times of need or…cherishing your body?"

Laughing seductively, she rubbed her body against him. "That would be lovely, since I would not wish to hear your chatter along with my own within my mind."

Liam traced the soft fullness of her mouth with his tongue. "Hungry?"

"Food or pleasure?"

"Both."

Abela kissed him thoroughly and then pushed away from his arms. Wandering back to the trees, she picked up her gown and proceeded to get dressed. She took her time braiding her long locks into one braid.

Liam was about to ask if she was able to magically dress herself, but remained silent. He had no wish to spoil the day with worry over her failing powers. Walking to her side, he quickly got dressed.

"Shoes?" He pointed to the discarded slipper boots on the grass.

Her smile was radiant. "Absolutely not." She twirled around in a small circle. "This day is meant to walk upon the land."

"Agreed." Reaching for her hand, Liam steered her toward the path that led away from the waterfall.

Liam chatted for most of the way. Yet when Abela continued to remain silent or give one-word responses, he halted their progress. "Is something wrong?"

She blinked as if in deep thought. "Why would you ask?"

He lifted her chin with his finger. "You're quiet."

"I'm enjoying the sound of your voice."

Liam studied her for several moments, and then placed her hand in the crook of his arm. "I believe you require food and drink."

"Are you always so perceptive, my warrior?"

"When it comes to the woman I love, yes."

"Then you are correct. I am thirsty."

"Your wish is my command." He maneuvered them toward the river.

When he approached, Liam knelt, cupped his hand into the cool water and brought some to her.

Abela sat on a boulder near the edge, eyeing him with disbelief. "I am not too weak to retrieve my own water."

"I'm merely assisting."

She sipped the water from his outstretched hands.

"More, kind sir."

Liam complied and brought more water to her lips. After several more handfuls, she waved him off.

"Refreshing, but not as sweet as the lakes from our own world."

Standing, Liam wiped his hands off on his trews. "Tsk, tsk, my lady. No complaints, although, I am in agreement about the taste."

"I'm not, simply stating a fact."

Liam chuckled and extended his hand to her. "Ready?"

"I guess our rest has come to an end."

Instantly, his composure went from mirth to worry. Kneeling in front of her, he gazed into her eyes. The rosy glow was absent from her cheeks, and she appeared tired. "You are weak."

"Ahh…I see you are making a statement and not asking a question."

He braced his hands on her knees. "How do you feel?"

"Content."

"Physically, *not* spiritually."

She sighed and glanced away. "Somewhat tired."

"Somewhat?" Liam stood and brought her along with him. "Tell me truthfully, Abela."

"How can I explain what I have never experienced? I long to stretch out and take a nap. Even walking the short distance we did has left me tired."

Liam rubbed a hand across his brow in thought. "You are not used to the human world. Perhaps there is a reason why only the Fenian Warriors are able to maintain their strength and powers here. I am glad we are returning to our home tomorrow."

226

"I'm not," she declared and pushed away from him. She hugged her arms around her body. "I know what we shall endure come tomorrow."

"Are you worried *or* afraid?"

She waved her hand in the air. "Bah! Never do I fear them. If I can hold my own against the great Aidan Kerrigan *and* my father, I can do so before the Fae council."

Liam stood and cupped her cheeks. "My brave princess."

"Always."

He brushed a feather-light kiss against her lips as tender as the summer breeze. "Why don't you remain here, and I'll fetch the food from the wagon."

Shaking her head, Abela started forward. "I will be all right. I have no wish to be parted from you."

"Brave and stubborn." Taking her hand, he led her away from the river and in the direction of their wagon.

The air was warm, with a light breeze. They remained quiet on the duration of their journey. By the time they reached the wagon, they could hear faint music from the camp of the travelers.

"Beautiful. So full of gaiety," commented Abela, slipping her hand free from his. She sniffed the air. "But I am happy we are not staying. I smell burnt animal flesh."

"It no longer bothers me. I simply squash the unpleasant odor." After retrieving the basket of food from the wagon and her cloak, Liam motioned for them to move out into the meadow away from the smells of the camp.

"Much better," declared Abela, inhaling deeply as they entered the shade of a few birch trees.

After placing her cloak at the base of a tree, Liam opened the basket and peered inside. "The good folk have provided more than I requested. Fresh bread, apples, berries, mushrooms, cheese, and something sweet." He lifted out a larger package and offered it to Abela. "It smells faintly of a honeyed cake."

Upon opening the package, Abela gasped. "Is that some kind of jam?"

Liam reached across and swiped with his finger at the sticky fruit oozing out from the side. "Care to guess what kind?"

When she placed her mouth over his finger, Liam let out a soft hiss.

"Mmm…strawberry," she replied. "My turn." Taking her finger, she portioned out some and held it outward for him.

Reaching for her hand, Liam took his time in savoring the tart fruit mixed with the taste of Abela. A crimson blush grew from her neck to her face. Liam removed the cake from her hands and scooted near her. Cupping her chin, he sought out her lips. "Delicious," he murmured against her skin.

Abela wrapped her arms around his neck. "Does this ever stop?"

Liam drew back and gazed at her. "What?"

She tilted her head to the side. "The desire to be in your arms, kissing and touching you."

His hands stilled. "In all my lifetime, I have never known such desire. I find I am another man when I am around you. One who wishes to cherish you every waking moment. Will it stop? No, Abela. It grows by the hour."

"Perchance it's only the lure of Midsummer," she

whispered, leaning her forehead against his. "Or maybe the travelers have put an enchantment over the food."

"You're wrong," he argued. "It's neither of those reasons."

Lifting her head, she asked, "How can you be so sure?"

He smiled fully. "Because this is what I felt all those years ago, except now I have tasted the forbidden fruit and will not be content with another."

Her lips trembled. "Nor I."

Liam showered her with kisses around her mouth and neck. "You are mine. *Forever.*"

Lost in each other's embrace, they never heard the approaching horses until they were upon them. When the hiss of steel filled the air, Liam bolted to a standing position in front of Abela. Surveying the area, he counted six armed men, all with swords extended. Keeping his hand on his sword at his waist, he tried to detect who was the leader.

Abela stood and placed a hand on his shoulder.

"Is there a reason you have your swords unsheathed? We are guests of the O'Malley," protested Liam.

One of the men dismounted and stalked toward them. "I know who you are, MacGregor."

Frowning, Liam stated, "We are at a disadvantage, since I do not know *your* name."

"No, I don't recall us being introduced. My brother dinnae include me in his discussions with the Fae warriors. He thought me beneath him."

Liam bristled at the man's words. "I can only surmise you are kin to O'Malley."

He snorted. "Aye. I am Peter O'Malley."

A tremor of unease settled within Liam. "Then why may I ask are you pointing your weapons at us, if you know we are guests of your brother?"

Peter's sinister laugh surrounded them. "Ye *were* guests, but I am now in control of our clan. My brother has grown weak. When word reached my ears ye were requesting the Treaty of Feahan, I knew it was time for my plan to take over. I have bided my time for the right moment."

"How did you know I wanted the treaty?" demanded Liam, tersely.

"I have my own spies." He nodded to another man. "Bind the woman."

"You touch her, and I'll rip out your heart before you take your next breath," warned Liam, glaring at the man.

"If you do, my man will use his blade on your woman," argued Peter.

"Truth, Abela?" Liam dared not glance at her, instead keeping his focus on the men in front of him. Had another man moved silently behind Abela, or was it a ruse to misdirect his attention?

"Yes," she affirmed, squeezing his shoulder. "He's holding a blade at my side."

Peter signaled to another man. "Remove his sword and bind him with the cuffs."

Liam's fury soon turned to shock when the man approached with Fae crystal cuffs and quickly placed them around his wrists—binding Liam's powers. Glancing over his shoulder, he noted Abela's wrists were bound with the same as well. Never before had Liam felt so exposed and helpless. She drew near his side, her eyes wide with fear.

Do not worry, I will protect you. He brushed the thought across her mind. She gave him a faint smile in acknowledgement.

Returning his attention back to Peter, he demanded, "Where did you acquire these from?"

Peter leveled a blade at Liam's chest. "Apparently there are those in your own world who are not happy with some of the new events. They seek to undo recent changes in their world and want no resistance or interference."

"You lie," protested Abela. "No one would ever defy the king."

His lip curled in disgust. "Wrong! And ye *princess*, will make a great bargain for wealth."

Liam clenched his fists. "You have made a grave error here today. You will incur the wrath of the entire Fae kingdom."

The man took a fist to Liam's jaw. He staggered but remained unfazed.

Peter spat on the ground in front of him. "As long as I have ye both, nothing shall happen to me and my men. Ye are the fool. With the power of certain Fae backing me, ye will do exactly as I say." He waved his men forward. "Let us retreat back to our camp. They can walk on foot."

Grasping the reins of his horse, Peter mounted the animal.

Liam clenched his jaw so tightly he feared it would snap. Who would dare go against the King of the Fae? His mind reeled, trying to fathom any coherent thought. Yet, only one remained. When he and Abela were freed, Liam would take a blade to the man's heart and burn the hearts of all the traitorous Fae involved.

"Why can't we ride one of the horses?" asked Liam.

Peter eyed him with contempt. "I am nae fool. Once ye are on a horse, ye can command the animal."

One of the men shoved him forward. Abela kept a steady pace beside him. He might be used to being shackled, but this treatment to her was unspeakable. Had their kingdom splintered in his absence? Surely Abela would have mentioned the dissension within the realm. Or maybe she was unaware due to her time in the temple.

With each step he took, Liam drew in the energy of the land into his body—trying to keep focused and remain calm. His singular purpose was to free Abela and find the Fae traitors.

"Drop your shields, Abela," he ordered within her mind.

She gave him a startled look. "Are you sure?"

"Yes. We need the aid of Conn and any other Fenian Warriors."

"How can you be certain he is coming after me—us?"

"Because nothing will stop him from protecting you. It doesn't matter if he is now the Prince of the Fae, I know your brother, and I can bet my life he is searching the cosmos for you."

She nodded. "Done."

"Good."

Onward they traveled in a southeast direction away from the O'Malley's camp. Had Peter already eliminated his brother? Family feuds left a bitter taste in his gut. He had no wish to become embroiled in a clan war. His gut soured more at the thought of his own world also choosing sides and dividing the kingdom.

As the hours bled into the next, the sun dipped in the late afternoon sky. Abela had stumbled twice, and her face had taken on an ashen color.

"What is wrong?"

"Weaker. Head...body hurts."

"Lean back and I'll scoop you into my arms."

"No."

"I can cradle you, Abela. Do not argue with me!"

She staggered and wiped her fingers across her brow. Stopping, she sighed and waited for him to take her into his arms.

"What are ye doing?" barked the man following behind them.

Ignoring the brute, Liam nodded to her and she fell back into his arms. Lifting her against his chest, she positioned herself and leaned her head against his shoulder.

"Release her," ordered the man.

"The princess has taken ill and cannot walk any ."

His captor punched him in the back. "I gave ye an order."

Liam reeled around. "What do you think will happen if your leader finds out you've let his bargaining piece come to harm? The princess is unable to continue on this arduous journey."

Uncertainty wavered in the man's eyes. Scratching his beard, he grunted a curse and motioned them forward.

"Rest," Liam uttered softly.

Abela sighed and closed her eyes.

When they finally reached a secluded area through a thick copse of trees, Liam crossed to a fallen log and gently placed Abela down. He took another count of how many men Peter had under his command, which at present had grown to ten. He also noted that his sword had been tossed to the ground beyond the trees. *Fools— weak men.* Did they fear the weapon?

"Water," she muttered.

Liam returned his attention to Abela and tucked a stray lock of hair away from her eyes. "Your wish is my command."

A smile tugged on the corners of her mouth, before she dropped her head forward.

Wasting no time, Liam stormed to where Peter was speaking with some of his men. The man who had accompanied them stepped in front of him, blocking his path. "Ye will wait until spoken to."

"Leave him be, Andrew," ordered Peter, pushing him aside. "He can do nae harm with these special cuffs."

"The princess has taken ill and requires fresh water," demanded Liam.

Peter glanced behind Liam at Abela. "Is this a ruse?"

"On my honor, I have not deceived you."

He waved a hand dismissively in the air. "I find it hard to fathom."

Liam dared to take a step toward the man. His fury rising. "The *princess* is not accustomed to your world. She has grown weaker since her arrival here. I'm only asking for a little water."

Peter scrubbed a hand over his face. "Someone fetch the Fae woman water!"

Grunts and curses ensued from the group of men, but soon, one of them made his way to her side.

"Thank you."

Peter snorted and returned to his men.

Liam retreated to Abela's side, taking a seat beside her. After she finished drinking the water from a flask, she handed it back to the man.

"Lean against my arm, *mo ghrá*."

"What is wrong with me?"

Worry infused Liam, but he would not allow it to show. "The human world is not to your liking."

"Definitely," she acknowledged. But what bothers me is who the traitor in our kingdom is."

He kissed the top of her head. "Can you think of anything that would cause this rift?"

"Yes…and no."

"Care to enlighten me?"

She shuddered against him. "No. When Conn arrives—I pray soon—he can explain further to you. Again, it is not my place."

"And my brother, Rory? You cannot share anything?"

"Forgive me, no."

Liam glanced upward. "Do not ask for forgiveness. All will be revealed once we are rescued from this insanity."

"Or worse," muttered Abela. "The traitorous Fae will show their faces first, and then we'll be doomed."

"Do not fear, *mo ghrá*, they are no match for a Fenian Warrior. Even one who is chained." *Goddess help them, for they have no idea the power I will unleash against them.*

Chapter Twenty-One

"I mistook the breeze as merely elemental and did not listen to the whisper of Mother Danu calling out my name."

~Diary of Princess Abela

A kaleidoscope of images flashed within her mind. Abela tried to sort out the colorful ones from the gray pictures in an attempt to divide them into two groups. The process was overwhelming and convoluted. Each attempt proved futile and she groaned in frustration. Perchance, she should give up and float away on a faery stone. Nevertheless, peace was not attainable and only an illusion.

Sharp pain pricked her arm, along with another voice trying to reason with her. By the Gods, how was she supposed to solve the riddle?

"Abela, *mo ghrá*, wake."

"No," she protested in a cracked voice.

"Then drink."

Cool water passed her dry lips and entered her body, soothing all the heat within. Her mind cleared, and she shook her head, trying to clear the cobwebs of a fragmented dream. Abela blinked in an attempt to fully open her eyes. Liam appeared in front of her in a haze. "Why is everything so hot here? Is the summer heat upon us?"

"Sweet Mother Danu, you are with fever," complained Liam.

"The Great Goddess refuses to answer me," she mumbled and closed her eyes.

"No," hissed out Liam. "Open your eyes, warrior princess."

Immediately complying, she gazed at him skeptically. "Warrior, no. Princess, yes." Taking in their surroundings, Abela noted it was dark. "If there is no sun, why am I so hot? Please unfasten my cloak and remove the garment."

"You are with fever and the night air is chilled."

"Ahh...yes. You did mention the fever." Abela rubbed a hand over her forehead and tried to settle her thoughts. "No rescue?"

"No. And I disagree. You are a magnificent warrior. Was it not you who dared to break me out of a Fae prison, and attempt to maneuver us through the Veil of Ages?"

She snorted and then coughed. "After many arguments and attempts to get the correct time-period and location through the Veil."

"Regardless, I have been in awe of your strength and abilities," countered Liam, settling her onto his lap.

She bit her lip and looked away. "I'm scared."

He kissed her cheek tenderly. "All warriors learn early on to harness their fear. If not, it will devour them and they will die."

"Another lesson to learn?" she asked, returning her attention to him.

"Is not life all about the lessons?"

She studied him. His eyes blazed in the twinkling starlight. "You are ever the scholar. You should consider working with the Bard of the Fae."

"Archie McKibben? He is far better suited for the position and does not require an assistant."

She shivered. "We need someone in the Fae realm. Most of the historians are ancient. I recall trying to procure a certain tome on ancient Scotland—" A coughing spasm wracked her body, and Abela fought to get control.

Liam brought the flask to her lips. "Take a few sips," he encouraged.

After drinking some more water, she waved him off. "As I was saying…they moved in slow, methodical steps to obtain the information I was seeking."

Dabbing at the corners of her mouth with part of her cloak, he asked, "Why would you want to learn about ancient Scotland?"

Abela nudged him. "I was thinking of you."

"Contrary to what you may think, those historians are vastly superior. Yes, they are old, but their knowledge also contains insight into our homeland of Taralyn." He kissed the top of her head. "You were determined to learn about my travels."

"Well, no one else would tell me anything, and I disagree. You'd be perfect as one of the prestigious historians." Abela unfastened the broach at the top of her cloak and shifted her position away from Liam. "You're too hot, and I ache everywhere."

"Turn completely away from me and straddle the log."

Sighing, Abela did as Liam suggested. When the side of his hands touched her shoulders, she hissed.

"Relax," he urged.

She nodded and permitted him to massage the

knots in a rolling movement from her neck and along her shoulders. After several minutes, her body began to unwind, and she allowed Liam to continue with his ministrations.

"Lean against me and try to get some more rest."

"Can't I just curl up on the ground?"

He didn't even answer. Instead, Liam pulled her against his body. "When you are feeling better and have rid yourself of this fever."

She pouted. "What a nuisance. I have never suffered this gravely ever before."

An owl hooted nearby, and she smiled. Closing her eyes, she tried to push the pain away within her head.

"Abela?"

"Yes?" she mumbled.

"You have hidden the Stone of Ages well?"

"Of course," she whispered. "Only a Fae can detect its placement."

"Wise, *mo ghrá*. Keep the cloak with you at all times."

"I will guard it with my life." Taking a deep sigh, Abela slipped into a blissful slumber.

****

Shards of pain continued to invade Abela's body as she attempted to open her eyes. Sunlight danced along the ground, and she ached to slump down upon its soft coolness. It teased and tormented her.

"Let me go," she pleaded.

"Shh…" whispered Liam against her cheek.

Once she'd welcomed his breath against her skin. Now it was like a burning poker. Lifting her hand, she attempted to swat at him.

"What's wrong?" she asked in a hoarse voice.

"The men are arguing. It seems as if they are unable to contact the Fae. They have been trying all night and into the early morning."

"Stupid humans." She cupped a hand over her mouth to stifle the giggle. Why did she ever become fascinated with the human world?

"Can you turn around?" he asked.

"Every cell in my body is screaming." However, Abela did as he requested. "By the Goddess," she moaned.

Shifting around, Liam retrieved the flask. Lifting it to her lips, she tried to take in some of the cooling liquid. "Throat hurts."

"You must stay hydrated. The fever has not abated."

Abela looked up at him. Slowly she reached out and touched his cheek with her fingers. "Say a prayer to Mother Danu."

He bent and kissed her nose. "She can still hear you, Abela."

She shook her head solemnly. "The Goddess has forsaken me."

"Never," he affirmed. "But I will add my prayers to yours."

Regardless of what Liam said, she knew in her heart Mother Danu had left her. Never once, had Abela heard her whispered words of comfort. Furthermore, she understood that her body was dying. Each hour a part of her life force faded away, vanishing into the land and leaving her weaker. In addition, she battled with the decision to keep this knowledge contained from Liam. She could not bear to burden the love of her life that without help, she would surely die in this world. She tried to fight the soothing call of the other side, but her body would not cooperate with her mind. The moment she lowered her shields, she thought Conn would somehow magically appear. Was he not searching for them? Had their father forbidden him from leaving the realm again?

She rubbed her temples. "So many questions."

"What answers do you seek?" asked Liam quietly, reaching for her hand.

"For one, where is my brother?"

Liam shrugged. "I am as much in the dark as you are. In fact more so, since I have no knowledge as to the current affairs of our kingdom."

Abela fought the urge to tell him everything. Perhaps she could share a small amount of knowledge to ease his mind. "Conn and your brother walked their own path—both were not easy ones either. Do not pass judgment on them when you see them."

He looked at her suspiciously. "Care to elaborate?"

"Sorry, no."

Liam's laughter sounded bitter, and he remained silent.

Abela lowered her head and sighed.

"I love you, *mo ghrá*. Remember my words always. Heart to heart…"

She lifted her head, doing her best to hold back the tears. "Blood to blood, my body and soul is forever yours."

He brought her hands to his lips. "Until my last breath."

Shouting and curses erupted from Peter, and they both turned at the heated conversation with his men.

"Will this ever end?" she muttered.

Liam snorted in contempt and kept his voice low. "They're furious over the absence of the Fae. Apparently they should have been here last evening. By my deductions, it sounds like more than one Fae. Something has gone wrong with Peter's plans. Or he reckons the Fae have mistook the time of the meeting, which in my opinion is incorrect. The Fae's timing is always impeccable. Peter suggests leaving to go to another rendezvous. One that the Fae suggested on another occasion."

"Wonderful. I do not relish moving once again on foot," she complained and tried stretching her legs out.

Peter pointed in their direction, and one of the men stormed forward. Liam immediately stood, taking a protective stance in front of Abela.

"Get out of my way," snapped the man, shoving Liam off to the side. "I'm to bring the woman. Ye are to remain here."

He grabbed a hold of her arm, and Abela winced. "I can stand," she protested feebly.

Liam's lip twisted in rage and attempted to block the man from leaving. "Where the princess goes, I follow. She is under *my* protection."

"Get out of my way," ordered the man, pulling her along with him.

"No!" roared Liam.

Peter barked out orders, and two other men charged toward Liam—swords extended.

"Stop," demanded Abela, trying to reason with her captor. "I will go, but do not harm him."

Liam continued to fight, until Peter charged forth and bashed him over the head with the hilt of his sword.

A chill of foreboding swept through Abela as she

screamed Liam's name, watching in stunned horror as he slumped to the ground. As she tried to yank free from the man, he tightened his grip. The pain radiated up her arm and into her neck. "Allow me to go to him. He's injured."

Peter marched toward her. "Silence!" Leveling his blade against her neck, he added, "If ye want him to live, ye will go willingly."

Though her body trembled, Abela lifted her chin in determination despite her fear. *I have never known hatred until this moment.* "I will cause you no further trouble." Though the words she spouted contained a lie.

"Good." He motioned to her captor. "Take her away. We will move onward."

The bile in her stomach threatened to heave onto the ground. Abela cast one more glance at Liam as Peter gave instructions for two of the men to bind Liam to a tree. Blood seeped down his face from the wound to his head, and she prayed he'd wake soon. How she yearned to see the spark of love in his eyes, if only for one last moment.

Blinking back the tears, she tried to focus on one single thought that Conn would find them. She had tried calling him, but was too weak to project her thoughts in search of her brother's mind. Searching the trees, Abela sent out messages to the animal kingdom in an effort to alert her brother if he should venture upon Liam first.

Her body was heavy as she stumbled ahead, trying to stay focused and push away the pain in her heart and limbs. With each step leading her farther away from Liam, a piece of her soul splintered like shards of glass.

The men continued to argue over the course of direction, believing they should have remained at the original destination agreed upon by them and the Fae. Peter overrode their complaints, stating there was a secondary location in the event something went wrong. Listening with intent, Abela tried to hear any mention of a Fae name. However, their language was garbled and the accent too thick with most of the men. If only she could concentrate more.

Almost stumbling over a tree root, she quickly righted herself and tried to keep pace with the men. A breeze lifted the hair on the nape of her neck and she sighed. It was a blessed relief to her scorching body. Glancing upward, she longed for a cool rain shower to douse the heat within her.

Minutes turned into hours, and her body screamed to stop this ruthless procession across the land. When Peter held up his hand to halt, Abela almost cried out in relief. Making her way to a yew tree, she slumped down.

Her captor kicked her leg with his boot. "Get up."

"I thought we were stopping," she argued and placed her palms upon the ground.

"Nae."

Clenching her jaw, Abela tried to draw energy from the land into her pain-wracked body. "I only require a few moments."

The man didn't respond. Instead, he yanked her to standing and pushed her forward.

Beads of sweat dotted her brow, and she wiped a hand across her forehead. Time was running out. Her body was failing. Yet she would fight until her last breath. Did not Liam call her a warrior? Now was the time to earn this badge of honor he had bestowed on her.

Glaring at the man, she stepped around him and walked onward.

Holding her palm up, she blew across the skin. *I love you, Liam. Never forget, my love. Seek me out at the gates of Tir na Og. I shall wait for you.*

Chapter Twenty-Two

"Destiny is fickle. One moment the path shines brightly in front of you. And the next, it tosses you into an abyss of pain."

~*Chronicles of Liam MacGregor*

Intense pain and screaming filled Liam's head. He shook in an attempt to rid the demons tormenting his mind. They continued in their merciless torture. His fingers sought to withdraw his blade and slice the tongue from the man bellowing in his ear, but he was unable to retrieve the sword.

"Wake up, you bloody fool!" bellowed the man.

Liam recognized that voice and fought the urge within his mind to sink back into the chasm of darkness. Fighting the wave of pain, he blinked and tried to focus on his surroundings.

His realty came crashing back into his memories, and he let out a strangled cry, "*Abela!*"

"Where is she?" demanded Conn, towering over him.

Wiping the blood away from his eye, he responded, "Gone with Peter O'Malley of the Irish Travelers and his men. He seeks to take over O'Malley's clan."

"You bastard! You have dishonored the Brotherhood. I should save us all the trouble and kill you where you sit."

Liam ignored Conn's ranting, expecting far worse. He leaned to the side and took in the appearance of his brother, Rory, Taran, and Ronan. "I see only the strongest have been dispatched to assist the Fae *Prince*."

Without warning, Conn leveled a fist to his jaw, and Liam's head slammed against the bark of the tree. Lights danced before his eyes, and he shook his head in an effort to focus.

His brother stepped forward. Withdrawing his dirk, he sliced through the ropes and freed Liam.

As Rory helped him to stand, he pointed to the crystal cuffs. "By the Gods, how? Have the Fae council guards arrived?"

Liam lifted his joined hands. "There is a traitor within our kingdom."

"You lie," spat out Conn, grabbing his tunic. "Your dishonesty is unforgiveable."

Arching a brow, Liam countered, "For what purpose? I just told you Peter O'Malley has Abela. He has done this with the help of someone *within* the Fae realm. Peter was the one who possessed the cuffs to bind both Abela and myself. So tell me, my *prince*, where would he obtain them?"

After releasing his hold, Conn took a step back, shock registering across his features. "Why would there be a division within the realm? This is madness!"

"Agreed," stated Liam dryly. "Apparently, there are some Fae who are not happy with the recent changes within the kingdom and aligned themselves with Peter and his men. Yet, I suspect there are more humans involved. Peter only had ten men with him." He shifted his stance and glanced at his brother.

Wariness reflected in his eyes. "Since Abela refused to share any knowledge of what has transpired between you and Rory, I can only surmise that much has happened since my time in seclusion. Would any like to share the recent events of what has occurred?"

Rory pointed to Conn. "Should *you* give him the particulars?"

Conn blew out a frustrated breath and rubbed a hand over his face. He looked at Ronan. "Alert the king immediately. Place extra guards around all the royal households. When all is completed, return to us. Furthermore, do not inform the king we have found Liam. If he even hears a whisper that Abela's been kidnapped by humans, he will ignite a war by entering this world."

Ronan gave a curt nod and snapped his fingers. In a flash of colors, the warrior vanished.

"Regardless of the circumstances, I judge it wise not to discuss what has happened to Rory and me. Our lives have indeed changed. I can share that not only have I claimed the throne to the kingdom, but also I am now the leader of the Fenian Warriors."

"I denoted the additional leader markings on your arms and the silver armbands that proclaim you the prince," Liam interrupted. "Why the secrecy? Were you forced at your trial to accept the throne?"

Rory and Conn exchanged glances.

When silence lingered like a black cloud, Liam sighed and lifted his hands. "Would you care to remove these?"

Conn eyed him skeptically. "No. You are under arrest for breaking out of prison. In addition, your crimes are great for bringing the princess into the mortal world."

He took a step near the prince. "We need to locate Abela."

Fisting his hands on his hips, Conn's eyes blazed silver. "And we shall, but not you. Furthermore, what gives you the right to call her thusly? She is a priestess of the temple, a princess, and *my* sister!"

"We waste valuable time arguing," protested Liam. "Remove these cuffs!"

"Rory, remove your brother from my presence, or I will be forced to take a blade to his tongue."

Liam refused to leave, and he gave Rory a warning look. "You will not be able to track her." He risked his life by revealing what he was going to confess to Conn and the others. But the sands of time were slipping away.

The prince smirked. "I have thus far."

"Only through the blood on the stones, and this is where it ends. I am your only hope now in tracking Abela," divulged Liam.

Silence ensued all around them. Liam registered that each warrior was trying to unravel what he had professed. He took a hesitant step back. "You require my aid in searching for *Abela*. I am the only one who can hear the whisper of her blood. I will not return to the Fae realm without her."

Conn slowly unsheathed his sword, the hiss of steel filling the air. "Your life is *mine*."

"Remember your vow," warned Rory and took a step toward the prince.

Liam showed no fear as he stared at Conn. "If you kill me, you will break the bond between Abela and me."

"No! This is an outrage! You have violated her!" roared Conn and punched the air with his fist.

The blast of power sent Liam flying back. He landed against the ground with a thud. Rolling over onto his knees, he tried to take in air as his lungs constricted from the blow. Waves of pain pounded his body, and he dug his hands into the land for healing.

"Get up, you bastard! You spout lies."

Standing on shaky limbs, Liam turned around. He did not fear Conn. No matter the man's rage, he had to get Conn to contain his fury until after they rescued Abela. "You cannot deny it to yourself what you already know in your heart—"

"Silence! Not one more word!"

Ignoring Conn's order, Liam continued, "We have spoken the binding vows. Abela is *mine*."

Instead of a blast of power, Conn leveled his blade against his heart. "I should end your pathetic life. You are not worthy of her."

Liam gave the man a weak smile. "On that we are in agreement. Nevertheless, I am in love with her," he paused and then continued, "In truth, I have *always* loved Abela. But it was your words so long ago that sent her fleeing from me."

Uncertainty clouded Conn's features, and he lowered his sword. He rubbed a hand over his brow. "How did you escape?"

"Abela used the magic of the temple and entered my prison. From there, *she* was the one who kidnapped me and brought us both into the mortal world."

"By the hounds! Why didn't you object? Surely you understood the risk she faced by committing or executing this crime," snapped Conn.

"At the time, she was garbed in material to shield her identity. I forced her to reveal herself once we were in the human world. She presented me with a proposition, and I accepted."

Conn, Rory, and Taran gaped at him in astonishment.

"Abela can be extremely convincing," professed Liam.

"But why would she do this for you and not for Conn?" asked Rory. "What possible meaning, unless…"

Liam nodded slowly. "She had no wish to see me die, since she has loved me for years, as well. Your destiny was on another path, and I assume she did not want to interfere. Whereas mine was ending in death."

"Sweet Mother Danu. I am the fool," muttered Conn, raking a hand through his hair. "I vaguely recall the time when she grew curious about the infamous MacGregor brothers. When she specifically wanted details pertaining about you—"

"You told her about my liaisons," interrupted Liam.

"Yours and Rory's exploits were legendary. It was my right as her brother," Conn objected.

"Nevertheless, I had not visited the Pleasure Gardens in many moons while I was seeing Abela."

Conn blew out a frustrated sigh.

Moving toward the prince, Liam held his hands outward. "I have no wish to stand here and debate the past with you. Not when time is diminishing for Abela. Regardless of how you feel about our relationship, we need to rescue her. She has grown weak with fever, and her magic is dwindling."

"Because she is *dying* in the human world," declared Conn.

Liam staggered back, the blow of Conn's words akin to a hammer to his soul. "I thought her merely *ill*...adjusting to the human world."

"Only the Fenian Warriors can travel within this realm. I have only just come upon this knowledge. We do not know how long she has either."

"But what about the Fae who work with the humans?" Liam retorted. "Apparently you are incorrect and Abela is merely ill."

The grave look Conn gave Liam only confirmed the worst scenario.

"Abela is dying. Any member of the royal family, except me, cannot travel above. It was part of the pact with the Milesians when we were sent underground after the great battle in Ireland. Though if the king knew of her situation, I believe he would enter this world and risk ending the life of everyone involved to rescue his daughter. I cannot fathom how the other Fae are maintaining their position above ground, unless they remain for brief periods of time here." Conn lifted his hand, and the crystal cuffs vanished from around Liam's wrists.

Liam rubbed his wrists in an effort to bring back the blood flow into his hands. He tried to ignore the agonizing fear swelling inside his heart of possibly losing Abela and refused to let panic cloud his warrior instincts. They would find her. "Then we waste time talking."

Conn pinched the bridge of his nose. "For now you have your freedom. Though once we have found Abela, you will be sent back to your prison." He glanced at

Liam. "Those are not my orders, but our king's."

Liam chose to remain silent, though he noted a questioning look on his brother's face. "Is there something you wish to ask?"

"Why did they separate you two?" inquired Rory.

"Apparently their Fae contact did not show up at the appointed time. They grew worried and decided to proceed with their alternate plan."

"Which is what?" inquired Taran, handing Liam a dirk.

Taking the blade and securing it within his belt at his waist, Liam responded, "To barter the princess for wealth."

"You do realize they have ignited a war by abducting Abela," acknowledged Conn.

Liam scanned the area, searching for his sword that one of the men discarded when they arrived. Quickly retrieving it, he returned to Conn's side. "Her rescue is imperative. If we can squelch this insanity and capture the Fae involved, then we can thwart a threat of war between our worlds."

Sheathing his sword, Conn adjusted his tunic. "My father's wrath will be far greater when he finds out there were traitorous Fae involved."

Liam said no more as he went to the last known place Abela had rested her body. He knelt on the ground and brushed his hand over the soft grass. Closing his eyes, he waited. When the first flutter of her heartbeat swept across his mind, Liam smiled and stood. "We shall proceed south."

"Can you be more specific?" asked Conn.

"Unless you are prepared to grant me my full powers, I cannot tell you exactly where she is located."

"Do you take me for a fool?"

"Regardless of no powers, I am still a Fenian Warrior," Liam argued. He grew tired of this sparring of words. "On my honor, once we have found Abela, I vow to return to my prison and await my trial."

Conn narrowed his eyes. Making a sign within the air, a blue crystal dagger appeared in his hand. "Bow your head and kneel."

Liam quickly complied. As Conn's first words entered his mind, the brush of power filled his body and mind. Inhaling deeply, the energy of his additional Fenian powers flowed to the depth of his soul. As he flexed his fingers, Liam placed his palms upon the ground. *Walk with us, Mother Danu. Help us to find your daughter.*

Rising, Liam inclined his head toward Conn. "Thank you."

After Conn enclosed them in a sphere of white light, he motioned to Liam. "Lead us to her."

Liam lifted his head to the sky and uttered the ancient words to transport them. In a soft whisper they vanished.

****

Abela blinked in an attempt to focus on her surroundings. Sunlight filtered through the thick canopy of trees and swept across the narrow path they traveled. Several rabbits dashed out of their way, and she tried to reach out mentally. However the pain and weakness in her limbs made the effort futile, and she finally relented.

Her only hope of survival depended on Liam finding her. She almost burst into tears when she felt the brush of his thoughts enter her mind. But the euphoria was quickly doused when one of the men prodded her forward with his sword, and she was unable to respond.

With shaking hands, she wiped her fingers across her slick brow. The fever continued to burn with a vengeance, and her vision became blurred.

"I will not die," she mumbled, and then burst out laughing. Who among her kidnappers cared?

"Be quiet," ordered the man behind her.

She gave him a scathing look over her shoulder. "Why?"

He lifted his hand as if to strike her and then clenched his fist. "Ye tempt fate, princess."

Shrugging, she returned her attention to the path in front of her. "I have done so all my life. If this is my ending, I shall not be silenced."

He grumbled a curse, but did not strike her.

The path finally opened up, and Abela shielded her eyes from the sun's intensity. More trees dotted the landscape around them as she staggered into the small clearing. Her mouth was parched, and the sun beat down upon her body. Fighting a wave of dizziness, she spouted, "Would any care to give me some water?"

Unable to continue with this relentless march through the land, Abela collapsed onto the ground. She'd rather die within the arms of Mother Danu than at the hands of these barbarians. "I cannot go any farther without liquid."

Peter dismounted from his horse and signaled to several other men. He dashed to her side. "What is wrong with her?" he snapped.

Her captor on her journey replied, "She is requesting more water."

"Then give her some! She is of no use to us if she dies!" Peter bellowed. "When she finishes, remove her out of sight. I will bargain with the Fae first."

The man grunted and removed his flask. Shoving it into her hands, he ordered, "Drink."

Abela removed the stopper and guzzled deeply. After wiping her mouth on her arm, she handed the flask back to the man. "Thank you."

Without a word, the man gripped her arm and yanked her to standing. "Move toward the trees."

Holding back the barb she wanted to fling out at him, Abela complied. The water did little to squelch the scorching fire within her, but at least her blurred vision had retreated. Crossing the clearing, she sighed as she retreated deep within the shade of the trees.

"Ye can halt here," he stated and pointed to one of the thick oak trees.

After she slumped down against the rough bark, Abela placed her palms upon the ground. She tried to draw forth some healing energy, but the weakness in her body was too overwhelming. Abela cast her sight outward. What traitorous Fae was involved? Would she be able to detect the person?

Voices drifted back to her, and she strained to pick up a note of familiarity.

Pressing her back fully against the ancient oak, she reached out within its spirit and closed her eyes. *Help me to part the limbs from the other trees, so that I may witness another.* The energy swirled around her, and Abela concentrated with all her last remaining strength. When a gentle breeze kissed her cheeks, she opened her eyes.

Through the thick tree limbs, a linear view

appeared before her vision. Traveling along the path within her second sight, she sought the center of the clearing. Her breath hitched as the traitor Fae stepped into view. Never had she fathom one so highly regarded in their realm would plot against her father the king.

She'd determined it was another lower Fae seeking recourse for some past deed done against him. Yet, this Fae *was* regarded and held a position of authority. When did her beautiful kingdom become divided? Had the prophecy truly begun? She recalled the stories from her mother and the seer. It would start with one high Fae—a division between above and below. Her mother had reassured her it would not take place in their life threads, but what if she was wrong? It could be what was happening now.

Abela dug her hands into the soft dirt as deep sorrow mixed with anger filled her. *Hurry, Liam. Time is fading for me and you must prevent a war.*

Chapter Twenty-Three

"It was foretold by a seer that if I ever witnessed the birth of a star, I would travel an unknown path. I did glimpse one on the celebration of my thousandth year of life."

~Diary of Princess Abela

Each of the Fenian Warriors steadily made their way across the open terrain. Conn kept them shielded from the humans as Liam led them onward to their destination. Lifting his fist to warn the others, Liam halted and scanned the area. The warriors fell behind him. Smoke billowed above the trees from a campfire, and the scent of charred meat permeated the area.

"Is Abela with them?" asked Conn quietly.

Closing his eyes, Liam concentrated. He gritted his teeth in frustration. "Someone is blocking our connection."

"Another Fae?" Conn withdrew his sword, glancing in all directions.

Dropping to the ground, Liam pressed both palms on the dirt. After extending his powers as far as he was able, he waited and tried to curb his growing impatience. *Hear my call. Feel my heart. I am coming for you, mo ghrá.*

From across the pulse of the land a light flutter of a heartbeat echoed back to him, and Liam exhaled slowly. He stood and faced Conn. "She is with them, but extremely weak. It took a great deal of energy for her to reach out to me."

Ronan appeared in a sliver of light. "All the royal households are secure."

"Any problems?" asked Conn.

"None."

Taran stepped forward. "How should we proceed?"

Conn brushed a hand over his chin. "We need to know the Fae involved, so that will be your task. Ronan, Rory, and I will battle the others." Conn glanced at Liam. "Your responsibility is securing Abela and transporting her to my chambers. Do not deviate to any other place in the kingdom. All the royal households are under the protection of the Fenian Warriors. Once there, you will find a woman. Her name is Ivy. Have her send for the healer and the Master Fae Apothecary. Present her with these coded words, Celtic Knot. She will understand my message."

"She should be transported to the temple. They have the most experienced healers," protested Liam.

"If you put her into the care of the priestesses, they may let her die since she has broken laws within the Order. I cannot risk the chance." Conn placed a firm hand on his shoulder. "Trust me."

"I agree," confirmed Rory, coming alongside Liam. "I know the Master Fae Apothecary well."

Uncertainty filled Liam. He sensed more to Conn's words, but this was not the time to dwell or argue for more information. "Then I will take her there."

Conn gave him a curt nod. "Let us move forward." With a flick of his wrist, he transported them behind the enemy's camp.

Liam noted four men positioned at a directional compass of north, south, east, and west. A few others were crouched near a fire eating. A wagon and horses were set back within the trees, surrounded by more men. Liam was correct. More humans had gathered. Two of the men had their backs to him, but were dressed in odd clothing. An odd sense of familiarity tugged at his mind. He tried to recall the memory. When one of the men turned sideways, blue markings adorned one side of his face.

Glancing at the other warriors, Liam asked, "When did the Milesians become embroiled in affairs of the Fae and humans?"

Conn's expression was a mask of stone. "None. I have not seen a Milesian since the final war that sent us underground. Their bloodline became mixed with the later people of Ireland, since they remained above."

"Nevertheless, several are present," interjected Ronan with contempt. "Ye can tell by the markings on one of them that they are from a warrior lineage."

Terror settled like a lodestone in Liam's gut. "We must quickly find Abela. They are within their rights to take her. She is a princess of the Fae and extremely valuable."

Conn glared at him. "I am well aware of the rights of the Milesians. However, they have already broken a law by conferring with another Fae outside of our kingdom *without* the knowledge of the king. Furthermore, I suspect their own king does not know of the betrayal within his realm."

"How can you be so sure?" demanded Liam, scanning the area.

Shrugging, Conn responded, "Call it intuition, but

this entire situation reeks of lesser individuals. Our realm has undergone some vast changes recently, and there have been a select few who have sought to thwart the new additions in our kingdom."

Liam tightened his grip on the hilt of his sword, frustrated with the limited knowledge of what had been happening in his absence. "No matter what has transpired, my concern is retrieving Abela and seeing her safely back to the kingdom. You can deal with the others."

"My brother is correct," acknowledged Rory and stepped forward. "We know what must be done. We will provide the distraction for Liam. It should not be difficult to locate the other Fae."

Conn pointed a warning finger at Rory. "No harm shall come to the Milesians. It would be a declaration of war, considering I am leading us on this mission. Our main focus is securing Abela and the other Fae." He glanced at all of them. "Are we in agreement?"

Rory, Taran, and Ronan gave curt nods in agreement.

Liam started forward and then paused. "When this is finished, I expect a full account of what has happened in our realm—be it at Abela's side or in my prison." He leveled a hard stare at Conn. "Swear it."

"On my honor," affirmed Conn. "As your prince *and* leader, all details will be given."

Snapping his fingers, Liam vanished.

Traveling over the ground in a flash of light, he followed Abela's faint heartbeat. As he came to a cluster of pine and oak trees, he settled behind them and cast his gaze out in all directions. Determined to keep himself shielded until he found Abela, he waited patiently.

Where are you, mo ghrá?

A slight coughing sound echoed to the right and Liam crouched low to the ground to get a better view of the footpath. Small critters scampered about, until his sight came upon a portion of Abela's body slumped next to a giant oak.

"Be quiet," hissed her captor.

Liam's lip curled in disgust as his gaze sought the man. He continued to survey the area, making sure no others were guarding Abela and then stood. When several other men stepped onto the path, Liam clenched his jaw and blended in with the tree. One of the Milesians had approached with a traveler.

"What is wrong with the woman? She doesn't look like a princess of anything," protested the Milesian and kicked her leg with his boot. "Are you attempting to barter with a peasant woman, instead of royalty?"

"Sweet Brigid! She appeared fine several hours ago, though was complaining of the heat, and walking," professed the traveler in apparent agitation. "I can assure ye that this is the Fae princess."

"Her hair is streaked with gray, and she is naught but skin and bones. This is *not* royalty. Our agreement is terminated. I must speak with your leader about this outrage." The Milesian shoved past the man and stormed to the clearing.

"Wa...wait," sputtered the man, running after him. "Speak with Peter before ye make your final decision."

Liam had no intention on waiting for Conn and the others to provide a distraction. A tremor of unease crept down his spine the moment they spoke of Abela's appearance. Making steady strides toward her, he was unprepared for the vision who greeted him.

He dropped to the ground in shock. "*Abela*," he uttered in a hoarse whisper, touching the gray strands that streaked through her once stunning ebony locks.

Her eyes fluttered open. Gone were the lavender hues he loved. In their depths were silver and gold specks. Her features were ashen and so withered, he barely recognized the woman that had stolen his heart. Her life force was evaporating.

She raised a frail hand. Her fingers trembled over his mouth. "Home," she mumbled and then collapsed into coughing spasms.

Liam's heart constricted. After swiftly sheathing his sword, he cradled her head against his chest until the seizures subsided. *You will not die, mo ghrá. Do you hear my words? I am taking you home. All will be well once you return.*

"Back away from the woman," ordered a male voice behind him.

Liam stood and turned around. He gazed into the sinister eyes of another Milesian. "I have no intention of releasing her *or* fighting you."

The man leveled his blade at Liam. "Then I will be forced to slay you."

"And start a war?" Liam shook his head. "I think not."

A flicker of wariness flashed briefly over the Milesian's features. The man pressed his blade center to Liam's heart. "She has already done so by entering this realm. And if you are the Fenian Warrior Peter O'Malley has told us about, you are without your powers and no threat to me."

He regarded the Milesian with contempt and

slowly lifted his hand. "I do not know where you came upon your information, but I am in full use of my powers." With a single thought, Liam dislodged the weapon from the man's hand and flung it outward.

Shock registered in the Milesian's eyes, and he stumbled back. Liam reached for his neck and lifted the man off the ground. Pure rage exploded inside him. "You have *trespassed* against the Fae kingdom by endeavoring to kidnap me and this woman. I take it as a sign of war! Your life is forfeit and by rights, mine."

"No, Liam, stop," uttered Abela in a cracked dry voice.

Her feeble voice scarcely registered within Liam's mind. His grip increased. "Give me the name of the Fae you are in league with?"

"Can…cannot speak his name."

"If you don't, I will pry it from your mind, leaving you incoherent for the rest of your life."

A turbulent war cry resounded in the distance alerting Liam that Conn and the others had come upon the enemy. "Your time is at an end. Answer me!"

The Milesian struggled for air, clawing at his face, and in a flash of blinding light disintegrated into ashes before Liam's eyes. Disbelief ripped through him as he shook his hand free of the last remnants of the man. "What just happened?" he muttered in shock. Even though he yearned to kill the man, Liam was not responsible for his death.

The sounds of battle echoed around him, snapping Liam out of his thoughts and his current situation. Turning around, he gently lifted Abela into his arms. Placing a soft kiss upon her brow, he whispered, "Do not leave me, *mo ghrá*."

In a shard of light, Liam transported them back into the Fae realm.

****

As Liam crept along the corridors of the Crystal Palace, he kept his shields around them. Passing several Fae, he remained focused on his progress. They spoke in hushed whispers as they skirted around a marble column. Liam swiftly ascended the polished amber stairs. An arched passageway filled with ivy and jasmine stood out in stark relief against the crystal walls, and he frowned in confusion. Was he in the wrong area? Beyond this lush foliage was Conn's chambers and in all of his time with the warrior, the area had remained untouched and clear. Slowly moving along the hallway, he came to a bend and peered around the corner. Noting the two Fenian Warriors positioned outside Conn's chambers, he let out a sigh of relief, grateful they were not royal guards.

Striding forth, he removed his shields. "Let me enter, Markus."

The warrior nodded. "The prince has alerted us of your coming." He knocked three times and then opened the massive oak doors.

Liam stepped inside and glanced around. The doors to the garden were open, and children's laughter spilled into the chamber. Abela moaned within his arms. "Hello?" he shouted. "Is Ivy here?"

He crossed the chamber and went to a cushioned bench. "Shh…you are home, *mo ghrá*."

"I am Ivy," answered the soft feminine voice behind him.

After brushing a lock of hair away from Abela's damp brow, he stood and faced the tiny woman. "I am

Liam MacGregor, and this is—"

"Oh my stars! *Abela*!" Ivy rushed to her side and knelt down. "What happened?"

Liam had no time to give an account on his beloved's condition. "Can you send for the Master Apothecary and the healer?" She glanced sharply at him, and he quickly added, "Conn told me to mention the words, Celtic Knot."

"Yes, yes." Ivy stood and crossed to the entrance. After giving Markus instructions in a hushed tone, she returned to Liam's side. "Give me a few moments to prepare a room."

He gave her a curt nod and watched her vanish down a corridor. Ivy's few moments turned into fifteen agonizing minutes as Liam paced in front of Abela. He was prepared to go in search of her, when she returned in a soft whisper. "Please follow me," she ordered.

He gathered Abela into his arms and proceeded down the corridor after Ivy. The woman led him into a small chamber already lit with candles. The air was permeated with the scent of rosemary and lavender.

Ivy gestured for Liam to settle Abela onto the bed. His beloved gasped as he propped more velvet pillows under her head. "Shh...all will be well."

A woman entered the room. She approached and dipped her head. "I am called, Aelish."

"I am aware of who you are, Lady Aelish. We met once long ago. I pray you can heal the princess. Where is the other healer?"

"I am the only one required. We do not want to alert anyone else. Permit me to make my examination alone with the *priestess*," suggested Aelish.

Liam bent and placed a kiss on Abela's cheek,

giving no care to who witnessed his display of emotion. He then turned to Aelish. "Alert me of your findings first."

Aelish clasped her hands together, surveying him skeptically. She peered over his shoulder at the other woman.

"Do as he requests," ordered Ivy and tugged on Liam's arm. "Let me offer you some food and drink."

"Don't bother," he argued, curious as to why Aelish would take orders from another Fae, especially from one who spoke with an odd accent. He pondered what part of the realm she belonged to.

"Nevertheless, it is the least I can do," she explained and moved to the door.

Liam hesitated, giving Abela one last look before following Ivy out of the chamber. As she led him down another corridor, he asked, "Did I hear children earlier? And if I may ask, what is your involvement with Prince Conn?"

Ivy paused before a stained-glass window. "Yes, there are children in the garden."

He found it odd she would profess the presence of the children, but nothing about herself. A blush stained her cheeks, and he realized he was staring at her. There was something different about the diminutive female. Her blonde hair was cropped short and there was an aura about her unlike any other Fae. *Not only Fae, but human!*

Liam staggered back, his back slamming into the wall. "You're *human*. Present day earth?" He surveyed the multi-colored pendant hanging around her neck filled with tears of a Fae, and all the pieces fell into place.

As if reading his thoughts, she acknowledged, "Yes, I *was* human. However, I now have the blood of the Fae within my veins. I am Conn's wife." She clasped the pendant. "This was from Conn."

The declaration was like a blow to his body, and Liam knelt on one knee. "*Princess* Ivy, I presume." He fisted his hand over his heart in reverence to her royalty status.

She placed her hand on his shoulder. "Please, just Ivy. And before you pass judgment on Conn, hear the story of his quest."

Liam glanced up into her eyes. "Can you not share it with me?"

"Only that he gave me his blood to save my life. But there were strings attached. And yes, we love each other very much. You must ask for the full account from him." She bit her lip. "Please get up."

Liam stood. Had the months turned into years? Though he was unaware of how much time passed in his seclusion, he had to ask, "Are the children yours?"

Ivy placed her hand in the crook of his arm, and the tension eased from Liam's body. "One is. Her name is Sorcha."

Liam sensed there was more Ivy wanted to say, but she remained silent as they continued along the corridor. She led him into Conn's inner chamber. "I will fetch you something to eat and drink. It is much quieter here than in the main chamber. The children can get loud with their antics."

"I am quite fond of children," he confessed and moved to an arched window. He could make out one of small girls chasing butterflies across the lush landscape, and he smiled. Another one sat content on the ground, waving her chubby hands in the air. "Which one is Sorcha?"

"The blonde-hair lass sitting down and observing."

He was going to inquire about the other one with dark locks, when a woman strolled across the garden. She was a vision, radiant and...something else. He placed his hands on the glass panes. "By the hounds, is she a human, too?"

"I'll be right back," replied Ivy slowly.

He turned abruptly. "Stay...princess."

A look of mischief shone in her eyes. "I suppose since you've already guessed, she is human, and the little girl flitting about with the butterflies is her daughter."

His mind reeled, and he collapsed onto the window bench. "The father?"

"Your brother, Rory," she responded and darted out of the chamber.

Liam raked a shaky hand through his hair. "No wonder there is a division in the realm. I would never have dreamed that two Fenian Warriors would go mad."

Chapter Twenty-Four

"Abela transformed my life into a rainbow of mosaic colors. If she dies, I will follow into the abyss."
~Chronicles of Liam MacGregor

His thoughts were scattered, and indecision battled inside Liam as he steadily made his way out of Conn's chamber and into the garden. Anger, betrayal, jubilation, and many more emotions clouded him as he stood at the entrance and gazed out at the scene below. Conn's secular garden retreat was always known to be vast, but Liam sensed the prince had expanded since he last visited a hundred years ago.

Approaching the woman slowly, he marveled at her beauty and more. There was an earthy quality about her, and he smiled. "My brother has married well," he whispered.

An ache settled inside his heart, and he longed to speak more with Rory. Soon, he would return to his prison, and he yearned to hear about his journey in finding love.

He clasped his hands behind his back. "Greetings."

The woman turned abruptly. She lifted her chin as if studying him.

"I am Liam MacGregor, Rory's brother."

"Aye, I ken who ye are," she responded with a smile and pointed to his arm. "I noted your armband, similar to Rory's."

Unclasping his hand, Liam touched the silver family relic. "I was unaware my brother had found his. He claimed to have lost it many years ago."

"Have ye not seen him?"

"Yes, but he was wearing clothing suitable for the century we were in. Furthermore, we had little time to discuss recent events." Liam stepped forward and bowed slightly. "Welcome to the family, Lady…"

She laughed. "Sweet Goddess! Where are my manners? I am Erina."

Liam took a hold of her hand and placed a kiss along her knuckles. "It is an honor. From what part of Scotland do you come from?"

"The village of Lindane," she responded, brushing a strand of hair away from her face.

"Ahh…Loch Etive on the west coast. I know the area well from my travels there."

"Aye," she beamed. "Rory has shared his stories with me."

The wee lass toddled over to her mother and hid among the folds of her gossamer gown. Her raven hair was similar to Rory's, and he marveled at how the butterflies hovered around her like a crown of jewels.

Liam knelt on one knee in front of her. "What is your name, child?"

She giggled. Reaching outward with her hand, she placed it center to his chest. *Angelica*

He blinked in fascination. "What a beautiful name." Liam traced a path across her cheek with his finger. "A rare gift to speak so young within a Fae's mind. I am your uncle."

She let out another burst of laughter and glanced

upward at her mother.

A few quiet moments passed before Erina nodded. "Yes, ye may go play with Sorcha. But please, no more flowers. I believe she has plenty around her."

Liam watched as the lass skipped away from her mother. "She possesses a unique gift."

"One of many," affirmed Erina. "She is to be the next Master Apothecary."

He brushed a hand down the back of his neck. "Part Fae *and* human. Our realm is indeed changing."

"So Rory has explained. Even Sorcha is special."

"Do tell," he drawled, glancing at the wee Fae who resembled Conn.

"She will become the next High Seer, but only after her mother, Ivy."

Liam snapped his attention to the woman and stared at her in disbelief. "Forgive my insensitive nature, but you're both *human*. How can this be?"

Erina shrugged. "I was raised by my grandmother, whom ye ken as Aelish." She gently touched his arm. "Mayhap, the Goddess has determined to set both Fae and human on a path joined together. Who are we to question the journey?"

"Or outcome," added Liam, stunned by the declaration that Aelish had raised her. *This is why the kingdom is divided. Fae allowing humans to enter the realm and marry would certainly cause friction.*

"There you are," stated Ivy, bringing forth a tray with food and drink onto the terrace. After setting it down, she made her way toward them. "I know you said you didn't want anything, but you must be exhausted, and I would never forgive myself for not being a proper hostess to one of Conn's dearest friends."

"Seriously?" Liam barked out in laughter, the sound foreign to him. "I deem he has severed our friendship after finding out Abela is now my wife."

Both women gaped at him.

Ivy was the first to recover her wits. "I think I need a dram of something more potent than the honeyed lemonade I brought." She hurried back up the steps and disappeared inside.

"Aye, I will take one, too," mumbled Erina.

"Make that three!" shouted Liam.

Ivy returned carrying a bottle under her arm and three glasses. Handing the bottle to Liam, she gave a glass to Erina and held onto the other two. "This calls for a celebration, and I don't think Conn will mind, regardless of how he might feel about his sister marrying you."

Liam snorted and held the bottle outward, studying the label. "Do you realize how old this rare bottle of whisky is, Princess Ivy? I appreciate the gesture, but will not partake."

She frowned and tapped her foot in irritation. "Yes, I do. It comes from my home town of Glennamore in Ireland. It was found along with several rare bottles of wine in the ruins of Castle Lintel. In addition, I have asked that you call me Ivy. It's beyond maddening that the rest of the kingdom bows or curtsies each time I wander away from the palace. I realize I am the princess of the realm, but among friends, I'd like to be just *Ivy*." She held the glasses outward. "Would you be so kind as to do the honors?"

Liam acknowledged her with a kiss on the cheek. "Since you insist." Retrieving his dirk from his belt, he removed the wax from the bottle. "Before I leave, you must share how you brought the great Conn MacRoich to the marriage pact."

Ivy gestured outward with her hand. "Simple. We fell in love."

Letting out a sigh, he poured a small amount of the amber liquid into all three glasses and then placed the bottle on the marble ledge. *Love.* How peculiar all three of them found the women they were destined to spend the rest of their lives with. Nonetheless, his was a somber contradiction. Liam's relationship with Abela was forbidden, and her life now in grave danger.

Ivy handed him his glass, snapping him out of his grim thoughts.

"Let me be the first to congratulate you on your marriage to the priestess," said Ivy.

"Aye," agreed, Erina. "May it be a blessed union."

How he yearned for the woman's blessing to come true. Tossing back the whisky, he savored its intense peaty flavor. The heat seared a path throughout his body, but Liam's mind battled against the inevitable, and a chill swept over him.

The possibility of a future without his beloved Abela.

"Aelish is one of our strongest healers," reassured Ivy, smiling at him.

He fingered the rim of the glass. "I pray we are not too late." He laughed bitterly. "I even used her blood to help transport us through the stones and the Veil of Ages. I suppose it did not help her current health situation."

Ivy glanced at Erina and then returned her attention to him. "We are both learning the lore of the Fae realm.

Yet, we are not privy to the knowledge of the Brotherhood."

"Even the future seer must have some wisdom about the Fenian Warriors," he professed dryly.

"Perhaps I have some insight into the warriors, but not about your laws."

"Regardless, Abela is fading from this world as we speak." Liam swept his gaze over the bucolic garden, trying to remain positive.

"If I may make a suggestion, I have prepared a room next to Abela's, so you'll be able to hear any news first."

Liam nodded slowly. "Yes, I would like to wait there. Thank you both for your warm welcome and for sharing how you came into *our* world." He placed his glass on the ledge and gestured for Ivy to move forward.

****

Liam stared at the starlight reflecting through the crystal ceiling. Unable to quiet his mind, he tried reaching out to Abela while resting on the divan. Not even a thread of acknowledgment made it back to him and worry infused his spirit. He placed his hands beneath his head and continued to survey the stars. How his beloved enjoyed sharing stories of all the dragons in the sky on their first days of courting. She knew all the ancient guardians' names, and she often teased him on his fading recollection.

"Can you not tell me at least ten names?" she asked, poking his toe with her foot.

Liam leaned against the tree. "Why should I? Once they departed from our realm, they were known as the Guardians or Great Dragons."

She took a step back and sadness swept over her delicate features. "You dishonor them by forgetting."

He shook his head solemnly. "Their names are emblazed on my soul—forever. I have no need to recite them out loud. Yet, I am truly amazed at your knowledge." Liam would never divulge his lack of memory to her. The names would always be within his spirit, but not mind.

Abela dipped a curtsy. "Why thank you for the compliment." She gave him one of her alluring smiles and strolled along the bank of the river.

"Where are you going?" he asked, pushing away from the tree.

Lifting her hand up to the night sky, she responded, "To teach you at least ten of the names and where they are located in the cosmos. It will be your lesson for tonight."

"Ahh...a challenge." He approached and walked alongside her. "Will there be a reward for my test?"

"Of course," she beamed. "I shall grant you one kiss."

Liam reached for her hand, bringing them both to a halt. "Only one? Are there not ten names?"

"We...well...yes. But what—"

He drew her near him and leaned close to her ear. "For each name I can recite, I will demand a kiss. Therefore, if I can recall ten, I shall take that many kisses."

Abela's mouth opened on a sigh. "Let the test begin," she whispered.

Liam rubbed a hand over his brow at the long-forgotten memory. "I can still remember their names, *mo ghrá.*" He sat and regarded all the ancient guardians, some gazing back down at him.

A crash resounded outside the chamber, and Liam jumped up from the divan. As he was about to exit the room, the door exploded into shards of wood. Swiftly withdrawing his sword, he started to move forward and then froze.

Liam dropped to one knee and placed his blade on the ground. "King Ansgar."

"I should kill you now!" bellowed the king, his eyes flashing with outrage.

"I believe the prince stated the same."

"Liam MacGregor, I charge you back to your prison to await your trial. Death will come soon thereafter. Guards remove his sword and escort this man to the Room of Reflection."

Standing, Liam stared into the face of fury. He dared not speak another word, but it was within his rights. "Will you not hear my account?"

"When my daughter is dying in the next chamber? I think not! You have brought dishonor to the Brotherhood and your family."

Liam staggered from the intensity of the king's words. Yet he was only honor-bound to one in his heart. Turmoil fought with duty to the Fae king. Liam had no more to lose. He only prayed the king would not strike him dead with what he was about to pronounce. "I would appreciate if I am alerted of Abela's condition."

"How dare you!" The king glared at him with disdain. "She is a priestess!"

"And my wife."

The blow of the king's power lifted Liam, and he struggled for air. Lights flashed before his eyes. The king's wrath swirled in a tempest around him, and the pressure built within his mind and body.

"I *forbid* you to utter her name. Furthermore, all power as a Fenian Warrior has been stripped from you," uttered King Ansgar with deadly calm. He released his powerful hold and Liam collapsed to the floor.

"Remove this Fae to his prison," demanded the king as he stormed away.

Liam fought for air as two of the guards approached. They gave him no time to stand, before whisking him away.

Once inside the Room of Reflection, they tossed him onto the floor and slammed the door. Liam sat and rubbed at his eyes vigorously, taking in deep calming breaths. Weakened from being stripped of his Fenian powers, he remained seated on the floor of his prison. As Liam glanced around his crystal enclosure, he sought out the corner where Abela had first approached him. His heart constricted, longing to see her once again step through the shadows.

He gazed upward at the night sky.

"My beloved, my life. Do not cross over to *Tir na Og*. Remember our love and fight. You are my warrior, my princess, *my wife*. There is no purpose without you. Do not leave me to a future that does not have you by my side."

Placing his palms on the ground on either side of his body, Liam closed his eyes. "Do not forget your daughter, Mother Danu. Keep her from passing over. If she goes into the Summerland, your warrior shall follow."

Chapter Twenty-Five

"During great times of sorrow in my life after Liam entered the Brotherhood, I sought out the music of the butterflies."

~*Diary of Princess Abela*

Why did walking this path take forever to reach the golden sunlight? Abela grew weary with each step forward. She paused on her journey and dug her toes into the moss-covered ground. The dew tickled her feet, and she laughed. Her voice reminded her of tinkling bells, so she laughed again. Cupping a hand over her mouth to squelch the gaiety, she glanced around and noted a rose-quartz bench.

A brief respite on her journey was what she required. Crossing the path dotted with flower petals, she wandered over to the beautifully carved bench and sat down. Her hand caressed the Celtic knots on the wood as she tried to recall where she had witnessed seeing them before. Were they adorned on a wall? Or a person? Her recollection was vague. Fog surrounded her memory, and she tapped her fingers to her temple to jog some fragmented image. It was a futile endeavor, doing nothing to restore what refused to be awakened within her mind.

Abela tucked her feet under her on the bench, and watched the branches of the trees sway with the warm gentle breeze. Roses, lilacs, and honeysuckle fought for space between the massive oak trees, and she marveled at their beauty. Inhaling deeply, she nearly swooned from their heady floral aroma, even as it soothed and caressed her mind.

The pulsing golden light beckoned her once again. She knew there was something magical beyond the radiance, but she was not ready to continue onward. This place was one of beauty. Were there others? She looked around, trying to catch a glimpse of another Fae, bird, or animal. Yet, none announced themselves.

"Perchance this is my own realm and path," she whispered.

Her voice was one filled with melody, and she pondered why it sounded unique here.

She cast her sight again to the carved etchings in the bench. Taking her finger, she traced the pattern in a continuous motion. However, the effort tired her quickly, and her head pounded from the struggle to recall anything.

A whisper of words floated to her, and Abela snapped her head up, searching in all directions. Removing herself from the bench, she studied the landscape in the opposite direction of the golden light. Nothing but shadows greeted her.

"Is someone there?" She stood on tiptoe, trying to discern any images.

She blew out a frustrated sigh. There was nothing but emptiness. She heard the words again, and this time they wove a thread of familiarity inside her mind. "I am here. Can you not speak more clearly? I am having trouble hearing your words."

Biting her lip, she almost started toward the bleak

abyss until pain seared into her body. Fear halted her progress, and she hugged her arms around her body. She had no wish to return to the agonizing assault she had suffered earlier. This is why she left the darkness of pain and took to the path of radiance.

"I cannot go back." Placing her hands over her ears, she whimpered. "Please stop speaking to me. I must find peace and you won't permit me to go. There is so much pain and suffering."

Tears smarted her eyes, and Abela turned toward the warmth of the light. The darkness was not a part of her future. The glowing path of bliss urged her forward. But with each step, the tears began to flow down her cheeks, and Abela was helpless to control them. Instead of happiness, sorrow engulfed her.

Nevertheless, she had sought this journey, and she refused to turn back. Peace from pain lured her to its warm embrace of light. If only she felt comforted by the thought.

When she finally approached the golden archway, shimmering lights danced all around the entrance. Once again, the words of someone speaking to her floated on a breeze, and she took a hesitant step back. A sliver of light teased her along the path.

"Am I ready to enter? Is this *Tir na Og*, the land of forever?"

Abela dropped to the ground, confused and wary. There was something she forgot to do from long ago. It niggled in the back recess of her mind. Her hands trembled as she placed them on the lush grass. Instinctively, she reached out with her thoughts to another she had long forgotten.

"Forgive me, Mother Danu."

"For what, my child?"

Startled, Abela drew back her hands. "You can hear me," she uttered on a choked sob.

"I have always heard you, sweet daughter."

Abela rubbed a hand over her brow. "I sense I have been trying to speak with you, but without any success."

"Your guilt has shut me out, daughter."

She tucked her legs under her. "Guilt? What did I do to cause such a grievance?"

"Touch the strand of light, daughter."

Abela lifted her hand. "I am scared."

"Truth, beauty, and love should never be feared. You saw the beauty in love, but feared in speaking your heart's truth to me. That is where your fear has taken root. That is where the wall was built with guilt around your heart, mind, and spirit. You kept me out, unable to hear my words. If you refuse to touch the light, you have chosen poorly and will walk alone."

"But I am alone."

"I am here within the light and speaking to you."

"If I know the truth, will I return to the darkness?"

"The pathway is always a choice in directions. Light cannot exist without the dark. The sun cannot rise without the moon slipping into the shadows. Each a reminder of the other in the cosmos."

Stretching her fingers toward the sliver of light, Abela watched the radiance travel upward through her arm and pierced into her heart with blazing heat. She gasped, but kept her hand within the glow. Images swirled in a kaleidoscope of various colors inside her mind, some foreign to her, and others significant.

When one emerged, steady and strong, her lips

trembled. *"Liam."* Abela lowered her head. "I was afraid to tell you, Mother Danu, for fear you would not be happy or allow me to leave the temple."

"Love is a precious gem, daughter. All you had to do was ask me. Instead of tears of happiness for you, I wept in sorrow."

****

Liam paced within his prison, endeavoring to remain calm. The long night slipped silently away and by dawn, there still remained no word on Abela's condition. Not one soul had visited him, and his worry increased with each passing hour. When the sun reached its zenith in the sky, he shouted his frustration and slammed the wall with his fists.

Hours later, he penned a missive. In it, he gave instructions to his brother, Rory, if she should live and he was sentenced to death. He gave no care about his own existence, save hers. His predicament was already doomed. In addition, he stated that the documents he had procured from King MacAlpin and Angus MacKay remained in Conn's chambers. Regardless, without the third one from Peter O'Malley, the king would never agree to hearing a plea. Therefore, he asked if Rory could return the two documents to their owners.

He halted and laughed bitterly. "You certainly would not consider listening to me now that you know about your daughter and me."

The walls became too confining as he observed the last rays of sunlight slipping into darkness. Liam stormed back to his desk. Bracing his hands on the wood, he tried to calm his breathing. How could he endure another day without any information on his beloved? He placed the heel of his palm over his heart, trying to ease the ache.

"Give me any news," he pleaded. "Even from you, Mother Danu."

He shook his head in irritation. "All I did was love her."

Taking a seat once again at his desk, he pulled forth another piece of parchment and quill. Liam had to remain steadfast in his belief Abela would survive. When she did recover, he had to reassure her to keep moving forward with her life. His hand shook as he formed the words on the sheet.

~My beloved wife,

Sadly, I have come to the crossroads once again in my life where I am without you. Regardless of our brief time together as husband and wife, our love will last until the last star fades from the cosmos. I have loved you since I drew your breath into my body after our first kiss. When I entered the Brotherhood, I hardened my heart and locked away our memories from the beginning. However, I was the fool. Time could not erase what you etched upon my soul. You have brought light into my life, and when I take my last breath, your name shall be on my lips. Keep my love wrapped around you during the dark days of despair you shall feel after I am gone.

Continue on your path, mo ghrá. Do not forget joy, laughter, knowledge, or love. I shall await you at the gates of Tir na Og.

Yours forever, heart to soul,

Liam~

Blowing a kiss over the words to bind their meaning, he reached for an envelope and tucked the parchment inside. Scribbling her name on the outside, he tucked it with the others for his brother.

The silence and solitude were chains around his heart, and Liam stood. Crossing the room, he went to the place Abela had first entered and sat down on the cold floor. There was nothing left for him to do. He hugged his knees to his chest and lowered his head. No comfort would he seek. No food or drink would he partake. No sleep would he obtain.

As Liam fought the tide of emotions, a stirring of another Fae entered his prison, and he lifted his head.

Rory stood leaning against the crystal wall. A look of utter misery was carved across his features.

"Tell me," ordered Liam in a low voice.

"I am sorry."

Liam stood abruptly and clenched his fists. "Tell me!"

His brother pushed away from the wall. "King Ansgar removed Abela from Conn's chambers and took her to the temple. The priestesses placed her in the cavern that leads to—"

"*Tir na Og*." Liam staggered. His heart pounded inside his chest, and the room blurred. "No, *no*!"

"I am sorry, brother."

He pointed a warning finger at Rory. "Don't you dare say the word."

"Abela is dead."

Liam's wave of despair waxed so deep, his anguished soul cried out for death and release. Letting out a guttural cry of sorrow, he ran to his desk, lifted it high, and tossed it across the room. It smashed in two, leaving a mess of strewn paperwork littered across the floor. His tormented soul could do nothing, as he continued to pitch anything in his path outward.

"She was mine!" he roared. "My *death* was ordained, not hers!"

Waves of pain coursed throughout his body, unable to fathom his beloved was gone. When he had hurled everything onto the floor, he ripped his tunic free from his body. He refused to utter the word of her demise.

His steps faltered as he went to the center of his prison and gazed upward, tears streaming down his face. His grief was akin to a blade through his heart, and he longed to rip it free from his chest.

Lifting his hands, he poured out his emotions. "Abela, do not enter the boat to *Tir na Og*. Do you hear me? I order you to stay at the gates! Return to me. Return to love." He wiped a hand over his face. "You have only begun to live. Choose life!"

Liam fisted his hands at his side, keeping his back to his brother. "Let me out of the chamber."

"You know I cannot."

He turned abruptly. "I have to see her. She is not listening to me in here."

Rory frowned in obvious confusion. "Liam…she is *gone*."

Liam crossed the room in two strides and yanked on Rory's tunic, shaking him. "Unless I see it for my own eyes, I *refuse* to believe your words."

His brother placed a firm hand on his shoulder. "Your pain is clouding you to the truth."

"Have you seen her? How do you know?" snapped Liam, shirking free from his hold. He found it difficult to draw in any breath, and he staggered back.

"The news comes from Conn through the king," answered Rory in a somber tone.

"But you must understand why I must see her," he

pleaded. What if it was Erina?"

Rory's eyes flashed in anger. "Since I have yet to give you my account, be careful the words you spout. I have witnessed the *death* of my wife. The first time was in 1605 when she was burnt at the stake. I can still recall the stench of her burning flesh."

His brother's declaration was like a blow to his body, and Liam's shoulders sagged with the weight of everything. "Forgive me," he whispered and trudged to the other side of the room. Slumping down against the crystal wall, he leveled his arms on his bent knees.

Rory joined him on the other side. "I first met Erina on a mission and fell in love. I was unable to save her from death the first time. When I returned to the Brotherhood, I kept all knowledge of what had occurred inside me, locked away." He let out a sigh and continued, "During my time in my Room of Reflection, I began to dream."

"We are unable to dream," countered Liam.

"Yes, but my soul was so tortured by her death that being in solitude exposed the veil of reality. I came close to entering the Realm of Sorrows."

Liam glanced in horror at his brother. "It is a wonder you are here today."

"Death was my path, until Conn sent me back to close the wounds left open by her death."

"Bastard!"

Rory lifted his hand to halt any further comments. "My sentiments at the time as well. Nevertheless, his plan succeeded with the help of an alternate element in the timeline that neither he nor myself had any knowledge of. In addition, Conn has had to travel his own quest. His was arduous, too."

"So I am the last," muttered Liam. He gazed upward.

"I've often pondered why the council took so long after Aidan's death to bring you to trial. Why did they choose now, especially after the battle we fought with the Dragon Knights? You should have been brought before the members long ago."

Liam lowered his head. "I can only surmise they had no idea what to do with me, or they waited for the opportunity to skewer three great Fenian Warriors at once. After Aileen released Aidan's ashes, along with her mother's in Loch Ness, I waited for a summons from the council. There was none." He sighed. "Perhaps if they had done so immediately, Ab...*the princess* would still be alive."

His brother nudged him. "I deem Abela would have attempted the rescue, regardless of the timing of your trial. She truly loved you, Liam. I have some other information to impart. Your trial is in the morning."

Closing his eyes, he muttered, "Finally." Exhaustion settled over Liam with the news. "Tell me how you overcame the shadows and rescued Erina."

In accordance of his brother's request, Rory spent the next hour giving him a detailed account of everything that had occurred. From almost losing Erina to the stake again, the birth of their daughter without his knowledge, and his quest to find himself on a walking journey in the Fae kingdom that led him to their parents' home.

Liam glanced sideways at his brother. "I am happy for you."

"I will fight for you at the council, along with all the Brotherhood," Rory avowed.

He arched a brow skeptically. "Even our prince?"

Rory sneered. "We have a traitor within and *he* will be exposed. Only Conn and Taran know his name."

Nodding slowly, Liam knew his time was ending. It no longer mattered to him. The others in the Brotherhood would seek vengeance for him. "Grant me a favor."

Standing, Rory asked, "If it is within my power."

"Use my sword to carve out the heart of the traitor."

"Done." In a flash of light, his brother vanished.

The cold blade of pain seared into his heart again, leaving Liam without breath and he lowered his head, letting the tears fall freely. *Wait for me at the gates, Abela. We shall both travel on the boat to Tir na Og. I am coming soon.*

Chapter Twenty-Six

"Of all the lessons in my life, Abela's gift of love was the most valuable."
                              ~Chronicles of Liam MacGregor

As he waited by the gilded doors leading into the chambers of the council, Liam brushed his fingers along the etchings on his armband. Words from long ago echoed within his mind. His father had spoken them to Liam and Rory before he presented the family heirlooms—one for each of them.

"Courage, honor, strength, protector, warrior, truth." They were carved by the ancient warriors on Taralyn. They were your ancestors. Wear them proudly as a sign of whom you each stand for in the realm.

"Forgive me father," uttered Liam softly, casting his gaze to where his brother stood speaking with another Fenian Warrior.

Rory paused and looked at him. After giving the warrior a curt nod, he crossed to Liam's side. "We are waiting for several other warriors to join us."

Liam shifted his stance, uneasy to learn there were others attending. "I am not comfortable with this. It is my trial, not theirs."

"They are coming as a sign of solidarity. You are not alone."

His brother was wrong. He was alone without

Abela in his life. "I have another request."

"Remove you from this place?"

Liam noticed a smile tugging on the corners of his brother's mouth. "I thought I was the humorous one in the family."

His brother nudged him. "Your character flaws have rubbed off on me." Then in a more somber tone added, "What is it you want me to do?"

Pointing to his armband, he replied, "Before I depart from this realm, remove my armband. You should have it in your possession after I die."

Rory's jaw clenched, and he touched his own. "I have no intention of seeing to your death. Nevertheless, if the time presents itself, I will be honored to retrieve the family relic."

"Thank you."

Ronan and Taran appeared, steadily making their way toward them.

"We shall stand by your side during your trial," professed Ronan. "The other Fenian Warriors are positioned around the corridors."

Liam shifted his stance. "I am honored, but there is no need."

"We can think of no other place we'd rather be than here."

"Agreed," affirmed Taran, placing a hand on Liam's shoulder. "The Brotherhood stands as a united front per Prince Conn's orders. Though none of us had to be ordered."

"Even with his sister's death?" Liam struggled for words, his grief too raw to speak her name.

Taran nodded slowly. "We all grieve, but this trial is insanity, given what has recently happened."

Before Liam could ask who the traitor was, the doors to the chambers opened. He straightened and glanced at those gathered. Taking a fist to his chest, he looked at each of his fellow warriors. "It has been an honor."

After each warrior gave him a salute, Liam entered. Walking across the expanse of the room, he stood directly in front of the council members. He clasped his hands behind his back, and swept his gaze to each Fae member. He noted the cool regard from some. Yet, others gave him a brief nod of acknowledgment.

Seneca stood. "This is not a trial for spectators. You are not welcome here at these proceedings."

Rory stepped forward. "We are here upon the request of Prince Conn's orders."

"The Prince has no authority here," she argued.

"You are correct, Lady Seneca." Another Fae emerged in a flash of light. "Yet, this one order you cannot rescind. It comes from King Ansgar, as well."

"Is there a reason why you are here giving me this news, Loran, and not the king?"

Loran slowly made his way toward Liam's side. "As you are aware, the king and queen are in mourning over the death of their daughter, Princess Abela."

Seneca sighed. "As is the entire kingdom. Are you here as counsel to the warrior?"

"No. I am here in *support* of his actions."

An audible gasp came forth from some of the members, and Seneca pursed her lips in obvious disapproval. "Noted, *Elder* Loran."

Liam smiled at his friend. "Thank you," he whispered.

"As I was not permitted at the trial of my friend,

Aidan, I vowed to be at yours."

Snapping her fingers, a golden leaflet appeared within Seneca's hand. "Fenian Warrior, Liam MacGregor, you are aware of the reason for this trial?"

Did she attempt to mock him? "Yes. But I request you state the full violation and then announce judgment."

Shock flitted briefly in her eyes, but she quickly composed herself. "You have no desire to state for the council why you did the crime?"

"I believe I was just in doing so and have no cause to profess for the members why I took a great noble Fenian Warrior—"

"Aidan Kerrigan was stripped of his status and immortality," interrupted Seneca tersely.

Ignoring her outburst, Liam continued, "As I was saying, a Fenian Warrior through the Veil of Ages to assist his daughter. The warrior had been stripped of his powers, but he was one of us. I see no crime in what I did."

"You warriors always twist the laws to meet your specific deeds," snapped Tulare.

"I concur," stated council member, Bonee. "However, I am willing to hear his reasons."

Tulare pointed a finger at Liam, but kept his gaze on the other members. "Why must they be above the laws? His death should have been swift after we were alerted of his crime."

Bonee settled back in his chair. "In this, I disagree. Does not our own law dictate that each Fae has a right to give their full account?"

Tulare glared at Liam. "The Fae refuses to give his account." He darted a glance at Seneca. "Pronounce his judgment and let us rid ourselves of this travesty."

"Travesty?" echoed Liam and unclasped his hands. "What you did to Aidan Kerrigan was a *travesty*." He pounded his chest. "He was my friend, mentor, and one of the greatest Fae warriors of our kingdom. He was banished from his own world, a world he had protected, loved, and treasured for a millennium."

"He impregnated a human," spat out Tulare in disgust.

"Enough!" Seneca ordered, glaring at the Fae. "You have gone too far, Tulare. Might I remind you that we now have humans living here in the realm?"

Tulare remained silent, but he cast daggers at Liam.

She returned her attention to Liam. "Regardless of what has occurred, I can see no other action for what is just by the rules in our kingdom. You disregarded a primary law within the Brotherhood. If you refuse to give your account, I am hereby ordered—"

The gilded doors opened, and the leaflet Seneca was holding fluttered onto the table. Liam glanced over his shoulder at the intrusion.

Queen Nuala entered, followed by Conn. Liam noted her poise, her set of chin, so like Abela's.

He immediately knelt on one knee. How could he ever cast his sight on the mother of his beloved? His heart pounded erratically, and he fought the wave of sorrow and shame covering him. In her darkest moment over the loss of her daughter, she came to set him free from the oath he had made so many moons ago.

She approached in front of him, placing a gentle hand on his shoulder. "Rise, my warrior."

He shook, trying to compose his emotions. "I am

not worthy."

"Do not ask me to beg or drop down in front of you, Liam MacGregor."

Inhaling deeply, he exhaled slowly and stood. Great sorrow reflected within her eyes. He had no words to give her at the moment. Instead, he dipped his head. "My queen."

"I release you from your oath, my warrior."

Liam nodded slowly, understanding the meaning of her statement.

Queen Nuala turned her attention to the council, who had all now stood. "It is time for the truth to be revealed."

"I am confused by your...*presence*," stammered Seneca.

The queen clasped her hands in front of her. "It is simple. Liam MacGregor could not account for his reasoning, since he swore an oath of silence to me."

"Continue, please."

"When my brother, Aidan, approached me one day many eons ago—"

"He was banished from the kingdom! Who brought him here?" demanded Tulare, glaring at everyone.

"I did," acknowledged Liam. "Please let *our* queen continue with her account."

"Agreed," stated Seneca. "There will be no further outbursts from anyone while the queen is speaking."

Queen Nuala gave a brief smile. "My brother requested my approval to journey back in time through the Veil of Ages to find his daughter, Aileen. Since she was part Fae and not aware of her gifts, she had stepped through a portal at Arbroath Abbey and landed in the 13th century. Although this was her destiny, her father feared for her safety. As a mother *and* queen, I understood his emotions and logic. After hearing his appeal, I granted him passage with Fenian Warrior, Liam MacGregor. If all went according to plan, Aidan was duly prepared to return and profess his account. He was willing to forfeit his life in order to spare Liam's. However, their plan did not go well, and Aidan died as a result of his wounds in a battle. I am here to set the record in accordance and exonerate this Fenian Warrior."

"Is the king aware of your interference?" asked Tulare.

"Yes," responded the queen, coolly. "But the decision was mine."

Seneca retrieved the leaflet from the table. She stared at the council members. "I hereby amend the judgment on Fenian Warrior, Liam MacGregor. Are we all in agreement?"

All but one accepted her final decree. Tulare shook his head. "I cannot in good faith accept this account in order to remove the death sentence from this Fae. Only the king has the power to interfere with the Brotherhood and even so, it is limited." He gestured outward. "This is unacceptable."

Conn stepped forward. "Since Seneca is our leader of the council, she has the right to overturn your objection."

Tulare looked down in contempt at Conn. "This is a mockery of a trial. You have no right or any of the other warriors to be present. Again, you manipulate the laws for your purpose. I propose we disband the Brotherhood and create a new order."

A chill swept through the room, and Loran tugged

on Liam's tunic. "Step back," he ordered in a low voice.

Confused by the elder's tone, he whispered, "What is happening?" He noted the other warriors had gathered around Conn.

The queen stood regally in the center as Liam followed the elder to the side of the room. "You are without your powers," muttered Loran. "Remain by my side."

Stunned into silence, Liam watched the scene unfold before them.

Conn flexed his hands. "I, Prince Conn, *leader* of the Fenian Warriors, hereby order your dismissal from the Fae council. You will be escorted to the king's prison—"

"How dare you!" shrieked Tulare. "This is an outrage! You have no power here. Leave at once."

Seneca looked cautiously at the other members. "I am appalled at this demonstration of power within these elite chambers. Explain yourself, Prince Conn."

"Tulare, Royal house of Meeghan is under arrest for crimes against the kingdom."

"Liar!" His face was a mask of rage. "If you do not leave now, I will call upon the guards to remove you and these warriors from the chambers."

Seneca lifted her hand. "Hold your words, council member, Tulare."

Conn kept his gaze fixed on Seneca. "Tulare is charged with treason against the Fae people, the kingdom, and our king. He has conspired with the humans and an enemy from long ago—the Milesians. Tulare was instrumental in the kidnapping of Liam and Princess Abela. If not for him, she would still be alive."

Tulare brought forth a ball of glowing energy and flung it outward at Conn. The prince swiftly deflected the energy, crushing it within his hand. Many of the council members gasped in stunned horror and a few stumbled away from Tulare. The council guards stormed into the chambers, but Queen Nuala halted their progress with a warning flash of power.

"Your power is great, but mine is from the king. I am here with his full support." Conn snapped his fingers and a pair of crystal cuffs appeared. "I have procured these from Peter O'Malley, who was forthcoming in his account on how he acquired these cuffs after I presented him bound and gagged to his clan and brother. You might recognize them as the ones you used on Liam MacGregor."

Tulare shook his fist in the air, his eyes blazing with hatred.

Smacking the table with her fist, Seneca regarded the council member with disdain. "Does the prince speak the truth? Have you turned traitor against your own people?"

His lip curled in disgust. "Yes!"

"Why?" she demanded. "This is betrayal of the worst kind."

In a gesture of defiance, he ripped his regal robe in half, flinging it across the room. "I have no desire to live in a realm where humans have ingrained themselves within. The Fae lineage is now sullied with human blood. We were once a noble and proud people. Now look at us!" He leveled a finger at Conn. "It is your father's fault for allowing your human female to live. The king has grown weak, allowing you and the other warriors to have free reign over this realm and the mortal world. You might be surprised there are those in the Milesian world who have argued against an alliance. You think to have your revenge, but this will not end with me."

"The Fae people are not above or below the other kingdoms. The seers have seen another path in the future. We cannot permit those who thwart our journey with evil, discrimination, and hatred to live here, regardless if they are human, Fae, *or* Milesian." Conn took a step forward. "And the King of the Milesians agrees."

"You know *nothing* about him," Tulare snarled, spittle flying everywhere.

"And you are the fool. He is meeting with *our* king as we debate this issue here."

The blood visibly drained from Tulare's face, and he staggered back. "No, no," he mumbled.

Liam started forward, but Loran firmly held him back. His hands clenched and unclenched, aching to wrap them around the traitorous Fae's neck. Fury swirled in a tempest around him, and he struggled to control his emotions. *I should rip your heart from your chest and let you watch as I turn it into ashes.* "Allow *me* to bind him," he suggested in a hoarse voice.

Conn beckoned him forward with a wave of his hand. After Liam approached by his side, Conn handed him the cuffs. Deep sadness reflected in his eyes. "For Abela," he whispered.

He gave him a curt nod and made his way slowly to Tulare.

The Fae thrust his hands outward at Liam in surrender. "I suppose you take great delight in subjecting me to this dishonor in front of my peers."

"On the contrary, I find this entire affair distasteful. You have brought dishonor upon yourself, Tulare." Liam snapped the cuffs in place. "You are not worthy to be among our people."

A vein throbbed at his temple, but Tulare remained silent. Conn gestured to the other Fenian warriors. "Escort him to the King's prison and alert the guards there that our mission has been fulfilled."

Taran and Ronan crossed the room. Each took a stance on either side of Tulare and in a shard of light vanished from the chambers. Some of the council members slumped into their chairs and others remained standing, speaking in hushed tones.

Seneca made her way to the queen. Bowing before her, she said, "I mourn with you in the loss of the princess."

"Thank you," responded the queen softly and walked to her son. She gave him a weak smile and vanished in a soft blur of lights.

Rory wandered to Liam's side. "You kept your vow, even if it meant your death."

Liam sighed heavily. "Aidan fully intended to present himself at my trial, along with the queen. When he died, I was bound by my honor to her to remain silent. I never knew the conversation she had with Aidan, or how he persuaded her to go along with his plan. She made me swear not to divulge anything before Aidan and I departed."

Chuckling softly, Rory replied, "It's simple. *Family*. Aidan was her brother—a bond more powerful than royalty. I would have done the same for you, as well."

Liam shrugged. "I suppose, but the royal family is

honor-bound by their own set of rules and edicts."

"Did Abela know?"

"No." Liam glanced at Conn. "Will he ever forgive me?"

"He has only mentioned attaining your freedom. There has been no reference of Abela from him."

Liam returned his attention to his brother. "I have no desire to return to the Brotherhood."

"Your grief is raw, Brother. Take some time to heal."

Despite Rory's words, Liam had no intention of ever stepping back inside the Brotherhood. His life was finished there. His future bleak.

His beloved dead.

Chapter Twenty-Seven

"I listened for the call of the phoenix, but grew disillusioned and lost. Therefore, I flew up to the clouds and drifted away from the anguish."

~Diary of Princess Abela

Peaceful, serene, bucolic. Rory's home was all those and more. His brother deserved his happiness. He had a loving, beautiful wife, and a cherished daughter. Laughter floated on the early spring breeze, and Liam found himself smiling. Angelica was a treasured gem. She danced, played, and enchanted anyone she encountered.

And yet, everything here reminded him of what he would never possess.

Liam swirled the wine in his cup, gazing into the dark liquid as if there was some great message of importance for him. For two days, he had fought grief and despair. They were now his constant companions, and he cloaked himself in misery. Downing the wine in one gulp, he wiped his mouth with the back of his hand.

Though his trial was over, Liam refused the summons to return to the Brotherhood and take his place in a new position as an elite warrior under the command of Prince Conn. In truth, he found it difficult to speak to the Fae. Conn was reserved in his comments after the trial, and Liam took it as a sign of his own grief over the death of his sister.

Liam pinched the bridge of his nose. Fatigue had settled within and he welcomed the wine's elixir in dulling his senses. He picked up the bottle, holding it up to the sunlight and squinted. "Empty," he muttered.

"You cannot drink away your sorrows," pronounced Rory, joining him on the ground.

Snorting, Liam tossed the bottle aside. "Advice from one who almost entered the Realm of Sorrows?" He snapped his fingers and a fresh bottle appeared. "I think not."

"Are you drunk?"

Liam cast his brother a suspicious look. "If I am, are you going to give me a lecture?"

"Aye, most assuredly."

Ignoring his brother, Liam opened the bottle and guzzled deeply. Afterward, he handed the bottle to Rory. "Either join me or leave."

Rory hesitated and then took the wine. Taking a sip, he held the bottle outward. "You've taken a bottle from the private stash of the council members? You do realize it's mixed with ambrosia from the Pleasure Gardens?"

Liam shrugged. "I figured it was within my rights. I have yet to be given a formal apology."

"Seneca has convened a meeting with the king. Until a new member has been chosen, she has requested Elder Loran to take the vacant position. In addition, he will oversee the new member. There shall be stricter rules within the order."

Waving a hand dismissively in the air, Liam spouted, "I say banish them all."

Rory took another sip of the wine. "No wonder

you're drunk. This drink is potent. Remember when we spent a week in the gardens, sipping ambrosia?"

"Among other pleasures, too." He sighed. "At the time I was trying to wipe a certain Fae minx from my blood."

"Why didn't you ever mention your attraction?"

Liam darted a glance at him. "Seriously? As I recall, you mentioned the story of how Conn took a fist to your jaw when you followed the princess one afternoon. I had no intention of spouting anything to *anyone*."

His brother chuckled and rubbed a hand over his chin. "Yes, but mine was lust. Yours, I believe was emotional."

"Years ago," muttered Liam, attempting to reach for the bottle of wine.

Rory held it away from him. "I think we're done with spirits *and* the past. Time to move forward."

"Leave me alone," he groaned and stood. The landscape blurred, and Liam scrubbed a hand over his face. "I believe it's time for me to leave."

"I agree." Rory stood and clamped a hand around his shoulders. "It is time for you to take a wee trip with me."

He eyed his brother warily. "I am not returning to the Brotherhood."

"We're not going there. When you are ready, you shall return."

"Never," countered Liam, attempting to free himself from Rory's grasp.

Rory gazed outward. "I have been overseeing the training of a certain young Dragon Knight."

"Jamie?"

"Aye. I am teaching him battle techniques and honing his powers. The fire dragon is strong within the lad. The time has come for him to further his studies." Rory glanced at him and tapped Liam on the head. "He requires a scholar."

"Me? What about Archie?"

Releasing his hold, Rory replied, "The Bard of the Fae has taught the young Dragon Knight as much as he is able. In truth, he should not be the one schooling the lad. You are a wise choice, Liam."

"It's too soon," he complained and moved away. There would be love and laughter in the home of Adam and Meggie MacFhearguis.

As if understanding his thoughts, Rory mentioned, "It would only be for a few days and then you can return home. Meet with the lad and discern what he requires in his mental learning. I understand you have yet to accept your Fenian powers. I can take you through the Veil until you've made a final decision, and arrangements can be made for you stay above without harm to your body."

Liam continued to watch his niece play as butterflies flitted in a dance of beauty around her. "When will…" He placed a hand over his heart in an effort to ease the pain. "When is the funeral procession?"

"They have left the ceremony to the priestesses in the temple. All deemed this would be for the best, since they still considered her a priestess. There will be no formal one within the kingdom."

Turning abruptly, he stared at his brother. "She should be *honored*, not hidden."

Rory nodded solemnly.

"When do we depart for Aonach Castle?" asked Liam.

"Tomorrow at dawn."

"Good." Liam strode past Rory, retrieving the bottle of wine as he made his way back to his own chambers. He required something to dull his senses further, especially during the long, bleak night hours when Abela's image haunted him.

****

Shielding his eyes from the intense glare of the morning sunlight, Liam surveyed the landscape around Aonach Castle. Peace had once again resided in this home of the Dragon Knights. The last time he visited was before the great battle to rid the world of the vile druid, Lachlan. It was a volatile time and required the Dragon Knights from the past—Meggie's brothers, and her husband, Adam, to help defeat the evil that was threatening the world. Liam, Conn, and Rory defied their own people by assisting the Dragon Knights. After achieving victory, they were bound in cuffs and sent to their respective prisons.

"A different view than the last time you were here, right?" Rory came alongside him and folded his arms over his chest.

"Most definitely. Though how is Adam adjusting to life in present day Scotland?"

Rory shrugged. "One day at a time with the help of Meggie and their children. He will never fully become one here. As a 13th century Scottish warrior, I believe his soul would rather return there."

Startled, Liam asked, "Is he not happy with Meggie?"

"Absolutely! If given the chance to return to the

past, he would swiftly decline. His true heart and soul is Meggie. He lost her once and vowed to never part from her again. I must confess, he is extremely happy to be finally working on the ancient ruins of his home."

"Leomhann," mused Liam.

"Yes. Meggie gifted him the castle with the proceeds of the money her brothers had stashed away for her. After the battle and the MacKay Dragon Knights returned to the past, Angus made a pact that each new generation of Dragon Knights would set aside their profits for Meggie and her descendants. She had amassed quite a sum and bought Leomhann Castle, and the MacFhearguis land surrounding the ruins."

"Ironic how this all came to fruition, don't you think?"

Rory sighed. "Considering Meggie's brother's sword was the catalyst for her death and each of her brothers had to seek their own redemption, yes I find it ironic *and* amazing."

Watching a hawk make lazy circles in the sky, Liam studied its flight. The bird appeared to take its own course, instead of drifting along in the warm draft of air. A flicker of awareness prickled along his senses. Liam clasped his hands behind his back and shielded his thoughts. He continued to watch with intent as the bird flew closer to them.

"Return to the Dragon Knight," ordered Liam.

"He has spoken to you?" asked Rory, stepping aside. "He did so on my first meeting here."

"I never gave him the chance," replied Liam. "If he tried to enter my mind, he might not like what's inside. His first lesson will be manners when it comes to entering one's thoughts. In addition, he used the hawk's vision to study us. The lad's magic is strong."

Rory barked out in laughter and pounded Liam's back. "This is exactly why you are needed here. Not only did he speak within my mind, but he has scared his own mother by entering her thoughts."

"You should have thwarted his attempt with a blast of energy," suggested Liam, keeping his focus on the retreating hawk and not the agonizing loss he felt within his soul. It was a darkness that consumed him daily.

"He's only a child."

"Then you're the fool, Brother. His mind and dragon are ancient. They have united."

"By the hounds! It is impossible." Rory fisted his hands on his hips.

"Contrary to what we've been led to believe in the legends, this young Dragon Knight has mastered the beast within. They made a pact. No one has ever done so at an early age. It takes years of training and respect."

"You were able to grasp all this knowledge from here? In such a brief time?"

Liam pointed to the sky. "Jamie may be strong, but he's young, inexperienced, and leaves a trail of mental power. He is wary."

"Of whom?"

"Two Fenian Warriors converging on a hill? I cannot say, yet, his concern is there." Liam nudged his brother. "Let us go greet the MacFhearguis clan."

In a whisper of light, both warriors vanished and appeared in front of the portcullis to Aonach Castle. Striding forth across the open gate, Liam glanced in all directions. The darkness that once clouded this place was replaced with beauty. Flowers grew in abundance near the entrance.

Dogs greeted them in welcome, and Rory responded with firm pats on the side. "This young wolfhound is Zeus and the other one is known as Odin."

Chuckling softly, Liam said, "Greek and Viking under one roof."

"Better them than the Celts, right?"

"Agreed."

The clang of steel halted their conversation.

"Should we venture to the lists?" recommended Rory.

Liam gestured outward. "Lead on."

When they approached, Liam was unprepared for the sight. Jamie MacFhearguis had grown tremendously since the last time he saw the lad. "How old now?"

"Six winters."

"He looks like a lad of *twelve*."

"There has never been a recorded account of any other Dragon Knight to have aged so quickly, either," remarked Rory. "Archie is keeping a daily record of Jamie's progress."

Liam examined father and son sparring in the lists, marveling at the strength of the younger knight. Adam was the stronger, but Jamie was holding his own against his father.

"And how is Adam adjusting to his dragon?"

Rory leaned near him. "Considering he only found out a few years ago, I can honestly say his is superior, as well. They united much sooner than we expected."

"Amazing." Liam's attention was soon directed to a younger lad standing on the bench and waving a wooden sword high in the air. His language was garbled, until Liam detected it was in ancient Latin." He nudged his brother. "Who is the newest Dragon Knight?"

"Alexander *Conn* MacKay MacFhearguis."

"Impressive."

"According to Meggie, the next two bairns will each have our names as well."

Liam folded his arms over his chest, content to observe the younger Dragon Knight. "Where did this knowledge of future children come from?"

"Jamie, through the Great Dragon."

Thunder rolled in the distance, and Liam narrowed his eyes. "Alexander has the power of the skies."

"Correct."

"Powerful," remarked Liam.

"I've deduced these Dragon Knights will become the most powerful in history. Archie is in agreement with my conclusion."

Uneasiness settled within Liam as he recalled the last time the Dragon Knights were the most powerful. It was during the 13th century with the MacKay clan, Jamie's uncles. "Has anyone mentioned this occurrence with the king or the seers?"

"Yes. Conn held a meeting after I met with Jamie. He wished to have another opinion before alerting the king. The seers have often stated this is a new bloodline of Dragon Knights."

"A new order," added Liam and brushed a hand down the back of his neck. "Do you think evil will try to enter this world sooner than in a thousand years?"

"I pray not," stated Rory in a hushed tone. We thought we were done when we vanquished the bastard several years ago."

Liam glanced at his brother skeptically. "A new order. A new bloodline. A *new* evil?"

"Gods and Goddesses protect us."

A burst of shouting brought their conversation to a halt, and they turned their attention to Adam leveling his blade to Jamie's chest. The lad had enclosed them both in a ring of fire, and his fire dragon hovered behind him. Adam was yelling at his son in Gaelic, ordering him to withdraw his dragon back into his body.

"Sweet Mother Goddess, what is Jamie doing?" Liam started forward, but Rory held him back.

"Let the older Dragon Knight command him. If we interfere, it will show Jamie's dragon that his father is weak and needs outside assistance."

"It's madness!" hissed Liam, but remained standing by his brother.

They continued to watch the battle of wills and strength unfold before them, until Adam's dragon emerged at the tip of his blade. The shadow dragon was furious—eyes flashing silver. Liam watched in stunned fascination as Adam grew several inches, towering even more over his son. Jamie relented and clenched his hand. The fire dragon retreated into his body, and the lad slumped to the ground.

"I have never witnessed a display of power so great," commented Liam. "I am relieved to know Archie is keeping an account. Even Adam has grown in strength and power."

"Yes. Especially since he is the elder," acknowledged Rory.

"But not the leader. Jamie will lead the next

battle."

Rory gestured him forward. "You are ever observant, Brother. Let's go greet them."

Alexander jumped down from the bench and raced to Rory. "Greetings! Yippee, ye have brought another warrior!"

Rory ruffled the lad's hair. "Alexander this is my brother, Liam."

Alexander gave him a mock salute. "Welcome to Aonach Castle."

Liam gave him a curt nod. "And how goes the training, Alexander?"

"Magnificent. I tried to force my dragon out to help my brother."

Liam arched a brow in disapproval. "Your first lesson, Alexander, is to control your emotions. Your dragon should never be unleashed in anger."

The lad narrowed his eyes as if trying to discern Liam's message. He tapped his chest. "If I am angry, he must stay inside?"

"Precisely."

Alexander tapped the sword on the ground. "But what if the enemy is attacking? Should I not release my dragon?"

A cold tendril of fear snaked down Liam's spine, and he refused to continue this path of conversation. "I pray you will live in peaceful times here."

The lad nodded slowly. "It is what we all wish for, also." He pointed to his brother, who was embracing his father. "Jamie says the darkness is coming."

Liam swiftly glanced at his brother, who remained silent. Returning his attention to the lad, Liam said, "I hope he is wrong."

"'Tis good to see ye," remarked Adam, striding forth with Jamie by his side.

Liam embraced the man. "And you, my friend. As well as Jamie." He reached for the lad, noting the uncertainty in his eyes. Liam attributed his sullen behavior to his verbal thrashing by his father.

"Are you here to oversee more training?" inquired Jamie, shifting uneasily.

"Yes. Rory thought it would be best if you acquired more knowledge from the Fae realm. Archie has taught you as much as possible, but you require more warrior wisdom."

Humor softened the lad's features, and his eyes grew bright. "It would be an honor for ye to teach me."

Smiling, Liam held out his arm. "Let us shake like warriors of old."

Jamie puffed out his chest and took Liam's outstretched arm. "I welcome your knowledge, Fenian Warrior."

Adam placed a hand on his son's shoulder. "Take Alexander into the castle and wash the stench of dirt off both of ye."

"Aye, Father."

Liam watched the two brothers depart the lists and then turned toward Adam. "What is this darkness that Jamie is referring to?"

Adam blew out a curse. "He speaks of another battle—one where I cannae fathom if it is within him *or* another threat of evil. This is all the knowledge he imparts to us."

"Then it is wise there will be two warriors enlisting in his training. His strength as a Dragon Knight is impressive in one so young, but his mind has yet to harness the power. He rules by emotion."

Adam raked a hand through his hair. "Ye are spouting nothing new."

Liam placed a hand on his friend's shoulder. "Do not worry. Whatever evil he must face, he will not be alone."

"Aye," affirmed Adam. "Let us go greet Meggie."

Liam gave the man a weak smile, trying to ignore the snaking fear of yet another battle to be fought by both Fae and humans.

Chapter Twenty-Eight

"As a Fenian Warrior, my deepest strength came from the power to control my emotions. After Abela died, I found myself adrift in a sea of misery and agony, unable to shake free from my wretched companions."
~*Chronicles of Liam MacGregor*

"I have heard ye are leaving us," commented Meggie, stepping alongside Liam near the loch's bank.

"I believe having two Fenian Warriors, especially ones that are brothers for a few months can be exhausting on Jamie. He requires time to digest the information I have taught him. I judge it best he train physically for several months and then have scholar lessons. Rory and I have deemed this wise, switching out his training and lessons."

She eyed him skeptically and pulled the shawl over her shoulders. "Is it true?"

Confused by her question, Liam asked, "What truth are you referring to, Meggie?"

"The darkness you hide within yourself. We all ken of Jamie's, but he has mentioned yours."

Liam muttered a curse. "Mine is different. Deep sorrow fills me over the loss of my wife. The lad knows *nothing* about loss and suffering, unless he is channeling those who have suffered from his ancestors. Yes, he witnessed pain from the evil druid, Lachlan, but his father saved him."

Meggie touched his arm. "I am sorry. Please forgive me. Ye never mention anything about her, except to say ye married and she died shortly afterward. The loss of a loved one is terrible for anyone, be it Fae or human."

A surge of pain shot through Liam, and he stepped away from Meggie. Each day the darkness of pain chipped away at his soul. Often he woke in the early morning, gasping for breath. As if someone was strangling him in a vice grip, punishing him for falling in love. His focus was faltering, and it was time to return home and attempt to heal. If not, his sanity might slip into a chasm of eternal pain.

Liam stared out at the expanse of water. Even the Great Dragon who dwelled deep within the loch could not bring him any words of comfort. The fortress of grief continued to build inside him. His hands trembled as he balled them into fists. "I must return home." He glanced over his shoulder. "My restraint of control is ebbing away. I need to regain a sense of purpose."

Meggie nodded slowly. "Rory has spoken about the difference of Fae and human emotions."

"How considerate," replied Liam dryly.

She bent and retrieved two rocks. Stepping toward the water, she explained, "This stone is like a human when dealing with turbulent emotions." Meggie tossed the stone outward, making it skip across the water several times. Pointing, she added, "Yet, the emotions of a Fae are felt keenly unlike any other here. Ye sense them deeply." She flung the other stone high into the air and they watched as it plunged into the loch with a resounding splash.

"Impressive comparison," he acknowledged.

Meggie returned to his side and placed a kiss on his cheek. "Go home and heal, Liam."

"What if I can't?" Liam had not wished to profess the question, but he found himself lacking in any firm control over his words, thoughts, and emotions.

Meggie pursed her lips in thought, studying the ground. Minutes ticked by and Liam thought it odd she did not answer him. When she finally lifted her head, she replied, "Then ye are nae good to us here. Jamie will reflect the darkness ye have kept hidden, exposing your weakness and flaws. I have nae wish to ever see my son take down a Fenian Warrior in an attempt to show how powerful he is and how weak ye are. I worry he would use your darkness to show his strength over a Fae. Ye must teach him the path of both—light and dark. Your darkness is consuming ye."

A chill of foreboding washed over Liam. "Even in a Fae's *darkest* moments, they can harness the most power. This will be my next lesson to your son when I return."

She angled her head at him. "A wise lesson, indeed, Liam. I look forward to your next visit."

Liam gave a slight bow. "Be well, Meggie."

"The same to ye, my friend."

He marveled at the woman as she strode through the thick pine trees, and also understood her own sorrow at losing her brothers. After the great battle, Angus, Duncan, Stephen, and Alastair MacKay had to return to their own time—the 13th century. Sadly, she, Adam, and their son, Jamie had to remain in the present.

"The new order of Dragon Knights has indeed been

reborn here in this century." Liam knelt on one knee and placed his palm upon the ground. Gazing outward at the loch, he uttered softly, "Keep them safe Great Dragon. Watch over them, Mother Danu. From the first shaft of sunlight until the first kiss of a moonbeam."

Rising slowly, Liam steadily made his way back to Aonach to say his farewells and depart for home.

****

"How much longer are you going to keep coming to your father's library?" inquired Liam's mother, Reena. "You cannot bury your head in the tomes here, seeking answers within your heart."

Liam closed the current book that occupied his thoughts and gazed intently at his mother. "And what do you purpose I do? Weep out in the gardens? Take up blacksmithing like Rory did when he agonized over the loss of his love?" His patience with his doting mother was grating on his nerves. "Perchance I should retreat to my chambers within the Brotherhood, so you will have no need to worry about me."

She leveled him a hard stare. "Where there will always be a reminder of *her*? Are not your chambers near the Royal House and gardens? Should I applaud this new decision? Have you taken a good look at your appearance? You are barely existing, my son."

He threw the book across the room. "Then pray tell me what to do? I'm obviously doing something wrong, since you correct me daily."

Her eyes filled with sorrow. "You have lost control, Liam. Coming home to wallow in your sorrow is consuming you." She stepped closer and cupped his cheek.

Liam flinched and backed away. "Do not give me

any comfort."

His mother vanished in a whisper of light.

Slamming his fists onto the oak desk, he let out a frustrated cry. "Why can't I find any solace?"

Deafening silence greeted him. Even Mother Danu had abandoned him. The months since he'd come back home had been filled with more despair. Anguish had been replaced with anger and malice. His anger at the humans and Milesians. And his malice was also directed at the king for removing his beloved to the temple of Mother Danu where she was allowed to die.

"Did not any endeavor to heal her?" he shouted.

He tore his gaze to the crystal stain-glass window. The bucolic scene outside made him nauseated. Beauty filled his parents' home, and he longed to leave. He should have never returned. His nails bit into the wood, letting the fury snake through his blood.

His last thread of discipline and training deserted him.

"I am living a lie! This life is not meant for me. My trial was a farce, and I should have been permitted to join my beloved." His voice shook with rage.

The walls of this home had become another prison, and he shuddered. Quickly removing his armband, he traced a path over the ancient words with his thumb. He placed it in the center of the desk and stepped aside.

Snapping his fingers, Liam magically transported to the western gate of the Fae realm. As he reappeared by the waterfall denoting the entrance to *Tir na Og*, he stripped free from his boots and removed his tunic.

Inhaling deeply, he exhaled on a sigh.

He studied the flowing water, cascading over the moss-covered rocky cliff. The waterfall fed into a graceful river that surged into the sea toward the land of forever. The last time he had been there was when they sent his father's body adrift out to sea. He touched the skin where he had removed his armband. The time for asking forgiveness was over, and his thoughts turned toward another.

"Where did they hold your ceremony, my beloved?" He pointed to a patch of violets. "Did they not think to tuck a few of your favorite flowers within your ebony locks? I think no...*not*, since there was no one there to share this knowledge." Liam choked back the emotion. "The entire kingdom should have paid homage to your life."

This place invoked serenity, and for the first time in many moons, Liam felt at peace. He started forward in the direction of the violets, pausing every so often to pluck another favorite flower he knew she favored.

Stopping before the lavender clusters, his eyes blurred. "I even penned a missive in prison to you. I should have been the one that died—not you—never you." He bent and grasped a few more, adding them to the others.

Returning his attention to the sea, he continued on his journey. He clutched the bouquet to his chest as he approached the shore. A crystal pillar marked the division between the entrance to the Fae realm and *Tir na Og*. It shimmered from the sun, illuminating the ancient words carved from long ago.

His body shook when he stepped on the glistening white ground. It was a mixture of stardust, fine crystals, and sand from his own homeland on Taralyn. His toes dug into the soft warmth, and Liam swallowed.

In a low voice, he sang the ancient words to call

forth the barge. "From this land to the next, from the rising sun, to the setting moons. The stars are my home beyond the glittering gates. I heed the call to return. Heart and soul shall be fused as one during my journey home."

A brilliant flash of light appeared on the horizon, and he spotted the vessel sailing toward the shore.

Liam took another step forward, the frothing water merely inches from his feet. "Are you waiting for me at the gates of *Tir na Og*, my beloved? Did you hear my voice call out to you?"

He brushed a hand over his brow, preparing to take the last step into the water and sealing his fate forever. If even a drop touched his skin, death would happen instantly, transporting him onto the barge and escorting him across the sea.

"I have heard you, my warrior."

Liam froze. Slowly, he glanced over his shoulder. "*Abela*," he uttered her name on a gut-wrenching sob for the first time since her death.

"Please do not step into the water," she pleaded and beckoned him toward her.

He blinked in confusion. "Are you a vision within my mind? Have I truly gone mad?" He pinched the bridge of his nose and then refocused his sight. "Move away from the shadow of the oak tree."

"Heart to heart, I am yours. Blood to blood, we are one." Abela stepped into the radiant sunlight. "I am as real as you are, Liam MacGregor, and I have no desire to watch you vanish forever. Please come away from the water."

Liam dropped the flowers and ran into her outstretched arms, crushing her body against his.

Closing his eyes, he inhaled her scent—one filled with all the flowers of their kingdom. "Abela, *Abela*." When he opened his eyes, he roamed her features, unable to fathom that she was standing before him. "You are here—*alive*."

"My warrior." A lone tear slipped down her cheek, and Liam brushed it away with the pad of his thumb.

Euphoria swept through him, and he covered her mouth hungrily. The kiss sang through his veins, healing the scars of her death and loss. Her moan resonated within him, and he deepened the kiss, filling her with all he had to give.

When he broke free, Liam lifted her high in the air and twirled her around. Abela's laughter filled him, the sound exhilarating.

Gently, he brought her back to the ground. "How?" he asked. "I thought you de...*dead*."

Abela cupped his face. "Almost," she whispered. Tears misted her eyes. "I kept hearing your voice. *You* brought me back, Liam."

"Sweet Goddess, I truly believed I had lost you! They took you away to the temple."

She brushed a lock of hair from his eyes. "I was lost for a long time. If not for the priestesses and Mother Danu, I would have slipped into death's embrace. They kept a vigil around me, along with my mother."

Liam frowned, confused and uncertain. "But I was told of your *death*. All mourned the loss of you."

"The priestesses deemed it necessary to inform the kingdom that I was dead, except for the king and queen. In reality, I was suspended between the land of the living and the spirit realm. Keeping me in the healing caverns within the temple was the only solution presented to my parents, even though the priestesses believed I would never return. They expected Mother Danu to take me into her loving embrace." She leaned her head on his chest. "Apparently my mother spoke to me constantly. Yet, the only words I was able to hear were from you. When I woke, your name was on my lips. It was many days later before I could even rise from my bed. The recovery was a slow process."

He tipped her chin up with his finger. "You heard my voice, because you are my *wife*, Abela."

Leaning to the side, she traced her tongue along the side of his neck, and his pulse raced. "Blood to blood, my husband. *Forever* we are linked."

Liam recaptured her lips in a firestorm of passion, thrusting his tongue inside the velvet softness of her mouth. Desire burned within his blood. Lifting her into his arms, Liam strode with intent away from the tree.

"Where are we going?" she asked, playing with his hair.

He surveyed her seductive pout. "To have a proper reunion."

She looked affronted. "I have no desire to be with anyone but you."

"Did I mention anyone else? And how did you manage to find me here?"

Wrapping her arms around his neck, she smiled. "I followed your voice. Though it was filled with sorrow, I knew where to find you."

He cursed softly. "There will be no more talk of dying or *Tir na Og*."

"Then what shall we discuss?" she inquired, trailing her tongue in a leisurely manner along the bottom of his lip.

Liam trembled from her touch, aching to bury himself deep within her. "Desires."

"Yours or mine?"

"Both."

"Then don't you think you should transport us to your chambers, instead of walking there?"

"Are you in a hurry?" he countered in amusement.

She breathed a kiss along the vein in his neck. "Yes."

Liam winked and in a blazing flash of light, he transported them far away from the great waterfall in the west.

Chapter Twenty-Nine

"My journey was uncertain, until I encountered my last thread on the loom of life."
                                        ~Diary of Princess Abela

Stretching fully, Abela wrapped a leg over Liam's naked hips, reveling in the hard planes of his body and inhaling his scent. Contentment filled her soul, and she pressed a kiss on his shoulder. Loving Liam MacGregor was the greatest adventure of her life.

"I love you, my warrior." Lifting her head, she gazed into his silver-blue eyes. Love reflected back within his own.

He caressed her backside in a leisurely manner, sending shivers of desire once again through her. "And I love you, *mo ghrá*."

Her fingers trailed down his arm. "Where is your armband?"

"On my father's desk."

She bolted upright. "If you removed the relic, then you fully intended to enter into the water? It is sacred to your family and denotes your lineage within the Royal house of Avieon on our homeland on Taralyn."

Liam winced. "Yes."

She smacked his arm and turned away from him.

He tugged on one of her curls. "I was fading from this existence. Eventually, I would have gone mad. I could not fathom you gone. I lost all self-control. It was the first time in my existence that I allowed the darkness of grief to invade my soul. I refused to harness the anguish."

"Life is precious," argued Abela. Glancing over her shoulder, she added, "However, I might have done the same. At least I reached you in time."

Liam placed one arm under his head. "Yes, you did. I will retrieve the armband in the morning. Amidst collecting the family relic, I must make apologies to my mother."

"Have you caused her distress?"

He closed his eyes on a sigh. "Horrifically so."

Poking him on his leg, she added, "Go this evening. Do not wait."

"As you wish, beloved."

Curling her knees to her chest, Abela gazed around his chamber. An oak tree was fashioned from all the pieces of wood in their realm—from a blend of rowan, yew, maple, birch, elm, pine, and oak. The creative carving expanded across the entire wall in a multi-layer of colors. Directly opposite was a tapestry of their ancient homeland of Taralyn during the full moons. Moonlight spilled over the entire kingdom in an illuminating effect. In awe of the work, she found something new as her gaze traveled over the embroidery. Candles graced an amber table at the end of his massive four-poster bed. The room spoke of the man, and Abela grew curious about the rest of his chambers here in the Crystal Palace.

"You have exquisite taste," she observed.

Liam pulled her back against him. "Wait until you see the rest of my chambers."

"Hmm...let me guess. Is there a library?"

"Massive. It contains all the tomes from the collection of Panilla."

"The great poet from our homeland? I thought the works were lost."

"I found them one day searching for a scroll on elixirs in the lower level of the Library of the Ancients."

"I would enjoy reading them." Abela nuzzled his neck. "I've heard that reading some of his poems can ignite arousal in a Fae."

In one swift move, Liam rolled her onto her back. His fingers trailed a path over her breasts and down her stomach. "Not as much as *my* words and touch."

When his fingers reached the most intimate part of Abela, she gasped in pleasure. "I'm not so sure. I...I...um...will have to read those poems for myself."

In slow circles, Liam continued to fondle and tease her. "No. I will read them to *you*."

"Yes, *yes*," she agreed, trying to grasp the elusive flame building within her body.

"For now, let me give you pleasure," he murmured against her neck, nipping at the soft spot below her ear. "I find I cannot get enough of you. I never want to part from you."

Abela closed her eyes on the sensations and surrendered herself to his ministrations. He stopped, and her eyes flew open. "*No*. Never." And in one fluid movement, he entered her body and she let out a groan.

The sensual dance continued, especially when she wrapped her legs around Liam's back, bringing him even deeper within her body. His thrusts were driving her wild. Raking her nails down his back, she arched madly against him. The tide of passion lifted and swept them into the stars, and she screamed his name.

Liam roared as his release poured into her body. Her skin tingled from her head to her toes, and the starlight shimmered all around them. Floating on a wave of ecstasy, they drifted back onto his bed. He held her quaking body, crooning words of love and endearments in her ear.

Sated and content, Abela closed her eyes.

Their quiet reunion was interrupted when Rory came charging through the outer chamber shouting. "What did you do to our mother?"

Abela scooted under the covers as Liam bolted out of the bed and met his brother at the entrance of his inner chamber. "I am going to make amends. For now, you must leave."

"You bastard!" Rory shoved him aside. "Is this how you honor the woman—*your wife*—who you loved and lost? By bringing another to your bed?"

"Wait!"

"Who is she?" demanded Rory, standing by the side of the bed. "Are you bringing other women back from the Pleasure Gardens?"

Abela let out a hiss of disapproval from under the fur coverings. She snapped her fingers to magically view the spectacle.

Liam folded his arms across his chest, giving no regard to his lack of clothing. "Contrary to what you've *assumed*, I can assure you that I have remained honorable to my beloved."

Rory regarded him like a specimen. "Have you gone mad? How many times must I tell you? She is—"

"Do *not* say that word," ordered Abela, tossing the

covers off her head and clutching them to her chest.

Rory's mouth opened and closed, resembling a gaping fish. He pointed a finger at her. "Im...*impossible*."

Abela pinched her arm in a mock display of being alive. "Yes, it is possible. I felt the pain."

Rory stumbled back, blinking several times. "Does Conn know? The king and queen?"

Plucking a rare piece of lint from the velvet covering, she replied, "Yes. Conn was made aware of my *awakening* early this morning by the king."

Rory charged out of the room.

"What is he doing now?" complained Abela.

Liam shrugged and went to a trunk by the side of the bed, retrieving a pair of trews. Hastily putting them on, he asked, "Would you like me to do the honors?"

Rolling her eyes, Abela snapped her fingers and a pale blue silken gown graced her body. Giving a light touch to her mussed hair, she magically transformed the mass into perfection. "I am fully in control of *all* my powers," she replied dryly.

"Good to hear."

After slipping out of the bed, she went and wrapped her arms around him. "I think we'd better go see what he's doing."

Liam groaned. "By all the noise, I believe he's searching for one of my rare bottles of single malt."

"What? No ambrosia from the Pleasure Gardens?" She winked and darted away from him.

"I find no humor in your question."

"Then I shall think of something else."

Abela strolled into the main chamber with Liam following closely behind her. True to what Liam had stated, his brother had flung open the doors to a massive cabinet. Three glasses were displayed next to a decanter, but Rory continued to explore and pull out other bottles.

"Is there something I can help you find," asked Liam, opening the doors that led out to the garden.

"I know you have a bottle from Alastair MacKay."

"I do, but it's mead, not whisky. You know he favors the sweet wine."

Rory arched a brow in question. "Are you sure? I can always resort to using magic to find it."

"You are forbidden to use any type of magic in my chambers, or have you forgotten our vows when we entered the Brotherhood?"

"Never. You made me swear in blood," acknowledged Rory, waving his hand about. "Why do you think I'm pulling out everything in this ancient cabinet? Your collection of glassware, iron and bronze vessels, *and* rare bottles of drink are more extensive than Conn's."

Abela continued to observe Rory in his quest to hunt for the elusive bottle. Liam's mouth twitched in humor while he stood to the side, offering no assistance.

Fresh, floral air streamed inside distracting her from the comical scene. "And here I thought Conn had a stunning vista. You've outdone yourself, Liam." She moved to the entrance and gazed outward. "Sweet Goddess, you have the golden swans in your lake. They've been missing from the royal gardens for years."

"Found it!" shouted Rory, triumphantly.

Liam approached from behind and swept back a

lock of hair from her neck. Leaning near, he whispered. "It will be our secret."

She shivered from his touch, aching to strip free and frolic out in his lush garden.

"This is a cause to celebrate," interrupted Rory carrying three glasses of whisky. Handing one to her and Liam, he lifted his high. "To life, love, renewal. A triad of happiness to you both always." He quickly tossed back the dram.

Taking a sip, Abela sputtered. "This is what you were searching for?" She held the glass outward. "It burns."

"It's an acquired taste, *mo ghrá*."

Handing Liam the rest of her drink, she countered, "I believe I'd like some of Alastair's mead, if there is any."

"Your wish is my command."

After setting his glass down, Rory stepped near her. Taking her hand, he placed a kiss along the knuckles. "I am greatly relieved to see you are once again in my brother's life. I feared he was descending to a place where no one would be able to reach him."

If only Rory knew how close his brother came to ending his life. "Thank you. It has been an adventure. Never could I have fathomed the path I took."

Dropping her hand, he smiled. "You are the first, besides the Fenian Warriors, to venture into the mortal world since we were escorted underground. I admire your strength. Many would have succumbed to death within hours." In a more somber tone, he added, "And I will be forever grateful to you in freeing my brother from his prison. Regardless of the circumstances, your adventurous journey led us to a plot which could have led to the downfall of the kingdom."

"I almost forgot!" She stole a glance at Liam. "I know who the traitor is!"

Liam crossed to her side and handed her a glass of mead. "Council member, Tulare."

Abela felt the blood leaving her face. Taking a sip of the honeyed mead, she tried to steady her racing heart. It was a memory she had tucked away. Tulare never glimpsed her that day, but she would always remember his vile nature standing next to several Milesians and Peter O'Malley.

"Let us move outside," suggested Liam. "There we can give you an account of everything."

When she stepped into the warmth of the sunlight, Abela exhaled slowly. Some of her memories remained clouded of her time in the mortal world when she became ill. Yet, this one image soared within her mind. She walked with intent toward the grassy area, needing to feel the touch of the ground on her skin. Finding a place near the water, she settled down on the ground and patted for the men to join her.

"How much do you remember?" asked Liam, softly.

Abela took another sip of the mead. "Fragments. Though with each new hour, I am finding my memories are binding, enabling me to recall more vividly my time above. I saw Tulare with the Milesians and Peter. I was stunned to witness him there and more so to see the Milesians."

"Thankfully, a war has been averted. Your father has met with the King of the Milesians. Another treaty has been drawn up. Both kings have witnessed, signed, and rescinded the previous one."

After finishing her drink, she placed it on the ground. "Do tell how they did this without including the others," she encouraged.

"Two treaties," interrupted Rory, leaning back on his forearms. "One between the kings, stating that if conflict arose between the realms, both races, Tuatha de Danann and the Milesians would combine forces to unite. This will keep the worlds safe. The other treaty is for all races, specifically in regards to the Fenian Warriors. If required, the Veil of Ages could be used by the warriors for use in special circumstances. And only with approval from the king himself." He paused. Wariness reflected within Rory's eyes.

She nudged his leg with her foot. "What do the others—Dragon Knights *and* Irish Travelers—say to this new treaty?"

Silence hovered around them, except for the hum of bees. Abela directed her gaze to Liam, who kept his attention on the swans. Her shoulders slumped. "They don't know."

"No, they do not," affirmed Liam, quietly.

"Have we truly become a divided realm? Did I do this?" She abruptly stood and hugged her arms around herself.

"It was inevitable," stated Liam, standing and placing his arms around her waist. "The path had begun when your brother, Conn fell in love with a human— Ivy. In truth, this new direction may have started years ago."

She sighed and leaned back against him. "This news is unsettling. I happen to like the Dragon Knights. At least the MacKays of Urquhart."

He kissed the top of her head. "I concur."

"So now what? The original treaties will be returned without their knowledge of the new ones?"

"Yes," offered Rory, coming to stand alongside them.

"But it will be a lie," she argued. "The shift of power has begun."

Both men remained silent, and Abela's heart grew heavy. Was this the path of the worlds? What was her part in all of this? Her lessons learned from the temple were for all people, regardless if they were human or Fae. Perhaps she could bring the teachings outside the sacred place for those to witness their healing purposes and knowledge. A thought to dwell on for another day.

Turning around in Liam's arms, she gave him a beaming smile. "For now let us celebrate peace in all the realms. There will always be conflict and strife, but good does triumph in the end."

"How right you are, beloved."

Rory leaned over and kissed her on the cheek. "With both your permissions, I will go forth and spread the good news that you are alive."

Abela laughed with content. "I anoint you with the task."

"Tell mother I shall visit her later," stated Liam, bringing Abela closer to him.

Rory gave him a mock salute. "She was second on my list. Erina will be overjoyed with the news."

"Unless Ivy has spoken with her already," admitted Abela. "Truth be told, I am puzzled why you did not hear the news directly from Conn."

Rory gave her a wink as he strolled away. "Erina and I were spending some alone time in the waters of Delfina."

"Isn't there a nickname for that place?" she shouted.

Rory's laughter resonated long after he vanished from their sight.

"Would you like to visit the *Lover's* waters, Abela?"

Abela's face heated as she turned slowly to meet Liam's sensual gaze. "Is it as pleasurable as many have whispered?"

He lowered his head and nipped on her lower lip. "I have never been, but the tales have been alluring."

His voice sent tremors of delight across her skin. "Why did you not go?"

Kissing her lips softly, he whispered, "I made a vow long ago that if I ever claimed you, the waters of Delfina would be a special place for us. I had no desire to share the unique experience with anyone else."

"*Oh*," she breathed out, falling in love with Liam all over again.

Chapter Thirty

"I heard the call of the songbird, and Abela emerged forth from the water. My soul sought hers, but our minds were wary."

~Chronicles of Liam MacGregor

Pacing the grand foyer of the king and queen's chambers, Liam pondered what he would say to Abela's parents. He had claimed Abela as his wife, without permission from his king and queen. Their daughter was royalty. Worse, she was a priestess from the temple, and he considered if he should have gone there first to speak with the High Priestess.

But none of it mattered now. Abela was his wife. Nevertheless, there was the subject of a ceremony, which his mother had pointed out after he made his apologies last evening. He never thought to ask Abela. Their reunion was a passionate one, exploring each other, and renewing what they both believed lost.

He raked a hand through his hair and straightened his tunic. Brushing his fingers over his armband, he then exhaled slowly. What he had endured was far more painful than this moment. His love for their daughter consumed his every waking moment. Her name was on his lips upon waking, filling him with a peace and contentment he had always yearned for in his life.

Smiling at his reflection in the gilded mirror

suspended on either side of the entrance, he let go of the fear and embraced what he knew. *I love you, Abela.*

As I love you, too, Liam.

Her voice floated within his thoughts as he advanced toward the doors. Clasping his hands behind his back, he waited. Time could never diminish what was in his heart, and he was prepared to wait all day in the foyer, if necessary.

However, his stay outside the chambers was short, and the amber doors opened.

Queen Nuala crossed the expanse of the room, holding out her hands toward him. "It is good to see you again, Liam."

Unprepared for the welcoming gesture, Liam knelt on one knee in reverence. "My queen."

She tapped him on the shoulder. "There is no need, Liam. Please rise."

After he complied, the queen placed a kiss on each of his cheeks. "Welcome."

Her informality left him without words to offer, so he gave her a weak smile. Lifting his gaze to the king, Liam understood there were going to be repercussions from Abela's father. The queen might have forgiven him, but his king reflected hesitancy in his stance and features. Recovering his voice, he inclined his head. "Thank you, my queen."

Her eyes held mirth. "*Nuala.*"

"As you wish."

The king snorted but made no motion to move forward.

Queen Nuala took Liam's arm, and proceeded to lead him toward her husband. "Do not be rude, Ansgar."

The king placed a hand over his heart. "Me? If it was not for this warrior, our daughter would not have been placed in danger."

"Might I remind you that I set Liam free," argued Abela, striding forth from the inner chamber. She went directly to her father, and placed her hand in the crook of his arm. "I find your brusque behavior unappealing and not like the king I understand so well. I have given my full account to you and mother."

His features softened somewhat. He patted her hand. "You risked a great deal, Abela. The priestesses were within their power to cast you out of the kingdom."

She lowered her head on a sigh. "As you have stated repeatedly, Father."

"The warrior should have returned you to the realm at once."

"And I gave you my reasons," she argued, darting the king a furious glance.

Liam grew weary of the sparring of words. Had they not been down this road of discussion already? He had no desire to watch a debate with his beloved as the target, as well as himself. He understood her father's devotion, but Abela was now his to guard and protect.

Removing the queen's arm from his, he walked over to Abela and her father. "If I may speak with you in private, King Ansgar, there is a matter which needs to be discussed."

The king regarded him for several moments and then gave a curt nod. "Follow me."

Liam grabbed Abela and kissed her soundly, trying to reassure her. "All will be well."

"Be careful," she whispered against his cheek.

He winked. "Always."

"Do not keep me waiting, warrior!" shouted the king.

Striding quickly down the corridor, Liam's steps slowed as the king took him into another area. Short circular steps led to a vast chamber, lit with candles. Books and scrolls lined the shelves all around him. He paused to take in the immeasurable collection of the king's library. His appreciation for the Fae King grew.

"I am impressed," Liam blurted out, unable to contain his exuberance.

"I have heard mentioned you are a scholar," remarked King Ansgar.

"Yes. I was appointed a scribe on my first assignment to the mortal world as a Fenian Warrior."

"Do tell," encouraged the king, removing a scroll from his desk.

Liam relaxed his stance. "It was during the early reign of King Brian Boru. He required someone who could give precise details during meetings with other chieftains. I remained in the background and committed to memory all words spoken, including observing reactions during the conversations. Afterward, I sat and wrote everything down on parchment for him."

The king tapped a finger on the parchment he held. "He was a great king, so I've been told. A wise man, indeed."

"Agreed. And I believe he would have found favor with you."

"Sprinkling me with compliments, warrior? It will not grant you any from me."

Liam arched a brow in amusement. "Never, my king. If I may speak freely?"

"Can I stop you?" The king wandered over to a massive golden globe of the Fae realm, supported by three uniquely carved oak dragons.

Liam straightened. "I have loved Abela for decades. I will guard, protect, shield, *and* cherish her forever. What has happened is in the past and cannot be undone."

The king eyed him skeptically. "Unless I undo the past."

"Not even you would dare to tamper with our threads on the loom of life." He hesitated and then continued, "And I would not allow you to take her from my heart."

"You would fight me on this, warrior?" His tone held a note of warning.

"With my life."

King Ansgar smiled and gestured Liam forward. "I have waited for the right warrior to claim my daughter. Only the strongest can stand by her side. She is destined for a future, one even she is unsure of at the moment. Regardless, she requires the strength, guidance, wisdom, and love of someone who will understand her. In addition, she requires a warrior who can profess to his king *and* her father his willingness to fight for her." Unfurling the parchment on his desk, he tapped the four corners to keep the document open.

Liam strode forth, overcome by elation within. He gazed upon the document, scanning the names. "A new order of Fenian Warriors?"

"Yes. You will be among the elite warriors. There is also another whose name I shall add. Yet, she will only be able to travel with her *husband*."

"Abela?" Liam wiped a hand over his brow,

tentative with this news. "She is unable to survive in the human world, so how is this possible?"

King Ansgar leaned against his desk. "After much deliberation with Conn, the elders, and Abela, we have concluded that it is time she enters the world to aid those in our teachings. She will continue to possess the Stone of Ages with you as her guardian."

Stunned by the news, Liam could not help but be concerned. The king had formally acknowledged and accepted him as Abela's husband. He'd hope to enter into another position within the kingdom after leaving the Brotherhood. The possibility of traveling into unknown dangerous situations, especially with his beloved, left him unsteady. Though it was a great honor, he pondered why Abela would have accepted. How could she think of returning to the human world when she almost died there?

The king shoved away from the desk. "I sense you have questions. Conn is waiting in the other room to speak with you. May I call him forth?"

Liam gave the king a slight bow. "Yes, please."

Conn magically appeared within the chamber. "About bloody time, Liam. I thought you'd never confess your love and fight for Abela in front of my father."

Folding his arms across his chest, Liam replied, "He may be your father, but he is my king. Did you suffer the same conflict with Ivy?"

The prince of the Fae narrowed his eyes and rubbed his chin in thought. "Good point. No."

"Has Abela agreed to these additional terms? Will she become part of the Brotherhood? I must admit to you both that I am uncertain of this new role, not only for myself, but my wife." He tried to keep the irritation out of his words and failed miserably.

Conn went and tapped a finger on the parchment. "Her name will never be included within the Brotherhood, though Abela will be linked. She is an exception. Since her husband is a Fenian Warrior—"

"What role shall I take part in this new order? Will I merely be a guard to accompany her on these missions?" He drew in a shaky breath. "What if something happens again? I will ask you once again, has Abela agreed to these terms? Because if she did, then I must speak with her first."

"If you had allowed me to finish, I am confident you will be in agreement. We require scholars in the human realm to assist Archie. There are many other kingdoms and with the threat of another division, the King of the Milesians and the Fae have agreed to combine knowledge for the good of all realms. Abela will be speaking to others about the Fae, but your position will be one of searching for rare documents and keeping an ear to the pulse of the land. We may have squashed the threat of war, but be assured there are others who will take their place."

"A spy and scholar," stated Liam, his curiosity now ignited.

"Precisely." Conn shifted his stance. "Furthermore, the king and queen have granted additional powers to Abela that will allow her to remain in the human world without suffering any harm. And to answer your main question, *your wife* will not move forward with any plans until you have given your consent. If you both do so, then there will be a private ceremony here in the king's chambers."

The thought of this new position was tempting and exhilarating. However, the past wounds of losing his beloved were still raw. All he wanted to do was protect Abela. Keep her safe from the growing tensions in the human world. Nevertheless, his wife was born a princess, served as a priestess, and became his warrior wife. She had proven countless times her strength and resilience on their journey.

As Liam tried to comprehend the new knowledge, he wove a single thought outward. *"If I agree to this new position from the king and Conn, will you obey my instructions when we are in the human world?"*

She chuckled softly within his mind. *"Obey is a strong word, husband. Can you choose another?"*

"Follow, comply, abide, conform? Which do you prefer?"

"Why don't you add submissive to your horrid list as well?"

Fighting the urge not to shout within her mind, he moved away from the prying eyes of Conn and the king. He braced his hands on the back of the massive chair by the hearth. *"Will you promise to listen to my instructions?"*

There was a lengthy pause. *"Yes. But I may have to interject my own from time to time."*

A smile tugged at the corners of his mouth. *"Then we are in agreement?"*

"Of course. And I will never venture out of the kingdom when I am carrying our child."

He gripped the chair fiercely. *"Ch...child? Are you telling me..."*

"No. Not yet." Her laughter of tinkling bells lingered long after she left his thoughts.

"Is all in agreement?" asked Conn, placing a hand on Liam's shoulder. "You look like you're in shock."

"Does Ivy do the same? Twist your guts into knots with the simplest words?"

Conn spared his father a glance, and then they both burst out in laughter. After giving Liam a firm shake, he stepped away. "Welcome to the world of wives and marriage, my friend."

"Thanks," he muttered, though it was good to hear Conn refer to him as a friend.

King Ansgar waved his hand outward, and the doors to the chamber opened. The queen entered, followed by Abela. His beloved's face glowed with happiness. She immediately went to Liam's side and clutched his hand.

He brought their joined hands to his chest. "Are you sure?"

"As long as you are by my side, yes."

Leaning near her cheek, he whispered, "*Always, beloved.*"

"Since this is a unique position, we are going to perform the ritual here in the king's chambers," stated Conn. "There will be another official one at the Brotherhood."

Liam brought their hands to his lips. Kissing her softly, he asked, "Ready?"

She nodded and smiled. "I do have one question which I'd like resolved before we proceed. It is for my mother and father."

The king eyed her warily. "Another request? Have we not granted you a pardon for breaking a law and freeing Liam from his prison? Or taking the Stone of Ages with you into the mortal realm, or using the powers gifted to you from the priestesses—"

"Forgive me for interrupting all my recent misgivings, but this one question has disturbed me greatly and I'd appreciate an explanation."

"What is your question, Abela?" asked her father.

"Why did you forbid anyone in the kingdom to inform Aileen Kerrigan—now MacKay—of her true heritage to the Fae? As you are aware, she knows the truth."

The king darted a glance at the queen. She moved across the room to his side. A silent communication seemed to pass between them, before he returned his attention to Abela. "When news reached the realm that Aidan had sired a daughter, one who was destined for greatness, we deemed it best at the time to enforce a mandate that no one should profess any knowledge of her link to the Fae."

The queen touched her husband's arm. "If I may add further?"

Smiling, he nodded.

"After I had a profound vision, I consulted the seer. She had seen the same future for Aileen. We worried that if she knew about her heritage, she would want to explore the kingdom. If Aidan had wished for his daughter to have this knowledge, he would have shared it with her. In my heart, I knew he never would. His last words were spoken tersely, and he vowed that his offspring would never know his true identity. He wanted to protect her from a people who had banished him from his world. Aileen's future was destined with the Dragon Knight, Stephen MacKay. We could not risk having her follow another direction."

"He did break part of his vow, but never mentioned

he was royalty. Aileen believes he knew his time was coming to an end," explained Abela.

Queen Nuala's eyes misted with unshed tears. "I know." She looked at her husband. "As much as we all have regrets with the decision to have Aidan leave the realm, his path was chosen. He forged a destiny for each of you standing in this room. Remember this well, especially when the king must ratify a new edict. There is always a purpose."

King Ansgar cupped his wife's chin and kissed her softly.

Silence lingered for several moments, and then he returned his attention to them. "Fenian Warrior, Liam MacGregor, and Princess Abela, please kneel."

After they both complied, Conn brought forth a blue crystal dagger. Tapping Liam on both shoulders, he then spoke the ancient words from their homeland. The power entered Liam, resonating in every cell of his body, and he lowered his head. The dragon guardians spoke to him within his mind, giving their approval with a breath of fire. The blazing truth of knowledge entered like a shaft of light, illuminating him with more wisdom, along with his Fenian powers that had been stripped from him by the king.

He barely registered the words spoken by Conn as he turned toward Abela. Lifting his head, he watched in awe as the prince wielded the additional power over his sister. Her head was bent, and her body enclosed in a sphere of pale blue light. When Conn asked a question, Abela responded in a voice he barely recognized. Not only would she be allowed to keep the powers from the temple, but also additional ones were bestowed on her today.

The air hummed with energy, swirling in a tempest of colors around them both.

King Ansgar proceeded forth. "By this declaration, I have witnessed, sealed, and approved this initiation. Rise Fenian Warrior and Princess of the Realm."

Liam brushed a kiss over her lips, yearning to escape to a more intimate area.

The queen approached and took Abela's other hand. "I believe it's time to leave, daughter."

Abela slipped free from Liam's grasp. "Yes, Mother."

Frowning, Liam started forward. "Where are you going, wife?"

She blew him a kiss. "To plan a wedding and feast."

He watched her vanish in a twinkling of lights. "But we are married!"

"Not formally within the kingdom," she whispered within his mind.

"Can the ceremony take place tomorrow?"

"Mother says in a week, and I cannot see you until then. I am the princess of the Fae and must have a formal wedding."

"You'd better be in my chambers, specifically my bed come the first star of the evening sky, wife."

"Is that a demand? What if I don't obey?"

"Then you will be punished."

"Hand, feather, or ice over my skin?"

Desire shot to his groin. *"All three."*

Her seductive laughter touched Liam, filling him with visions of yet to come.

Chapter Thirty-One

"As we venture forth on a new journey, our greatest trials will not be endured alone. We are determined to safeguard each other, bound by the laws of love for all eternity."
~Memoirs of Liam MacGregor and his wife, Abela

"Do you hear the whisper of the songbird calling your name, princess?" inquired High Priestess, Meena, as she draped the small cloak woven with feathers willingly donated from all the birds in the realm over her shoulders.

"Yes, High Priestess. She greeted me as the first light of dawn danced across the valley floor of the kingdom."

Abela brushed her hand across the delicate softness, marveling at the intricate pattern of colors. Only the palest were chosen, so they would shimmer in the soft morning light. They added a contrast to her ivory gown with amethysts magically sewn around the edges of her sleeves and hem. The back of the gown dipped low, so that all would see her new markings from the priestesses. Ancient Celtic patterns spiraled down her spine, each with a whispered blessing from all the women. Her long tresses were braided and woven around her head in an elegant crown. She allowed one long curl to lie gracefully over the front of her right shoulder, knowing how much Liam adored them.

The High Priestess reached for Abela's circlet, fashioned with seed pearls and crystals. The woman secured it firmly on her head and stepped back. "The songbird sings a melody fit for traveling. Your destiny awaits outside of this realm. Your time here was part of your journey. You have served us well."

Turning toward the woman, Abela bowed her head. "I ask for your blessing on this new path in my life."

The woman stunned Abela by cupping her face and placed a kiss on each cheek. "A blessing from me and Mother Danu. May light and love grace your life, princess. We were honored by your presence during your time within the temple."

Abela reached for her bouquet of violets and star jasmine. She had plucked the flowers from the garden by the temple earlier as she watched the new day begin. Slowly allowing her gaze to travel over the valley below the temple, her heart constricted. Never would she be allowed back inside. Once she stepped across the threshold, the doors would be sealed.

She had asked and been granted one last night within the sacred temple and would treasure every moment. A special feast had been prepared and each of the priestesses bestowed a blessing over her. The lore of the teachings of Mother Danu was safely tucked inside her mind and heart.

Bringing the flowers to her face, she inhaled their heady floral scent.

When the bells chimed in the distance, Abela lifted her head and smiled. One by one, the priestesses appeared in front of her. They would escort her to the steps of the Cathedral of Trees. From there Abela would walk the crystal steps to the top. Ninety steps for each of the nine dragons who were among the first that accompanied the Fae to the human world.

Taking a deep breath in, she released it slowly. "You may proceed."

"I shall meet you at the fountain," stated the High Priestess, and in a whisper of light, she vanished.

Stepping forward, Abela glanced behind her one last time. Silently, the doors to the temple closed, never to be opened for her again.

Returning her attention to the path in front of her, she moved along the smooth polished stones down the side of the hill. The procession led her past gardens, teeming with lush foliage. Onward they traveled through the arches and several bridges by the royal palace. She angled her head to view the swans gliding peacefully down the river, oblivious to her or the others. Their feathers of gold, silver, rose, and white glistened in the sunlight. With each step she took, Abela's heart raced in anticipation.

"Liam MacGregor." She uttered his name on a prayer. Earlier she had sealed off her thoughts from him. The time was one of preparation in solitude.

Her warrior. The only man who had the ability to stir her anger and joy all at the same time. From the moment his lips touched hers, she had given him her heart forever. Yet the journey took much longer than she had anticipated. Once he was lost to her, Liam had gone to another world and path as a Fenian Warrior.

Now he belonged to her. Heart, mind, body, and soul.

As they neared the Cathedral of Trees, she noted the banners fluttering in the warm early spring breeze.

Winter had thawed in time to welcome the spring growth, and a variety of bluebells, primroses, foxgloves, and sweet peas waved in greeting. Halting before the first step, she slowly lifted her head and watched the priestesses ascend into the cathedral.

When the first trumpet blared, Abela started forward. Though they were hidden in daylight, she felt the ancient guardians of the night sky surround her. They whispered blessings and brushed warmth over her. The power continued to lift her, and as she made it to the open doors of the cathedral, her skin tingled. Striding down a path littered with rose petals, she acknowledged those who dipped their head as she passed by them.

The massive oak, pine, and rowan trees towered inside, each illuminated with glittering lights on their branches. In the center was the huge fountain on a moss-covered mound. Generation after generation of Fae had come to this fountain to proclaim their union with another. Some chose to bathe in the waters, others sought to dip their fingers. It was the source of water from their homeland. A sacred place of bonding.

Abela observed the interior, seeking, searching for one particular Fae warrior.

Her breath caught, and she clutched her bouquet to her chest when Liam appeared from the side of one of the trees. He gave her a smile that sent her pulse racing.

She drank in the sensuality of his physique. His pants and sleeveless tunic were also in ivory, yet, the edges were trimmed in silver and green patterns, denoting his royal family of Avieon. His hair hung in soft waves past his shoulders, and she yearned to run into his arms. Abela's gaze roamed his features, taking in the seductive glint within his eyes and full lips that contained a smile only for her. Her face heated, and she fought to keep her hands from touching her cheeks. He was perfection in every way.

Immediately, she released the barrier between them within her mind.

"You are a vision that makes my blood burn like the fires of Caldron." The soft burr of his voice inside her mind had her trembling.

"With one kiss I can quench your fire, warrior."

"No. The satiny softness of your lips will only ignite a firestorm more powerful than you have witnessed. And I will demand more than one."

As her strides led her closer to him, she continued to keep her focus on Liam. *"Have you missed me?"*

His growl came swift. *"You tortured me all night long with your silence."*

Abela bit her lower lip. *"Absence makes the desire grow stronger, does it not?"*

"You're teasing me, mo ghrá."

"I have yet to begin, my husband."

Extending her hand to him, Liam grasped it firmly. He loomed dark and powerful over her. *"This will be a quick ceremony."*

She chuckled low. *"Not according to my mother and father who are glaring at us on our left."*

"You are already my wife. This is merely a formality."

Abela regarded him with a speculative gaze. *"Then let us proceed, before our king intercedes."*

Taking her hand, Liam tucked it in the crook of his arm and led her up the steps to the fountain. From the moment he noted Abela striding regally forth through the trees, his heart had slammed against his chest. Her beauty radiated all around her, and he was unable to contain himself. Liam had tried to remain patient, but when his body could no longer stay rooted to one spot, he bolted past his brother and Conn to fetch his beloved.

He steered her toward the side of the fountain, never releasing his hold on her. As she bent to place her bouquet of flowers on the crystal ledge, Liam's mouth became dry. Did she understand the markings that traveled from her upper to lower back? "Are you aware of the sensual design within these knots?" he whispered against her ear.

Her smile was as intimate as a kiss. "Yes, because I asked for that particular marking. It denotes sensuality for my *one* true love."

"I will enjoy feasting my way down your back."

A rosy glow splashed across her cheeks. "My skin is already aching for your touch."

High Priestess Meena emerged on the other side of the fountain and all passionate discussion ceased. Liam squeezed her hand.

"You have both come freely to the Mother and to the Fae. We, your people, rejoice in your union. Fenian Warrior and princess stand before us. This is a time of renewal and change. Our world is growing, evolving, and with your unification a new door opens. Each will venture out into the human world."

The High Priestess inclined her head toward Abela. "Royal daughter of King Ansgar and Queen Nuala, you were born under the ninth star, of the ninth month, in the ninth year of your parents' reign. Though you were born second, your path will lead to greatness. As for you Fenian Warrior, your strength and wisdom shall exceed those within the Brotherhood. With this marriage bond, a new responsibility is tasked upon you. Though this woman is no longer a priestess, she is a favored one by the Goddess. May you both visit the sacred waters near the temple for guidance."

Liam glanced at Abela, trying to discern if she knew anything about this special gift. *"Did you know?"*

She shook her head, confusion marring her features. *"I understood I would never be allowed near the temple again."*

High Priestess Meena gave a slight smile. "It is our wedding gift to you both."

Fisting a hand over his chest, Liam bowed. "My thanks."

"With mine, as well," uttered Abela softly.

They watched as the High Priestess departed from the area, making her way to the other priestesses.

Turning Abela around to face him, Liam placed her hand over his heart. "Do you feel the beat of my heart? This is where my love for you resides. Safe, warm, secure. We were fated so many moons ago, but were not ready for the journey. I now ask you to walk beside me. My body will shield and protect you. My heart shall forever cherish and love you. And my soul will seek yours at the gates of *Tir na Og*, only when it is time."

He lifted his hand high, whispering the ancient words of star fire. In a flash, a tiny star crystal appeared inside his palm. Presenting it to her, he said, "From the nine ancient guardians who grace the night sky. I asked and they have graciously given you this gem as protection on all your travels—be it in the human or

Fae realm."

Abela let out an audible gasp, as she took the gift. "It is warm."

"To always remind you of the breath of fire and that you are never alone."

Her eyes brimmed with unshed tears. "A treasured keepsake." She blew across the crystal and a silver chain magically appeared, securing the gem in place. "Once I place this around my neck, it shall never be parted from me." Slipping the chain over her head, she gazed up at him.

After removing her hand from his chest, Abela took his and placed it centered to her heart. Her gaze never wavered as she spoke, "My warrior, my husband, my lover, *my friend*. It was our friendship in the beginning that built the foundation of our love. My soul called out to yours in a spark of light. I kept my love hidden until it was time for it to mature and blossom. The candle of my love for you will never extinguish. It shines as bright as the stars in the cosmos. Even when their light fades, mine shall continue to illuminate. May our roots grow deep in love and the branches of our journey reach out in harmony as one."

She took another step closer. "In front of all these witnesses, I present you with the obsidian dagger of light and dark." Abela removed her hand from his chest and blew across her palm. The blade appeared magically. "You now possess the royal dagger, passed down to each generation within the royal family."

"I am not royalty, Abela," he argued softly. "It belongs to Conn. The power it contains should only be in the hands of the king *or* prince. It can only be used in times of war, though it cannot thwart the Dark One from entering our realm again."

Presenting the blade outward to him, she shook her head. "This was given to me on my 100th birthday by my father. If you recall, it was a rare occurrence for twins to be born in the realm. Therefore, *the king* deemed it wise that my future husband and children should carry the obsidian dagger. Two *royal* lines were formed on the day of our births. You are now part of that royal line with me."

Overcome with emotions, Liam found himself unable to speak. When his fingers made contact with the dagger, cold and heat surged through his skin. He regarded it for a few moments, understanding the power it contained—the ability to bring forth destruction as well as rebirth to the land. After securing it firmly under his belt on his tunic, he grasped Abela around the waist. "Two souls…"

"One love."

Liam brushed his fingers across her cheek. "A lifetime to cherish."

"Until we surrender to the mists."

Taking her hand in his, he submerged them in the bubbling water. A spray of water misted over their joined hands, and they both smiled. Liam released her hand, and they knelt on the soft ground. Mother Danu's whispered blessing poured through them, and the warmth of her love enveloped Liam.

Love, hope, renewal. A trial of fire they both endured. Regardless of their journey, their love had endured their trials together. Liam would gladly do it all over again for the woman who was now his wife.

As they both stood, he glanced around at those who were gathered. His brother, Rory and wife, Erina. Their daughter, Angelica, waved to him from her father's arms. He swept his gaze to Conn. Warrior, leader, prince, *and* his friend. There he stood with his wife, Ivy, and their daughter, Sorcha, tucked against his chest, fast asleep.

If anyone had professed their futures several years ago, he deemed they would have all fled to the outer reaches of the cosmos of time. Love had been their paths, though arduous and treacherous at times. He nodded and smiled at both of the warriors.

Three destinies fulfilled.

Abela's fingers grazed across his chin, snapping him out of his thoughts. He grasped her hand and kissed each scented, delicate finger. "I love you fiercely."

Her smile was a moonbeam of promises yet to be rewarded. "As you should, my husband."

Taking her in his arms, Liam placed feather-like kisses over her face between each whispered word of endearment. Her body trembled against him, and when her lips parted on a sigh, he captured her mouth with savage intensity.

They barely registered the shouts of elation from those within the cathedral. When someone nudged him on the back, he finally broke free from his wife's embrace.

"Welcome to the family," Conn pronounced.

Liam gazed down at Abela. "A beautiful family, indeed."

Others started forward, but Liam kept a firm arm around his wife. He had no desire to part from her. Each person acknowledged them with a kiss or bow in passing. Some of the Fae dusted stardust over them as they swept past them in a procession, and his heart swelled.

And as the trumpets heralded the wedding celebration of Liam MacGregor and Princess Abela, he bent near his beloved and whispered, "I have made arrangements to leave the feasting early."

"How is that possible?" She smiled and nodded to another Fae. "Wonderful, here comes my mother and father." Abela darted a glance at him. "Quick, get that mischievous glint out of your eyes. My father will understand its meaning instantly."

"Nope."

She rolled her eyes. "Sweet Goddess, you're now in a playful mood?"

"Yep."

"Can't you wait until these formalities are over?"

He winked at her. "Be careful, wife, or I may whisk you away."

She looked aghast at him. "You would not dare."

"Ahh...A challenge has been tossed out and I accept."

"If you move a muscle, I will freeze you where you stand," she hissed out.

Liam roared with laughter. When she started to protest, he silenced any further outburst with a searing kiss.

Epilogue

Abela tossed another blackberry into her mouth in between regaling Liam with yet another story she had heard—about how upset the king was over their early departure from the wedding feast. True, he did have his brother Rory arrange for their early exodus. But Liam judged he had done his best after one full day of feasting, drinking, and storytelling. King Ansgar should have been proud of him for his endurance.

He stretched out upon the ground and leaned back against the ancient oak tree bordering the river adjacent to his parents' home, fascinated with every aspect of his wife. Her gossamer lavender gown did nothing to hide her satiny skin underneath, and he found himself growing hard once again.

She gestured her hand outward in annoyance. "Did you know he even ordered Conn to bring you back? Mind you, he never said anything about me, but I'm positive there was a message in there somewhere for Conn to escort me back to the wedding table."

"As if Conn would agree," he replied dryly.

She snorted. "Clearly you know him well, since he *ignored* our father and escorted Ivy to the dancing along the royal lake."

"It has been eons since we have danced along the water," he admitted, trying to change the current topic of conversation and put the focus on them.

Her mouth opened and then snapped shut. Sprawling out on the lush grass onto her stomach, she reached for another blackberry from the silver bowl.

An array of tempting delicacies was spread out on trays and bowls. The empty bottle of honeyed ambrosia set in a chilled container, and Liam pondered fetching another one. Nevertheless, of all the enticing dishes set out before them, there was only one who had him craving a delicious sweet nectar. *Abela.*

Holding the tiny morsel out in front of her, she remarked, "Do you remember the fresh strawberries and blackberries we gathered on Beltaine? Then made ourselves nauseated by smothering them with thick, sweet cream that we made ourselves?"

He smiled knowingly. "If I recall, you were not feeling well the next morning. My recollection was the night before. Do you remember the game we played?"

She bit down on the blackberry and some of the juices stained her lips. "Yes," she answered in a rush.

"After dipping a variety of fruits in the sweet cream, I fed them to you when you answered each of my questions correctly."

"And then licked the leftover cream from my lips," she added in a throaty whisper.

The image of that provocative evening came slamming into his thoughts. "I have a confession."

"Do tell," she purred.

"I almost took your virginity that evening."

Rolling over, Abela sat up. "I'm shocked, Liam MacGregor." A glint of humor shone in her eyes.

Swiftly diverting his attention to a pair of wild geese gliding across the river, he added, "Yet, we were not ready so long ago."

"True words spoken."

When he glanced back at her, her smile had faded and she appeared crestfallen. "That was the night I fell in love with you."

Liam held out his hands to her. "Come here, *mo ghrá*."

She scrambled over to his waiting arms and curled up in his lap. He tugged at the loose curl from the braided mass around her head. With deft skill, Liam removed the crystal pins securing her braids in place. "A lot of work—" she explained.

He placed a finger over her pouting lips. "Shh...allow me the pleasure." After dropping the pins on the ground, he went to work unraveling each braid.

Sighing in obvious pleasure, she leaned her head forward against his chest as he massaged her scalp.

"Feels good," she mumbled.

Cupping her chin, his gaze roamed over her features. "There shall be no more unhappiness when we speak of the past. It was our journey. Regardless of the obstacles, and near death situations, we overcame them all. You are here with me. Those trials of the past are gone. We have our entire lives to map out. I shall love and cherish you forever."

Abela wrapped her arms around his neck and straddled his thighs. "Oh, Liam, my heart is full with love. Thank you for reminding me. There is much to do in the human realm. First, I wish to visit Aileen and the other wives of the Dragon Knights. Since Aileen is a healer, I consider it wise to have the Master Apothecary accompany us on our first official business."

Liam arched a brow. "Have you spoken to Aelish about this new venture?"

"Yes. At our wedding feast. Actually, she was the one who approached me and inquired about Aileen. She regretted not being able to assist the woman in the Fae healing practices. This will be a welcomed opportunity."

"And I have no doubt Aileen will appreciate the mentoring from the Master Apothecary and the chance to see you, as well."

Abela trailed a finger over the markings on his chest. "Exactly. But we should not concern ourselves with leaving for the human world just yet. This is a time of rest."

Liam's gaze dipped from her luscious lips to the pert rosy nipples pressing against her sheer gown. "I concur. We should take this time to indulge our fantasies and treasure the time alone."

Leaning forward, she nipped along the vein in his neck. "Fantasies? I am intrigued."

He cupped her full warm breasts. "Would you like to visit the waters of Delfina?"

She rocked slowly over his swollen erection. "I have heard that making love within the waters brings exquisite pleasure."

"Unspeakable passion. More heady than within the stars. You can feel the fervor of the other person you are with, increasing your sensitivity."

Her eyes glittered with desire and as Liam bent his head for a kiss, she whispered, "Take me there, my warrior."

"With pleasure, my Fae minx."

And with a wave of his hand, they vanished in a soft mist of light and love.

Note from the Author

I have never had a story developed so quickly as *Trial of a Warrior*. Princess Abela stunned me one cold winter morning when she stepped forth within my thoughts *and* Liam's prison. Uncertainty filled me as I fought against her choice for the heroine. Yet, she refused to leave, and I yielded to her demands. After all, she is royalty.

In the end, it was a perfect match.

Liam and Abela took me on an amazing adventure. I allowed these characters to involve me—the writer— on their epic journey. I hope you've enjoyed their story as much as I loved writing the tale. We also learned that the greatest Fenian Warrior, Aidan Kerrigan, had his own secret—the queen's brother! Did I know this important fact? No. The warrior chose not to reveal his particular lineage with me until now.

And this my friends is what happens in the life of a writer. Some elements of a story unfold immediately before we hit the first keystroke. However, there are times when you have nothing, and when you sit down to begin, the characters reveal the story to you.

Next in the *Legends of the Fenian Warriors*? Who else but the greatest legend of the Fae kingdom. Aidan Kerrigan—*Destiny of a Warrior*! Learn what really happened when the kingdom's most revered warrior (and oldest) defies his own people for the love of a human. You first met this ancient warrior as Aileen Kerrigan's father in *Dragon Knight's Medallion, Order of the Dragon Knights, Book 2.*

Until then, may your dreams be filled with Irish charm and Highland mists.

Coming in 2019

DESTINY OF A WARRIOR

For a sneak preview just turn the page…

Prologue

In the beginning...when the world was new, Fae and humans lived peacefully together, but as the centuries passed, fear and distrust evolved. The Fae continued to love the humans, but they believed it was time to safeguard the realms. Therefore, they appointed the Fenian Warriors to protect the domain between human and faery. But most importantly, these warriors were only to assist the humans and steer a new course in the mortal world.

When evil threatened to destroy a clan, country, or civilization, the Fae council called upon these warriors. This group of elite Fae had the power to travel through the Veil of Ages, supporting those in need. They were not to alter the timeline or what the Fae believed to be the life strings of a human. To do so, would be catastrophic.

Ancient and powerful, the Brotherhood of the Fenian Warriors was second only to the Fae King and Queen's powers. They have lived amongst us for thousands of years—watching, aiding, guiding. They could live in the guise of a professor, lawyer, knight, tavern owner, or a simple farmer.

Whatever was required, the warriors did so without complaint. If so much as a whisper of negativity reached their leader, they were banished from the Brotherhood.

In the early formation of the Fenian Warriors, many were chosen to enter the Brotherhood. Yet, some argued as to who should lead this vast number of Fae. A council of nine Fae elders was appointed to oversee the debate regarding a leader. The elders agreed that whoever was chosen had to have qualities that were impeccable. No blemish had to stain his life history.

They were given nine days to make their decision. In the end, one Fae stood out in stark contrast to all those who were considered. It was a unanimous decision.

Aidan Kerrigan, older brother to Queen Nuala, was deemed the perfect Fae to govern the Fenian Warriors. His code of ethics rivaled none. Steadfast and loyal to his people and the Brotherhood, not one could find fault in him. In addition, his royal bloodline was vast, and he was one of the few to be born on their homeland of Taralyn within the great cosmos.

So on the summer festival marking the five thousandth year of the Fae living on earth, King Ansgar made Aidan the supreme leader over the Brotherhood. He was bestowed with more powers, making him almost an equal to the King of the Fae.

Over the centuries, admiration grew for the leader of the Fenian Warriors. Honorable, loyal, brave, courageous—words uttered by all when his name was mentioned.

Until one day, when the sun and moon became one on both worlds, and a shift in the Fae realm transpired.

The Fae forgot about the prophecy. No one cared about the whispers on a darkened midday. Nor did any seek out the seer for her wisdom or heard the weeping of the priestesses within the temple of Mother Danu.

The warm air turned frigid in seconds, and not one Fae paused to understand the meaning of what was about to occur.

Yet, one human female did notice in her world.

When she stumbled along a path one spring afternoon in awe of the glorious solar eclipse, the Fates shredded the loom of two individuals—one human and the other a Fae.

The rift in their lives would be glorious *and* catastrophic. Neither would be prepared for the future they faced, or the impact they would have for future generations.

In the end, their fated meeting would bring about the greatest downfall of one of the most revered warriors ever.

And the Fae realm would never be the same again.

Chapter One

*Beneath the Hill of Tara, Ireland, Early spring—
the season of growth and renewal in the Fae realm*

His fingers moved deftly over the hilt of his sword,
aching to unsheathe the blade and sever the hand from
the warrior's body. Watching the scene unfold in the
training camp below, Aidan Kerrigan drew in a sharp
hiss. The wind slapped at his face, mocking him to
make his move against the defiant Fae. Branches
smacked his back in an effort to sway him from his
concealment within the trees. He barely registered the
wolf's low growl behind him.

Nevertheless, Aidan was a seasoned warrior, not
some young lad showing off his prowess in front of his
peers and those others whom Aidan had fashioned into
hardened Fenian Warriors. No, he would not rush in,
though his instinct begged him to do so. He would
choose the right moment to reveal himself.

"Why is there always one who defies my orders?"
he uttered with contempt.

And the question Aidan posed was immediately
answered.

"Because this is how you pluck those who are
unworthy to continue with their training in the
Brotherhood."

Aidan gripped the hilt more firmly, refusing to

acknowledge his friend and kept his sight riveted on the scene below. "Then explain why those not *worthy* are the ones who possess the most power?"

"Power is intoxicating. Even the strongest cannot deflect the energy all the time."

Arching a brow, Aidan glanced sharply at the Fae. "Do you speak from experience, Flynn? Or was this part of your elusive training when you left the Brotherhood to study under the king's guards?"

A shadow of annoyance passed briefly over his friend's features. "Intoxication in any form is a hindrance to the Fae. Power can fill our bodies, flood our veins, and heightened our senses."

"As with any drug, woman, *or* libation," countered Aidan, releasing his grip on the sword. "This is why I order all initiates to undergo a year without all three. If I deem they cannot control their *basic* urges, then they are not creditable to continue with their training."

"So with the first brush of Fenian power, you believe they should harness the intensity of the feeling?"

Shifting his stance, Aidan clasped his hands behind his back. "Instantly. With one thought, a warrior could obliterate a man into ashes within seconds in the human world. The power should not control the warrior. Are you wavering from your own training, Flynn?"

His friend rubbed a hand over his jaw. "Until my last breath, I shall always recall the rush of power when it first entered my body after the seclusion."

"You did not answer my question."

"No. But for a fraction of a second, I almost let lose the power," Flynn acknowledged.

Aidan eyed his friend warily. What possessed him

to make such a confession? And why now? "Is there a reason you're admitting this declaration?"

Flynn sighed heavily. "It is a pity. Loman is a strong warrior. In addition, he is blood kin to my own royal house. I only sought to share my story in hopes you would find mercy and allow him to remain."

"Yours was a split-second indecisiveness." Aidan cast his hand outward. "This warrior making a mock display of authority over the others is vastly different. There is no comparison. Furthermore, Loman continues to build the energy without thought to the repercussions. As you know me so well, Flynn, I give *no* mercy to any warrior in training."

His friend shifted his stance, but remained silent.

The wolf padded around in front of Aidan.

"Your companion's interest has grown," commented Flynn.

Aidan shrugged. "Even the animal can sense the misuse of power."

"Or his next feast."

The wolf as well as Aidan snapped their gazes toward Flynn.

"This wolf is a higher species than those animals in the human world," declared Aidan.

"You should not have brought him into the Fae realm," argued Flynn.

The wolf snickered and returned its attention to the group of Fae below.

Aidan fought the smile forming on his mouth. "The man or beast? Which one should not have been permitted into the kingdom?"

Flynn arched a brow. "Are they not one and the same?"

"His clan is interested in observing the training we do with the young warriors. It was the same with the Dragon Knights. We brought them here for a short time to witness and learn." Aidan waved a hand dismissively. "Dragons, wolves, does it matter?"

"I'd rather deal with dragons," admitted Flynn, folding his arms across his chest.

Aidan chuckled softly. When he requested to bring a member from Clan Sutherland to the Fae realm to survey the training within the Brotherhood, all argued against the preposterous idea. The council judged it unsafe to have a Highlander from the Wolves of Sutherland wander among the Fae and animals, striking at any for his meal. Regardless of Aidan's assurance that they did not act upon their predatory instinct to kill for their meal, the council denied his appeal.

Therefore, Aidan took his petition to the king and won. The council was not pleased.

Apparently, Flynn regarded the wolf as a hunter and not an elite warrior, trained in the art of all forms of combat. He had yet to share with his friend that Magnar was also the war chieftain for his clan.

"He has made a vow not to *devour* any Fae while in our homeland," Aidan remarked.

"I do not find your statement amusing," stated Flynn dryly. "Can he not observe in human form?"

In a soft blur of gray shadows, the wolf shimmered into a man. Fisting his hands on his hips, he glared at Flynn—all seven feet of him and totally naked. "Will ye be more comfortable now that I am in my human skin?"

"I was *comfortable* before," argued Flynn.

Magnar sniffed the air. "Liar."

Flynn's eyes flashed silver, and he took a step toward the man.

Aidan put a fist to his mouth to stifle the laughter, eager to watch the display of power between his friends. "Be warned, Magnar moves as fast as you or I."

"Ahh…it has been eons since I've challenged anyone in the training lists," professed Flynn.

Magnar relaxed his stance. "And I only accept those I consider *worthy* to confront."

"Arrogant bastard."

"Aye, but do ye not have any *Fae* curse words?"

Flynn shrugged. "You would not comprehend their meaning."

"It will be a pleasure beating ye in the lists." Magnar's smile turned predatory as he shifted back into his wolf form.

Aidan smacked his friend on the shoulder. "Save the event for when I can gather the other warriors."

Flynn pinched the bridge of his nose. "A spectator sport was not what I intended to—"

A blast of power had both men stumbling back. Aidan was the first to recover as he scanned the area below. Loman had increased the sphere of energy into a massive swirling globe, effectively showing off his power. However, he was unable to control the building orb, and the sparks of energy bolted outward in all directions.

A word about the author...

Award-winning Scottish paranormal romance author, Mary Morgan resides in Northern California, with her own knight in shining armor. However, during her travels to Scotland, England, and Ireland, she left a part of her soul in one of these countries and vows to return.

Mary's passion for books started at an early age along with an overactive imagination. She spent far too much time daydreaming and was told quite often to remove her head from the clouds. It wasn't until the closure of Borders Books, where Mary worked, that she found her true calling—writing romance. Now, the worlds she created in her mind are coming to life within her stories.

If you enjoy history, tortured heroes, and a wee bit of magic, then time-travel within the pages of her books.

Visit Mary's website where you'll find links to all of her books, blog, and pictures of her travels.

http://www.marymorganauthor.com

Other books by Mary Morgan

Order of the Dragon Knights ~
Dragon Knight's Sword, Book 1
Dragon Knight's Medallion, Book 2
Dragon Knight's Axe, Book 3
Dragon Knight's Shield, Book 4
Dragon Knight's Ring, Book 5
~*~

Legends of the Fenian Warriors ~
Quest of a Warrior, Book 1
Oath of a Warrior, Book 2
~*~

Holiday Romances ~
A Magical Highland Solstice
A Highland Moon Enchantment

www.ingramcontent.com/pod-product-compliance
Lightning Source LLC
Chambersburg PA
CBHW050026030726
47506CB00001B/145